"Back to back they stand, eyeing their foes over the gleam of sharpened steel...

Lean Times in Lankhmar
The Adventures of Fafhrd and the Gray Mouser

Follow the giant barbarian Fafhrd and his diminutive ally the Gray Mouser as they travel the mysterious, exotic world of Nehwon in search of riches and glory. From the top of Nehwon's highest mountain to the deepest catacomb of subterranean Quarmall they journey, even exploring times and worlds beyond Nehwon itself.

Praise for the Fritz Leiber and his Lankhmar: The Adventures of Fafhrd and the Gray Mouser series!

"Fritz Leiber's tales of Fafhrd and the Gray mouser are virtually a genre unto themselves. Urbane, idiosyncratic, comic, erotic and human, spiked with believable action and the eerie creations of a master fantasist, they make most of today's fantasy look plodding and dull."
  —William Gibson

"Intense...exotic...made up of all kinds of dusty magic..."
  —Brian Aldiss

"Glowing imagination melds with gorgeous language...Leiber's back: Rejoice!"
  —Harlan Ellison

"I...fervently urge you to get hold of *Ill Met in Lankhmar* as soon as it can be decently arranged..."
—Gahan Wilson
Realms of Fantasy

"...long overdue...if you need an excuse to re-read some of the finest heroic fantasy ever written, here it is."
—*Science Fiction Chronicle*

"His themes are handled with a maturity and depth uncommon in the genre."
— *Philadelphia Inquirer*

"A literate and effective writer, Leiber is one of the two best fantasists to come out of the pulps—the other is Bradbury—but he remains under-appreciated."
—*Publishers Weekly*

"Solid entertainment"
—*Kirkus Review*

"One of science fiction's most endearingly comic, mock-heroic series...Fafhrd and the Gray Mouser [are a] much-loved duo."
—*Booklist*

"Outlandish tales told with finesse...there is plenty of swordplay, to be sure, but Leiber also brings an emotional reality to these characters that is often funny and quite touching...Enjoyable and worthwhile."
—*San Francisco Chronicle*

"[these] adventures...are sure to add some swash to your buckle!"
—*Des Moines Sunday Register*

"Sword and sorcery fans can rejoice in White Wolf's new edition of Fritz Leiber's classic Fafhrd and the Gray Mouser stories...White Wolf has done an exemplary job of reprinting and packaging Leiber's work...this collection is clearly a classic."
—*Middlesex News*

FRITZ LEIBER'S
LEAN TIMES IN LANKHMAR

Lean Times in Lankhmar
A White Wolf, Inc. Publication

Cover Art: Mike Mignola

Book Design: Michael Scott Cohen and Michelle Prahler

Copyright © Fritz Leiber, 1996. All rights reserved.

For information address:
White Wolf Publishing,
735 Park North Boulevard, Suite 125,
Clarkston, GA 30021.
www.white-wolf.com

This volume is dedicated to the memory of Fritz Leiber.

CONTENTS

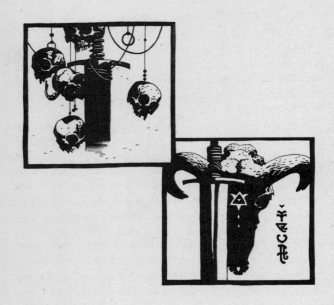

FAFhRD AND The GRAY MOUSER
BY
RAYMOND E. FEIST

Fafhrd and the Gray Mouser. They are easily two of the finest creations in the history of modern fantasy. Before them were few characters with recognizable human foibles. Save for the flaws in Lancelot, you didn't see a lot of foibles in most fantasy heroes.

Fantasy, before Fritz gave birth to these two originals, was almost exclusively the domain of stout hearted knights embarked upon quests to stem the tide of evil. The exception to that over-generalization was R.E. Howard's Conan, who was far less a hero than he was a force of nature; while his heart was not always pure, his lack of nobility was a result of his history and culture, not any moral flaw. Conan's confrontations with evil were almost always a case of happenstance rather than by any design. But the other heroes of fantasy were constantly on the lookout for evil to confront.

Fafhrd, the giant from the frozen north, and The Gray Mouser, the diminutive sneak-thief, were too full of their own needs and desires to be caught up in any concerns over good versus evil, let alone choosing sides. They were too busy striving to keep body and soul together to dwell upon such esoteric issues. No existential angst for these two; there wasn't enough time in the day to consider universal order while they were struggling to stay alive.

All the elements of the fantasy genre are present in Fritz's stories, and a few that other writers haven't attempted, but at the heart of these stories is a very recognizable human component: this human "city mouse and country mouse" pair found a brotherhood that was based upon genuine human feelings; a love for one another that rose naturally from bitter isolation and a desire to stay free of unwelcome ties, yet admitted to a basic human drive to connect with another human being. Despite their poses as rugged individualists, and an occasional attempt on the part of one to turn a profit at the other's expense, they were loyal to one another in a way few could understand. Their friendship was inviolate.

Pacts with inhuman wizards, duels will deadly foes, run-ins with mad monarchs, and much more are the stuff of the Fafhrd and Gray Mouser tales. Lankhmar—smoky, dirty, crowded, host to ever depravity imagined—is typical of their haunts, a strange place populated by unusual denizens, with danger lurking behind even the most prosaic façade.

But what makes these characters unique is the unsurpassed story telling of Fritz. For while the cast of characters is improbable to the extreme, their ambitions, hopes, fears, and passions are recognizable, and their predicaments become all the more engaging because Fritz made you care about his not-quite-heroes.

Most of us in this field today are constantly being compared to J.R.R. Tolkien. This is a marketing device and has no bearing on reality. Most of us, if asked, admit that Fritz Leiber is our spiritual father, and for the most part, we're sweating to keep up with the "Grand Old Man," let alone overtake him.

These stories will show you why this is true.

AUThOR'S FOREWORD

Book Three of the Fafhrd-Mouser Saga knits together three stories written around 1960 with the first ever to be written: "Adept's Gambit," completed in 1936 but not published until 1947 (in the Arkham House book *Night's Black Agents*). The knitting is done by the two very short stories—*"Their Mistress, the Sea"* and *"The Wrong Branch,"* both written in 1968, which function chiefly as picaresque bridging episodes between *"The Cloud of Hate," "Lean Times in Lankhmar"* (both set in that city), *"When the Sea-King's Away"* (set under the Inner Sea), and *"Adept's Gambit"* (set in historic Hellenistic times, which requires a spot of magical space- and time-travel).

It is worth noting that "Adept's Gambit" was shown in manuscript to the master teller of supernatural tales H. P. Lovecraft during the brief period (less than four months, November 1936 to February 1937) when the New England fantasist was corresponding voluminously with the author, his wife, Jonquil Stephens Leiber (who had first written HPL, starting it all off), and his friend and colleague Harry Otto Fischer. Some of this correspondence appears in the fifth volume of Lovecraft's *Selected Letters* (Arkham House 1976) which also contains Lovecraft's last letter, uncompleted at the time of his death (March 15, 1937). This letter, to his long-time friend James F. Morton, covers in some detail a dozen or so topics, including Fafhrd and the Mouser:

There will shortly be circulated among the gang (you can be on the list if you like) a remarkable unpublished novelette by young Leiber—*Adept's Gambit*, rejected by Wright and now under revision according to my suggestions. It is a very brilliant piece of fantastic imagination—with suggestions of Cabell, Beckford, Dunsany, and even Two-Gun Bob—and ought to see publication some day. Being wholly out of the cheap tradesman tradition, it has small chance of early magazine placement—hence the idea of circulation amongst the members of the circle. This novelette is part of a very unusual mythcycle spontaneously evolved in the correspondence of Leiber and his closest friend—Harry O. Fischer of lately-inundated Louisville. Fischer has also come within my congested epistolary circle and is in some ways even more remarkable than Leiber—he has more imaginative fertility, though less concentrated emotional power and philosophic insight. Their mythcycle, originally started by Fischer, involves my own pantheon of Yog-Sothoth, Cthulhu, etc., and revolves around the adventures of two roving characters (Fafhrd the Viking, modelled after Leiber—who is six feet four—and the Gray Mouser, modelled after the diminutive Fischer) in vague congeries of fabulous and half fabulous worlds of the remote past. Fischer's parts of this cycle are vivid but unformulated and disjointed, so that at present Leiber—the better craftsman—is the only publicly visible author of the pair. *Adept's Gambit* is laid in Syria of the earlier Hellenistic period, but soon moves away from Tyre and Ephesus to a fabulous mountain realm of inland Asia. Fischer's wife is an accomplished artist, and has made several very effective pastel drawings of some of the inconceivable Entities in the Fafhrd-Mouser cycle.

Actually, Lovecraft's suggestions for revision were not extensive, mostly matters of word-choice: "move" instead of "activate," "fascinating" rather than "intriguing." In his enthusiasm for things Lovecraftian the author did introduce into the story a few references to Yog-Sothoth and Nyarlathotep, but soon deleted them completely on the urgings of his wife and Fischer, who for once found themselves in agreement on a point. But Lovecraft's extreme devotion to careful research, literary purity, and painstaking craftsmanship made a lifelong impression on him.

—Fritz Leiber, San Francisco
August 28, 1977

FRITZ LEIBER'S
LANKhMAR

BOOK III
SWORDS IN THE MIST

CONTENTS BOOK III

IV: WHEN THE SEA-KING'S AWAY

Of the delusions and lascivious imaginings of seamen athirst and erotically starved—or else of a magic mightier than the weight of all the world's waters. Of land tunnels and sea tunnels, of water wells in earth and air wells in water, of cliffs paper-thin and oceans at war. Of the Triple Goddess at work in Nehwon, or at play. Of a masked black sea-witch and her magical toys. Of two luscious sea-queens and their outré harem guard. Together with a compendium of practical information useful to those who must walk, not on water, but—without diving garb—down, through, and under the aqueous element.

V: THE WRONG BRANCH

The devious workings of the Sea-King's curse. A swimming race between men and sharks and how it was betted on. Of noisome Ilthmar. Of Doors between distant worlds. A warning to all to avoid side-paths when visiting Ningauble of the Seven Eyes in his caverns, and of how this wise rule was broken upon one occasion.

VI: ADEPT'S GAMBIT

In his gambits, a chess-player sacrifices pawn or piece to checkmate his adversary. But in his games, a black magician, in order to triumph, may sacrifice living pieces and even himself the player.

1. *Tyre* Of a humiliating enchantment which robbed Fafhrd and the Gray Mouser of all girls, except Chloe the cross-eyed Greek. And of how the Mouser fell into love, though not with Chloe.

2. *Ningauble*   Of a visit by the two heroes to the Gossiper of the Gods, to find a cure for their girl-denying enchantment. Of a word-war of maneuver between Ningauble and the Mouser, with mention of four infamous handmaidens of Ishtar and a dwarf who was richly compensated for his deformity, of the Friday concubine of the satrap Philip, and of like matters.

3. *The Woman Who Came*   How on Ningauble's advice and to make a magic to restore them, Fafhrd and the Mouser went on a multiple quest to procure the Shroud of Ahriman, the aphrodisiacal mummy of the Demon Pharaoh, the Cup from which Socrates drank the hemlock, a sprig from the primal Tree of Life, and The Woman Who Would Come When She Was Ready.

4. *The Lost City*   Of the heroes' cautious courting of shy, sly Ahura. Of the rift she naughtily digged between them. Of the journey they made, all three together. Of the Mouser's theory of Ahura's sex, and of how he felt it disproved in the moment of proving it. Of a saving gale, a messenger-bat, and the making of a great magic.

5. *Anra Devadoris*   Of a fastidious stranger named the Dark Gift of Demons. Of the most taxing sword fight in the Gray Mouser's duel-starred life. Of the stranger's filthy bed.

6. *The Mountain*   Of a demon peak that preyed on its countryside, and of a demon castle atop that peak. Of the follies of heroes and of a quest resumed.

7. *Ahura Devadoris*   The spoken story of the Bright Gift of Demons. Of a tyranny more intimate and absolute than that of a wizard over his concubine-acolyte. Of the mixings of magics and whoredoms. Of a Tyrian orgy and its frightful close.

8. *The Old Man Without a Beard*   Ahura's weird tale concluded. Of a sorcerer, his student, and their evil curriculum. Of an especially close confinement suffered by Ahura.

9. *The Castle Called Mist*   Of a vast edifice alive or stretching into other dimensions. Horrors innumerable. End of Ahura's tale. Fate of the Old Man. A final duel and a final revelation. Lankhmar once more in view.

FRITZ LEIBER'S
LANKHMAR

THE CLOUD OF HATE

I

Muffled drums beat out a nerve-scratching rhythm, and red lights flickered hypnotically in the underground Temple of Hates, where five thousand ragged worshipers knelt and abased themselves and ecstatically pressed foreheads against the cold and gritty cobbles as the trance took hold and the human venom rose in them.

The drumbeat was low. And save for snarls and mewlings, the inner pulsing was inaudible. Yet together they made a hellish vibration which threatened to shake the city and land of Lankhmar and the whole world of Nehwon.

Lankhmar had been at peace for many moons, and so the hates were greater. Tonight, furthermore, at a spot halfway across the city, Lankhmar's black-togaed nobility celebrated with merriment and feasting and twinkling dance the betrothal of their Overlord's daughter to the Prince of Ilthmar, and so the hates were redoubled.

The single-halled subterranean temple was so long and wide and at the same time so irregularly planted with thick pillars that at no point could a person see more than a third of the way across it. Yet it had a ceiling so low that at any point a man standing tall could have brushed it with his fingertips—except that here all groveled. The air was swooningly fetid. The dark bent backs of the hate-ensorceled worshipers made a kind of hummocky dark ground, from which the nitre-crusted stone pillars rose like gray tree trunks.

The masked Archpriest of the Hates lifted a skinny finger. Parchment-thin iron cymbals began to clash in unison with the drums and the furnace-red flickerings, wringing to an unendurable pitch the malices and envies of the blackly enraptured communicants.

Then in the gloom of that great slitlike hall, dim pale tendrils began to rise from the dark hummocky ground of the bent backs, as though a white, swift-growing ghost-grass had been seeded there. The tendrils, which in another world might have been described as ectoplasmic, quickly multiplied, thickened, lengthened, and then coalesced into questing white serpentine shapes, so that it seemed as if tongues of thick river-fog had come licking down into this subcellar from the broad-flowing river Hlal.

The white serpents coiled past the pillars, brushed the low ceiling, moistly caressed the backs of their devotees and source, and then in turn coalesced to pour up the curving black hole of a narrow spiral stairway, the stone steps of which were worn almost to chutelike smoothness—a sinuously billowing white cylinder in which a redness lurked. And all the while the drums and cymbals did not falter for a single beat, nor did the Hell-light tenders cease to crank the wooden wheels on which shielded, red-burning candles were affixed, nor did the eyes of the Archpriest flicker once sideways in their wooden mask, nor did one mesmerized bent soul look up.

Along a misted alley overhead there was hurrying home to the thieves' quarter a beggar girl, skinny-frail of limb and with eyes big as a lemur's peering fearfully from a tiny face of elfin beauty. She saw the white pillar, slug-flat now, pouring out between the bars of a window-slit level with the pavement, and although there were thick chilly tendrils of river-fog already following her, she knew that this was different.

She tried to run around the thing, but swift almost as a serpent striking, it whipped across to the opposite wall, barring her way. She ran back, but it outraced her and made a U, penning her against the unyielding wall. Then she only stood still and shook as the fog-serpent narrowed and grew denser and came wreathing around her. Its tip swayed like the head of a poisonous snake preparing to strike and then suddenly dipped toward her breast. She stopped shaking then and her head fell back and the pupils rolled up in her lemurlike eyes so that they showed only great whites, and she dropped to the pavement limp as a rag.

The fog-serpent nosed at her for a few moments, then as though irked at finding no life remaining, flipped her over

on her face, and went swiftly questing in the same direction
the river-fog itself was taking: across city toward the homes
of the nobles and the lantern-jeweled palace of the Overlord.

Save for an occasional fleeting red glint in the one, the
two sorts of fog were identical.

Beside a dry stone horse-trough at the juncture of five
alleys, two men curled close to either side of a squat brazier
in which a little charcoal glowed. The spot was so near the
quarter of the nobles that the sounds of music and laughter
came at intervals, faintly, along with a dim rainbow-glow of
light. The two men might have been a hulking beggar and a
small one, except that their tunics and leggings and cloaks,
though threadbare, were of good stuff, and scabbarded
weapons lay close to the hand of each.

The larger said, "There'll be fog tonight. I smell it coming
from the Hlal." This was Fafhrd, brawny-armed, pale and
serene of face, reddish gold of hair.

For reply the smaller shivered and fed the brazier two small
gobbets of charcoal and said sardonically, "Next predict
glaciers!—advancing down the Street of the Gods, by
preference." That was the Mouser, eyes wary, lips quirking,
cheeks muffled by gray hood drawn close.

Fafhrd grinned. As a tinkling gust of distant song came
by, he asked the dark air that carried it, "Now why aren't we
warmly cushioned somewhere inside tonight, well drunk and
sweetly embraced?"

For answer the Gray Mouser drew from his belt a ratskin
pouch and slapped it by its drawstrings against his palm. It
flattened as it hit and nothing chinked. For good measure
he writhed at Fafhrd the backs of his ten fingers, all ringless.
Fafhrd grinned again and said to the dusky space around
them, which was now filled with the finest mist, the fog's
forerunner, "Now that's a strange thing. We've won I know
not how many jewels and oddments of gold and electrum in

our adventurings—and even letters of credit on the Guild of the Grain Merchants. Where have they all flown to?—the credit-letters on parchment wings, the jewels jetting fire like tiny red and green and pearly cuttlefish. Why aren't we rich?"

The Mouser snorted, "Because you dribble away our get on worthless drabs, or oftener still pour it out for some noble whim—some plot of bogus angels to storm the walls of Hell. Meantime I stay poor nursemaiding you."

Fafhrd laughed and retorted, "You overlook your own whimsical imprudences, such as slitting the Overlord's purse and picking his pocket too the selfsame night you rescued and returned him his lost crown. No, Mouser, I think we're poor because—" Suddenly he lifted an elbow and flared his nostrils as he snuffed the chill moist air. "There's a taint in the fog tonight," he announced.

The Mouser said dryly, "I already smell dead fish, burnt fat, horse dung, tickly lint, Lankhmar sausage gone stale, cheap temple incense burnt by the ten-pound cake, rancid oil, moldy grain, slaves' barracks, embalmers' tanks crowded to the black brim, and the stink of a cathedral full of unwashed carters and trulls celebrating orgiastic rites—and now you tell me of a taint!"

"It is something different from all those," Fafhrd said, peering successively down the five alleys. "Perhaps the last..." His voice trailed off doubtfully, and he shrugged.

Strands of fog came questing through small high-set street-level windows into the tavern called the Rats' Nest, interlacing curiously with the soot-trail from a failing torch, but unnoticed except by an old harlot who pulled her patchy fur cloak closer at her throat. All eyes were on the wrist game being played across an ancient oaken table by the famed bravo Gnarlag and a dark-skinned mercenary almost as big-thewed as he. Right elbows firmly planted and right hands bone-squeezingly gripped, each strained to force the back of the other's wrist down against the ringed and scarred and carved and knife-stuck wood. Gnarlag, who scowled sneeringly, had the advantage by a thumb's length.

One of the fog-strands, as though itself a devotee of the wrist game and curious about the bout, drifted over Gnarlag's shoulder. To the old harlot the inquisitive fog-strand looked redly-veined—a reflection from the torches, no doubt, but she prayed it brought fresh blood to Gnarlag.

The fog-finger touched the taut arm. Gnarlag's sneering look turned to one of pure hate, and the muscles of his forearm seemed to double in thickness as he rotated it more than a half turn. There was a muffled snap and a gasp of anguish. The mercenary's wrist had been broken.

Gnarlag stood up. He knocked to the wall a wine cup offered him and cuffed aside a girl who would have embraced him. Then grabbing up his two swords on their thick belt from the bench beside him, he strode to the brick stairs and up out of the Rats' Nest. By some trick of air currents, perhaps, it seemed that a fog-strand rested across his shoulders like a comradely arm.

When he was gone, someone said, "Gnarlag was ever a cold and ungrateful winner." The dark mercenary stared at his dangling hand and bit back groans.

"So tell me, giant philosopher, why we're not dukes," the Gray Mouser demanded, unrolling a forefinger from the fist on his knee so that it pointed across the brazier at Fafhrd. "Or emperors, for that matter, or demigods."

"We are not dukes because we're no man's man," Fafhrd replied smugly, settling his shoulders against the stone horse-trough. "Even a duke must butter up a king, and demigods the gods. We butter no one. We go our own way, choosing our own adventures—and our own follies! Better freedom and a chilly road than a warm hearth and servitude."

"There speaks the hound turned out by his last master and

not yet found new boots to slaver on," the Mouser retorted with comradely sardonic impudence. "Look you, you noble liar, we've labored for a dozen lords and kings and merchants fat. You've served Movarl across the Inner Sea. I've served the bandit Harsel. We've both served this Glipkerio, whose girl is tied to Ilthmar this same night."

"Those are exceptions," Fafhrd protested grandly. "And even when we serve, we make the rules. We bow to no man's ultimate command, dance to no wizard's drumming, join no mob, hark to no wildering hate-call. When we draw sword, it's for ourselves alone. *What's that?*"

He had lifted his sword for emphasis, gripping it by the scabbard just below the guard, but now he held it still with the hilt near his ear.

"It hums a warning!" he said tersely after a moment. "The steel twangs softly in its sheath!"

Chuckling tolerantly at this show of superstition, the Mouser drew his slimmer sword from its light scabbard, sighted along the blade's oiled length at the red embers, spotted a couple of dark flecks and began to rub at them with a rag.

When nothing more happened, Fafhrd said grudgingly as he laid down his undrawn sword, "Perchance only a dragon walked across the cave where the blade was forged. Still, I don't like this tainted mist."

Gis the cutthroat and the courtesan Tres had watched the fog coming across the fantastically peaked roofs of Lankhmar until it obscured the low-swinging yellow crescent of the moon and the rainbow glow from the palace. Then they had lit the cressets and drawn the blue drapes and were playing at throw-knife to sharpen their appetites for a more intimate but hardly kinder game.

Tres was not unskillful, but Gis could somersault the weapon a dozen or thirteen times before it stuck in wood and throw as truly between his legs as back over his shoulder without mirror. Whenever he threw the knife so it struck very near Tres, he smiled. She had to remind herself that he was not much more evil than most evil men.

A frond of fog came wreathing between the blue drapes and touched Gis on the temple as he prepared to throw. "The blood in the fog's in your eye-whites!" Tres cried, staring at him weirdly. He seized the girl by the ear and, smiling hugely, slashed her neck just below her dainty jaw. Then, dancing out of the way of the gushing blood, he delicately snatched up his belt of daggers and darted down the curving stairs to the street, where he plunged into a warmhearted fog that was somehow as full of rage as the strong wine of Tovilyis is of sugar, a veritable cistern of wrath. His whole being was bathed in sensations as ecstatic as those strong but fleeting ones the tendril's touch on his temple had loosed from his brain. Visions of daggered princesses and skewered serving maids danced in his head. He stepped along happily, agog with delicious anticipations, beside Gnarlag of the Two Swords, knowing him at once for a hate-brother, sacrosanct, another slave of the blessed fog.

Fafhrd cupped his big hands over the brazier and whistled the gay tune sifting from the remotely twinkling palace. The Mouser, now reoiling the blade of Scalpel against the mist, observed, "For one beset by taints and danger-hums, you're very jolly."

"I like it here," the Northerner asserted. "A fig for courts and beds and inside fires! The edge of life is keener in the street—as on the mountaintop. Is not imagined wine sweeter than wine?" ("Ho!" the Mouser laughed, most sardonically.) "And is not a crust of bread tastier to one an-hungered than larks' tongues to an epicure? Adversity makes the keenest appetite—the clearest vision."

"There spoke the ape who could not reach the apple," the

Mouser told him. "If a door to paradise opened in that wall there, you'd dive through."

"Only because I've never been to paradise," Fafhrd swept on. "Is it not sweeter now to hear the music of Innesgay's betrothal from afar than mingle with the feasters, jig with them, be cramped and blinkered by their social rituals?"

"There's many a one in Lankhmar gnawn fleshless with envy by those sounds tonight," the Mouser said darkly. "I am not gnawn so much as those stupid ones; I am more intelligently jealous. Still, the answer to your question: no!"

"Sweeter by far tonight to be Glipkerio's watchman than his pampered guest," Fafhrd insisted, caught up by his own poetry and hardly hearing the Mouser.

"You mean we serve Glipkerio *free?*" the latter demanded loudly. "Aye, there's the bitter core of all freedom: no pay!"

Fafhrd laughed, came to himself, and said almost abashedly, "Still, there is something in the keenness and the watchman part. We're watchmen not for pay, but solely for the watching's sake! Indoors and warm and comforted, a man is blind. Out here we see the city and the stars, we hear the rustle and the tramp of life, we crouch like hunters in a stony blind, straining our senses for—"

"Please, Fafhrd, no more danger signs," the Mouser protested. "Next you'll be telling me there's a monster a-drool and a-stalk in the streets, all slavering for Innesgay and her betrothal-maids, no doubt. And perchance a sword-garnished princeling or two, for appetizer."

Fafhrd gazed at him soberly and said, peering around through the thickening mist, "When I am *quite* sure of that, I'll let you know."

The twin brothers Kreshmar and Skel, assassins and alleybashers by trade, were menacing a miser in his hovel when the red-veined fog came in after them. As swiftly as ambitious men take last bite and wine-swig at a family dinner when unexpectedly summoned to the emperor's banquet board, the two finished their business. Kreshmar neatly bludgeoned a crater in the miser's skull while Skel thrust into his belt the one small purse of gold they had thus far extorted from the ancient man now turning to corpse. They stepped briskly outside, their swords a-swing at their hips, and into the fog, where they marched side-by-side with Gnarlag and Gis in the midst of the compact pale mass that moved almost indistinguishably with the river-fog and yet intoxicated them as surely as if it were a clouded white wine of murder and destruction, zestfully sluicing away all natural cautions and fears, promising an infinitude of thrilling and most profitable victims.

Behind the four marchers, the false fog thinned to a single glimmering thread, red as an artery, silver as a nerve, that led back unbroken around many a stony corner to the Temple of the Hates. A pulsing went ceaselessly along the thread, as nourishment and purpose were carried from the temple to the marauding fog mass and to the four killers, now doubly hate-enslaved, marching along with it. The fog mass moved purposefully as a snow-tiger toward the quarter of the nobles and Glipkerio's rainbow-lanterned palace above the breakwater of the Inner Sea.

Three black-clad police of Lankhmar, armed with metal-capped cudgels and weighted wickedly-barbed darts, saw the thicker fog mass coming and the marchers in it. The impression to them was of four men frozen in a sort of pliant ice. Their flesh crawled. They felt paralyzed. The fog fingered them, but almost instantly passed them by as inferior material for its purpose.

Knives and swords licked out of the fog mass. With never a cry the three police fell, their black tunics glistening with a fluid that showed red only on their sallow slack limbs. The fog mass thickened, as if it had fed instantly and richly on its victims. The four marchers became almost invisible from the outside, though from the inside they saw clearly enough.

Far down the longest and most landward of the five alleyways, the Mouser saw by the palace-glimmer behind him the white mass coming, shooting questing tendrils before it, and cried gaily, "Look, Fafhrd, we've company! The fog comes all the twisty way from the Hlal to warm its paddy paws at our little fire."

Fafhrd, frowning his eyes, said mistrustfully, "I think it masks other guests."

"Don't be a scareling," the Mouser reproved him in a fey voice. "I've a droll thought, Fafhrd: what if it be not fog, but the smoke of all the poppy-gum and hemp-resin in Lankhmar burning at once? What joys we'll have once we are sniffing it! What dreams we'll have tonight!"

"I think it brings nightmares," Fafhrd asserted softly, rising in a half crouch. Then, "Mouser, the taint! And my sword tingles to the touch!" The questingmost of the swiftly advancing fog-tendrils fingered them both then and seized on them joyously, as if here were the two captains it had been seeking, the slave leadership which would render it invincible.

The two blood-brothers tall and small felt to the full then the intoxication of the fog, its surging bittersweet touch-song of hate, its hot promises of all bloodlusts forever fulfilled, an uninhibited eternity of murder-madness.

Fafhrd, wineless tonight, intoxicated only by his own idealisms and the thought of watchmanship, was hardly touched by the sensations, did not feel them as temptations at all.

The Mouser, much of whose nature was built on hates and envies, had a harder time, but he too in the end rejected the fog's masterful lures—if only, to put the worst interpretation on it, because he wanted always to be the source of his own evil and would never accept it from another, not even as a gift from the archfiend himself.

The fog shrank back a dozen paces then, cat-quick, like a vixenishly proud woman rebuffed, revealing the four marchers in it and simultaneously pointing tendrils straight at the Mouser and Fafhrd.

It was well for the Mouser then that he knew the membership of Lankhmar's underworld to the last semiprofessional murderer and that his intuitions and reflexes were both arrow-swift. He recognized the smallest of the four—Gis with his belt of knives—as also the most immediately dangerous. Without hesitation he whipped Cat's Claw from its sheath, poised, aimed, and threw it. At the same instant Gis, equally knowledgeable and swift of thought and speedy of reaction, hurled one of his knives.

But the Mouser, forever cautious and wisely fearful, snatched his head to one side the moment he'd made his throw, so that Gis's knife only sliced his ear flap as it hummed past.

Gis, trusting too supremely in his own speed, made no similar evasive movement—with the result that the hilt of Cat's Claw stood out from his right eye socket an instant later. For a long moment he peered with shock and surprise from his other eye, then slumped to the cobbles, his features contorted in the ultimate agony. Kreshmar and Skel swiftly drew their swords and Gnarlag his two, not one whit intimidated by the winged death that had bitten into their comrade's brain.

Fafhrd, with a fine feeling for tactics on a broad front, did not draw sword at first but snatched up the brazier by one of its three burningly hot short legs and whirled its meager red-glowing contents in the attackers' faces.

This stopped them long enough for the Mouser to draw Scalpel and Fafhrd his heavier cave-forged sword. He wished he could do without the brazier—it was much too hot—but seeing himself opposed to Gnarlag of the Two Swords, he contented himself with shifting it jugglingly to his left hand.

Thereafter the fight was one swift sudden crisis. The three

attackers, daunted only a moment by the spray of hot coals and quite uninjured by them, raced forward surefootedly. Four truly-aimed blades thrust at the Mouser and Fafhrd.

The Northerner parried Gnarlag's right-hand sword with the brazier and his left-hand sword with the guard of his own weapon, which he managed simultaneously to thrust through the bravo's neck.

The shock of that death-stroke was so great that Gnarlag's two swords, bypassing Fafhrd one to each side, made no second stroke in their wielder's death-spasm. Fafhrd, conscious now chiefly of an agonizing pain in his left hand, chucked the brazier away in the nearest useful direction—which happened to be at Skel's head, spoiling that one's thrust at the Mouser, who was skipping nimbly back at the moment, though not more swiftly than Kreshmar and Skel were attacking.

The Mouser ducked under Kreshmar's blade and thrust Scalpel up through the assassin's ribs—the easy way to the heart—then quickly whipped it out and gave the same measured dose of thin steel to the dazedly staggering Skel. Then he danced away, looking around him dartingly and holding his sword high and menacing.

"All down and dead," Fafhrd, who'd had longer to look, assured him. "Ow, Mouser, I've burnt my fingers!"

"And I've a dissected ear," that one reported, exploring cautiously with little pats. He grinned. "Just at the edge, though." Then, having digested Fafhrd's remark, "Serves you right for fighting with a kitchen boy's weapon!"

Fafhrd retorted, "Bah! If you weren't such a miser with the charcoal, I'd have blinded them all with my ember cast!"

"And burnt your fingers even worse," the Mouser countered pleasantly. Then, still more happy-voiced, "Methought I heard gold chink at the belt of the one you brazier-bashed. Skel...yes, alleybasher Skel. When I've recovered Cat's Claw—"

He broke off because of an ugly little sucking sound that ended in a tiny *plop*. In the hazy glow from the nobles' quarter they saw a horridly supernatural sight: the Mouser's bloody dagger poised above Gis's punctured eye socket, supported only by a coiling white tentacle of the fog which had masked their attackers and which had now grown still more dense, as if it had sucked supreme nutriment—as indeed it had— from its dead servitors in their dying.

Eldritch dreads woke in the Mouser and Fafhrd: dreads of the lightning that slays from the storm-cloud, of the giant sea-serpent that strikes from the sea, of the shadows that coalesce in the forest to suffocate the mighty man lost, of the black smoke-snake that comes questing from the wizard's fire to strangle.

All around them was a faint clattering of steel against cobble: other fog-tentacles were lifting the four dropped swords and Gis's knife, while yet others were groping at that dead cutthroat's belt for his undrawn weapons.

It was as if some great ghost squid from the depths of the Inner Sea were arming itself for combat.

And four yards above the ground, at the rooting point of the tentacles in the thickened fog, a red disk was forming in the center of the fog's body, as it were—a reddish disk that looked moment by moment more like a single eye large as a face.

There was the inescapable thought that as soon as that eye could see, some ten beweaponed tentacles would thrust or slash at once, unerringly.

Fafhrd stood terror-bemused between the swiftly-forming eye and the Mouser. The latter, suddenly inspired, gripped Scalpel firmly, readied himself for a dash, and cried to the tall northerner, "Make a stirrup!"

Guessing the Mouser's stratagem, Fafhrd shook his horrors and laced his fingers together and went into a half crouch. The Mouser raced forward and planted his right foot in the stirrup Fafhrd had made of his hands and kicked off from it just as the latter helped his jump with a great heave—and a simultaneous "Ow!" of extreme pain.

The Mouser, preceded by his exactly aimed sword, went straight through the reddish ectoplasmic eye disk, dispersing it entirely. Then he vanished from Fafhrd's view as suddenly and completely as if he had been swallowed up by a snowbank.

An instant later the armed tentacles began to thrust and slash about, at random and erratically, as blind swordsmen might. But since there were a full ten of them, some of the strokes came perilously close to Fafhrd and he had to dodge and duck to keep out of the way. At the rutch of his shoes on the cobbles the tentacle-wielded swords and knives began to aim themselves a little better, again as blind swordsmen might, and he had to dodge more nimbly—not the easiest or safest work for a man so big. A dispassionate observer, if such had been conceivable and available, might have decided the ghost squid was trying to make Fafhrd dance.

Meanwhile on the other side of the white monster, the Mouser had caught sight of the pinkishly silver thread and, leaping high as it lifted to evade him, slashed it with the tip of Scalpel. It offered more resistance to his sword than the whole fog-body had and parted with a most unnatural and unexpected *twang* as he cut it through.

Immediately the fog-body collapsed and far more swiftly than any punctured bladder—rather it fell apart like a giant white puffball kicked by a giant boot—and the tentacles fell to pieces, too, and the swords and knives came clattering down harmlessly on the cobbles, and there was a swift fleeting rush of stench that made both Fafhrd and the Mouser clap hand to nose and mouth.

After sniffing cautiously and finding the air breathable again, the Mouser called brightly, "Hola there, dear comrade! I think I cut the thing's thin throat, or heart string, or vital nerve, or silver tether, or birth cord, or whatever the strand was."

"Where did the strand lead back to?" Fafhrd demanded.

"I have no intention of trying to find that out," the Mouser assured him, gazing warily over his shoulder in the direction from which the fog had come. "You try threading the Lankhmar labyrinth if you want to. But the strand seems as gone as the thing."

"Ow!" Fafhrd cried out suddenly and began to flap his hands. "Oh you small villain, to trick me into making a stirrup of my burnt hands!"

The Mouser grinned as he poked about with his gaze at the nastily slimed cobbles and the dead bodies and the scattered hardware. "Cat's Claw must be here somewhere," he muttered, "and I did hear the chink of gold...."

"You'd feel a penny under the tongue of a man you were strangling!" Fafhrd told him angrily.

At the Temple of the Hates, five thousand worshipers began to rise up weakly and groaningly, each lighter of weight by some few ounces than when he had first bowed down. The drummers slumped over their drums, the lantern-crankers over their extinguished red candles, and the lank Archpriest wearily and grimly lowered his head and rested the wooden mask in his clawlike hands.

At the alley-juncture, the Mouser dangled before Fafhrd's face the small purse he had just slipped from Skel's belt.

"My noble comrade, shall we make a betrothal gift of it to sweet Innesgay?" he asked liltingly. "And rekindle the dear little brazier and end this night as we began it, savoring all the matchless joys of watchmanship and all the manifold wonders of—"

"Give it here, idiot boy!" Fafhrd snarled, snatching the chinking thing for all his burnt fingers. "I know a place where they've soothing salves—and needles too, to stitch up the notched ears of thieves—and where both the wine and the girls are sharp and clean!"

FRITZ LEIBER'S
LANKhMAR

LEAN TIMES IN LANKhMAR

II

Once upon a time in Lankhmar, City of the Black Toga, in the world of Nehwon, two years after the Year of the Feathered Death, Fafhrd and the Gray Mouser parted their ways.

Exactly what caused the tall brawling barbarian and the slim elusive Prince of Thieves to fall out, and the mighty adventuring partnership to be broken, is uncertainly known and was at the time the subject of much speculation. Some said they had quarreled over a girl. Others maintained, with even greater unlikelihood, that they had disagreed over the proper division of a loot of jewels raped from Muulsh the Moneylender. Srith of the Scrolls suggests that their mutual cooling off was largely the reflection of a supernatural enormity existing at the time between Sheelba of the Eyeless Face, the Mouser's demonic mentor, and Ningauble of the Seven Eyes, Fafhrd's alien and multiserpentine patron.

The likeliest explanation, which runs directly counter to the Muulsh Hypothesis, is simply that times were hard in Lankhmar, adventures few and uninviting, and that the two heroes had reached that point in life when hard-pressed men desire to admix even the rarest quests and pleasurings with certain prudent activities leading either to financial or to spiritual security, though seldom if ever to both.

This theory—that boredom and insecurity, and a difference of opinion as to how these dismal feelings might best be dealt with, chiefly underlay the estrangement of the twain…this theory may account for and perhaps even subsume the otherwise ridiculous suggestion that the two comrades fell out over the proper spelling of Fafhrd's name, the Mouser perversely favoring a simple Lankhmarian equivalent of "Faferd" while the name's owner insisted that only the original mouth-filling agglomeration of consonants could continue to satisfy his ear and eye and his semiliterate, barbarous sense of the fitness of things. Bored and insecure men will loose arrows at dust motes.

Certain it is that their friendship, though not utterly fractured, grew very cold and that their life-ways, though both continuing in Lankhmar, diverged remarkably.

Gray Mouser entered the service of one Pulg, a rising racketeer of small religions, a lord of Lankhmar's dark underworld who levied tribute from the priests of all godlets seeking to become gods—on pain of various unpleasant, disturbing and revolting things happening at future services of the defaulting godlet. If a priest didn't pay Pulg, his miracles were sure to misfire, his congregation and collection fall off sharply, and it was quite possible that a bruised skin and broken bones would be his lot.

Accompanied by three or four of Pulg's buddies and frequently a slim dancing girl or two, the Mouser became a familiar and newly-ominous sight in Lankhmar's Street of the Gods which leads from the Marsh Gate to the distant docks and the Citadel. He still wore gray, went close-hooded, and carried Cat's Claw and Scalpel at his side, but the dagger and curving sword kept in their sheaths. Knowing from of old that a threat is generally more effective than its execution, he limited his activities to the handling of conversations and cash. "I speak for Pulg—Pulg with a *guh!*" was his usual opening. Later, if holy men grew recalcitrant or overly keen in their bargaining and it became necessary to maul saintlets and break up services, he would sign the bullies to take disciplinary measures while he himself stood idly by, generally in slow sardonic converse with the attendant girl or girls and often munching sweetmeats. As the months passed, the Mouser grew fat and the dancing girls successively more slim and submissive-eyed.

Fafhrd, on the other hand, broke his longsword across his knee (cutting himself badly in the act), tore from his garments the few remaining ornaments (dull and worthless scraps of metal) and bits of ratty fur, forswore strong drink and all allied pleasures (he had been on small beer and womanless for some time), and became the sole acolyte of Bwadres, the sole priest of Issek of the Jug. Fafhrd let his beard grow until it was as long as his shoulder-brushing hair, he became lean and hollow-cheeked and cavern-eyed, and his voice changed from bass to tenor, though *not* as a result of the distressing mutilation which some whispered he had inflicted upon himself—these last knew he had cut himself but lied wildly as to where.

The gods *in* Lankhmar (that is, the gods and candidates for divinity who dwell or camp, it may be said, in the Imperishable City, not the gods *of* Lankhmar—a very different and most secret and dire matter)...the gods *in* Lankhmar sometimes seem as if they must be as numberless as the grains of sand in the Great Eastern Desert. The vast majority of them began as men, or more strictly the memories of men who led ascetic, vision-haunted lives and died painful, messy deaths. One gets the impression that since the beginning of time an unending horde of their priests and apostles (or even the gods themselves, it makes little difference) have been crippling across that same desert, the Sinking Land, and the Great Salt Marsh to converge on Lankhmar's low, heavy-arched Marsh Gate—meanwhile suffering by the way various inevitable tortures, castrations, blindings and stonings, impalements, crucifixions, quarterings and so forth at the hands of eastern brigands and Mingol unbelievers who, one is tempted to think, were created solely for the purpose of seeing to the running of that cruel gauntlet. Among the tormented holy throng are a few warlocks and witches seeking infernal immortality for their dark satanic would-be deities and a very few proto-goddesses—generally maidens reputed to have been enslaved for decades by sadistic magicians and ravished by whole tribes of Mingols.

Lankhmar itself and especially the earlier-mentioned street serves as the theater or more precisely the intellectual and artistic testing-ground of the proto-gods after their more material but no more cruel sifting at the hands of the brigands and Mingols. A new god (his priest or priests, that is) will begin at the Marsh Gate and more or less slowly work his way up the Street of the Gods, renting a temple or preempting a few yards of cobbled pavement here and there, until he has found his proper level. A very few win their way to the region adjoining the Citadel and join the aristocracy of the gods in Lankhmar—transients still, though resident there for centuries and even millennia (the gods *of* Lankhmar are as jealous as they are secret). Far more godlets, it can justly be said, play a one-night-stand near the Marsh Gate and abruptly disappear, perhaps to seek cities where the audiences are less critical. The majority work their way about halfway up the Street of the Gods and then slowly work their way down again, resisting bitterly every inch and yard, until they once more reach the Marsh Gate and vanish forever from Lankhmar and the memories of men.

Now Issek of the Jug, whom Fafhrd chose to serve, was one of the most lowly and unsuccessful of the gods, godlets rather, in Lankhmar. He had dwelt there for about thirteen years, during which time he had traveled only two squares up the Street of the Gods and was now back again, ready for oblivion. He is not to be confused with Issek the Armless, Issek of the Burnt Legs, Flayed Issek, or any other of the numerous and colorfully mutilated divinities of that name. Indeed, his unpopularity may have been due in part to the fact that the manner of his death—racking—was not deemed particularly spectacular. A few scholars have confused him with Jugged Issek, an entirely different saintlet whose claim to immortality lay in his confinement for seventeen years in a not overly roomy earthenware jar. The Jug (Issek of the Jug's Jug) was supposed to contain Waters of Peace from the Cistern of Cillivat—but none apparently thirsted for them. Indeed, had you sought for a good example of a has-been who has never really been anything, you could hardly hit on a better choice than Issek of the Jug, while Bwadres was the very type of the failed priest—sere, senile, apologetic and mumbling. The reason that Fafhrd attached to Bwadres, rather than to any one of a vast number of livelier holy men with better prospects, was that he had seen Bwadres pat a deaf-and-dumb child on the head *while* (so far as Bwadres could have known) *no one was looking* and the incident (possibly unique in Lankhmar) had stuck in the mind of the barbarian. But otherwise Bwadres was a most unexceptional old dodderer. However, after Fafhrd became his acolyte, things somehow began to change.

In the first place, and even if he had contributed nothing else, Fafhrd made a very impressive one-man congregation from the very first day when he turned up so ragged-looking and bloody (from the cuts breaking his longsword). His near seven-foot height and still warlike carriage stood out mountainously among the old women, children and assorted riff-raff who made up the odorous, noisy, and vastly fickle crowd of worshipers at the Marsh Gate end of the Street of the Gods. One could not help thinking that if Issek of the Jug could attract one such worshiper the godlet must have unsuspected virtues. Fafhrd's formidable height, shoulder breadth and bearing had one other advantage: he could maintain claim to a very respectable area of cobbles for Bwadres and Issek merely by stretching himself out to sleep on them after the night's services were over.

It was at this time that oafs and ruffians stopped elbowing Bwadres and spitting on him. Fafhrd was most pacific in his new personality—after all, Issek of the Jug was notably a godlet of peace—but Fafhrd had a fine barbaric feeling for the proprieties. If anyone took liberties with Bwadres or disturbed the various rituals of Issek-worship, he would find himself lifted up and set down somewhere else, with an admonitory thud if that seemed called for—a sort of informal one-stroke bastinado.

Bwadres himself brightened amazingly as a result of this wholly unexpected respite granted him and his divinity on the very brink of oblivion. He began to eat more often than twice a week and to comb his long skimpy beard. Soon his senility dropped away from him like an old cloak, leaving of itself only a mad stubborn gleam deep in his yellowly crust-edged eyes, and he began to preach the gospel of Issek of the Jug with a fervor and confidence that he had never known before.

Meanwhile Fafhrd, in the second place, fairly soon began to contribute more to the promotion of the Issek of the Jug cult than his size, presence, and notable talents as a chucker-out. After two months of self-imposed absolute silence, which he refused to break even to answer the simplest questions of Bwadres, who was at first considerably puzzled by his gigantic convert, Fafhrd procured a small broken lyre, repaired it and began regularly to chant the Creed and History of Issek of the Jug at all services. He competed in no way with Bwadres, never chanted any of the litanies or presumed to bless in Issek's name; in fact he always kneeled and resumed silence while serving Bwadres as acolyte, but seated on the cobbles at the foot of the service area while Bwadres meditated between rituals at the head, he would strike melodious chords from his tiny lyre and chant away in a rather high-pitched, pleasing, romantically vibrant voice.

Now as a Northerner boy in the Cold Waste, far poleward of Lankhmar across the Inner Sea, the forested Land of the Eight Cities and the Trollstep Mountains, Fafhrd had been trained in the School of the Singing Skalds (so called, although they chanted rather than sang, because they pitched their voices tenor) rather than in the School of the Roaring Skalds (who pitched their voices bass). This assumption of a childhood-inculcated style of elocution, which he also used in answering the few questions his humility would permit him to notice, was the real and sole reason for the change in Fafhrd's voice that was made the subject of gossip by those who had known him as the Gray Mouser's deep-voiced swordmate.

As delivered over and over by Fafhrd, the History of Issek of the Jug gradually altered, by small steps which even Bwadres could hardly cavil at had he wished, into something considerably more like the saga of a Northern hero, though toned down in some respects. Issek had not slain dragons and other monsters as a child—that would have been against his Creed—he had only sported with them, swimming with leviathan, frisking with behemoth, and flying through the trackless spaces of air on the backs of wivern, griffin and hippogryph. Nor had Issek as a man scattered kings and emperors in battle, he had merely dumbfounded them and their quaking ministers by striding about on fields of poisoned sword-points, standing at attention in fiery furnaces, and treading water in tanks of boiling oil—all the while delivering majestic sermons on brotherly love in perfect, intricately rhymed stanzas. Bwadres' Issek had expired quite quickly, though with some kindly parting admonitions, after being disjointed on the rack. Fafhrd's Issek (now *the* Issek) had broken seven racks before he began seriously to weaken. Even when, supposedly dead, he had been loosed and had got his hands on the chief torturer's throat there had been enough strength remaining in them alone so that he had been able to strangle the wicked man with ease, although the latter was a champion of wrestlers among his people. However, Fafhrd's Issek had not done so—again it would have been quite against his Creed—he had merely broken the torturer's thick brass band of office from around his trembling neck and twisted it into an exquisitely beautiful symbol of the Jug before finally permitting his own ghost to escape from him into the eternal realms of spirit, there to continue its wildly wonderful adventurings.

Now, since the vast majority of the gods *in* Lankhmar, arising from the Eastern Lands or at least from the kindredly decadent southern country around Quarmall, had been in their earthly incarnations rather effete types unable to bear more than a few minutes of hanging or a few hours of impalement, and with relatively little resistance to molten lead or showers of barbed darts, also not given overly to composing romantic poetry or to dashing exploits with strange beasts, it is hardly to be wondered that Issek of the Jug, as interpreted by Fafhrd, swiftly won and held the attention and soon thereafter also the devotion of a growing section of the usually unstable, gods-dazzled mob. In particular, the vision of Issek of the Jug rising up with his rack, striding about with it on his back, breaking it, and then calmly waiting with arms voluntarily stretched above his head until another rack could be readied and attached to him…that vision, in particular, came to occupy a place of prime importance in the dreams and daydreams of many a porter, beggar, drab scullion, and the brats and aged dependents of such.

As a result of this popularity, Issek of the Jug was soon not only moving up the Street of the Gods for a second time—a rare enough feat in itself—but also moving at a greater velocity than any god had been known to attain in the modern era. Almost every service saw Bwadres and Fafhrd able to move their simple altar a few more yards toward the Citadel end as their swelling congregations overflowed areas temporarily sacred to gods of less drawing power, and frequently latecoming and tireless worshipers enabled them to keep up services until the sky was reddening with the dawn—ten or twelve repetitions of the ritual (and the yardage gain) in one night. Before long the makeup of their congregations had begun to change. Pursed and then fatter-pursed types showed up: mercenaries and merchants, sleek thieves and minor officials, jeweled courtesans and slumming aristocrats, shaven philosophers who scoffed lightly at Bwadres' tangled arguments and Issek's irrational Creed but who were secretly awed by the apparent sincerity of the ancient man and his giant poetical acolyte…and with these monied newcomers came, inevitably, the iron-tough hirelings of Pulg and other such hawks circling over the fowl yards of religion.

Naturally enough, this threatened to pose a considerable problem for the Gray Mouser.

So long as Issek, Bwadres and Fafhrd stayed within hooting range of the Marsh Gate, there was nothing to worry about. There when collection time came and Fafhrd circled the congregation with cupped hands, the take, if any, was in the form of moldy crusts, common vegetables past their prime, rags, twigs, bits of charcoal, and—very rarely, giving rise to shouts of wonder—bent and dinted greenish coins of brass. Such truck was below the notice of even lesser racketeers than Pulg, and Fafhrd had no trouble whatever in dealing with the puny and dull-witted types who sought to play Robber King in the Marsh Gate's shadow. More than once the Mouser managed to advise Fafhrd that this was an ideal state of affairs and that any considerable further progress of Issek up the Street of the Gods could lead only to great unpleasantness. The Mouser was nothing if not cautious and most prescient to boot. He liked, or firmly believed he liked, his newly-achieved security almost better than he liked himself. He knew that, as a recent hireling of Pulg, he was still being watched closely by the Great Man and that any appearance of continuing friendship with Fafhrd (for most outsiders thought they had quarreled irrevocably) might someday be counted against him. So on the occasions when he drifted down the Street of the Gods during off-hours— that is, by daylight, for religion is largely a nocturnal, torchlit business in Lankhmar—he would never seem to speak to Fafhrd directly. Nevertheless he would by seeming accident end up near Fafhrd and, while apparently engaged in some very different private business or pleasure (or perhaps come secretly to gloat over his large enemy's fallen estate—that was the Mouser's second line of defense against conceivable accusations by Pulg) he would manage considerable conversations out of the corner of his mouth, which Fafhrd would answer, if at all, in the same way—though in his case presumably from abstraction rather than policy.

"Look, Fafhrd," the Mouser said on the third of such occasions, meanwhile pretending to study a skinny-limbed pot-bellied beggar girl as if trying to decide whether a diet of lean meat and certain calisthenics would bring out in her a rare gaminesque beauty. "Look, Fafhrd, right here you have what you want, whatever that is—I think it's a chance to patch up poetry and squeak it at fools—but whatever it is, you must have it here near the Marsh Gate, for the only thing in the world that is not near the Marsh Gate is money, and you tell me you don't want that—the more fool you!—but let me tell you something: if you let Bwadres get any nearer the Citadel, yes even a pebble's toss, you will get money whether you want it or not, and with that money you and Bwadres will buy something, also willy-nilly and no matter how tightly you close your purse and shut your ears to the cries of the hawkers. That thing which you and Bwadres will buy is trouble."

Fafhrd answered only with a faint grunt that was the equivalent of a shoulder shrug. He was looking steadily down past his bushy beard with almost cross-eyed concentration at something his long fingers were manipulating powerfully yet delicately, but that the large backs of his hands concealed from the Mouser's view. "How is the old fool, by the by, since he's eating regularly?" the Mouser continued, leaning a hair closer in an effort to see what Fafhrd was handling. "Still stubborn as ever, eh? Still set on taking Issek to the Citadel? Still as unreasonable about…er…business matters?"

"Bwadres is a good man," Fafhrd said quietly.

"More and more that appears to be the heart of the trouble," the Mouser answered with a certain sardonic exasperation. "But look, Fafhrd, it's not necessary to change Bwadres' mind—I'm beginning to doubt whether even Sheelba and Ning, working together, could achieve that cosmic revolution. You can do by yourself all that needs to be done. Just give your poetry a little downbeat, add a little defeatism to Issek's Creed—even you must be tired by now of all this ridiculous mating of northern stoicism to southern masochism, and wanting a change. One theme's good as another to a true artist. Or, simpler still, merely refrain from moving Issek's altar up the street on your big night...or even move down a little!—Bwadres gets so excited when you have big crowds that the old fool doesn't know which direction you're going, anyhow. You could progress like the well-frog. Or, wisest of all, merely prepare yourself to split the take before you hand over the collection to Bwadres. I could teach you the necessary legerdemain in the space of one dawn, though you really don't need it—with those huge hands you can palm anything."

"No," said Fafhrd.

"Suit yourself," the Mouser said very very lightly, though not quite unfeelingly. "Buy trouble if you will, death if you must. Fafhrd, what *is* that thing you're fiddling with? No, don't hand it to me, you idiot! Just let me glimpse it. By the Black Toga!—what *is* that?"

Without looking up or otherwise moving, Fafhrd had cupped his hands sideways, much as if he were displaying in the Mouser's direction a captive butterfly or beetle—indeed it did seem at first glimpse as if it were a rare large beetle he was cautiously baring to view, one with a carapace of softly burnished gold.

"It is an offering to Issek," Fafhrd droned. "An offering made last night by a devout lady who is wed in spirit to the god."

"Yes, and to half the young aristos of Lankhmar too and not all in spirit," the Mouser hissed. "I know one of Lessnya's double-spiral bracelets when I see it. Reputedly given her by the Twin Dukes of Ilthmar, by the by. What did you have to do to her to get it?—stop, don't answer. I know...recite poetry! Fafhrd, things are far worse than I dreamed. If Pulg knew you were already getting gold…" He let his whisper trail off. "But what have you *done* with it?"

"Fashioned it into a representation of the Holy Jug," Fafhrd answered, bowing his head a shade farther and opening his hands a bit wider and tipping them a trifle.

"So I see," the Mouser hissed. The soft gold had been twisted into a remarkably smooth strange knot. "And not a bad job at all. Fafhrd, how you keep such a delicate feeling for curves when for six months you've slept without them against you is quite beyond me. Doubtless such things go by opposites. Don't speak for a moment now, I'm getting an idea. And by the Black Scapula!—a good one! Fafhrd, you must give me that trinket so that I may give it to Pulg. No—please hear me out and then think this through!—not for the gold in it, not as a bribe or as part of a first split—I'm not asking that of you or Bwadres—but simply as a keepsake, a presentation piece. Fafhrd, I've been getting to know Pulg lately, and I find he has a strange sentimental streak in him— he likes to get little gifts, little trophies, from his…er…customers, we sometimes call them. These curios must always be items relating to the god in question— chalices, censers, bones in silver filigree, jeweled amulets, that sort of thing. He likes to sit looking at his shelves of them and dream. Sometimes I think the man is getting religion without realizing it. If I should bring him this bauble he would—I know!—develop an affection for Issek. He would tell me to go easy on Bwadres. It would probably even be possible to put off the question of tribute money for…well, for three more squares at least."

"No," said Fafhrd.

"So be it, my friend. Come with me, my dear, I am going to buy you a steak." This second remark was in the Mouser's regular speaking voice and directed, of course, at the beggar girl, who reacted with a look of already practiced and rather languorous affright. "Not a fish steak either, puss. Did you know there were other kinds? Toss this coin to your mother, dear, and come. The steak stall is four squares up. No, we won't take a litter—you need the exercise. *Farewell—Death-seeker!*"

Despite the wash-my-hands-of-you tone of this last whisper, the Gray Mouser did what he could to put off the evil night of reckoning, devising more pressing tasks for Pulg's bullies and alleging that this or that omen was against the immediate settling of the Bwadres account—for Pulg, alongside his pink streak of sentimentality, had recently taken to sporting a gray one of superstition.

There would have been no insurmountable problem at all, of course, if Bwadres had only had that touch of realism about money matters that, when a true crisis arises, is almost invariably shown by even the fattest, greediest priest or the skinniest, most unworldly holy man. But Bwadres was stubborn—it was probably, as we have hinted, the sole remaining symptom, though a most inconvenient one, of his only seemingly cast-off senility. Not one rusty iron *tik* (the smallest coin of Lankhmar) would he pay to extortioners— such was Bwadres' boast. To make matters worse, if that were possible, he would not even *spend* money renting gaudy furniture or temple space for Issek, as was practically mandatory for gods progressing up the central stretch of the street. Instead he averred that every tik collected, every bronze agol, every silver smerduk, every gold rilk, yes every diamond-in-amber gludditch!—would be saved to buy for Issek the finest temple at the Citadel end, in fact the temple of Aarth the Invisible All-Listener, accounted one of the most ancient and powerful of all the gods *in* Lankhmar.

Naturally, this insane challenge, thrown out for all to hear, had the effect of still further increasing Issek's popularity and swelled his congregations with all sorts of folk who came, at first at least, purely as curiosity seekers. The odds on how far Issek would get up the Street how soon (for they regularly bet on such things in Lankhmar) began to switch wildly up and down as the affair got quite beyond the shrewd but essentially limited imaginations of bookmakers. Bwadres took to sleeping curled in the gutter around Issek's coffer (first an old garlic bag, later a small stout cask with a slit in the top for coins) and with Fafhrd curled around him. Only one of them slept at a time, the other rested but kept watch.

At one point the Mouser almost decided to slit Bwadres' throat as the only possible way out of his dilemma. But he knew that such an act would be the one unforgivable crime against his new profession—it would be bad for business—and certain to ruin him forever with Pulg and all other extortioners if ever traced to him even in faintest suspicion. Bwadres must be roughed up if necessary, yes even tortured, but at the same time he must be treated in all ways as a goose who laid golden eggs. Moreover, the Mouser had a presentiment that putting Bwadres out of the way would not stop Issek. Not while Issek had Fafhrd.

What finally brought the affair to a head, or rather to its first head, and forced the Mouser's hand was the inescapable realization that if he held off any longer from putting the bite on Bwadres for Pulg, then rival extortioners—one Basharat in particular—would do it on their own account. As the Number One Racketeer of Religions in Lankhmar, Pulg certainly had first grab, but if he delayed for an unreasonable length of time in making it (no matter on what grounds of omens or arguments about fattening the sacrifice), then Bwadres was anybody's victim—Basharat's in particular, as Pulg's chief rival.

So it came about, as it so often does, that the Mouser's efforts to avert the evil nightfall only made it darker and stormier when it finally came down.

When at last that penultimate evening did arrive, signalized by a final warning sent Pulg by Basharat, the

Mouser, who had been hoping all along for some wonderful last-minute inspiration that never came, took what may seem to some a coward's way out. Making use of the beggar girl whom he had named Lilyblack, and certain other of his creatures, he circulated a rumor that the Treasurer of the Temple of Aarth was preparing to decamp in a rented black sloop across the Inner Sea, taking with him all funds and ample valuables, including a set of black-pearl-crusted altar furnishings, gift of the wife of the High Overlord, on which the split had not yet been made with Pulg. He timed the rumor so that it would return to him, by unimpeachable channels, just after he had set out for Issek's spot with four well-armed bullies.

It may be noted, in passing, that Aarth's Treasurer actually was in monetary hot waters and really had rented a black sloop. Which proved not only that the Mouser used good sound fabric for his fabrications, but also that Bwadres had by landlords' and bankers' standards made a very sound choice in selecting Issek's temple-to-be—whether by chance or by some strange shrewdness co-dwelling with his senile stubbornness.

The Mouser could not divert his whole expeditionary force, for Bwadres must be saved from Basharat. However, he was able to split it with the almost certain knowledge that Pulg would consider his action the best strategy available at the moment. Three of the bullies he sent on with firm instructions to bring Bwadres to account, while he himself raced off with minimum guard to intercept the supposedly fleeing and loot-encumbered treasurer.

Of course the Mouser *could* have made himself part of the Bwadres-party, but that would have meant he would have had personally to best Fafhrd or be bested by him, and while the Mouser wanted to do everything possible for his friend he wanted to do just a little bit more than that (he thought) for his own security.

Some, as we have suggested, may think that in taking this way out the Gray Mouser was throwing his friend to the wolves. However, it must always be remembered that the Mouser knew Fafhrd.

The three bullies, who did not know Fafhrd (the Mouser had selected them for that reason), were pleased with the turn of events. An independent commission always meant the chance of some brilliant achievement and so perhaps of promotion. They waited for the first break between services, when there was inevitably considerable passing about and jostling. Then one, who had a small ax in his belt, went straight for Bwadres and his cask, which the holy man also used as altar, draping it for the purpose with the sacred garlic bag. Another drew sword and menaced Fafhrd, keeping sound distance from and careful watch on the giant. The third, adopting the jesting, rough-and-ready manner of the master of the show in a bawdy house, spoke ringing warnings to the crowd and kept a reasonably watchful eye on them. The folk of Lankhmar are so bound by tradition that it was unthinkable that they would interfere with any activities as legitimate as those of an extortioner—the Number One Extortioner, too—even in defense of a most favored priest, but there are occasional foreigners and madmen to be dealt with (though in Lankhmar even the madmen generally respect the traditions).

No one in the congregation saw the crucial thing that happened next, for their eyes were all on the first bully, who was lightly choking Bwadres with one hand while pointing his ax at the cask with the other. There was a cry of surprise and a clatter. The second bully, lunged forward toward Fafhrd, had dropped his sword and was shaking his hand as if it pained him. Without haste Fafhrd picked him up by the slack of his garments between his shoulder blades, reached the first bully in two giant strides, slapped the ax from his hand, and picked him up likewise.

It was an impressive sight: the giant, gaunt-cheeked, bearded acolyte wearing his long robe of undyed camel's hair (recent gift of a votary) and standing with knees bent and feet wide-planted as he held aloft to either side a squirming bully.

But although indeed a most impressive tableau, it presented a made-to-order opening for the third bully, who instantly unsheathed his scimitar and, with an acrobat's smile and wave to the crowd, lunged toward the apex of the obtuse angle formed by the juncture of Fafhrd's legs.

The crowd shuddered and squealed with the thought of the poignancy of the blow.

There was a muffled *thud*. The third bully dropped *his* sword. Without changing his stance Fafhrd swept together the two bullies he was holding so that their heads met with a loud *thunk*. With an equally measured movement he swept them apart again and sent them sprawling to either side, unconscious, among the onlookers. Then stepping forward, still without seeming haste, he picked up the third bully by neck and crotch and pitched him a considerably greater distance into the crowd, where he bowled over two of Basharat's henchmen who had been watching the proceedings with great interest.

There was absolute silence for three heartbeats, then the crowd applauded rapturously. While the tradition-bound Lankhmarians thought it highly proper for extortioners to extort, they also considered it completely in character for a strange acolyte to work miracles, and they never omitted to clap a good performance.

Bwadres, fingering his throat and still gasping a little, smiled with simple pleasure and when Fafhrd finally acknowledged the applause by dropping down cross-legged to the cobbles and bowing his head, the old priest launched instantly into a sermon in which he further electrified the crowd by several times hinting that, in his celestial realms,

Issek was preparing to visit Lankhmar in person. His acolyte's routing of the three evil men Bwadres attributed to the inspiration of Issek's might—to be interpreted as a sort of foretaste of the god's approaching reincarnation.

The most significant consequence of this victory of the doves over the hawks was a little midnight conference in the back room of the Inn of the Silver Eel, where Pulg first warmly praised and then coolly castigated the Gray Mouser.

He praised the Mouser for intercepting the Treasurer of Aarth, who it turned out *had* just been embarking on the black sloop, not to flee Lankhmar, though, but only to spend a water-guarded weekend with several riotous companions and one Ilala, High Priestess of the goddess of the same name. However, he *had* actually taken along several of the black-pearl-crusted altar furnishings, apparently as a gift for the High Priestess, and the Mouser very properly confiscated them before wishing the holy band the most exquisite of pleasures on their holiday. Pulg judged that the Mouser's loot amounted to just about twice the usual cut, which seemed a reasonable figure to cover the Treasurer's irregularity.

He rebuked the Mouser for failing to warn the three bullies about Fafhrd and omitting to instruct them in detail on how to deal with the giant.

"They're your boys, son, and I judge you by their performance," Pulg told the Mouser in fatherly matter-of-fact tones. "To me, if they stumble, you flop. You know this Northerner well, son; you should have had them trained to meet his sleights. You solved your main problem well, but you slipped on an important detail. I expect good strategy from my lieutenants, but I demand flawless tactics."

The Mouser bowed his head.

"You and this Northerner were comrades once," Pulg continued. He leaned forward across the dinted table and drew down his lower lip. "You're not still soft on him, are you, son?"

The Mouser arched his eyebrows, flared his nostrils and slowly swung his face from side to side.

Pulg thoughtfully scratched his nose. "So we come tomorrow night," he said. "Must make an example of Bwadres—an example that will stick like Mingol glue. I'd suggest having Grilli hamstring the Northerner at the first onset. Can't kill him—he's the one that brings in the money. But with ankle tendons cut he could still stump around on his hands and knees and be in some ways an even better drawing card. How's that sound to you?"

The Mouser slitted his eyes in thought for three breaths. Then, "Bad," he said boldly. "It gripes me to admit it, but this Northerner sometimes conjures up battle-sleights that even I can't be sure of countering—crazy berserk tricks born of sudden whim that no civilized man can anticipate. Chances are Grilli could nick him, but what if he didn't? Here's my reed—it lets you rightly think that I may still be soft on the man, but I give it because it's my best reed: let me get him drunk at nightfall. Dead drunk. Then he's out of the way for certain."

Pulg frowned. "Sure you can deliver on that, son? They say he's forsworn booze. And he sticks to Bwadres like a giant squid."

"I can detach him," the Mouser said. "And this way we don't risk spoiling him for Bwadres' show. Battle's always uncertain. You may plan to hock a man and then have to cut his throat."

Pulg shook his head. "We also leave him fit to tangle with our collectors the next time they come for the cash. Can't get him drunk every time we pick up the split. Too complicated. And looks very weak."

"No need to," the Mouser said confidently. "Once Bwadres starts paying, the Northerner will go along."

Pulg continued to shake his head. "You're guessing, son," he said. "Oh, to the best of your ability, but still guessing. I want this deal bagged up strongly. An example that will stick, I said. Remember, son, the man we're really putting on this show for tomorrow night is Basharat. He'll be there, you can bet on it, though standing in the last row, I imagine—did you hear how your Northerner dumped two of his boys? I liked that." He grinned widely, then instantly grew serious again. "So we'll do it my way, eh? Grilli's very sure."

The Mouser shrugged once, deadpan. "If you say so. Of course, some Northerners suicide when crippled. I don't think *he* would, but he might. Still, even allowing for that, I'd say our plan has four chances in five of working out perfectly. Four in five."

Pulg frowned furiously, his rather piggy red-rimmed eyes fixed on the Mouser. Finally he said, "*Sure* you can get him drunk, son? Five in five?"

"I can do it," the Mouser said. He had thought of a half dozen additional arguments in favor of his plan, but he did not utter them. He did not even add, "Six in six," as he was tempted to. He was learning.

Pulg suddenly leaned back in his chair and laughed, signing that the business part of their conference was over. He tweaked the naked girl standing beside him. "Wine!" he ordered. "No, not that sugary slop I keep for customers—didn't Zizzi instruct you?—but the real stuff from behind the green idol. Come, son, pledge me a cup, and then tell me a little about this Issek. I'm interested in him. I'm interested in 'em all." He waved loosely at the darkly gleaming shelves of religious curios in the handsomely carved traveling case rising beyond the end of the table. He frowned a very different frown from his business one. "There are more things in this world than we understand," he said sententiously. "Did you know that, son?" The Great Man shook his head, again very differently. He was swiftly sinking into his most deeply metaphysical mood. "Makes me wonder, sometimes. You and I, son, know that these"—He waved again at the case—"are toys. But the feelings that men have toward them...they're real, eh?—and they can be strange. Easy to understand part of those feelings—brats shivering at bogies, fools gawking at a show and hoping for blood or a bit of undressing—but there's another part that's strange. The priests bray nonsense, the people groan and pray, and then something comes into existence. I don't know what that something is—I wish I did, I think—but it's strange." He shook his head. "Makes any man wonder. So drink your wine, son—watch his cup, girl, and don't let it empty—and talk to me about Issek. I'm interested in 'em all, but right now I'd like to hear about him."

He did not in any way hint that for the past two months he had been watching the services of Issek for at least five nights a week from behind a veiled window in various lightless rooms along the Street of the Gods. And that was something that not even the Mouser knew about Pulg.

So as a pinkly opalescent, rose-ribboned dawn surged up the sky from the black and stinking Marsh, the Mouser sought out Fafhrd. Bwadres was still snoring in the gutter, embracing Issek's cask, but the big barbarian was awake and sitting on the curb, hand grasping his chin under his beard. Already a few children had gathered at a respectful distance, though no one else was abroad.

"That the one they can't stab or cut?" the Mouser heard one of the children whisper.

"That's him," another answered.

"I'd like to sneak up behind him and stick him with this pin."

"I'll bet you would!"

"I guess he's got iron skin," said a tiny girl with large eyes.

The Mouser smothered a guffaw, patted that last child on the head, and then advanced straight to Fafhrd and, with a grimace at the stained refuse between the cobbles, squatted fastidiously on his hams. He still could do it easily, though his new belly made a considerable pillow in his lap. He said without preamble, speaking too low for the children to hear, "Some say the strength of Issek lies in love, some say in honesty, some say in courage, some say in stinking hypocrisy. I believe I have guessed the one true answer. If I am right, you will drink wine with me. If I am wrong, I will strip to my loincloth, declare Issek my god and master, and serve as acolyte's acolyte. Is it a wager?"

Fafhrd studied him. "It is done," he said.

The Mouser advanced his right hand and lightly rapped Fafhrd's body twice through the soiled camel's hair—once in the chest, once between the legs. Each time there was a faint *thud* with just the hint of a *clank*. "The cuirass of Mingsward and the groin-piece of Gortch," the Mouser pronounced. "Each heavily padded to keep them from ringing. Therein lie Issek's strength and invulnerability. They wouldn't have fit you six months ago."

Fafhrd sat as one bemused. Then his face broke into a large grin. "You win," he said. "When do I pay?"

"This very afternoon," the Mouser whispered, "when Bwadres eats and takes his forty winks." He rose with a light grunt and made off, stepping daintily from cobble to cobble. Soon the Street of the Gods grew moderately busy and for awhile Fafhrd was surrounded by a scattering of the curious, but it was a very hot day for Lankhmar. By midafternoon the Street was deserted; even the children had sought shade.

Bwadres droned through the Acolyte's Litany twice with Fafhrd, then called for food by touching his hand to his mouth—it was his ascetic custom always to eat at this uncomfortable time rather than in the cool of the evening.

Fafhrd went off and shortly returned with a large bowl of fish stew. Bwadres blinked at the size of it, but tucked it away, belched, and curled around the cask after an admonition to Fafhrd. He was snoring almost immediately.

A hiss sounded from the low wide archway behind them.

Fafhrd stood up and quietly moved into the shadows of the portico. The Mouser gripped his arm and guided him toward one of several curtained doorways.

"Your sweat's a flood, my friend," he said softly. "Tell me, do you really wear the armor from prudence, or is it a kind of metal hair-shirt?"

Fafhrd did not answer. He blinked at the curtain the Mouser drew aside. "I don't like this," he said. "It's a house of assignation. I may be seen and then what will dirty-minded people think?"

"Hung for the kid, hung for the goat," the Mouser said lightly. "Besides, you haven't been seen—yet. In with you!"

Fafhrd complied. The heavy curtains swung to behind them, leaving the room in which they stood lit only by high louvers. As Fafhrd squinted into the semidarkness, the Mouser said, "I've paid the evening's rent on this place. It's private, it's near. None will know. What more could you ask?"

"I guess you're right," Fafhrd said uneasily. "But you've spent too much rent money. Understand, my little man, I can have only one drink with you. You tricked me into that— after a fashion you did—but I pay. But only one cup of wine, little man. We're friends, but we have our separate paths to tread. So only one cup. Or at most two."

"Naturally," purred the Mouser.

The objects in the room grew in the swimming gray blank of Fafhrd's vision. There was an inner door (also curtained), a narrow bed, a basin, a low table and stool, and on the floor beside the stool several portly short-necked large-eared shapes. Fafhrd counted them and once again his face broke into a large grin.

"Hung for a kid, you said," he rumbled softly in his old bass voice, continuing to eye the stone bottles of vintage. "I see four kids, Mouser." The Mouser echoed himself.

"Naturally."

By the time the candle the Mouser had fetched was

guttering in a little pool, Fafhrd was draining the third "kid." He held it upended above his head and caught the last drop, then batted it lightly away like a large feather-stuffed ball. As its shards exploded from the floor, he bent over from where he was sitting on the bed, bent so low that his beard brushed the floor, and clasped the last "kid" with both hands and lifted it with exaggerated care onto the table. Then taking up a very short-bladed knife and keeping his eyes so close to his work that they were inevitably crossed, he picked every last bit of resin out of the neck, flake by tiny flake.

Fafhrd no longer looked at all like an acolyte, even a misbehaving one. After finishing the first "kid" he had stripped for action. His camel's hair robe was flung into one corner of the room, the pieces of padded armor into another. Wearing only a once-white loincloth, he looked like some lean doomful berserk, or a barbaric king in a bath-house. For some time no light had been coming through the louvers. Now there was a little—the red glow of torches. The noises of night had started and were on the increase—thin laughter, hawkers' cries, various summonses to prayer…and Bwadres calling "Fafhrd!" again and again in his raspy long-carrying voice. But that last had stopped some time ago.

Fafhrd took so long with the resin, handling it like gold leaf, that the Mouser had to fight down several groans of impatience. But he was smiling his soft smile of victory. He did move once—to light a fresh taper from the expiring one. Fafhrd did not seem to notice the change in illumination. By now, it occurred to the Mouser, his friend was doubtless seeing everything by that brilliant light of spirits of wine which illumines the way of all brave drunkards.

Without any warning the Northerner lifted the short knife high and stabbed it into the center of the cork.

"Die, false Mingol!" he cried, withdrawing the knife with a twist, the cork on its point. "I drink your blood!" And he lifted the stone bottle to his lips.

After he had gulped about a third of its contents, by the Mouser's calculation, he set it down rather suddenly on the table. His eyeballs rolled upward, all the muscles of his body quivered with the passing of a beatific spasm, and he sank back majestically, like a tree that falls with care. The frail bed creaked ominously but did not collapse under its burden.

Yet this was not quite the end. An anxious crease appeared between Fafhrd's shaggy eyebrows, his head tilted up and his bloodshot eyes peered out menacingly from their eagle's nest of hair, searching the room.

Their gaze finally settled on the last stone bottle. A long rigidly-muscled arm shot out, a great hand shut on the top of the bottle and placed it under the edge of the bed and did not leave it. Then Fafhrd's eyes closed, his head dropped back with finality and, smiling, he began to snore.

The Mouser stood up and came over. He rolled back one of Fafhrd's eyelids, gave a satisfied nod, then gave another after feeling Fafhrd's pulse, which was surging with as slow and strong a rhythm as the breakers of the Outer Sea. Meanwhile the Mouser's other hand, operating with an habitual deftness and artistry unnecessary under the circumstances, abstracted from a fold in Fafhrd's loincloth a gleaming gold object he had earlier glimpsed there. He tucked it away in a secret pocket in the skirt of his gray tunic.

Someone coughed behind him.

It was such a deliberate-sounding cough that the Mouser did not leap or start, but only turned around without changing the planting of his feet in a movement slow and sinuous as that of a ceremonial dancer in the Temple of the Snake.

Pulg was standing in the inner doorway, wearing the black-and-silver striped robe and cowl of a masker and holding a black, jewel-spangled vizard a little aside from his face. He was looking at the Mouser enigmatically.

"I didn't think you could do it, son, but you did," he said

softly. "You patch your credit with me at a wise time. Ho, Wiggin, Quatch! Ho, Grilli!"

The three henchmen glided into the room behind Pulg, garbed in garments as somberly gay as their master's. The first two were stocky men, but the third was slim as a weasel and shorter than the Mouser, at whom he glared with guarded and rivalrous venom. The first two were armed with small crossbows and shortswords, but the third had no weapon in view.

"You have the cords, Quatch?" Pulg continued. He pointed Fafhrd. "Then bind me this man to the bed. See that you secure well his brawny arms."

"He's safer unbound," the Mouser started to say, but Pulg cut in on him with, "Easy, son. You're still running this job, but I'm going to be looking over your shoulder; yes, and I'm going to be revising your plan as you go along, changing any detail I choose. Good training for you. Any competent lieutenant should be able to operate under the eyes of his general, yes, even when other subordinates are listening in on the reprimands. We'll call it a test."

The Mouser was alarmed and puzzled. There was something about Pulg's behavior that he did not at all understand. Something discordant, as if a secret struggle were going on inside the master extortioner. He was not obviously drunk, yet his piggy eyes had a strange gleam. He seemed most fey.

"How have I forfeited your trust?" the Mouser asked sharply.

Pulg grinned skewily. "Son, I'm ashamed of you," he said. "High Priestess Ilala told me the *full* story of the black sloop—how you sublet it from the Treasurer in return for allowing him to keep the pearl tiara and stomacher. How you had Ourph the Mingol sail it to another dock. Ilala got mad at the Treasurer because he went cold on her or scared and wouldn't give her the black gewgaws. That's why she came to me. To cap it, your Lilyblack spilled the same story to Grilli here, whom she favors. Well, son?"

The Mouser folded his arms and threw back his head. "You said yourself the split was sufficient," he told Pulg. "We can always use another sloop."

Pulg laughed low and rather long. "Don't get me wrong," he said at last. "I like my lieutenants to be the sort of men who'd want a bolt-hole handy—I'd suspect their brains if they didn't. I *want* them to be the sort of men who worry a lot about their precious skins, but only after worrying about my hide first! Don't fret, son. We'll get along—I think. Quatch! Is he bound yet?"

The two burlier henchmen, who had hooked their crossbows to their belts, were well along with their job. Tight loops of rope at chest, waist and knees bound Fafhrd to the bed, while his wrists had been drawn up level with the top of his head and tightly laced to the sides of the bed. Fafhrd still snored peacefully on his back. He had stirred a little and groaned when his hand had been drawn away from the bottle under the bed, but that was all. Wiggin was preparing to bind the Northerner's ankles, but Pulg signed it was enough.

"Grilli!" Pulg called. "Your razor!"

The weasel-like henchman seemed merely to wave his hand past his chest and—lo!—there was a gleaming square-headed blade in it. He smiled as he moved toward Fafhrd's naked ankles. He caressed the thick tendons under them and looked pleadingly at Pulg.

Pulg was watching the Mouser narrowly.

The Mouser felt an unbearable tension stiffening him. He must do something! He raised the back of his hand to his mouth and yawned.

Pulg pointed at Fafhrd's other end. "Grilli," he repeated, "shave me this man! Debeard and demane him! Shave him like an egg!" Then he leaned toward the Mouser and said in a sort of slack-mouthed confidential way, "I've heard of these barbs that it draws their strength. Think you so? No matter, we'll see."

Slashing of a lusty man's head-and-face hair and then shaving him close takes considerable time, even when the barber is as shudderingly swift as Grilli and as heedless of the dim and flickering light. Time enough for the Mouser to assess the situation seventeen different ways and still not find its ultimate key. One thing shone through from every angle: the irrationality of Pulg's behavior. Spilling secrets…accusing a lieutenant in front of henchmen…proposing an idiot "test"…wearing grotesque holiday clothes…binding a man dead drunk…and now this superstitious nonsense of shaving Fafhrd—why, it was as if Pulg were fey indeed and performing some eerie ritual under the demented guise of shrewd tactics.

And there was one thing the Mouser was certain of: that when Pulg got through being fey or drugged or whatever it was, he would never again trust any of the men who had been through the experience with him, including—most particularly!—the Mouser. It was a sad conclusion—to admit that his hard-bought security was now worthless—yet it was a realistic one and the Mouser perforce came to it. So even while he continued to puzzle, the small man in gray congratulated himself on having bargained himself so disastrously into possession of the black sloop. A bolt-hole might soon be handy indeed, and he doubted whether Pulg had discovered where Ourph had concealed the craft. Meanwhile he must expect treachery from Pulg at any step and death from Pulg's henchmen at their master's unpredictable whim. So the Mouser decided that the less *they* (Grilli in particular) were in a position to do the Mouser or anyone else damage, the better.

Pulg was laughing again. "Why, he looks like a new-hatched babe!" the master extortioner exclaimed. "Good work, Grilli!"

Fafhrd did indeed look startlingly youthful without any hair above that on his chest, and in a way far more like what most people think an acolyte should look. He might even have appeared romantically handsome except that Grilli, in perhaps an excess of zeal, had also shorn naked his eyebrows—which had the effect of making Fafhrd's head, very pale under the vanished hair, seem like a marble bust set atop a living body.

Pulg continued to chuckle. "And no spot of blood—no, not one! That is the best of omens! Grilli, I love you!"

That was true enough too—in spite of his demonic speed, Grilli had not once nicked Fafhrd's face or head. Doubtless a man thwarted of the opportunity to hamstring another would scorn any lesser cutting—indeed, consider it a blot on his own character. Or so the Mouser guessed.

Gazing at his shorn friend, the Mouser felt almost inclined to laugh himself. Yet this impulse—and along with it his lively fear for his own and Fafhrd's safety—was momentarily swallowed up in the feeling that something about this whole business was very wrong—wrong not only by any ordinary standards, but also in a deeply occult sense. This stripping of Fafhrd, this shaving of him, this binding of him to the rickety narrow bed…wrong, wrong, wrong! Once again it occurred to him, more strongly this time, that Pulg was unknowingly performing an eldritch ritual.

"Hist!" Pulg cried, raising a finger. The Mouser obediently listened along with the three henchmen and their master. The ordinary noises outside had diminished, for a moment almost ceased. Then through the curtained doorway and the red-lit louvers came the raspy high voice of Bwadres beginning the Long Litany and the mumbling sigh of the crowd's response.

Pulg clapped the Mouser hard on the shoulder. "He is about it! 'Tis time!" he cried. "Command us! We will see, son, how well you have planned. Remember, I will be watching over your shoulder and that it is my desire that you strike at the end of Bwadres' sermon when the collection is taken." He frowned at Grilli, Wiggin and Quatch. "Obey this, my lieutenant!" he warned sternly. "Jump at his least command!—save when I countermand. Come on, son, hurry it up, start giving orders!"

The Mouser would have liked to punch Pulg in the middle of the jeweled vizard which the extortioner was just now again lifting to his face—punch his fat nose and fly this madhouse of commanded commandings. But there was Fafhrd to be considered—stripped, shaved, bound, dead drunk, immeasurably helpless. The Mouser contented himself with starting through the outer door and motioning the henchmen and Pulg too to follow him. Hardly to his surprise—for it was difficult to decide what behavior would have been surprising under the circumstances—they obeyed him.

He signed Grilli to hold the curtain aside for the others. Glancing back over the smaller man's shoulder, he saw Quatch, last to leave, dip to blow out the taper and under cover of that movement snag the two-thirds full bottle of wine from under the edge of the bed and lug it along with him. And for some reason that innocently thievish act struck the Mouser as being the most occultly wrong thing of all the supernally off-key events that had been occurring recently. He wished there were some god in which he had real trust so that he could pray to him for enlightenment and guidance in the ocean of inexplicably strange intuitions engulfing him. But unfortunately for the Mouser there was no such divinity. So there was nothing for it but to plunge all by himself into that strange ocean and take his chances—do without calculation whatever the inspiration of the moment moved him to do.

So while Bwadres keened and rasped through the Long Litany against the sighing responses of the crowd (and an uncommonly large number of catcalls and boos), the Mouser was very busy indeed, helping prepare the setting and place the characters for a drama of which he did not know more than scraps of the plot. The many shadows were his friends in this—he could slip almost invisibly from one shielding darkness to another—and he had the trays of half the hawkers in Lankhmar as a source of stage properties.

Among other things, he insisted on personally inspecting the weapons of Quatch and Wiggin—the shortswords and their sheaths, the small crossbows and the quivers of tiny quarrels that were their ammunition—most wicked-looking short arrows. By the time the Long Litany had reached its wailing conclusion, the stage was set, though exactly when and where and how the curtain would rise—and who would be the audience and who the players—remained uncertain.

At all events it was an impressive scene: the long Street of Gods stretching off toward a colorful torchlit dolls' world of distance in either direction, low clouds racing overhead, faint ribbons of mist gliding in from the Great Salt Marsh, the rumble of far distant thunder, bleat and growl of priests of gods other than Issek, squealing laughter of women and children, leather-lunged calling of hawkers and news-slaves, odor of incense curling from temples mingling with the oily aroma of fried foods on hawkers' trays, the reek of smoking torches, and the musk and flower smells of gaudy ladies.

Issek's audience, augmented by the many drawn by the tale of last night's doings of the demon acolyte and the wild predictions of Bwadres, blocked the Street from curb to curb, leaving only difficult gangway through the roofed porticos to either side. All levels of Lankhmarian society were represented—rags and ermine, bare feet and jeweled sandals, mercenaries' steel and philosophers' wands, faces painted with rare cosmetics and faces powdered only with dust, eyes of hunger, eyes of satiety, eyes of mad belief and eyes of a skepticism that hid fear.

Bwadres, panting a little after the Long Litany, stood on the curb across the Street from the low archway of the house where the drunken Fafhrd slept bound. His shaking hand rested on the cask that, draped now with the garlic bag, was both Issek's coffer and altar. Crowded so close as to leave him almost no striding space were the inner circles of the congregation—devotees sitting cross-legged, crouched on knees, or squatting on hams.

The Mouser had stationed Wiggin and Quatch by an overset fishmonger's cart in the center of the Street. They passed back and forth the stone bottle Quatch had snared, doubtless in part to make their odorous post more bearable, though every time the Mouser noted their bibbing he had a return of the feeling of occult wrongness.

Pulg had picked for his post a side of the low archway in front of Fafhrd's house, to call it that. He kept Grilli beside him, while the Mouser crouched nearby after his preparations were complete. Pulg's jeweled mask was hardly exceptional in the setting; several women were vizarded and a few of the other men—colorful blank spots in the sea of faces.

It was certainly not a calm sea. Not a few of the audience seemed greatly annoyed at the absence of the giant acolyte (and had been responsible for the boos and catcalls during the Litany), while even the regulars missed the acolyte's lute and his sweet tenor tale-telling and were exchanging anxious questions and speculations. All it took was someone to shout, "Where's the acolyte?" and in a few moments half the audience was chanting, "We want the acolyte! We want the acolyte!"

Bwadres silenced them by looking earnestly up the Street with shaded eyes, pretending he saw one coming, and then suddenly pointing dramatically in that direction, as if to signal the approach of the man for whom they were calling. While the crowd craned their necks and shoved about, trying to see what Bwadres was pretending to—and incidentally left off chanting—the ancient priest launched into his sermon.

"I will tell you what has happened to my acolyte!" he cried. "Lankhmar has swallowed him. Lankhmar has gobbled him up—Lankhmar the evil city, the city of drunkenness and lechery and all corruption—Lankhmar, the city of the stinking black bones!"

This last blasphemous reference to the gods *of* Lankhmar (whom it can be death to mention, though the gods *in* Lankhmar may be insulted without limit) further shocked the crowd into silence.

Bwadres raised his hands and face to the low-racing clouds.

"Oh, Issek, compassionate mighty Issek, pity thy humble servitor who now stands friendless and alone. I had one acolyte, strong in thy defense, but they took him from me. You told him, Issek, much of your life and your secrets, he had ears to hear it and lips to sing it, but now the black devils have got him! Oh, Issek, have pity!"

Bwadres spread his hands toward the mob and looked them around.

"Issek was a young god when he walked the earth, a young god speaking only of love, yet they bound him to the rack of torture. He brought Waters of Peace for all in his Holy Jug, but they broke it." And here Bwadres described at great length and with far more vividness than his usual wont (perhaps he felt he had to make up for the absence of his skald-turned-acolyte) the life and especially the torments and death of Issek of the Jug, until there was hardly one among the listeners who did not have vividly in mind the vision of Issek on his rack (succession of racks, rather) and who did not feel at least sympathetic twinges in his joints at the thought of the god's suffering.

Women and strong men wept unashamedly, beggars and scullions howled, philosophers covered their ears.

Bwadres wailed on toward a shuddering climax. "As you yielded up your precious ghost on the eighth rack, oh, Issek, as your broken hands fashioned even your torturer's collar into a Jug of surpassing beauty, you thought only of us, oh, Holy Youth. You thought only of making beautiful the lives of the most tormented and deformed of us, thy miserable slaves."

At those words Pulg took several staggering steps forward from the side of the archway, dragging Grilli with him, and dropped to his knees on the filthy cobbles. His black-and-silver striped cowl fell back on his shoulders and his jeweled black vizard slipped from his face, which was thus revealed as unashamedly coursing with tears.

"I renounce all other gods," the boss extortioner gasped between sobs. "Hereafter I serve only gentle Issek of the Jug."

The weasely Grilli, crouching contortedly in his efforts to avoid being smirched by the nasty pavement, gazed at his master as at one demented, yet could not or still dared not break Pulg's hold on his wrist.

Pulg's action attracted no particular attention— conversions were a smerduk a score at the moment—but the Mouser took note of it, especially since Pulg's advance had brought him so close that the Mouser could have reached out and patted Pulg's bald pate. The small man in gray felt a certain satisfaction or rather relief—if Pulg had for some time been a secret Issek-worshiper, then his feyness might be explained. At the same time a gust of emotion akin to pity went through him. Looking down at his left hand the Mouser discovered that he had taken out of its secret pocket the gold bauble he had filched from Fafhrd. He was tempted to put it softly in Pulg's palm. How fitting, how soul-shaking, how *nice* it would be, he thought, if at the moment the floodgates of religious emotion burst in him, Pulg were to receive this truly beautiful memento of the god of his choice. But gold is gold, and a black sloop requires as much upkeep as any other color yacht, so the Mouser resisted the temptation.

Bwadres threw wide his hands and continued, "With dry throats, oh, Issek, we thirst for thy Waters. With gullets burning and cracked, thy slaves beg for a single sip from thy Jug. We would ransom our souls for one drop of it to cool us in this evil city, damned by black bones. Oh, Issek, descend to us! Bring us thy Waters of Peace! We need you, we want you. Oh, Issek, come!"

Such was the power and yearning in that last appeal that the whole crowd of kneeling worshipers gradually took it up, chanting with all reverence, louder and louder, in an unendingly repeated, self-hypnotizing response: "We want Issek! We want Issek!"

It was that mighty rhythmic shouting which finally penetrated to the small conscious core of Fafhrd's wine-deadened brain where he lay drunk in the dark, though Bwadres' remarks about dry throats and burning gullets and healing drops and sips may have opened the way. At any rate, Fafhrd came suddenly and shudderingly awake with the one thought in his mind: another drink—and the one sure memory: that there was some wine left.

It disturbed him a little that his hand was not still on the stone bottle under the edge of the bed, but for some dubious reason up near his ear.

He reached for the bottle and was outraged to find that he could not move his arm. Something or someone was holding it.

Wasting no time on petty measures, the large barbarian rolled his whole body over mightily, with the idea of at once wrenching free from whatever was holding him and getting under the bed where the wine was.

He succeeded in tipping the bed on its side and himself with it. But *that* didn't bother him, it didn't shake up his numb body at all. What *did* bother him was that he couldn't sense any wine nearby—smell it, see it squintily, bump his head into it…certainly not the quart or more he remembered having safeguarded for just such an emergency as this.

At about the same time he became dimly aware that he was somehow *attached* to whatever he'd been sleeping on—especially his wrists and shoulders and chest.

However, his legs seemed reasonably free, though somewhat hampered at the knees, and since the bed happened to have fallen partly on the low table and with its head braced against the wall, the blind twist-and-heave he gave now actually brought him to his feet and the bed with him.

He squinted around. The curtained outer doorway was an oblong of lesser darkness. He immediately headed for it. The bed foiled his first efforts to get through, bringing him up short in a most exasperating manner, but by ducking and by turning edgewise he finally managed it, pushing the curtain ahead of him with his face. He wondered muddily if he were paralyzed, the wine he'd drunk all gone into his arms, or if some warlock had put a spell on him. It was certainly degrading to have to go about with one's wrists up about one's ears. Also, his head and cheeks and chin felt unaccountably chilly—possibly another evidence of black magic.

The curtain dragged off his head finally, and he saw ahead of him a rather low archway and—vaguely and without being at all impressed by them—crowds of people kneeling and swaying.

Ducking down again, he lumbered through the archway and straightened up. Torchlight almost blinded him. He stopped and stood there blinking. After a bit his vision cleared a little, and the first person he saw that meant anything to him was the Gray Mouser.

He remembered now that the last person he had been drinking with was the Mouser. By the same token—in this matter Fafhrd's maggoty mind worked very fast indeed—the Mouser must be the person who had made away with his quart or more of midnight medicine. A great righteous anger flamed in him and he took a very deep breath.

So much for Fafhrd and what *he* saw.

What the *crowd* saw—the god-intoxicated, chanting, weeping crowd—was very different indeed.

They saw a man of divine stature strapped with hands high to a framework of some sort. A mightily muscled man, naked save for a loincloth, with a shorn head and face that, marble white, looked startlingly youthful. Yet with the expression on that marble face of one who is being tortured.

And if anything else were needed (truly, it hardly was) to convince them that here was the god, the divine Issek, they had summoned with their passionately insistent cries, then it was supplied when that nearly seven-foot-tall apparition called out in a deep voice of thunder:

"Where is the jug? WHERE IS THE JUG?"

The few people in the crowd who were still standing dropped instantly to their knees at that point or prostrated themselves. Those kneeling in the opposite direction switched around like startled crabs. Two score persons, including Bwadres, fainted, and of these the hearts of five stopped beating forever. At least a dozen individuals went permanently mad, though at the moment they seemed no different from the rest—including (among the twelve) seven philosophers and a niece of Lankhmar's High Overlord. As one, the members of the mob abased themselves in terror and ecstasy—groveling, writhing, beating breasts or temples, clapping hands to eyes and peering fearfully through hardly parted fingers as if at an unbearably bright light.

It may be objected that at least a few of the mob should have recognized the figure before them as that of Bwadres' giant acolyte. After all, the height was right. But consider the differences: The acolyte was full-bearded and shaggy-maned; the apparition was beardless and bald—and strangely so, lacking even eyebrows. The acolyte had always gone robed; the apparition was nearly naked. The acolyte had always used a sweetly high voice; the apparition roared harshly in a voice almost two octaves lower.

Finally, the apparition was bound—to a torture rack,

surely—and calling in the voice of one being tortured for his Jug.

As one, the members of the mob abased themselves.

With the exception of the Gray Mouser, Grilli, Wiggin, and Quatch. They knew well enough who faced them. (Pulg knew too, of course, but he, most subtle-brained in some ways and now firmly converted to Issekianity, merely assumed that Issek had chosen to manifest himself in the body of Fafhrd and that he, Pulg, had been divinely guided to prepare that body for the purpose. He humbly swelled with the full realization of the importance of his own position in the scheme of Issek's reincarnation.)

His three henchmen, however, were quite untouched by religious emotions. Grilli for the moment could do nothing as Pulg was still holding his wrist in a grip of fervid strength.

But Wiggin and Quatch were free. Although somewhat dull-brained and little used to acting on their own initiative, they were not long in realizing that the giant who was supposed to be kept out of the way so that he would not queer the game of their strangely-behaving master and his tricky gray-clad lieutenant had appeared. Moreover, they well knew what jug Fafhrd was shouting for so angrily, and since they also knew they had stolen and drunken it empty, they likely also were moved by guilty fears that Fafhrd might soon see them, break loose, and visit vengeance upon them.

They cranked up their crossbows with furious haste, slapped in quarrels, knelt, aimed, and discharged the bolts straight at Fafhrd's naked chest. Several persons in the mob noted their action and shrieked at its wickedness.

The two bolts struck Fafhrd's chest, bounced off, and dropped to the cobbles—quite naturally enough, as they were two of the fowling quarrels (headed merely with little knobs of wood and used for knocking down small birds) with which the Mouser had topped off their quivers.

The crowd gasped at Issek's invulnerability and cried for joy and amazement.

However, although fowling quarrels will hardly break a man's skin, even when discharged at close range, they nevertheless sting mightily even the rather numb body of a man who has recently drunk numerous quarts of wine. Fafhrd roared in agony, punched out his arms convulsively, *and broke the framework to which he was attached.*

The crowd cheered hysterically at this further proper action in the drama of Issek which his acolyte had so often chanted.

Quatch and Wiggin, realizing that their missile weapons had somehow been rendered innocuous, but too dull-witted or wine-fuddled to see anything either occult or suspicious in the manner of that rendering, grabbed at their shortswords and rushed forward at Fafhrd to cut him down before he could finish detaching himself from the fragments of the broken bed—which he was now trying to do in a puzzled way.

Yes, Quatch and Wiggin rushed forward, but almost immediately came to a halt—in the very strange posture of men who are trying to lift themselves into the air by heaving at their own belts.

The shortswords would not come out of their scabbards. Mingol glue is indeed a powerful adhesive, and the Mouser had been most determined that, however little else he accomplished, Pulg's henchmen should be put in a position where they could harm no one.

However, he had been able to do nothing in the way of pulling Grilli's fangs, as the tiny man was most sharp-witted himself, and Pulg had kept him closely at his side. Now almost foaming at the mouth in vulpine rage and disgust, Grilli broke loose from his god-besotted master, whisked out his razor, and sprang at Fafhrd, who at last had clearly realized what was encumbering him and was having a fine time breaking the last pesky fragments of the bed over his knee or by the leverage of foot against cobble—to the accompaniment of the continuing wild cheers of the mob.

But the Mouser sprang rather more swiftly. Grilli saw him coming, shifted his attack to the gray-clad man, feinted twice and loosed one slash that narrowly missed. Thereafter he lost blood too quickly to be interested in attempting any further fencing. Cat's Claw is narrow, but it cuts throats as well as any other dagger (though it does not have a sharply curved or barbed tip, as some literal-minded scholars have claimed).

The bout with Grilli left the Mouser standing very close to Fafhrd. The little man realized he still held in his left hand the golden representation of the Jug fashioned by Fafhrd, and that object now touched off in the Mouser's mind a series of inspirations leading to actions that followed one another very much like the successive figures of a dance.

He slapped Fafhrd back-handed on the cheek to attract the giant's attention. Then he sprang to Pulg, sweeping his left hand in a dramatic arc as if conveying something from the naked god to the extortioner, and lightly placed the golden bauble in the supplicating fingers of the latter. (One of those times had come when all ordinary scales of value fail—even for the Mouser—and gold is—however briefly— of no worth.)

Recognizing the holy object, Pulg almost expired in ecstasy.

But the Mouser had already skipped on across the Street. Reaching Issek's coffer-altar, beside which Bwadres was stretched unconscious but smiling, he twitched off the garlic bag and sprang upon the small cask and danced upon it, hooting to further attract Fafhrd's attention and then pointing at his own feet.

Fafhrd saw the cask, all right, as the Mouser had intended he should, and the giant did not see it as anything to do with Issek's collections (the thought of all such matters was still wiped from his mind) but simply as a likely source of the liquor he craved. With a glad cry he hastened toward it across

the Street, his worshipers scuttling out of his way or moaning
in beatific ecstasy when he trod on them with his naked feet.
He caught up the cask and lifted it to his lips.

To the crowd it seemed that Issek was drinking his own
coffer—an unusual yet undeniably picturesque way for a god
to absorb his worshipers' cask offerings.

With a roar of baffled disgust Fafhrd raised the cask to
smash it on the cobbles, whether from pure frustration or with
some idea of getting at the liquor he thought it held is hard
to say, but just then the Mouser caught his attention again.
The small man had snatched two tankards of ale from an
abandoned tray and was pouring the heady liquid back and
forth between them until the high-piled foam trailed down
the sides.

Tucking the cask under his left arm—for many drunkards
have a curious prudent habit of absentmindedly hanging onto
things, especially if they may contain liquor—Fafhrd set out
again after the Mouser, who ducked into the darkness of the
nearest portico and then danced out again and led Fafhrd in
a great circle all the way around the roiling congregation.

Literally viewed it was hardly an edifying spectacle—a large
god stumbling after a small gray demon and grasping at a
tankard of beer that just kept eluding him—but the
Lankhmarians were already viewing it under the guise of two
dozen different allegories and symbolisms, several of which
were later written up in learned scrolls.

The second time through the portico Issek and the small
gray demon did not come out again. A large chorus of mixed
voices kept up expectant and fearful cries for some time, but
the two supernatural beings did not reappear.

Lankhmar is full of mazy alleyways, and this stretch of the
Street of the Gods is particularly rich in them, some of them
leading by dark and circuitous routes to localities as distant
as the docks.

But the Issekians—old-timers and new converts alike—

largely did not even consider such mundane avenues in analyzing their god's disappearance. Gods have their own doorways into and out of space and time, and it is their nature to vanish suddenly and inexplicably. Brief reappearances are all we can hope for from a god whose chief life-drama on earth has already been played, and indeed it might prove uncomfortable if he hung around very long, protracting a Second Coming—too great a strain on everybody's nerves for one thing.

The large crowd of those who had been granted the vision of Issek was slow in dispersing, as might well have been expected—they had much to tell each other, much about which to speculate and, inevitably, to argue.

The blasphemous attack of Quatch and Wiggin on the god was belatedly recalled and avenged, though some already viewed the incident as part of a general allegory. The two bullies were lucky to escape with their lives after an extensive mauling.

Grilli's corpse was unceremoniously picked up and tossed in next morning's Death Cart. End of *his* story.

Bwadres came out of his faint with Pulg bending solicitously over him—and it was largely these two persons who shaped the subsequent history of Issekianity.

To make a long or, rather, complex story simple and short, Pulg became what can best be described as Issek's grand vizier and worked tirelessly for Issek's greater glory—always wearing on his chest the god-created golden emblem of the Jug as the sign of his office. He did not upon his conversion to the gentle god give up his old profession, as some moralists might expect, but carried it on with even greater zeal than before, extorting mercilessly from the priests of all gods other than Issek and grinding them down. At the height of its success, Issekianity boasted five large temples in Lankhmar, numerous minor shrines in the same city, and a swelling priesthood under the nominal leadership of Bwadres, who was lapsing once more into general senility.

Issekianity flourished for exactly three years under Pulg's viziership. But when it became known (due to some incautious babblings of Bwadres) that Pulg was not only conducting under the guise of extortion a holy war on all other gods *in* Lankhmar, with the ultimate aim of driving them from the city and if possible from the world, but that he even entertained murky designs of overthrowing the gods *of* Lankhmar or at least forcing them to recognize Issek's overlordship…when all this became apparent, the doom of Issekianity was sealed. On the third anniversary of Issek's Second Coming, the night descended ominous and thickly foggy, the sort of night when all wise Lankhmarians hug their indoor fires. About midnight awful screams and piteous howlings were heard throughout the city, along with the rending of thick doors and the breaking of heavy masonry— preceded and followed, some tremulously maintained, by the clicking tread of bones on the march. One youth who peered out through an attic window lived long enough before he expired in gibbering madness to report that he had seen striding through the streets a multitude of black-togaed figures, sooty of hand, foot and feature and skeletally lean.

Next morning the five temples of Issek were empty and defiled and his minor shrines all thrown down, while his numerous clergy, including his ancient high priest and overweeningly ambitious grand vizier, had vanished to the last member and were gone beyond human ken.

Turning back to a dawn exactly three years earlier we find the Gray Mouser and Fafhrd clambering from a cranky, leaky skiff into the cockpit of a black sloop moored beyond the Great Mole that juts out from Lankhmar and the east bank of the River Hlal into the Inner Sea. Before coming aboard, Fafhrd first handed up Issek's cask to the impassive and sallow-faced Ourph and then with considerable satisfaction pushed the skiff wholly underwater.

The cross-city run the Mouser had led him on, followed by a brisk spell of galley-slave work at the oars of the skiff (for which he indeed looked the part in his lean near-nakedness) had quite cleared Fafhrd's head of the fumes of wine, though it now ached villainously. The Mouser still looked a bit sick from his share in the running—he was truly in woefully bad trim from his months of lazy gluttony.

Nevertheless the twain joined with Ourph in the work of upping anchor and making sail. Soon a salty, coldly refreshing wind on their starboard beam was driving them directly away from the land and Lankhmar. Then while Ourph fussed over Fafhrd and bundled a thick cloak about him, the Mouser turned quickly in the morning dusk to Issek's cask, determined to get at the loot before Fafhrd had opportunity to develop any silly religious or Northernly-noble qualms and perhaps toss the cask overboard.

The Mouser's fingers did not find the coin-slit in the top—it was still quite dark—so he upended the pleasantly heavy object, crammed so full it did not even jingle. No coin-slit in that end either, seemingly, though there was what looked like a burned inscription in Lankhmarian hieroglyphs. But it was still too dark for easy reading and Fafhrd was coming up behind him, so the Mouser hurriedly raised the heavy hatchet he had taken from the sloop's tool rack and bashed in a section of wood.

There was a spray of stingingly aromatic fluid of most familiar odor. *The cask was filled with brandy—to the absolute top, so that it had not gurgled.*

A little later they were able to read the burnt inscription. It was most succinct: "Dear Pulg—Drown your sorrows in this—Basharat."

It was only too easy to realize how yesterday afternoon the Number Two Extortioner had had a perfect opportunity to effect the substitution—the Street of the Gods deserted, Bwadres almost druggedly asleep from the unaccustomedly large fish dinner, Fafhrd gone from his post to guzzle with the Mouser.

"That explains why Basharat was not on hand last night," the Mouser said thoughtfully.

Fafhrd was for throwing the cask overboard, not from any disappointment at losing loot, but because of a revulsion at its contents, but the Mouser set aside the cask for Ourph to close and store away—he knew that such revulsions pass. Fafhrd, however, extorted the promise that the fiery fluid only be used in direst emergency—as for burning enemy ships.

The red dome of the sun pushed above the eastern waves. By its ruddy light Fafhrd and the Mouser really looked at each other for the first time in months. The wide sea was around them, Ourph had taken the lines and tiller, and at last nothing pressed. There was an odd shyness in both their gazes—each had the sudden thought that he had taken his friend away from the life-path he had chosen in Lankhmar, perhaps the life-path best suited to his treading.

"Your eyebrows will grow back—I suppose," the Mouser said at last, quite inanely.

"They will indeed," Fafhrd rumbled. "I'll have a fine shock of hair by the time you've worked off that belly."

"Thank you, Egg-Top," the Mouser replied. Then he gave a small laugh. "I have no regrets for Lankhmar," he said, lying mightily, though not entirely. "I can see now that if I'd stayed I'd have gone the way of Pulg and all such Great Men—fat, power-racked, lieutenant-plagued, smothered with false-hearted dancing girls, and finally falling into the arms of religion. At least I'm saved that last chronic ailment, which is worse than the dropsy." He looked at Fafhrd narrowly. "But how of you, old friend? Will you miss Bwadres and your cobbled bed and your nightly tale-weaving?"

Fafhrd frowned as the sloop plunged on northward and the salt spray dashed him.

"Not I," he said at last. "There are always other tales to be woven. I served a god well, I dressed him in new clothes, and then I did a third thing. Who'd go back to being an acolyte after being so much more? You see, old friend, I really was Issek."

The Mouser arched his eyebrows. "You were?"

Fafhrd nodded twice, most gravely.

FRITZ LEIBER'S
LANKHMAR

THEIR MISTRESS,
THE SEA

III

The next few days were not kind to the Mouser and Fafhrd. To begin with, both got seasick from their many months ashore. Between gargantuan groaning retches, Fafhrd monotonously berated the Mouser for having tricked him out of asceticism and stolen from him his religious vocation. While in the intervals of his vomiting, the Gray Mouser cursed Fafhrd back, but chiefly excoriated himself for having been such a fool as to give up the soft life in Lankhmar for sake of a friend.

During this period—brief in reality, an eternity to the sufferers—Ourph the Mingol managed sails and tiller. His impassive, wrinkle-netted face forever threatened to break into a grin, yet never did, though from time to time his jet eyes twinkled.

Fafhrd, first to recover, took back command from Ourph and immediately started ordering an endless series of seamanlike exercises: reefings, furlings, raisings, and changing of sails; shiftings of ballast; inspection of crawl-spaces for rats and roaches; luffings, tackings, jibings, and the like.

The Mouser swore feebly yet bitterly as these exercises sent both Ourph and Fafhrd clumping all over the deck, often across his prone body, and changed the steady pitch and roll of the *Black Treasurer*, to which he'd been getting accustomed, into unpredictable jitterbuggings which awakened nausea anew.

Whenever Fafhrd left off this slave-driving, he would sit cross-legged, deaf to the Mouser's sultry swearing, and silently meditate, his gaze directed at first always toward Lankhmar, but later more and more toward the north.

When the Mouser at last recovered, he forswore all food save watery gruel in small measures, and scorning Fafhrd's nautical exercises, began grimly to put himself through a variety of gymnastical ones until he collapsed sweating and panting—yet only waiting until he had his breath back to begin again.

It was an odd sight to see the Mouser walking about on his hands while Ourph raced forward to change the set of the jib and Fafhrd threw his weight on the tiller and bellowed, "Hard a-lee!"

Yet at odd moments now and then, chiefly at sunset, when they each sipped a measure of water tinted with sweet wine—the brandy being still under interdict—they began to reminisce and yarn together, only a little at first, then for longer and longer periods.

They spoke of piratings, both inflicted and suffered. They recalled notable storms and calms, sighting of mysterious ships which vanished in fog or distance, never more to be seen. They talked of sea monsters, mermaids, and oceanic devils. They relived the adventure of their crossing of the Outer Sea to the fabled Western Continent, which of all Lankhmarts only Fafhrd, the Mouser, and Ourph know to be more than legend.

Gradually the Mouser's belly melted and a bristly lawn of hair grew on Fafhrd's pate, cheeks, and chin, and around his mouth. Life became happenings rather than afflictions. They lived as well as saw sunsets and dawns. The stars became friendly. Above all, they began to match their rhythms to those of the sea, as if she were someone they lived and voyaged with, rather than sailed upon.

But their water and stores began to run low, the wine ran out, and they lacked even suitable clothing—Fafhrd in particular.

Their first piratical foray ended in near disaster. The small and lubberly-sailing merchant ship they approached most subtly at dawn suddenly bristled with brown-helmeted pikemen and slingers. It was a Lankhmar bait-ship, designed to trap pirates.

They escaped only because the trap was sprung too soon and the *Black Treasurer* was able to outsail the bait-ship, transformed into a speedy goer by proper handling. At that,

Ourph was struck senseless by a slung stone, and Fafhrd had two ribs cracked by another.

Their next sea-raid was only a most qualified success. The cutter they conquered turned out to be manned by five elderly Mingol women, witches by profession, they said, and bound on a fortune-telling and trading voyage to the southern settlements around Quarmall.

The Mouser and Fafhrd exacted from them a modest supply of water, food, and wine, and Fafhrd took several silk and fur tunics, some silver-plated jewelry, a longsword and ax which he fancied, and leather to make him boots. However, they left the surly women by no means destitute and forcibly prevented Ourph from raping even one of them, let alone all five as he had boastfully threatened.

They departed then, somewhat ashamed, to the tune of the witchwomen's chanting curses—most venomous ones, calling down on Fafhrd and the Mouser all the worst evils of air and earth, fire and water. Their failure to curse Ourph also, made the Mouser wonder whether the witch-women were not angriest because Ourph had been prevented in his most lascivious designs.

Now that the *Black Treasurer* was somewhat better provisioned, Fafhrd began to talk airily about voyaging once again across the Outer Sea, or toward the Frozen Sea north of No-Ombrulsk, there to hunt the polar tiger and white-furred giant worm.

That was the last straw to Ourph, who was a most even-tempered, sweet old man—for a Mingol. Overworked, skull-bashed, thwarted of a truly unusual amorous opportunity for one of his age, and now threatened with idiot-far-voyagings, he demanded to be set ashore.

The Mouser and Fafhrd complied. All this while the *Black Treasurer* had been southwesting along Lankhmar's northwestern coast. So it was near the small village of Earth's End that they put landside the old Mingol, who was still cursing them grumblingly, despite the gifts with which they had loaded him.

After consultation, the two heroes decided to set course straight north, which would land them in the forested Land of the Eight Cities at the city of Ool Hrusp, whose Mad Duke had once been their patron.

The voyage was uneventful. No ships were sighted. Fafhrd cut, sewed, and nailed himself boots, which he footed with spikes, perhaps from some dream of mountaineering. The Mouser continued his calisthenics and read *The Book of Aarth*, *The Book of Lesser Gods*, *the Management of Miracles*, and a scroll titled *Sea Monsters* from the sloop's small but select library.

Nights they would lazily talk for hours, feeling nearest then to the stars, the sea, and each other. They argued as to whether the stars had existed forever or been launched by the gods from Nehwon's highest mountain—or whether, as current metaphysics asserted, the stars were vast firelit gems set in islands at the opposite end of the great bubble (in the waters of eternity) that was Nehwon. They disputed as to who was the world's worst warlock: Fafhrd's Ningauble, the Mouser's Sheelba, or—barely conceivably—some other sorcerer.

But chiefly they talked of their mistress, the sea, whose curving motions they loved again, and to whose moods they now felt preternaturally attuned, particularly in darkness. They spoke of her rages and caressings, her coolths and unending dancings, sometimes lightly footing a minuet, some times furiously a-stamp, and her infinitude of secret parts.

The west wind gradually lessened, then shifted to a fluky east wind. Stores were once more depleted. At last they admitted to each other that they couldn't fetch Ool Hrusp on this reach, and they contented themselves with sailing to intercept the Claws—the narrow but mountainously rocky end of the Eastern Continent's great western-thrusting northern peninsula, comprised of the Land of the Eight Cities, the Cold Waste, and numerous grim and great mountain ranges. The east wind died entire one midnight. The *Black Treasurer* floated in a calm so complete it was as if their aqueous mistress had fallen into a trance. Not a breath stirred. They wondered what the morrow would show, or bring.

FRITZ LEIBER'S
LANKhMAR

SEA KING STORY

WhEN ThE SEA-KING'S AWAY

IV

Stripped to his loincloth, underbelt, and with amulet pouch a-dangle under his chin, the Gray Mouser stretched lizardlike along the bowed sprit of the sloop *Black Treasurer* and stared straight down into the hole in the sea. Sunlight unstrained by slightest wisp of cloud beat hotly on his deep-tanned back, but his belly was cold with the magic of the thing.

All around about, the Inner Sea lay calm as a lake of mercury in the cellar of a wizard's castle. No ripple came from the unbounded horizon to south, east and north, nor rebounded from the endless vertically-fluted curtain of creamy rock that rose a bowshot to the west and was a good three bowshots high, which the Mouser and Fafhrd had only yesterday climbed and atop which they had made a frightening discovery. The Mouser could have thought of those matters, or of the dismal fact that they were becalmed with little food and less water (and a tabooed cask of brandy) a weary sail west from Ool Hrusp, the last civilized port on this coast—or uncivilized either. He could have wondered about the seductive singing that had seemed to come from the sea last night, as of female voices softly improvising on the themes of waves hissing against sand, gurgling melodiously among rocks, and screaming wind-driven against icy coasts. Or he could perhaps best have pondered on Fafhrd's madness of yesterday afternoon, when the large Northerner had suddenly started to babble dogmatically about finding for himself and the Mouser "girls under the sea" and had even begun to trim his beard and brush out his brown otterskin tunic and polish his best male costume jewelry so as to be properly attired to receive the submarine girls and arouse their desires. There was an old Simorgyan legend, Fafhrd had insisted, according to which on the seventh day of the seventh moon of the seventh year of the Sevens-Cycle the king of the sea journeyed to the other end of the earth, leaving his opalescently beautiful green wives and faintly silver-scaled slim concubines free to find them lovers if they could...and this, Fafhrd had stridently asserted he knew by the spectral calm and other occult tokens, was the place of the sea-king's home and the eve of the day!

In vain had the Mouser pointed out to him that they had not sighted an even faintly feminine-looking fish in days, that there were absolutely no islets or beaches in view suitable for commerce with mermaids or for the sunbathing and primping of loreleis, that there were no black hulks whatever of wrecked pirate ships drifting about that might conceivably have fair captives imprisoned below decks and so technically "under the sea," that the region beyond the deceptive curtain-wall of creamy rock was the last from which one could expect girls to come, that—to sum it up—the *Black Treasurer* had not fetched the faintest sort of girl-blink either to starboard or larboard for weeks. Fafhrd had simply replied with crushing conviction that the sea-king's girls were there down below, that they were now preparing a magic channel or passageway whereby air-breathers might visit them, and that the Mouser had better be ready like himself to hasten when the summons came.

The Mouser had thought that the heat and dazzle of the unremitting sun—together with the sudden intense yearnings normal to all sailormen long at sea—must have deranged Fafhrd, and he had dug up from the hold and unsuccessfully coaxed the Northerner to wear a wide-brimmed hat and slitted ice-goggles. It had been a great relief to the Mouser when Fafhrd had fallen into a profound sleep with the coming of night, though then the illusion—or reality—of the sweet siren-singing had returned to trouble his own tranquillity.

Yes, the Mouser might well have thought of any of these matters, Fafhrd's prophetic utterances in particular, while he lay poised but unsweating in the hot sun along the stout bowsprit of the *Black Treasurer*, yet the fact is that he had mind only for the jade marvel so close that he could almost reach down a hand and touch the beginning of it.

It is well to approach all miracles and wonders by gradual

stages or degrees, and we can do this by examining another aspect of the glassy seascape of which the Mouser also might well have been thinking—but wasn't.

Although untroubled by swell, wavelet or faintest ripple or quiver, the Inner Sea around the sloop was not perfectly flat. Here and there, scatteredly, it was dimpled with small depressions about the size and shape of shallow saucers, as if giant invisible featherweight water-beetles were standing about on it—though the dimples were not arranged in any six-legged or four-legged or even tripod patterns. Moreover, a slim stalk of air seemed to go down from the center of each dimple for an indefinite distance into the water, quite like the tiny whirlpool that sometimes forms when the turquoise plug is pulled in the brimful golden bathtub of the Queen of the East (or the drain unstoppered in a bathtub of any humbler material belonging to any lowlier person)—except that there was no whirling of water in this case, and the air stalks were not twisted and knotted but straight, as though scores of slim-bladed rapiers with guards like shallow saucers but all as invisible as air had been plunged at random into the motionless waters around the *Black Treasurer*. Or as though a sparse forest of invisible lily pads with straight invisible stems had sprung up around the sloop.

Imagine such an air-stalked dimple magnified so that the saucer was not a palm's breadth but a good spearcast across and the rodlike sword-straight stalk not a fingernail's width but a good four feet, imagine the sloop slid prow-foremost down into that shallow depression but stopping just short of the center and floating motionless there, imagine the bowsprit of the slightly tilted ship projecting over the exact center of the central tube or well of air, imagine a small, stalwart, nut-brown man in a gray loincloth lying along the bowsprit, his feet braced against the foredeck rails, and looking straight down the tube...and you have the Gray Mouser's situation exactly!

To be in the Mouser's situation and peering down the tube was very fascinating indeed, an experience calculated to drive other thoughts out of any man's mind—or even any woman's! The water here, a bowshot from the creamy rock-wall, was green, remarkably clear, but too deep to allow a view of the bottom—soundings taken yesterday had shown it to vary between six score and seven score feet. Through this water the well-size tube went down as perfectly circular and as smooth as if it were walled with glass; and indeed the Mouser would have believed that it was so walled—that the water immediately around it had been somehow frozen or hardened without altering in transparency—except that at the slightest noise, such as the Mouser's coughing, little quiverings would run up and down it in the form of a series of ring-shaped waves.

What power prevented the tremendous weight of the sea from collapsing the tube in an instant, the Mouser could not begin to imagine.

Yet it was endlessly fascinating to peer down it. Sunlight transmitted through the sea water illuminated it to a considerable depth brightly if greenishly, and the circular wall played odd tricks with distance. For instance, at this moment the Mouser, peering down slantwise through the side of the tube, saw a thick fish as long as his arm swimming around it and nosing up to it. The shape of the fish was very familiar yet he could not at once name it. Then thrusting his head out to one side and peering down at the same fish through the clear water alongside the tube, he saw that the fish was three times the length of his body—in fact, a shark. The Mouser shivered and told himself that the curved wall of the tube must act like the reducing lenses used by a few artists in Lankhmar.

On the whole, though, the Mouser might well have decided in the end that the vertical tunnel in the water was an illusion born of sun-glare and suggestion and have put on the ice-goggles and stuffed his ears with wax against any more siren-singing and then perhaps swigged at the forbidden brandy and gone to sleep, except for certain other circumstances footing the whole affair much more firmly in reality. For instance, there was a knotted rope securely tied to the bowsprit and hanging down the center of the tube, and this rope creaked from time to time with the weight on it, and also there were threads of black smoke coming out of the watery hole (these were what made the Mouser cough), and last but not least there was a torch burning redly far down in the hole—so far down its flame looked no bigger than a candle's—and just beside the flame, somewhat obscured by its smoke and much tinied by distance, was the upward-peering face of Fafhrd!

The Mouser was inclined to take on faith the reality of anything Fafhrd got mixed up with, certainly anything that Fafhrd got physically into—the near-seven-foot Northerner was much too huge a hulk of solid matter to be picturable as strolling arm-in-arm with illusions.

The events leading up to the reality-footing facts of the rope, the smoke, and Fafhrd down the air-well had been quite simple. At dawn the sloop had begun to drift mysteriously among the water dimples, there being no perceptible wind or current. Shortly afterward it had bumped over the lip of the large saucer-shaped depression and slid to its present position with a little rush and then frozen there, as though the sloop's bowsprit and the hole were mutually desirous magnetic poles coupling together. Thereafter, while the Mouser had watched with eyes goggling and teeth a-chatter, Fafhrd had sighted down the hole, grunted with stolid satisfaction, slung the knotted rope down it, and then proceeded to array himself, seemingly with both war and love in mind—pomading his bushy hair and beard, perfuming his hairy chest and armpits, putting on a blue silk tunic under the gleaming one of otterskin and all his silver-plated necklaces, armbands, brooches and rings as well, but also strapping longsword and ax to his sides and lacing on his spiked boots. Then he had lit a long thin torch of resinous pine in the galley firebox, and when it was flaming bravely he had, despite the Mouser's solicitous cries and tugging protests, gone out on the bowsprit and lowered himself into the hole, using thumb and forefinger of his right hand to grip the torch and the other three fingers of that hand, along with his left hand, to grip the rope. Only then had he spoken, calling on the Mouser to make ready and follow him if the Mouser were more hot-blooded man than cold-blooded lizard.

The Mouser had made ready to the extent of stripping off most of his clothing—it had occurred to him it would be necessary to dive for Fafhrd when the hole became aware of its own impossibility and collapsed—and he had fetched to the foredeck his own sword Scalpel and dagger Cat's Claw in their case of oiled sealskin with the notion they might be needed against sharks. Thereafter he had simply poised on the bowsprit, as we have seen, observing Fafhrd's slow descent and letting the fascination of it all take hold of him.

At last he dipped his head and called softly down the hole, "Fafhrd, have you reached bottom yet?" frowning at the ring-shaped ripples even this gentle calling sent traveling down the hole and up again by reflection.

"What did you say?"

Fafhrd's answering bellow, concentrated by the tube and coming out of it like a solid projectile, almost blasted the Mouser off the bowsprit. Far more terrifying, the ring-ripples accompanying the bellow were so huge they almost seemed to close off the tube—narrowing it from four to two or three feet at any rate and dashing a spray of drops up into the Mouser's face as they reached the surface, lifting the rim upward as if the water were elastic, and then were reflected down the tube again.

The Mouser closed his eyes in a wince of horror, but when he opened them the hole was still there, and the giant ring-ripples were beginning to abate.

Only a shade more loudly than the first time, but much more poignantly, the Mouser called down, "Fafhrd, don't do that again!"

"What?"

This time the Mouser was prepared for it—just the same it was most horrid to watch those huge rings traveling up and down the tube in an arrow-swift green peristalsis. He firmly resolved to do no more calling, but just then Fafhrd started to speak up the tube in a voice of more rational volume—the rings produced were hardly thicker than a man's wrist.

"Come on, Mouser! It's Easy! You only have to drop the last six feet!"

"Don't drop it, Fafhrd!" the Mouser instantly replied. "Climb back up!"

"I already have! Dropped, I mean. I'm on the bottom! Oh, Mouser!"

The last part of Fafhrd's call was in a voice so infused with a mingled awe and excitement that the Mouser immediately asked back down, "What? 'Oh Mouser'—what?"

"It's wonderful, it's amazing, it's fantastic!" the reply came back from below—but this time very faintly all of a sudden, as if Fafhrd had somehow gone around an impossible bend or two in the tube.

"*What* is, Fafhrd?" the Mouser demanded—and this time his own voice raised moderate rings. "Don't go away, Fafhrd. But what *is* down there?"

"Everything!" the answer came back, not quite so faint this time.

"Are there girls?" the Mouser queried.

"A whole world!"

The Mouser sighed. The moment had come, he knew, as it always did, when outward circumstances and inner urges commanded an act, when curiosity and fascination tipped the scale of caution, when the lure of a vision and an adventure became so great and deep-hooking that he must respond to it or have his inmost self-respect eaten away.

Besides, he knew from long experience that the only way to extricate Fafhrd from the predicaments into which he got himself was to go fetch the perfumed and be-sworded lout!

So the Mouser sprang up lightly, clipped to his underbelt his sealskin-cased weapons, hung beside them in loops a short length of knotted line with a slip-noose tied in one end, made sure that the sloop's hatches were securely covered and even that the galley fire was tightly boxed, rattled off a short scornful prayer to the gods *of* Lankhmar, and lowered himself off the bowsprit and down into the green hole.

The hole was chilly, and it smelled of fish, smoke, and Fafhrd's pomade. The Mouser's main concern as soon as he got in it, he discovered to his surprise, was not to touch its glassy sides. He had the feeling that if he so much as lightly brushed it, the water's miraculous "skin" would rupture, and he would be engulfed—rather as an oiled needle floating on a bowl of water in its tiny hammock of "water skin" is engulfed and sinks when one pinks it. He descended rapidly knot by knot, supporting himself by his hands, barely touching his toes to the rope below, praying there would be no sway and that he would be able to check it if it started. It occurred to him he should have told Fafhrd to guy the rope at the bottom if he possibly could and above all have warned him not to shout up the tube while the Mouser descended—the thought of being squeezed by those dread water-rings was almost too much to bear. Too late now—any word now would only too surely bring a bellow from the Northerner in reply.

First fears having been thus inspected, though by no means banished, the Mouser began to take some note of his surroundings. The luminous green world was not just one emerald blank as it had seemed at first. There was life in it, though not in the greatest abundance: thin strands of

scalloped maroon seaweed, near-invisible jellyfish trailing
their opalescent fringes, tiny dark skates hovering like bats,
small silvery backboned fish gliding and darting—some of
them, a blue-and-yellow-ringed and black-spotted school,
even contesting lazily over the *Black Treasurer's* morning
garbage, which the Mouser recognized by a large pallid beef
bone Fafhrd had gnawed briefly before tossing overside.

Looking up, he was hard put not to gasp in horror. The
hull of the sloop, pressing down darkly, though pearled with
bubbles, looked seven times higher above him than the
distance he had descended by his count of the knots. Looking
straight up the tube, however, he saw that the circle of deep
blue sky had not shrunk correspondingly, while the bowsprit
bisecting it was still reassuringly thick. The curve of the tube
had shrunk the sloop as it had the shark. The illusion was
most weird and foreboding, nonetheless.

And now as the Mouser continued his swift descent, the
circle overhead did grow smaller and more deeply blue,
becoming a cobalt platter, a peacock saucer, and finally no
more than a strange ultramarine coin that was the converging
point of the tube and rope and in which the Mouser thought
he saw a star flash. The Gray One puffed a few rapid kisses
toward it, thinking how like they were to a drowning man's
last bubbles. The light dimmed. The colors around him faded,
the maroon seaweed turned gray, the fish lost their yellow
rings, and the Mouser's own hands became blue as those of a
corpse. And now he began to make out dimly the sea bottom,
at the same extravagant distance below as the sloop was
above, though immediately under him the bottom was oddly
veiled or blanketed and only far off could he make out rocks
and ridged stretches of sand.

His arms and shoulders ached. His palms burned. A
monstrously fat grouper swam up to the tube and followed
him down it, circling. The Mouser glared at it menacingly,
and it turned on its side and opened an impossibly large moon

crescent of mouth. The Mouser saw the razor teeth and realized it was the shark he'd seen or another like it, tinied by the lens of the tube. The teeth clashed, some of them inside the tube, only inches from his side. The water's "skin" did not rupture disastrously, although the Mouser got the eerie impression that the "bite" was bleeding a little water into the tube. The shark swam off to continue its circling at a moderate distance, and the Mouser refrained from any more menacing looks.

Meanwhile the fishy smell had grown stronger, and the smoke must have been getting thicker too, for now the Mouser coughed in spite of himself, setting the water rings shooting up and down. He fought to suppress an anguished curse—and at that moment his toes no longer touched rope. He unloosed the extra coil from his belt, went down three more knots, tightened the slip-noose above the second knot from the bottom, and continued on his way.

Five handholds later his feet found a footing in cold muck. He gratefully unclenched his hands, working his cramped fingers, at the same time calling "Fafhrd!" softly but angrily. Then he looked around.

He was standing in the center of a large low tent of air, which was floored by the velvety sea-muck in which he had sunk to his ankles and roofed by the leadenly gleaming undersurface of the water—not evenly though, but in swells and hollows with ominous downward bulges here and there. The air-tent was about ten feet high at the foot of the tube. Its diameter seemed at least twenty times that, though exactly how far the edges extended it was impossible to judge for several reasons: the great irregularity of the tent's roof, the difficulty of even guessing at the extent of some outer areas where the distance between water-roof and muck-floor was measurable in inches, the fact that the gray light transmitted from above hardly permitted decent vision for more than two dozen yards, and finally the circumstance that there was considerable torch-smoke in the way here and there, writhing in thick coils along the ceiling, collecting in topsy-turvy pockets, though eventually gliding sluggishly up the tube.

What fabulous invisible "tent-poles" propped up the ocean's heavy roof the Mouser could no more conceive than the force that kept the tube open.

Writhing his nostrils distastefully, both at the smoke and the augmented fishy smell, the Mouser squinted fiercely around the tent's full circumference. Eventually he saw a dull red glow in the black smudge where it was thickest, and a little later Fafhrd emerged. The reeking flame of the pine torch, which was still no more than half consumed, showed the Northerner bemired with sea-muck to his thighs and hugging gently to his side with his bent left arm a dripping mess of variously gleaming objects. He was stooped over somewhat, for the roof bulged down where he stood.

"Blubber brain!" the Mouser greeted him. "Put out that torch before we smother! We can see better without it. Oh, oaf, to blind yourself with smoke for the sake of light!"

To the Mouser there was obviously only one sane way to extinguish the torch—jab it in the wet muck underfoot—but Fafhrd, though evidently most agreeable to the Mouser 's suggestion in a vacantly smiling way, had another idea. Despite the Mouser's anguished cry of warning, he casually thrust the flaming stick into the watery roof.

There was a loud hissing and a large downward puff of steam and for a moment the Mouser thought his worst dreads had been realized, for an angry squirt of water from the quenching point struck Fafhrd in the neck. But when the steam cleared it became evident that the rest of the sea was not going to follow the squirt, at least not at once, though now there was an ominous lump, like a rounded tumor, in the roof where Fafhrd had thrust the torch, and from it water ran steadily in a stream thick as a quill, digging a tiny crater where it struck the muck below.

"Don't do that!" the Mouser commanded in unwise fury.

"This?" Fafhrd asked gently, poking a finger through the ceiling next to the dripping bulge. Again came the angry squirt, diminishing at once to a trickle, and now there were two bulges closely side by side, quite like breasts.

"Yes, *that*—not again," the Mouser managed to reply, his voice distant and high because of the self-control it took him not to rage at Fafhrd and so perhaps provoke even more reckless probings.

"Very well, I won't," the Northerner assured him. "Though," he added, gazing thoughtfully at the twin streams, "it would take those dribblings years to fill up this cavity."

"Who speaks of years down here?" the Mouser snarled at him. "Dolt! Iron Skull! What made you lie to me? 'Everything' was down here, you said—'a whole world.' And what do I find? Nothing! A miserable little cramp-roofed field of stinking mud!" And the Mouser stamped a foot in rage, which only splashed him foully, while a puffed, phosphorescent-whiskered fish expiring on the mire looked up at him reproachfully.

"That rude treading," Fafhrd said softly, "may have burst the silver-filigreed skull of a princess. 'Nothing,' say you? Look you then, Mouser, what treasure I have digged from your stinking field."

And as he came toward the Mouser, his big feet gliding gently through the top of the muck for all the spikes on his boots, he gently rocked the gleaming things cradled in his left arm and let the fingers of his right hand drift gently among them.

"Aye," he said, "jewels and gauds undreamed by those who sail above, yet all teased by me from the ooze while I sought another thing."

"What other thing, Gristle Dome?" the Mouser demanded harshly, though eyeing the gleaming things hungrily.

"The path," Fafhrd said a little querulously, as if the Mouser must know what he meant. "The path that leads from some corner or fold of this tent of air to the sea-king's girls. These things are a sure promise of it. Look you, here, Mouser." And he opened his bent left arm a little and lifted out most delicately with thumb and fingertips a life-size metallic mask.

Impossible to tell in that drained gray light whether the metal were gold or silver or tin or even bronze and whether the wide wavy streaks down it, like the tracks of blue-green sweat and tears, were verdigris or slime. Yet it was clear that it was female, patrician, all-knowing yet alluring, loving yet cruel, hauntingly beautiful. The Mouser snatched it eagerly yet angrily and the whole lower face crumpled in his hand, leaving only the proud forehead and the eyeholes staring at him more tragically than eyes.

The Mouser flinched back, expecting Fafhrd to strike him, but in the same instant he saw the Northerner turning away and lifting his straight right arm, index finger a-point, like a slow semaphore.

"You were right, oh Mouser!" Fafhrd cried joyously. "Not only my torch's smoke but its very light blinded me. See! See the path!"

The Mouser's gaze followed Fafhrd's pointing. Now that the smoke was somewhat abated and the torch-flame no longer shot out its orange rays, the patchy phosphorescence of the muck and of the dying sea-things scattered about had become clearly visible despite the muted light filtering from above.

The phosphorescence was not altogether patchy, however. Beginning at the hole from which the knotted rope hung, a path of unbroken greenish-yellow witch-fire a long stride in width led across the muck toward an unpromising-looking corner of the tent of air where it seemed to disappear.

"Don't follow it, Fafhrd," the Mouser automatically enjoined, but the Northerner was already moving past him, taking frightening long dreamlike strides. By degrees his cradling arm unbent, and one by one his ooze-won treasures began to slip from it into the muck. He reached the path and started along it, placing his spike-soled feet in the very center.

"Don't follow it, Fafhrd," the Mouser repeated—a little hopelessly, almost whiningly, it must be admitted. "Don't follow it, I say. It leads only to squidgy death. We can still go back up the rope, aye, and take your loot with us."

But meanwhile he himself was following Fafhrd and snatching up, though more cautiously than he had the mask, the objects his comrade let slip. It was not worth the effort, the Mouser told himself as he continued to do it: though they gleamed enticingly, the various necklaces, tiaras, filigreed breast-cups and great-pinned brooches weighed no more and were no thicker than plaitings of dead ferns. He could not equal Fafhrd's delicacy, and they fell apart at his touch.

Fafhrd turned back to him a face radiant as one who dreams sleeping of ultimate ecstasies. As the last ghost-gaud slipped from his arm, he said, "They are nothing—no more than the mask—mere sea-gnawed wraiths of treasure. But oh, the promise of them, Mouser! Oh, the promise!"

And with that he turned forward again and stooped under a large downward bulge in the low leaden-hued roof.

The Mouser took one look back along the glowing path to the small circular patch of sky-light with the knotted rope falling in the center of it. The twin streams of water coming from the two "wounds" in the ceiling seemed to be coming more strongly—where they hit, the muck was splashing. Then he followed Fafhrd.

On the other side of the bulge the ceiling rose again to more than head-height, but the walls of the tent narrowed in sharply. Soon they were treading along a veritable tunnel in the water, a leaden arch-roofed passageway no wider than the phosphorescently yellow-green path that floored it. The tunnel curved just enough now to left, now to right, so that there was no seeing any long distance ahead. From time to time the Mouser thought he heard faint whistlings and moanings echoing along it. He stepped over a large crab that was backing feebly and saw beside it a dead man's hand emerging from the glowing muck, one shred-fleshed finger pointing the way they were taking.

Fafhrd half turned his head and muttered gravely, "Mark me, Mouser, there's magic in this somewhere!"

The Mouser thought he had never in his life heard a less necessary remark. He felt considerably depressed. He had long given up his puerile pleadings with Fafhrd to turn back—he knew there was no way of stopping Fafhrd short of grappling with him, and a tussle that would invariably send them crashing through one of the watery walls of the tunnel was by no means to his liking. Of course, he could always turn back alone. Still…

With the monotony of the tunnel and of just putting one foot after the other into the clinging muck and withdrawing it with a soft *plop*, the Mouser found time to become oppressed too with the thought of the weight of the water overhead. It was as though he walked with all the ships of the world on his back. His imagination would picture nothing but the tunnel's instant collapse. He hunched his head into his shoulders, and it was all he could do not to drop to his elbows and knees and then stretch himself face down in the muck with the mere anticipation of the event.

The sea seemed to grow a little whiter ahead, and the Mouser realized the tunnel was approaching the underreaches of the curtain-wall of creamy rock he and Fafhrd had climbed yesterday. The memory of that climb let his imagination escape at last, perhaps because it fitted with the urge that he and Fafhrd somehow lift themselves out of their present predicament.

It had been a difficult ascent, although the pale rock had proved hard and reliable, for footholds and ledges had been few, and they had had to rope up and go by way of a branching chimney, often driving pitons into cracks to create a support where none was—but they had had high hopes of finding fresh water and game, too, likely enough, so far west of Ool Hrusp and its hunters. At last they had reached the top, aching and a little blown from their climb and quite ready to throw themselves down and rest while they surveyed the landscape of grassland and stunted trees that they knew to be characteristic of other parts of this most lonely peninsula stretching southwestward between the Inner and Outer Seas.

Instead they had found…nothing. Worse than nothing, in a way, if that were possible. The longed-for top proved to be the merest edge of rock, three feet wide at the most and narrower some places, while on the other side the rock descended even more precipitously than on the side which they had climbed—indeed it was deeply undercut in large areas—and for an equal or rather somewhat greater distance. From the foot of this dizzying drop a wilderness of waves, foam and rocks extended to the horizon.

They had found themselves clinging a-straddle to a veritable rock curtain, paper-thin in respect to its height and horizontal extent, between the Inner and what they realized must be the Outer Sea, which had eaten its way across the unexplored peninsula in this region but not yet quite broken through. As far as eye could see in either direction the same situation obtained, though the Mouser fancied he could make out a thickening of the wall in the direction of Ool Hrusp.

Fafhrd had laughed at the surprise of the thing— gargantuan bellows of mirth that had made the Mouser curse him silently for fear the mere vibrations of his voice might shatter and tumble down the knife-edged saddle on which they perched. Indeed the Mouser had grown so angry with Fafhrd's laughter that he had sprung up and nimbly danced a jig of rage on the rock-ribbon, thinking meanwhile of wise Sheelba's saying: "Know it or not, man treads between twin abysses a tightrope that has neither beginning nor end."

Having thus expressed their feeling of horrified shock, each in his way, they had surveyed the yeasty sea below more rationally. The amount of surf and the numbers of emergent rocks showed it to be more shallow for some distance out— even likely, Fafhrd had opined, to drain itself at low tide, for his moon-lore told him that tides in this region of the world must at the moment be near high. Of the emergent rocks, one in particular stood out: a thick pillar two bowshots from the curtain wall and as high as a four-story house. The pillar was spiraled by ledges that looked as if they were in part of human cutting, while set in its thicker base and emerging from the foam there appeared an oddly crisscrossed weed-fringed rectangle that looked mightily like a large stout door—though where such a door might lead and who would use it were perplexing questions indeed.

Then, since there was no answering that question or others, and since there was clearly no fresh water or game to be had from this literal shell of a coast, they had descended back to the Inner Sea and the *Black Treasurer*, though now each time they had driven a piton it had been with the fear that the whole wall might split and collapse.

"'Ware rocks!"

Fafhrd's warning cry pulled the Mouser out of his waking memory-dream—dropped him in a split instant as if it were from the upper reaches of the creamy curtain-wall to a spot almost an equal distance below its sea-gnarled base. Just ahead of him three thick lumpy daggers of rock thrust down inexplicably through the gray watery ceiling of the tunnel. The Mouser shudderingly wove his head past them, as Fafhrd must have, and then looking beyond his comrade he saw more rocky protuberances encroaching on the tunnel from all sides—saw, in fact, as he strode on, that the tunnel was changing from one of water and muck to one roofed, walled and floored with solid rock. The water-born light faded away behind them, but the increasing phosphorescence natural to the animal life of a sea cavern almost compensated for it, boldly outlining their wet stony way and here and there glowing with especial brilliance and variety of color from the bands, portholes, feelers and eye-rings of many a dying fish and crawler.

The Mouser realized they must be passing far under the curtain-wall he and Fafhrd had climbed yesterday and that the tunnel ahead must be leading under the Outer Sea they had seen tossing with billows. There was no longer that immediate oppressive sense of a crushing weight of ocean overhead or of brushing elbows with magic. Yet the thought that if the tube, tent and tunnel behind them should collapse, then a great gush of solid water would rush into the rock tunnel and engulf them, was in some ways even worse. Back under the water roof he'd had the feeling that even if it should collapse he might reach the surface alive by bold swimming and conceivably drag the cumbered Fafhrd up with him. But here they'd be hopelessly trapped.

True, the tunnel seemed to be ascending, but not enough or swiftly enough to please the Mouser. Moreover, if it did finally emerge, it would be to that shattering welter of foam they'd peered down at yesterday. Truly, the Mouser found it hard to pick between his druthers, or even to have any druthers at all. His feelings of depression and doom gradually sank to a new and perhaps ultimate nadir, and in a desperate effort to wrench them up he deliberately imagined to himself the zestiest tavern he knew in Lankhmar—a great gray cellar all a-flare with torches, wine streaming and spilling, tankards and coins a-clink, voices braying and roaring, poppy fumes a-twirl, naked girls writhing in lascivious dances....

"Oh, Mouser...!"

Fafhrd's deep and feelingful whisper and the Northerner's large hand against his chest halted the Mouser's plodding, but whether it fetched his spirit back below the Outer Sea or simply produced a fantastic alteration in its escapist imagining, the Gray One could not at once be sure.

They were standing in the entrance to a vast submarine grotto that rose in multiple steps and terraces toward an indefinite ceiling from which cascaded down like silver mist aglow about thrice the strength of moonlight. The grotto reeked of the sea like the tunnel behind them; it was likewise scattered with expiring fish and eels and small octopuses; mollusks tiny and huge clustered on its walls and corners between weedy draperies and silver-green veils; while its various niches and dark circular doorways and even the stepped and terraced floor seemed shaped in part at least by the action of rushing waters and grinding sand.

The silver mist did not fall evenly but concentrated itself in swirls and waves of light on three terraces. The first of these was placed centrally and only a level stretch separated it from the tunnel's mouth. Upon this terrace was set a great stone table with weed-fringed sides and mollusk-crusted legs. A great golden basin stood on one end of this table and two golden goblets beside the basin.

Beyond the first terrace rose a second uneven flight of steps with areas of menacing shadow pressing upon it from either side. Behind the areas of darkness were a second and third terrace that the silvery light favored. The one on the right— Fafhrd's side, to call it that, for he stood to the right in the tunnel mouth—was walled and arched with mother-of-pearl, almost as if it were one gigantic shell, and pearly swells rose from its floor like heaped satin pillows. The one on the Mouser's side, slightly below, was backed by an arras of maroon seaweed that fell in wide scalloped strands and billowed on the floor. From between these twin terraces the flight of irregular steps or ledges continued upward into a third area of darkness.

Shifting shadows and dark wavings and odd gleamings hinted that the three areas of darkness might be occupied; there was no doubt that the three bright terraces were. On the upper terrace on Fafhrd's side stood a tall and opulently beautiful woman whose golden hair rose in spiral masses like a shell and whose dress of golden fishnet clung to her pale greenish flesh. Her fingers showed greenish webs between them, and on the side of her neck as she turned were faint scorings like a fish's gills.

On the Mouser's side was a slimmer yet exquisitely feminine creature whose silver flesh seemed to merge into silver scales on shoulders, back and flanks under her robe of filmy violet and whose short dark hair was split back from her low forehead's center by a scalloped silver crest a hand's breadth high. She too showed the faint neck-scorings and finger-webs.

The third figure, standing a-crouch behind the table, was sexlessly scrawny, with an effect of wiry old age, and either gowned or clad closely in jet black. A shock of rope-thick hairs dark red as iron rust covered her head while her gills and finger-webs were starkly apparent.

Each of these women wore a metal mask resembling in form and expression the eaten-away one Fafhrd had found in the muck. That of the first figure was gold; of the second, silver; of the third, green-splotched sea-darkened bronze.

The first two women were still, not as if they were part of a show but as though they were observing one. The scrawny black sea-witch was vibrantly active, although she hardly moved on her black-webbed toes except to shift position abruptly and ever so slightly now and then. She held a short whip in either hand, the webs folded outside her bent knuckles, and with these whips she maintained and directed the swift spinning of a half dozen objects on the polished tabletop. What these objects were it was impossible to say, except that they were roughly oval. Some by their semitransparency as they spun might have been large rings or saucers, others actual tops by their opacity. They gleamed silver and green and golden, and they spun so swiftly and moved in such swift intersecting orbits as they spun that they seemed to leave gleaming wakes of spin in the misty air behind them. Whenever one would flag in its spinning and its true form begin to blink into visibility, she'd bring it back up to speed again with two or three rapid whip slashes; or should one veer too close to the table's edge or the golden basin, or threaten to collide with another, she'd redirect its orbit with deft lashings; now and again, with incredible skill, she'd flick one so that it jumped high in the air and then flick it again at landing so that it went on spinning without a break, leaving above it an evanescent loop of silvery air-spin.

These whirring objects made the pulsing moans and whistles the Mouser had heard along the tunnel.

As he watched them now and listened to them, the Gray One became convinced—partly because the silvery curving tubes of spin made him think of the air shaft he'd rope-climbed and the air-tunnel he'd plodded—that these spinning things were a crucial part of the magic that had created and held open the path through the Inner Sea behind them, and that once they should cease whirring then the shaft and tent and tunnel would collapse and the waters of the Inner Sea speed through the rock-tunnel into this grotto.

And indeed the scrawny black sea-witch looked to the Mouser as though she'd been whipping her tops for hours and—more to the point—would be able to keep on whipping them for hours more. She showed no signs of her exertion save the rhythmic rise and fall of her breastless chest and the extra whistle of breath through the mouth-slit of her mask and the gape and close of her gills.

Now she seemed for the first time to see him and Fafhrd, for without leaving off her whipping she thrust her bronze mask toward them, red ropes a-spill across its green-blotched forehead, and glared at them—hungrily, it seemed. Yet she made them no other menace, but after a searching scrutiny jerked back her head twice, to left and to right, as if for a sign that they should go past her. At the same time the green and silver queens beckoned to them languorously.

This woke the Mouser and Fafhrd from their dazed watching, and they complied eagerly enough, though in passing the table the Mouser sniffed wine and paused to take up the two golden goblets, handing one to his comrade. They drained them despite the green hue of the drink, for the stuff smelled right and was fiery sweet yet tart. The black witch took no note of them, but went on whipping her gleaming, mist-waked tops.

As he drank, the Mouser noted that the tabletop was of purple-splotched, creamy marble polished to an exquisite smoothness. He also saw into the golden bowl. It held no store of green wine, but was filled almost to the brim with a crystal fluid that might or might not have been water. On the fluid floated a model, hardly a finger long, of the hull of a black boat. A tiny tube of air seemed to go down from its prow.

But there was no time for closer looking, for Fafhrd was moving on. The Mouser stepped up into his area of shadow to the left as Fafhrd had done to the right…and as he so stepped, there sidled from the shadows before him two bluely pallid men armed each with a pair of wave-edged knives. They were sailors, he judged from their pigtails and shuffling gait, although they were both naked, and they were indisputably dead—by token of their unhealthy color, their carelessness of the thick slime streaking them, the way their bulging eyes showed only whites and the bottom crescent of the irises, and the fact that their hair, ears, and other portions of their anatomies looked somewhat fish-chewed. Behind them waddled a scimitar-wielding dwarf with short spindle legs and monstrous head and gills—a veritable walking embryo. His great saucer eyes too were the upturned ones of a dead thing, which did not make the Mouser feel any easier as he whisked Scalpel and Cat's Claw out of their sealskin case, for the three converged on him confidently where he stood and rapidly shifted to block his way as he sought to circle behind them.

It was probably just as well that the Mouser had at that moment no attention to spare for his comrade's predicament. Fafhrd's area of shadow was black as ink toward the wall, and as the Northerner strode through the margin of it past a ridged and man-sized knob of rock rising from the ledges and between him and the Mouser, there lifted from the further blackness—like eight giant serpents rearing from their lair— the thick, sinuous, crater-studded arms of a monstrous octopus. The sea-beast's movement must have struck internal sparks, for it simultaneously flashed into a yellow-streaked purplish iridescence, showing Fafhrd its baleful eyes large as plates, its cruel beak big as the prow of an overturned skiff, and the rather unlikely circumstance that the end of each mighty tentacle wrapped powerfully around the hilt of a gleaming broadsword.

Snatching at his own sword and ax, Fafhrd backed away from the be-weaponed squid against the ridged knob of rock. Two of the ridges, being the vertical shell-edges of a mollusk four feet across, instantly closed on the slack of his otterskin tunic, firmly holding him there.

Greatly daunted but determined to live nevertheless, the Northerner swung his sword in a great figure eight, the lower loop of which almost nicked the floor, while the upper loop rose above his head like a tall arching shield. This double-petaled flower of steel baffled the four blades or so with which the octopus first came chopping at him rather cautiously, and as the sea monster drew back his arms for another volley of slashes, Fafhrd's left arm licked out with his ax and chopped through the nearest tentacle.

His adversary hooted loudly then and struck repeatedly with all his swords, and for a space it looked as though Fafhrd's universal parry must surely be pierced, but then the ax licked out again from the center of the sword-shield, once, twice, and two more tentacle tips fell and the swords they gripped with them. The octopus drew back then out of reach and sprayed a great mist-cloud of stinking black ink from its tube, under cover of which it might work its will unseen on the pinned Northerner, but even as the blinding mist billowed toward him Fafhrd hurled his ax at the huge central head. And although the black fog hid the ax almost as soon as it left his hand, the heavy weapon must have reached a vital spot, for immediately the octopus hurled its remaining swords about the grotto at random (fortunately striking no one although they made a fine clatter) as its tentacles thrashed in dying convulsions.

Fafhrd drew a small knife, slashed his otterskin tunic down the front and across the shoulders, stepped out of it with a contemptuous wave to the mollusk as if to say, "Have it for supper if you will," and turned to see how his comrade fared. The Mouser, bleeding greenly from two trivial wounds in ribs and shoulder, had just finished severing the major tendons of his three hideous opponents—this having proved the only way to immobilize them when various mortal wounds had slowed them in no way at all nor caused them to bleed one drop of blood of any color.

He smiled sickishly at Fafhrd and turned with him toward the upper terraces. And now it became clear that the Green and Silver Ones were at least in one respect true queens, for they had not fled the prodigious battles as lesser women might, but abided them and now waited with arms lightly outstretched. Their gold and silver masks could not smile, but their bodies did, and as the two adventurers mounted toward them from the shadow into the light (the Mouser's little wounds changing from green to red, but Fafhrd's blue tunic staying pretty inky) it seemed to them that veily finger webs and light neck-scorings were the highest points of female beauty. The lights faded somewhat on the upper terraces, though not on the lower where the monotonous six-toned music of the tops kept reassuringly on, and the two heroes entered each into that dark lustrous realm where all thoughts of wounds are forgotten and all memories of even the zestiest Lankhmar wine-cellar grow flat, and the Sea, our cruel mother and loving mistress, repays all debts.

A great soundless jar, as of the rock-solid earth moving, recalled the Mouser to his surroundings. Almost simultaneously the whir of one of the tops mounted to a high-pitched whine ending in a tinkly crash. The silver light began to pulse and flicker wildly throughout the grotto. Springing to his feet and looking down the steps, the Mouser saw a memory-etching sight: the rust-topped black sea-witch whipping wildly at her rebellious tops, which leaped and bounded about the table like fierce silver weasels, while through the air around her from all sides but chiefly from the tunnel there converged an arrow-swift flight of flying fish, skates, and ribbon-edged eels, all inky black and with tiny jaws agape.

At that instant Fafhrd seized him by the shoulder and jerked him fully around, pointing up the ledges. A silver lightning flash showed a great cross-beamed, weed-fringed door at the head of the rocky stairs. The Mouser nodded violently—meaning he understood it resembled and must be the door they had yesterday seen from the ribbony cliff summit—and Fafhrd, satisfied his comrade would follow him, dashed toward it up the ledges.

But the Mouser had a different thought and darted in the opposite direction in the face of an ominous wet reeking wind. Returning a dozen lightning-flashes later, he saw the green and silver queens disappearing into round black tunnel mouths in the rock to either side of the terrace and then they were gone.

As he joined Fafhrd in the work of unsettling the crossbars of the great weedy door and drawing its massive rusty bolts, it quivered under a portentous triple knocking as though someone had smote it thrice with a long-skirted cloak of chain mail. Water squirted under it and through the lower third of the central vertical crack. The Mouser looked behind him then, with the thought that they might yet have to seek another avenue of escape…and saw a great white-headed pillar of water jetting more than half the height of the grotto from the mouth of the tunnel connecting with the Inner Sea. Just then the silver cavern-light went out, but almost immediately other light spilled from above. Fafhrd had heaved open half of the great door. Green water foamed about their knees and subsided. They fought their way through, and as the great door slammed behind them under a fresh surge of water, they found themselves sloshing about on a wild beach blown with foam, swimming with surf, and floored chiefly with large flat water-worn oval rocks like giants' skipping stones. The Mouser, turned shoreward, squinted desperately at the creamy cliff two bowshots away, wondering if they could possibly reach it through the mounting tide and climb it if they did.

But Fafhrd was looking seaward. The Mouser again felt himself shoulder-grabbed, spun around, and this time dragged up a curving ledge of the great tower-rock in the base of which was set the door through which they had just emerged. He stumbled, cutting his knees, but was jerked ruthlessly on. He decided that Fafhrd must have some very good reason for so rudely enjoining haste and thereafter did his best to hurry without assistance at Fafhrd's heels up the spiraling ramplike ledge. On the second circling he stole a seaward look, gasped, and increased the speed of his mad dizzy scramble.

The stony beach below was drained and only here and there patched with huge gouts of spume, but roaring toward them from outer ocean was a giant wave that looked almost half as high as the pillar they were mounting—a great white wall of water flecked with green and brown and studded with rocks—a wave such as distant earthquakes send charging across the sea like a massed cavalry of monsters. Behind that wave came a taller one, and behind that a third taller still.

The Mouser and Fafhrd were three gasping circles higher when the stout tower shuddered and shook to the crashing impact of the first giant wave. Simultaneously the landward door at its base burst open from within and the cavern-traveling water from the Inner Sea gushed out creamily to be instantly engulfed. The crest of the wave caught at Fafhrd's and the Mouser's ankles without quite tripping them or much slowing their progress. The second and third did likewise, although they had gained another circle before each impact. There was a fourth wave and a fifth, but no higher than the third. The two adventurers reached the stumpy summit and cast themselves down on it, clutching at the still-shaking rock and slewing around to watch the shore—Fafhrd noting the astonishing minor circumstance that the Mouser was gripping between his teeth in the corner of his mouth a small black cigar.

The creamy curtain-wall shuddered at the impact of the first wave and great cracks ran across it. The second wave shattered it, and it fell into the third with an explosion of spray, displacing so much salt water that the return wave almost swamped the tower, its dirty crest tugging at the Mouser's and Fafhrd's fingers and licking along their sides. Again the tower shook and rocked beneath them but did not fall, and that was the last of the great waves. Fafhrd and the Mouser circled down the spiraling ledges until they caught up with the declining sea, which still deeply covered the door at the tower's base. Then they looked landward again, where the mist raised by the catastrophe was dissipating.

A full half mile of the curtain-wall had collapsed from base to crest, its shards vanishing totally beneath the waves, and through that gap the higher waters of the Inner Sea were pouring in a flat sullen tide that was swiftly obliterating the choppy aftermath of the earthquake waves from the Outer Sea.

On this wide river in the sea the *Black Treasurer* appeared from the mist riding straight toward their refuge rock.

Fafhrd cursed superstitiously. Sorcery working against him he could always accept, but magic operating in his favor he invariably found disturbing.

As the sloop drew near, they dove together into the sea, reached it with a few brisk strokes, scrambled aboard, steered it past the rock, and then lost no time in toweling and dressing their nakedness and preparing hot drink. Soon they were looking at each other over steaming mugs of grog. The brandy keg had been broached at last.

"Now that we've changed oceans," Fafhrd said, "we'll raise No-Ombrulsk in a day with this west wind."

The Mouser nodded and then smiled steadily at his comrade for a space. Finally he said, "Well, old friend, are you sure that is all you have to say?"

Fafhrd frowned. "Well, there's one thing," he replied somewhat uncomfortably after a bit. "Tell me, Mouser, did your girl ever take off her mask?"

"Did yours?" the Mouser asked back, eyeing him quizzically.

Fafhrd frowned "Well, more to the point," he said gruffly, "did any of it really happen? We lost our swords and duds but we have nothing to show for it."

The Mouser grinned and took the black cigar from the corner of his mouth and handed it to Fafhrd.

"This is what I went back for," he said, sipping his grog. "I thought we needed it to get our ship back, and perhaps we did."

It was a tiny replica, carved in jet with the Mouser's teeth marks deeply indenting it near the stern, of the *Black Treasurer*.

FRITZ LEIBER'S LANKHMAR

THE WRONG BRANCH

V

It is rumored by the wise-brained rats which burrow the citied earth and by the knowledgeable cats that stalk its shadows and by the sagacious bats that wing its night and by the sapient zats which soar through airless space, slanting their metal wings to winds of light, that those two swordsmen and blood-brothers, Fafhrd and the Gray Mouser, have adventured not only in the World of Nehwon with its great empire of Lankhmar, but also in many other worlds and times and dimensions, arriving at these through certain secret doors far inside the mazy caverns of Ningauble of the Seven Eyes—whose great cave, in this sense, exists simultaneously in many worlds and times. It is a Door, while Ningauble glibly speaks the languages of many worlds and universes, loving the gossip of all times and places.

In each new world, the rumor goes, the Mouser and Fafhrd awaken with knowledge and speaking skills and personal memories suitable to it, and Nehwon then seems to them only a dream and they know not its languages, though it is ever their primal homeland.

It is even whispered that on one occasion they lived a life in that strangest of worlds variously called Gaia, Midgard, Terra, and Earth, swashbuckling there along the eastern shore of an inner sea in kingdoms that were great fragments of a vasty empire carved out a century before by one called Alexander the Great.

So much Srith of the Scrolls has to tell us. What we know from informants closer to the source is as follows:

After Fafhrd and the Gray Mouser escaped from the sea-king's wrath, they set a course for chilly No-Ombrulsk, but by midnight the favoring west wind had shifted around into a blustering northeaster. It was Fafhrd's judgment, at which the Mouser sneered, that this thwarting was the beginning of the sea-king's revenge on them. They perforce turned tail (or stern, as finicky sailormen would have us say) and ran south under jib alone, always keeping the grim mountainous coast in view to larboard, so they would not be driven into the trackless Outer Sea, which they had crossed only once in their lives before, and then in dire circumstance, much farther south.

Next day they reentered the Inner Sea by way of the new strait that had been created by the fall of the curtain rocks. That they were able to make this perilous and uncharted passage without holing the *Black Treasurer*, or even scraping her keel, was cited by the Mouser as proof that they had been forgiven or forgotten by the sea-king, if such a formidable being indeed existed. Fafhrd, contrariwise, murkily asserted that the sea-queen's weedy and polygynous husband was only playing cat and mouse with them, letting them escape one danger so as to raise their hopes and then dash them even more devilishly at some unknown future time.

Their adventurings in the Inner Sea, which they knew almost as well as a queen of the east her turquoise and golden bathing pool, tended more and more to substantiate Fafhrd's pessimistic hypothesis. They were becalmed a score of times and hit by three-score sudden squalls. They had thrice to outsail pirates and once best them in bloody hand-to-hand encounter. Seeking to reprovision in Ool Hrusp, they were themselves accused of piracy by the Mad Duke's harbor patrol, and only the moonless night and some very clever tacking— and a generous measure of luck—allowed the *Black Treasurer* to escape, its side bepricked and its sails transfixed with arrows enough to make it resemble a slim aquatic ebon hedgehog, or a black needlefish.

Near Kvarch Nar they did manage to reprovision, though only with coarse food and muddy river water. Shortly thereafter the seams of the *Black Treasurer* were badly strained and two opened by glancing collision with an underwater reef which never should have been where it was. The only possible point where they could careen and mend their ship was the tiny beach on the southeast side of the Dragon Rocks, and it took them two days of nip-and-tuck sailing and bailing to get them there with deck above water.

Whereupon while one patched or napped, the other must
stand guard against inquisitive two- and three-headed
dragons and even an occasional monocephalic. When they
got a cauldron of pitch seething for final repairs, the dragons
all deserted them, put off by the black stuff's stink—a
circumstance which irked rather than pleased the two
adventurers, since they hadn't had the wit to keep a pot of
pitch a-boil from the start. (They were most touchy and
thin-skinned now from their long run of ill fortune.)

A-sail once more, the Mouser at long last agreed with
Fafhrd that they truly had the sea-king's curse on them and
must seek sorcerous aid in getting it removed—because if they
merely forsook sea for land, the sea-king might well pursue
them through his allies the Rivers and the Rainstorms, and
they would still be under the full curse whenever they again
took to ocean.

It was a close question as to whether they should consult
Sheelba of the Eyeless Face, or Ningauble of the Seven Eyes.
But since Sheelba laired in the Salt Marsh next to the city
of Lankhmar, where their recent close connection with Pulg
and Issekianity might get them into more trouble, they
decided to consult Ningauble in his caverns in the low
mountains behind Ilthmar.

Even the sail to Ilthmar was not without dangers. They
were attacked by giant squids and by flying fish of the
poison-spined variety. They also had to use all their sailor
skill and expend all the arrows which the Ool Hruspians
had given them, in order to stand off yet one more pirate
attack. The brandy was all drunk.

As they were anchoring in Ilthmar harbor, the *Black
Treasurer* literally fell apart like a joke-box, starboard side
parting from larboard like two quarters of a split melon,
while the mast and cabin, weighted by the keel, sank
speedily as a rock.

Fafhrd and Mouser saved only the clothes they were in,

their swords, dirk, and ax. And it was well they hung onto the latter, for while swimming ashore they were attacked by a school of sharks, and each man had to defend self and comrade while swimming encumbered. Ilthmarts lining the quays and moles cheered the heroes and the sharks impartially, or rather as to how they had laid their money, the odds being mostly three-to-one against both heroes surviving, with various shorter odds on the big man, the little man, or one or the other turning the trick.

Ilthmarts are a somewhat heartless people and much given to gambling. Besides, they welcome sharks into their harbor, since it makes for an easy way of disposing of common criminals, robbed and drunken strangers, slaves grown senile or otherwise useless, and also assures that the shark-god's chosen victims will always be spectacularly received.

When Fafhrd and the Mouser finally staggered ashore panting, they were cheered by such Ilthmarts as had won money on them. A larger number were busy booing the sharks.

The cash they got by selling the wreckage of the *Black Treasurer* was not enough to buy or hire them horses, though sufficient to provide food, wine, and water for one drunk and a few subsequent days of living.

During the drunk they more than once toasted the *Black Treasurer*, a faithful ship which had literally given its all for them, worked to death by storms, pirate attacks, the gnawing of sea-things, and other sacraments of the sea-king's rage. The Mouser drank curses on the sea-king, while Fafhrd crossed his fingers. They also had more or less courteously to fight off the attentions of numerous dancing girls, most of them fat and retired.

It was a poor drunk, on the whole. Ilthmar is a city in which even a minimally prudent man dare not sleep soused, while the endless repetitions of its rat-god, more powerful even than its shark-god, in sculptures, murals, and smaller decor (and in large live rats silent in the shadows or a-dance in the alleys) make for a certain nervousness in newcomers after a few hours.

Thereafter it was a dusty two-day trudge to the caverns of Ningauble, especially for men untrained to tramping by many months a-sea and with the land becoming sandy desert toward the end.

The coolth of the hidden-mouthed rocky tunnel leading to Ningauble's deep abode was most welcome to men weary, dry, and powdered with fine sand. Fafhrd, being the more knowledgeable of Ningauble and his mazy lair, led the way, hands groping above and before him for stabilities and sharp rock edges which might inflict grievous head-bashings and other wounds. Ningauble did not approve the use by others of torch or candle in his realm.

After avoiding numerous side-passages they came to a Y-shaped branching. Here the Mouser, pressing ahead, made out a pale glow far along the left-hand branch and insisted they explore that tunnel.

"After all," he said, "if we find we've chosen wrong, we can always come back."

"But the right-hand branch is the one leading to Ningauble's auditorium," Fafhrd protested. "That is, I'm almost certain it is. That desert sun curdled my brain."

"A plague on you for a pudding-head and a know-not know," the Mouser snapped, himself irritable still from the heat and dryness of their tramping, and strode confidently a-crouch down the left-hand branch. After two heartbeats, Fafhrd shrugged and followed.

The light grew ever more coolly bright ahead. Each experienced a brief spell of dizziness and a momentary unsettling of the rock underfoot, as if there were a very slight earthquake.

"Let's go back," Fafhrd said.

"Let's at least see," the Mouser retorted. "We're already there."

A few steps more and they were looking down another slope of desert. Just outside the entrance arch there stood with preternatural calm a richly-caparisoned white horse, a smaller black one with silver harness buckles and rings and a sturdy mule laden with water-bags, pots, and parcels looking as though they contained provender for man and four-foot beast. By each of the saddles hung a bow and quiver of arrows, while to the white horse's saddle was affixed a most succinct note on a scrap of parchment:

The sea-king's curse is lifted. Ning.

There was something very strange about the writing, though neither could wholly define wherein the strangeness lay. Perhaps it was that Ningauble had written down the sea-king as Poseidon, but that seemed a most acceptable alternate. And yet...

"It is most peculiar of Ningauble," Fafhrd said, his voice sounding subtly odd to the Mouser and to himself too, "— most peculiar to do favors without demanding much information and even service in return."

"Let us not look gift-steeds in the mouth," the Mouser advised. "Nor even a gift mule, for that matter."

The wind had changed while they had been in the tunnels, so that it was not now blowing sultry from the east, but cool from the west. Both men felt greatly refreshed, and when they discovered that one of the mule's bags contained not branch water, but delicious strong water, their minds were made up. They mounted, Fafhrd the white, the Mouser the black, and single-footed confidently west, the mule tramping after.

A day told them that something unusual had happened, for they did not fetch Ilthmar or even the Inner Sea.

Also, they continued to be bothered by something strange about the words they were using, though each understood the other clearly enough.

In addition, both realized that something was happening to his memories and even common knowledge, though they did not at first reveal to each other this fear. Desert game was plentiful, and delicious when broiled, enough to quiet wonderings about an indefinable difference in the shape and coloration of the animals. And they found a rarely sweet desert spring.

It took a week, and also encounter with a peaceful caravan of silk-and-spice merchants, before they realized that they were speaking to each other not in Lankhmarese, pidgin Mingol, and Forest Tongue, but in Phoenician, Aramaic, and Greek; and that Fafhrd's childhood memories were not of the Cold Waste, but of lands around a sea called Baltic; the Mouser's not of Tovilyis, but Tyre; and that here the greatest city was not called Lankhmar, but Alexandria.

And even with those thoughts, the memory of Lankhmar and the whole world of Nehwon began to fade in their minds, become a remembered dream or series of dreams.

Only the memory of Ningauble and his caverns stayed sharp and clear. But the exact nature of the trick he had played on them became cloudy.

No matter, the air here was sharp and clean, the food good, the wine sweet and addling, the men built nicely enough to promise interesting women. What if the names and the new words seemed initially weird? Such feelings diminished even as one thought about them.

Here was a new world, promising unheard-of adventures. Though even as one thought "new," it became a world more familiar.

They cantered down the white sandy track of their new, yet foreordained, destiny.

FRITZ LEIBER'S
LANKHMAR

ADEPT'S GAMBIT

VI

1. *Tyre*

It happened that while Fafhrd and the Gray Mouser were dallying in a wine shop near the Sidonian Harbor of Tyre, where all wine shops are of doubtful repute, a long-limbed yellow-haired Galatian girl lolling in Fafhrd's lap turned suddenly into a wallopingly large sow. It was a singular occurrence, even in Tyre. The Mouser's eyebrows arched as the Galatian's breasts, exposed by the Cretan dress that was the style revival of the hour, became the uppermost pair of slack white dugs, and he watched the whole proceeding with unfeigned interest.

The next day four camel traders, who drank only water disinfected with sour wine, and two purple-armed dyers, who were cousins of the host, swore that no transformation took place and that they saw nothing, or very little out of the ordinary. But three drunken soldiers of King Antiochus and four women with them, as well as a completely sober Armenian juggler, attested the event in all its details. An Egyptian mummy-smuggler won brief attention with the claim that the oddly garbed sow was only a semblance, or phantom, and made dark references to visions vouchsafed men by the animal gods of his native land, but since it was hardly a year since the Seleucids had beaten the Ptolemies out of Tyre, he was quickly shouted down. An impecunious traveling lecturer from Jerusalem took up an even more attenuated position, maintaining that the sow was not a sow, or even a semblance, but only the semblance of a semblance of a sow.

Fafhrd, however, had no time for such metaphysical niceties. When, with a roar of disgust not unmingled with terror, he had shoved the squealing monstrosity halfway across the room so that it fell with a great splash into the water tank, it turned back again into a long-limbed Galatian girl and a very angry one, for the stale water in which the sow had floundered drenched her garments and plastered down her yellow hair (the Mouser murmured, "Aphrodite!") and the sow's uncorsetable bulk had split the tight Cretan waist. The stars of midnight were peeping through the skylight above the tank, and the wine cups had been many times refilled, before her anger was dissipated. Then, just as Fafhrd was impressing a reintroductory kiss upon her melting lips, he felt them once again become slobbering and tusky. This time she picked herself up from between two wine casks and, ignoring the shrieks, excited comments, and befuddled stares as merely part of a rude mystification that had been carried much too far, she walked with Amazonian dignity from the room. She paused only once, on the dark and deep-worn threshold, and then but to hurl at Fafhrd a small dagger, which he absentmindedly deflected upward with his copper goblet, so that it struck full in the mouth a wooden satyr on the wall, giving that deity the appearance of introspectively picking his teeth.

Fafhrd's sea-green eyes became likewise thoughtful as he wondered what magician had tampered with his love life. He slowly scanned the wine shop patrons, face by sly-eyed face, pausing doubtfully when he came to a tall, dark-haired girl beyond the water tank, finally returning to the Mouser. There he stopped, and a certain suspiciousness became apparent in his gaze.

The Mouser folded his arms, flared his snub nose, and returned the stare with all the sneering suavity of a Parthian ambassador. Abruptly he turned, embraced and kissed the cross-eyed Greek girl sitting beside him, grinned wordlessly at Fafhrd, dusted from his coarse-woven gray silk robe the antimony that had fallen from her eyelids, and folded his arms again.

Fafhrd began softly to beat the base of his goblet against the butt of his palm. His wide, tight-laced leather belt, wet with the sweat that stained his white linen tunic, creaked faintly.

Meanwhile murmured speculation as to the person responsible for casting a spell on Fafhrd's Galatian eddied around the tables and settled uncertainly on the tall, dark-haired girl, probably because she was sitting alone and therefore could not join in the suspicious whispering.

"She's an odd one," Chloe, the cross-eyed Greek, confided to the Mouser. "Silent Salmacis they call her, but I happen to know that her real name is Ahura."

"A Persian?" asked the Mouser.

Chloe shrugged. "She's been around for years, though no one knows exactly where she lives or what she does. She used to be a gay, gossipy little thing, though she never would go with men. Once she gave me an amulet, to protect me from someone, she said—I still wear it. But then she was away for a while," Chloe continued garrulously, "and when she came back she was just like you see her now—shy, and tight-mouthed as a clam, with a look in her eyes of someone peering through a crack in a brothel wall."

"Ah," said the Mouser. He looked at the dark-haired girl, and continued to look, appreciatively, even when Chloe tugged at his sleeve. Chloe gave herself a mental bastinado for having been so foolish as to call a man's attention to another girl.

Fafhrd was not distracted by this byplay. He continued to stare at the Mouser with the stony intentness of a whole avenue of Egyptian colossi. The cauldron of his anger came to a boil.

"Scum of wit-weighted culture," he said, "I consider it the nadir of base perfidy that you should try out on me your puking sorcery."

"Softly, man of strange loves," purred the Mouser. "This unfortunate mishap has befallen several others besides yourself, among them an ardent Assyrian warlord whose paramour was changed into a spider between the sheets, and an impetuous Ethiop who found himself hoisted several yards into the air and kissing a giraffe. Truly, to one who knows the literature, there is nothing new in the annals of magic and thaumaturgy."

"Moreover," continued Fafhrd, his low-pitched voice loud in the silence, "I regard it an additional treachery that you should practice your pig-trickery on me in an unsuspecting moment of pleasure."

"And even if I should choose sorcerously to discommode your lechery," hypothesized the Mouser, "I do not think it would be the woman that I would metamorphose."

"Furthermore," pursued Fafhrd, leaning forward and laying his hand on the large sheathed dirk beside him on the bench, "I judge it an intolerable and direct affront to myself that you should pick a Galatian girl, member of a race that is cousin to my own."

"It would not be the first time," observed the Mouser portentously, slipping his fingers inside his robe, "that I have had to fight you over a woman."

"But it would be the first time," asserted Fafhrd, with an even greater portentousness, "that you had to fight me over a pig!"

For a moment he maintained his belligerent posture, head lowered, jaw outthrust, eyes slitted. Then he began to laugh.

It was something, Fafhrd's laughter. It began with windy snickers through the nostrils, next spewed out between clenched teeth, then became a series of jolting chortles, swiftly grew into a roar against which the barbarian had to brace himself, legs spread wide, head thrown back, as if against a gale. It was a laughter of the storm-lashed forest or the sea, a laughter that conjured up wide visions, that seemed to blow from a more primeval, heartier, lusher time. It was the laugh of the Elder Gods observing their creature man and noting their omissions, miscalculations and mistakes.

The Mouser's lips began to twitch. He grimaced wryly, seeking to avoid the infection. Then he joined in.

Fafhrd paused, panted, snatched up the wine pitcher, drained it.

"Pig-trickery!" he bellowed, and began to laugh all over again.

The Tyrian riffraff gawked at them in wonder—astounded, awestruck, their imaginations cloudily stirred.

Among them, however, was one whose response was noteworthy. The dark-haired girl was staring at Fafhrd avidly, drinking in the sound, the oddest sort of hunger and baffled curiosity—and calculation—in her eyes.

The Mouser noticed her and stopped his laughter to watch.

Mentally Chloe gave herself an especially heavy swipe on the soles of her bound, naked feet. Fafhrd's laughter trailed off. He blew out the last of it soundlessly, sucked in a normal breath, hooked his thumbs in his belt.

"The dawn stars are peeping," he commented to the Mouser, ducking his head for a look through the skylight. "It's time we were about the business."

And without more ado he and Mouser left the shop, pushing out of their way a newly arrived and very drunken merchant of Pergamum, who looked after them bewilderedly, as if he were trying to decide whether they were a tall god and his dwarfish servitor, or a small sorcerer and the great-thewed automaton who did his bidding.

Had it ended there, two weeks would have seen Fafhrd claiming that the incident of the wine shop was merely a drunken dream that had been dreamed by more than one— a kind of coincidence with which he was by no means unfamiliar. But it did not. After "the business" (which turned out to be much more complicated than had been anticipated, evolving from a fairly simple affair of Sidonian smugglers into a glittering intrigue studded with Cilician pirates, a kidnapped Cappadocian princess, a forged letter of credit on a Syracusian financier, a bargain with a female Cyprian slave-dealer, a rendezvous that turned into an ambush, some priceless tomb-filched Egyptian jewels that no one ever saw, and a band of Idumean brigands who came galloping out of the desert to upset everyone's calculations) and after Fafhrd and the Gray Mouser had returned to the soft embraces and sweet polyglot of the seaport ladies, pig-trickery befell Fafhrd once more, this time ending in a dagger brawl with some men who thought they were rescuing a pretty Bithynian girl from death by salty and odorous drowning at the hands of a murderous red-haired giant—Fafhrd had insisted on dipping the girl, while still metamorphosed, into a hogshead of brine remaining from pickled pork. This incident suggested to the Mouser a scheme he never told Fafhrd: namely, to engage an amiable girl, have Fafhrd turn her into a pig, immediately sell her to a butcher, next sell her to an amorous merchant when she had escaped the bewildered butcher as a furious girl, have Fafhrd sneak after the merchant and turn her back into a pig (by this time he ought to be able to do it merely by making eyes at her), then sell her to another butcher and begin all over again. Low prices, quick profits.

For a while Fafhrd stubbornly continued to suspect the Mouser, who was forever dabbling in black magic and carried a gray leather case of bizarre instruments picked from the pockets of wizards and recondite books looted from Chaldean libraries—even though long experience had taught Fafhrd that the Mouser seldom read systematically beyond the prefaces in the majority of his books (though he often unrolled the later portions to the accompaniment of penetrating glances and trenchant criticisms) and that he was never able to evoke the same results two times running with his enchantments. That he could manage to transform two of Fafhrd's lights of love was barely possible; that he should get a sow each time was unthinkable. Besides, the thing happened more than twice; in fact, there never was a time when it did not happen. Moreover, Fafhrd did not really believe in magic, least of all the Mouser's. And if there was any doubt left in his mind, it was dispelled when a dark and satiny-skinned Egyptian beauty in the Mouser's close embrace was transformed into a giant snail. The Gray One's disgust at the slimy tracks on his silken garments was not to be mistaken, and was not lessened when two witnesses, traveling horse doctors, claimed that they had seen no snail, giant or ordinary, and agreed that the Mouser was suffering from an obscure kind of wet rot that induced hallucinations in its victim, and for which they were prepared to offer a rare Median remedy at the bargain price of nineteen drachmas a jar.

Fafhrd's glee at his friend's discomfiture was short-lived, for after a night of desperate and far-flung experimentation, which, some said, blazed from the Sidonian harbor to the Temple of Melkarth a trail of snail tracks that next morning baffled all the madams and half the husbands in Tyre, the Mouser discovered something he had suspected all the time, but had hoped was not the whole truth: namely, that Chloe alone was immune to the strange plague his kisses carried.

Needless to say, this pleased Chloe immensely. An arrogant self-esteem gleamed like two clashing swords from her crossed eyes, and she applied nothing but costly scented oil to her poor, mentally bruised feet—and not only mental oil, for she quickly made capital of her position by extorting enough gold from the Mouser to buy a slave whose duty it was to do very little else. She no longer sought to avoid calling the Mouser's attention to other women, in fact she rather enjoyed doing so, and the next time they encountered the dark-haired girl variously called Ahura and Silent Salmacis, as they were entering a tavern known as the Murex Shell, she volunteered more information.

"Ahura's not so innocent, you know, in spite of the way she sticks to herself. Once she went off with some old man— that was before she gave me the charm—and once I heard a primped-up Persian lady scream at her, 'What have you done with your brother?' Ahura didn't answer, just looked at the woman coldly as a snake, and after a while the woman ran out. Brr! You should have seen her eyes!"

But the Mouser pretended not to be interested.

Fafhrd could undoubtedly have had Chloe for the polite asking, and Chloe was more than eager to extend and cement in this fashion her control over the twain. But Fafhrd's pride would not allow him to accept such a favor from his friend, and he had frequently in past days, moreover, railed against Chloe as a decadent and unappetizing contemplator of her own nose.

So he perforce led a monastic life and endured contemptuous feminine glares across the drinking table and fended off painted boys who misinterpreted his misogyny and was much irritated by a growing rumor to the effect that he had become a secret eunuch priest of Cybele. Gossip and speculation had already fantastically distorted the truer accounts of what had happened, and it did not help when the girls who had been transformed denied it for fear of hurting their business. Some people got the idea that Fafhrd had committed the nasty sin of bestiality and they urged his prosecution in the public courts. Others accounted him a fortunate man who had been visited by an amorous goddess in the guise of a swine, and who thereafter scorned all earthly girls. While still others whispered that he was a brother of Circe and that he customarily dwelt on a floating island in the Tyrrhenian Sea, where he kept cruelly transformed into pigs a whole herd of beautiful shipwrecked maidens. His laughter was heard no more, and dark circles appeared in the white skin around his eyes, and he began to make guarded inquiries among magicians in hopes of finding some remedial charm.

"I think I've hit on a cure for your embarrassing ailment," said the Mouser carelessly one night, laying aside a raggedy brown papyrus. "Came across it in this obscure treatise, 'The Demonology of Isaiah ben Elshaz.' It seems that whatever change takes place in the form of the woman you love, you should continue to make love to her, trusting to the power of your passion to transform her back to her original shape."

Fafhrd left off honing his great sword and asked, "Then why don't you try kissing snails?"

"It would be disagreeable and, for one free of barbarian prejudices, there is always Chloe."

"Pah! You're just going with her to keep your self-respect. I know you. For seven days now you'd had thoughts for no one but that Ahura wench."

"A pretty chit, but not to my liking," said the Mouser icily. "It must be your eye she's the apple of. However, you really should try my remedy; I'm sure you'd prove so good at it that the shes of all the swine in the world would come squealing after you."

Whereupon Fafhrd did go so far as to hold firmly at arm's length the next sow his pent passion created, and feed it slops in the hope of accomplishing something by kindness. But in the end he had once again to admit defeat and assuage with owl-stamped Athenian silver didrachmas an hysterically angry Scythian girl who was sick at the stomach. It was then that an ill-advised curious young Greek philosopher suggested to the Northman that the soul or inward form of the thing loved is alone of importance, the outward form having no ultimate significance.

"You belong to the Socratic school?" Fafhrd questioned gently.

The Greek nodded.

"Socrates was the philosopher who was able to drink unlimited quantities of wine without blinking?"

Again the quick nod.

"That was because his rational soul dominated his animal soul?"

"You are learned," replied the Greek, with a more respectful but equally quick nod.

"I am not through. Do you consider yourself in all ways a true follower of your master?"

This time the Greek's quickness undid him. He nodded, and two days later he was carried out of the wine shop by friends, who found him cradled in a broken wine barrel, as if newborn in no common manner. For days he remained drunk, time enough for a small sect to spring up who believed him a reincarnation of Dionysus and as such worshipped him. The sect was dissolved when he became half sober and delivered his first oracular address, which had as its subject the evils of drunkenness.

The morning after the deification of the rash philosopher, Fafhrd awoke when the first hot sunbeams struck the flat roof on which he and the Mouser had chosen to pass the night. Without sound or movement, suppressing the urge to groan out for someone to buy him a bag of snow from the white-capped Lebanons (over which the sun was even now peeping) to cool his aching head, he opened an eye on the sight that he in his wisdom had expected: the Mouser sitting on his heels and looking at the sea.

"Son of a wizard and a witch," he said, "it seems that once again we must fall back upon our last resource."

The Mouser did not turn his head, but he nodded it once, deliberately.

"The first time we did not come away with our lives," Fafhrd went on.

"The second time we lost our souls to the Other Creatures," the Mouser chimed in, as if they were singing a dawn chant to Isis.

"And the last time we were snatched away from the bright dream of Lankhmar."

"He may trick us into drinking the drink, and we not awake for another five hundred years."

"He may send us to our deaths and we not to be reincarnated for another two thousand," Fafhrd continued.

"He may show us Pan, or offer us to the Elder Gods, or whisk us beyond the stars, or send us into the underworld of Quarmall," the Mouser concluded.

There was a pause of several moments.

Then the Gray Mouser whispered, "Nevertheless, we must visit Ningauble of the Seven Eyes."

And he spoke truly, for as Fafhrd had guessed, his soul was hovering over the sea dreaming of dark-haired Ahura.

2: *Ningauble*

So they crossed the snowy Lebanons and stole three camels, virtuously choosing to rob a rich landlord who made his tenants milk rocks and sow the shores of the Dead Sea, for it was unwise to approach the Gossiper of the Gods with an overly dirty conscience. After seven days of pitching and tossing across the desert, furnace days that made Fafhrd curse Muspelheim's fire gods, in whom he did not believe, they reached the Sand Combers and the Great Sand Whirlpools, and warily slipping past them while they were only lazily twirling, climbed the Rocky Islet. The city-loving Mouser ranted at Ningauble's preference for "a godforsaken hole in the desert," although he suspected that the Newsmonger and his agents came and went by a more hospitable road than the one provided for visitors, and although he knew as well as Fafhrd that the Snarer of Rumors (especially the false, which are the more valuable) must live as close to India and the infinite garden lands of the Yellow Men as to barbaric Britain and marching Rome, as close to the heaven-steaming trans-Ethiopian jungle as to the mystery of lonely tablelands and star-scraping mountains beyond the Caspian Sea.

With high expectations they tethered their camels, took torches, and fearlessly entered the Bottomless Caves, for it was not so much in the visiting of Ningauble that danger lay as in the tantalizing charm of his advice, which was so great that one had to follow wherever it led.

Nevertheless Fafhrd said, "An earthquake swallowed Ningauble's house and it stuck in his throat. May he not hiccup."

As they were passing over the Trembling Bridge spanning the Pit of Ultimate Truth, which could have devoured the light of ten thousand torches without becoming any less black, they met and edged wordlessly past a helmeted, impassive fellow whom they recognized as a far-journeying Mongol. They speculated as to whether he too were a visitor of the Gossiper, or a spy—Fafhrd had no faith in the clairvoyant powers of the seven eyes, averring that they were merely a sham to awe fools and that Ningauble's information was gathered by a corps of peddlers, panders, slaves, urchins, eunuchs, and midwives, which outnumbered the grand armies of a dozen kings.

They reached the other side with relief and passed a score of tunnel mouths, which the Mouser eyed most wistfully.

"Mayhap we should choose one at random," he muttered, "and seek yet another world. Ahura's not Aphrodite, nor yet Astarte—quite."

"Without Ning's guidance?" Fafhrd retorted. "And carrying our curses with us? Press on!"

Presently they saw a faint light flickering on the stalactited roof, reflected from a level above them. Soon they were struggling toward it up the Staircase of Error, an agglomeration of great rough rocks. Fafhrd stretched his long legs; the Mouser leaped catlike. The little creatures that scurried about their feet, brushed their shoulders in slow flight, or merely showed their yellow, insatiably curious eyes from crevice and rocky perch multiplied in number, for they were nearing the Arch-eavesdropper.

A little later, having wasted no time in reconnoitering,

they stood before the Great Gate, whose iron-studded upper reaches disdained the illumination of the tiny fire. It was not the gate, however, that interested them, but its keeper, a monstrously paunched creature sitting on the floor beside a vast heap of potsherds, and whose only movement was a rubbing of what seemed to be his hands. He kept them under the shabby but voluminous cloak which also completely hooded his head. A third of the way down the cloak, two large bats clung. Fafhrd cleared his throat. The movement ceased under the cloak.

Then out of the top of it sinuously writhed something that seemed to be a serpent, only in place of a head it bore an opalescent jewel with a dark central speck. Nevertheless, one might finally have judged it a serpent, were it not that it also resembled a thick-stalked exotic bloom. It restlessly turned this way and that until it pointed at the two strangers. Then it went rigid, and the bulbous extremity seemed to glow more brightly. There came a low purring, and five similar stalks twisted rapidly from under the hood and aligned themselves with their companion. Then the six black pupils dilated.

"Fat-bellied rumor monger!" hailed the Mouser nervously. "Must you forever play at peep show?"

For one could never quite get over the faint initial uneasiness that came with meeting Ningauble of the Seven Eyes.

"That is an incivility, Mouser," a voice from under the hood quavered thinly. "It is not well for men who come seeking sage counsel to cast fleers before them. Nevertheless, I am today in a merry humor and will give ear to your problem. Let me see, now, what world do you and Fafhrd come from?"

"Earth, as you very well know, you king of shreds of lies and patches of hypocrisy," the Mouser retorted thinly, stepping nearer. Three of the eyes closely followed his advance, while a fourth kept watch on Fafhrd.

At the same time, "Further incivilities," Ningauble

murmured sadly, shaking his head so that his eyestalks jogged. "You think it easy to keep track of the times and spaces and of the worlds manifold? And speaking of time, is it not time indeed that you ceased to impose on me, because you once got me an unborn ghoul that I might question it of its parentage? The service to me was slight, accepted only to humor you; and I, by the name of the Spoorless God, have repaid it twenty times over."

"Nonsense, Midwife of Secrets," retorted the Mouser, stepping forward familiarly, his gay impudence almost restored. "You know as well as I that deep in your great paunch you are trembling with delight at having a chance to mouth your knowledge to two such appreciative listeners as we."

"That is as far from the truth as I am from the Secret of the Sphinx," commented Ningauble, four of his eyes following the Mouser's advance, one keeping watch on Fafhrd, while the sixth looped back around the hood to reappear on the other side and gaze suspiciously behind them.

"But, Ancient Tale-bearer, I am sure you have been closer to the Sphinx than any of her stony lovers. Very likely she first received her paltry riddle from your great store."

Ningauble quivered like jelly at this tickling flattery.

"Nevertheless," he piped, "today I am in a merry humor and will give ear to your question. But remember that it will almost certainly be too difficult for me."

"We know your great ingenuity in the face of insurmountable obstacles," rejoined the Mouser in the properly soothing tones.

"Why doesn't your friend come forward?" asked Ningauble, suddenly querulous again.

Fafhrd had been waiting for that question. It always went against his grain to have to behave congenially toward one who called himself the Mightiest Magician as well as the Gossiper of the Gods. But that Ningauble should let hang from his shoulders two bats whom he called Hugin and Munin in open burlesque of Odin's ravens, was too much for him. It was more a patriotic than religious matter with Fafhrd. He believed in Odin only during moments of sentimental weakness.

"Slay the bats or send them slithering and I'll come, but not before," he dogmatized.

"Now I'll tell you nothing," said Ningauble pettishly, "for, as all know, my health will not permit bickering."

"But, Schoolmaster of Falsehood," purred the Mouser, darting a murderous glance at Fafhrd, "that is indeed to be regretted, especially since I was looking forward to regaling you with the intricate scandal that the Friday concubine of the satrap Philip withheld even from her body slave."

"Ah well," conceded the Many-Eyed One, "it is time for Hugin and Munin to feed."

The bats reluctantly unfurled their wings and flew lazily into the darkness.

Fafhrd stirred himself and moved forward, sustaining the scrutiny of the majority of the eyes, all six of which the Northman considered artfully manipulated puppet-orbs. The seventh no man had seen, or boasted of having seen, save the Mouser, who claimed it was Odin's other eye, stolen from sagacious Mimer—this not because he believed it, but to irk his Northern comrade.

"Greetings, Snake Eyes," Fafhrd boomed.

"Oh, is it you, Hulk?" said Ningauble carelessly. "Sit down, both, and share my humble fire."

"Are we not to be invited beyond the Great Gate and share your fabulous comforts too?"

"Do not mock me, Gray One. As all know, I am poor, penurious Ningauble."

So with a sigh the Mouser settled himself on his heels, for he well knew that the Gossiper prized above all else a reputation for poverty, chastity, humility, and thrift, therefore playing his own doorkeeper, except on certain days when the Great Gate muted the tinkle of impious sistrum and the lascivious wail of flute and the giggles of those who postured in the shadow shows.

But now Ningauble coughed piteously and seemed to shiver and warmed his cloaked members at the fire. And the shadows flickered weakly against iron and stone, and the little creatures crept rustling in, making their eyes wide to see and their ears cupped to hear; and upon their rhythmically swinging, weaving stalks pulsated the six eyes. At intervals, too, Ningauble would pick up, seemingly at random, a potsherd from the great pile and rapidly scan the memorandum scribbled on it, without breaking the rhythm of the eyestalks or, apparently, the thread of his attention. The Mouser and Fafhrd crouched on their hams.

As Fafhrd started to speak, Ningauble questioned rapidly, "And now, my children, you had something to tell me concerning the Friday concubine—"

"Ah, yes, Artist of Untruth," the Mouser cut in hastily. "Concerning not so much the concubine as three eunuch priests of Cybele and a slave-girl from Samos—a tasty affair of wondrous complexity, which you must give me leave to let simmer in my mind so that I may serve it up to you skimmed of the slightest fat of exaggeration and with all the spice of true detail."

"And while we wait for the Mouser's mind-pot to boil," said Fafhrd casually, at last catching the spirit of the thing, "you may the more merrily pass the time by advising us as to a trifling difficulty." And he gave a succinct account of their tantalizing bedevilment by sow- and snail-changed maidens.

"And you say that Chloe alone proved immune to the spell?" queried Ningauble thoughtfully, tossing a potsherd to the far side of the pile. "Now that brings to my mind—"

"The exceedingly peculiar remark at the end of Diotima's

FRITZ LEIBER   143 fourth epistle to Socrates?" interrupted the Mouser brightly. "Am I not right, Father?"

"You are not," replied Ningauble coldly. "As I was about to observe, when this tick of the intellect sought to burrow the skin of my mind, there must be something that throws a protective influence around Chloe. Do you know of any god or demon in whose special favor she stands, or any incantation or rune she habitually mumbles, or any notable talisman, charm, or amulet she customarily wears or inscribes on her body?"

"She did mention one thing," the Mouser admitted diffidently after a moment. "An amulet given her years ago by some Persian, or Greco-Persian girl. Doubtless a trifle of no consequence."

"Doubtless. Now, when the first sow-change occurred, did Fafhrd laugh the laugh? He did? That was unwise, as I have many times warned you. Advertise often enough your connection with the Elder Gods and you may be sure that some greedy searcher will come crawling from the pit."

"But what is our connection with the Elder Gods?" asked the Mouser, eagerly, though not hopefully. Fafhrd grunted derisively.

"Those are matters best not spoken of," Ningauble ordained. "Was there anyone who showed a particular interest in Fafhrd's laughter?"

The Mouser hesitated. Fafhrd coughed. Thus prodded, the Mouser confessed, "Oh, there was a girl who was perhaps a trifle more attentive than the others to his bellowing. A Persian girl. In fact, as I recall, the same one who gave Chloe the amulet."

"Her name is Ahura," said Fafhrd. "The Mouser's in love with her."

"A fable!" the Mouser denied laughingly, double-daggering Fafhrd with a superstitious glare. "I can assure you, Father, that she is a very shy, stupid girl, who cannot possibly be concerned in any way with our troubles."

"Of course, since you say so," Ningauble observed, his voice icily rebuking. "However, I can tell you this much: the one who has placed the ignominious spell upon you is, insofar as he partakes of humanity, a man…"

(The Mouser was relieved. It was unpleasant to think of dark-haired, lithe Ahura being subjected to certain methods of questioning which Ningauble was reputed to employ. He was irked at his own clumsiness in trying to lead Ningauble's attention away from Ahura. Where she was concerned, his wit failed him.)

"…and an adept," Ningauble concluded. "Yes, my sons, an adept—a master practitioner of blackest magic without faintest blink of light."

The Mouser started. Fafhrd groaned, "Again?"

"Again," Ningauble affirmed. "Though why, save for your connection with the Elder Gods, you should interest those most recondite of creatures, I cannot guess. They are not men who wittingly will stand in the glaringly illuminated foreground of history. They seek—"

"But who is it?" Fafhrd interjected.

"Be quiet, Mutilator of Rhetoric. They seek the shadows, and surely for good reason. They are the glorious amateurs of high magic, disdaining practical ends, caring only for the satisfaction of their insatiable curiosities, and therefore doubly dangerous. They are…"

"But what's his name?"

"Silence, Trampler of Beautiful Phrases. They are in their fashion fearless, irreligiously considering themselves the coequals of destiny and having only contempt for the Demigoddess of Chance, the Imp of Luck, and the Demon of Improbability. In short, they are adversaries before whom you should certainly tremble and to whose will you should unquestionably bow."

"But his name, Father, his name!" Fafhrd burst out, and the Mouser, his impudence again in the ascendant, remarked, "It is he of the Sabihoon, is it not, Father?"

"It is not. The Sabihoon are an ignorant fisher folk who inhabit the hither shore of the far lake and worship the beast god Wheen, denying all others," a reply that tickled the Mouser, for to the best of his knowledge he had just invented the Sabihoon.

"No, his name is..." Ningauble paused and began to chuckle. "I was forgetting that I must under no circumstances tell you his name."

Fafhrd jumped up angrily. "What?"

"Yes, children," said Ningauble, suddenly making his eye stalks staringly rigid, stern, and uncompromising. "And I must furthermore tell you that I can in no way help you in this matter..." (Fafhrd clenched his fists) "...and am very glad of it too..." (Fafhrd swore) "...for it seems to me that no more fitting punishment could have been devised for your abominable lecheries, which I have so often bemoaned..." (Fafhrd's hand went to his sword hilt) "...in fact, if it had been up to me to chastise you for your manifold vices, I would have chosen the very same enchantment..." (But now he had gone too far; Fafhrd growled, "Oh, so it is you who are behind it!" ripped out his sword and began to advance slowly on the hooded figure) "...Yes, my children, you must accept your lot without rebellion or bitterness..." (Fafhrd continued to advance) "...Far better that you should retire from the world as I have and give yourselves to meditation and repentance..." (The sword, flickering with firelight, was only a yard away) "...Far better that you should live out the rest of this incarnation in solitude, each surrounded by his faithful band of sows or snails..." (The sword touched the ragged robe) "...devoting your remaining years to the promotion of a better understanding between mankind and the lower animals. However—" (Ningauble sighed and the sword hesitated) "...if it is still your firm and foolhardy intention to challenge this adept, I suppose I must aid you with what little advice I can give, though warning you that it will plunge you into maelstroms of trouble and lay upon you geases you will grow gray in fulfilling, and incidentally be the means of your deaths."

Fafhrd lowered his sword. The silence in the black cave grew heavy and ominous. Then, in a voice that was distant yet resonant, like the sound that came from the statue of Memnon at Thebes when the first rays of the morning sun fell upon it, Ningauble began to speak.

"It comes to me, confusedly, like a scene in a rusted mirror; nevertheless, it comes, and thus: You must first possess yourselves of certain trifles. The shroud of Ahriman, from the secret shrine near Persepolis—"

"But what about the accursed swordsmen of Ahriman, Father?" put in the Mouser. "There are twelve of them. Twelve, Father, and all very accursed and hard to persuade."

"Do you think I am setting toss-and-fetch problems for puppy dogs?" wheezed Ningauble angrily. "To proceed: You must secondly obtain powdered mummy from the Demon Pharaoh, who reigned for three horrid and unhistoried midnights after the death of Ikhnaton—"

"But, Father," Fafhrd protested, blushing a little, "you know who owns that powdered mummy, and what she demands of any two men who visit her."

"Shhh! I'm your elder, Fafhrd, by eons. Thirdly, you must get the cup from which Socrates drank the hemlock; fourthly, a sprig from the original Tree of Life, and lastly..." He hesitated as if his memory had failed him, dipped up a potsherd from the pile, and read from it: "And lastly, you must procure the woman who will come when she is ready."

"What woman?"

"The woman who will come when she is ready." Ningauble tossed back the fragment, starting a small landslide of shards.

"Corrode Loki's bones!" cursed Fafhrd, and the Mouser said, "But, Father, no woman comes when she's ready. She always waits."

Ningauble sighed merrily and said, "Do not be downcast, children. Is it ever the custom of your good friend the Gossiper to give simple advice?"

"It is not," said Fafhrd.

"Well, having all these things, you must go to the Lost City of Ahriman that lies east of Armenia—whisper not its name—"

"Is it Khatti?" whispered the Mouser.

"No, Blowfly. And furthermore, why are you interrupting me when you are supposed to be hard at work recalling all the details of the scandal of the Friday concubine, the three eunuch priests, and the slave girl from Samos?"

"Oh truly, Spy of the Unmentionable, I labor at that until my mind becomes a weariness and a wandering, and all for love of you." The Mouser was glad of Ningauble's question, for he had forgotten the three eunuch priests, which would have been most unwise, as no one in his senses sought to cheat the Gossiper of even a pinch of misinformation promised.

Ningauble continued, "Arriving at the Lost City, you must seek out the ruined black shrine, and place the woman before the great tomb, and wrap the shroud of Ahriman around her, and let her drink the powdered mummy from the hemlock cup, diluting it with a wine you will find where you find the mummy, and place in her hand the sprig from the Tree of Life, and wait for the dawn."

"And then?" rumbled Fafhrd.

"And then the mirror becomes all red with rust. I can see no further, except that someone will return from a place which it is unlawful to leave, and that you must be wary of the woman."

"But, Father, all this scavenging of magical trumpery is a

great bother," Fafhrd objected. "Why shouldn't we go at once to the Lost City?"

"Without the map on the shroud of Ahriman?" murmured Ningauble.

"And you still can't tell us the name of the adept we seek?" the Mouser ventured. "Or even the name of the woman? Puppy dog problems indeed! We give you a bitch, Father, and by the time you return her, she's dropped a litter."

Ningauble shook his head ever so slightly, the six eyes retreated under the hood to become an ominous multiple gleam, and the Mouser felt a shiver crawl on his spine.

"Why is it, Riddle-Vendor, that you always give us half knowledge?" Fafhrd pressed angrily. "Is it that at the last moment our blades may strike with half force?"

Ningauble chuckled.

"It is because I know you too well, children. If I said one word more, Hulk, you could be cleaving with your great sword—at the wrong person. And your cat-comrade would be brewing his child's magic—the wrong child's magic. It is no simple creature you foolhardily seek, but a mystery, no single identity but a mirage, a stony thing that has stolen the blood and substance of life, a nightmare crept out of dream."

For a moment it was as if, in the far reaches of that nighted cavern, something that waited stirred. Then it was gone.

Ningauble purred complacently, "And now I have an idle moment, which, to please you, I will pass in giving ear to the story that the Mouser has been impatiently waiting to tell me."

So, there being no escape, the Mouser began, first explaining that only the surface of the story had to do with the concubine, the three priests, and the slave girl; the deeper portion touching mostly, though not entirely, on four infamous handmaidens of Ishtar and a dwarf who was richly compensated for his deformity. The fire grew low and a little, lemurlike creature came edging in to replenish it, and the hours stretched on, for the Mouser always warmed to his own tales. There came a place where Fafhrd's eyes bugged with astonishment, and another where Ningauble's paunch shook like a small mountain in earthquake, but eventually the tale came to an end, suddenly and seemingly in the middle, like a piece of foreign music.

Then farewells were said and final questions refused answer, and the two seekers started back the way they had come. And Ningauble began to sort in his mind the details of the Mouser's story, treasuring it the more because he knew it was an improvisation, his favorite proverb being, "He who lies artistically, treads closer to the truth than ever he knows."

Fafhrd and the Mouser had almost reached the bottom of the boulder stair when they heard a faint tapping and turned to see Ningauble peering down from the verge, porting himself with what looked like a cane and rapping with another.

"Children," he called, and his voice was tiny as the note of the lone flute in the Temple of Baal, "it comes to me that something in the distant spaces lusts for something in you. You must guard closely what commonly needs no guarding."

"Yes, Godfather of Mystification."

"You will take care?" came the elfin note. "Your beings depend on it."

"Yes, Father."

And Ningauble waved once and hobbled out of sight. The little creatures of his great darkness followed him, but whether to report and receive orders or only to pleasure him with their gentle antics, no man could be sure. Some said that Ningauble had been created by the Elder Gods for men to guess about and so sharpen their imaginations for even tougher riddles. None knew whether he had the gift of foresight, or whether he merely set the stage for future events with such a bewildering cunning that only an efreet or an adept could evade acting the part given him.

3. The Woman Who Came

After Fafhrd and the Gray Mouser emerged from the Bottomless Caves into the blinding upper sunlight, their trail for a space becomes dim. Material relating to them has, on the whole, been scanted by annalists, since they were heroes too disreputable for classic myth, too cryptically independent ever to let themselves be tied to a folk, too shifty and improbable in their adventurings to please the historian, too often involved with a riffraff of dubious demons, unfrocked sorcerers, and discredited deities—a veritable underworld of the supernatural. And it becomes doubly difficult to piece together their actions during a period when they were engaged in thefts requiring stealth, secrecy, and bold misdirection. Occasionally, however, one comes across the marks they left upon the year.

For instance, a century later the priests of Ahriman were chanting, although they were too intelligent to believe it themselves, the miracle of Ahriman's snatching of his own hallowed shroud. One night the twelve accursed swordsmen saw the blackly scribbled shroud rise like a pillar of cobwebs from the altar, rise higher than mortal man, although the form within seemed anthropoid. Then Ahriman spoke from the shroud, and they worshipped him, and he replied with obscure parables and finally strode giantlike from the secret shrine.

The shrewdest of the century-later priests remarked, "I'd say a man on stilts, or else—" (happy surmise!) "—one man on the shoulders of another."

Then there were things that Nikri, body slave to the infamous False Laodice, told the cook while she anointed the bruises of her latest beating. Things concerning two strangers who visited her mistress, and the carousal her mistress proposed to them, and how they escaped the black eunuch scimitarmen she had set to slay them when the carousal was done. "They were magicians, both of them," Nikri averred, "for at the peak of the doings they transformed my lady into a hideous, wiggly-horned sow, a horrid chimera of snail and swine. But that wasn't the worst, for they stole her chest of aphrodisiac wines. When she discovered that the demon mummia was gone with which she'd hoped to stir the lusts of Ptolemy, she screamed in rage and took her back-scratcher to me. Ow, but that hurts!"

The cook chuckled.

But as to who visited Hieronymus, the greedy tax farmer and connoisseur of Antioch, or in what guise, we cannot be sure. One morning he was found in his treasure room with his limbs stiff and chill, as if from hemlock, and there was a look of terror on his fat face, and the famous cup from which he had often caroused was missing, although there were circular stains on the table before him. He recovered but would never tell what had happened.

The priests who tended the Tree of Life in Babylon were a little more communicative. One evening just after sunset they saw the topmost branches shake in the gloaming and heard the snick of a pruning knife. All around them, without other sound or movement, stretched the desolate city, from which the inhabitants had been herded to nearby Seleucia three-quarters of a century before and to which the priests crept back only in great fear to fulfill their sacred duties. They instantly prepared, some of them to climb the Tree armed with tempered golden sickles, others to shoot down with gold-tipped arrows whatever blasphemer was driven forth, when suddenly a large gray batlike shape swooped from the Tree and vanished behind a jagged wall. Of course, it might conceivably have been a gray-cloaked man swinging on a thin, tough rope, but there were too many things whispered about the creatures that flapped by night through the ruins of Babylon for the priests to dare pursuit.

Finally Fafhrd and the Gray Mouser reappeared in Tyre,

and a week later they were ready to depart on the ultimate stage of their quest. Indeed, they were already outside the gates, lingering at the landward end of Alexander's mole, spine of an ever-growing isthmus. Gazing at it, Fafhrd remembered how once an unintroduced stranger had told him a tale about two fabulous adventurers who had aided mightily in the foredoomed defense of Tyre against Alexander the Great more than a hundred years ago. The larger had heaved heavy stone blocks on the attacking ships, the smaller had dove to file through the chains with which they were anchored. Their names, the stranger had said, were Fafhrd and the Gray Mouser. Fafhrd had made no comment.

It was near evening, a good time to pause in adventurings, to recall past escapades, to hazard misty, wild, rosy speculations concerning what lay ahead. "I think any woman would do," insisted the Mouser bickering. "Ningauble was just trying to be obscure. Let's take Chloe."

"If only she'll come when she's ready," said Fafhrd, half smiling.

The sun was dipping ruddy-golden into the rippling sea. The merchants who had pitched shop on the landward side in order to get first crack at the farmers and inland traders on market day were packing up wares and taking down canopies.

"Any woman will eventually come when she's ready, even Chloe," retorted the Mouser. "We'd only have to take along a silk tent for her and a few pretty conveniences. No trouble at all."

"Yes," said Fafhrd, "We could probably manage it without more than one elephant."

Most of Tyre was darkly silhouetted against the sunset, although there were gleams from the roofs here and there, and the gilded peak of the Temple of Melkarth sent a little water-borne glitter track angling in toward the greater one of the sun. The fading Phoenician port seemed entranced, dreaming of past glories, only half listening to today's news of Rome's implacable eastward advance, and Philip of Macedon's loss of the first round at the Battle of the Dog's Heads, and now Antiochus preparing for the second, with Hannibal come to help him from Tyre's great fallen sister Carthage across the sea.

"I'm sure Chloe will come if we wait until tomorrow," the Mouser continued. "We'll have to wait in any case, because Ningauble said the woman wouldn't come until she was ready."

A cool little wind came out of the wasteland that was Old Tyre. The merchants hurried; a few of them were already going home along the mole, their slaves looking like hunchbacks and otherwise misshapen monsters because of the packs on their shoulders and heads.

"No," said Fafhrd, "we'll start. And if the woman doesn't come when she's ready, then she isn't the woman who will come when she's ready, or if she is, she'll have to hump herself to catch up."

The three horses of the adventurers moved restlessly, and the Mouser's whinnied. Only the great camel, on which were slung the wine-sacks, various small chests, and snugly wrapped weapons, stood sullenly still. Fafhrd and the Mouser casually watched the one figure on the mole that moved against the homing stream; they were not exactly suspicious, but after the year's doings they could not overlook the possibility of death-dealing pursuers, taking the form either of accursed swordsmen, black eunuch scimitarmen, gold-weaponed Babylonian priests, or such agents as Hieronymus of Antioch might favor.

"Chloe would have come on time, if only you'd helped me persuade her," argued the Mouser. "She likes you, and I'm sure she must have been the one Ningauble meant, because she has that amulet which works against the adept."

The sun was a blinding sliver on the sea's rim, then went

under. All the little glares and glitters on the roofs of Tyre winked out. The Temple of Melkarth loomed black against the fading sky. The last canopy was being taken down, and most of the merchants were more than halfway across the mole. There was still only one figure moving shoreward.

"Weren't seven nights with Chloe enough for you?" asked Fafhrd. "Besides, it isn't she you'll be wanting when we kill the adept and get this spell off us."

"That's as it may be," retorted the Mouser. "But remember we have to catch our adept first. And it's not only I whom Chloe's company could benefit."

A faint shout drew their attention across the darkling water to where a lateen-rigged trader was edging into the Egyptian Harbor. For a moment they thought the landward end of the mole had been emptied. Then the figure moving away from the city came out sharp and black against the sea, a slight figure, not burdened like the slaves.

"Another fool leaves sweet Tyre at the wrong time," observed the Mouser. "Just think what a woman will mean in those cold mountains we're going to, Fafhrd, a woman to prepare dainties and stroke your forehead."

Fafhrd said, "It isn't your forehead, little man, you're thinking of."

The cool wind came again, and the packed sand moaned at its passing. Tyre seemed to crouch like a beast against the threats of darkness. A last merchant searched the ground hurriedly for some lost article.

Fafhrd put his hand on his horse's shoulder and said, "Come on."

The Mouser made a last point. "I don't think Chloe would insist on taking the slave girl to oil her feet, that is, if we handled it properly."

Then they saw that the other fool leaving sweet Tyre was coming toward them, and that it was a woman, tall and slender, dressed in stuffs that seemed to melt into the waning light, so that Fafhrd found himself wondering whether she truly came from Tyre or from some aerial realm whose inhabitants may venture to earth only at sunset. Then, as she continued to approach at an easy, swinging stride, they saw that her face was fair and that her hair was raven; and the Mouser's heart gave a great leap, and he felt that this was the perfect consummation of their waiting, that he was witnessing the birth of an Aphrodite, not from the foam but the dusk, for it was indeed his dark-haired Ahura of the wine shops, no longer staring with cold, shy curiosity, but eagerly smiling.

Fafhrd, not altogether untouched by similar feelings, said slowly, "So you are the woman who came when she was ready."

"Yes," added the Mouser gaily, "and did you know that in a minute more you'd have been too late."

4: The Lost City

During the next week, one of steady northward journeying along the fringe of the desert, they learned little more of the motives or history of their mysterious companion than the dubious scraps of information Chloe had provided. When asked why she had come, Ahura replied that Ningauble had sent her, that Ningauble had nothing to do with it and that it was all an accident, that certain dead Elder Gods had dreamed her a vision, that she sought a brother lost in a search for the Lost City of Ahriman; and often her only answer was silence, a silence that seemed sometimes sly and sometimes mystical. However, she stood up well to hardship, proved a tireless rider, and did not complain at sleeping on the ground with only a large cloak snuggled around her. Like some especially sensitive migratory bird, she seemed possessed of an even greater urge than their own to get on with the journey.

Whenever opportunity offered, the Mouser paid assiduous court to her, limited only by the fear of working a snail change. But after a few days of this tantalizing pleasure, he noticed that Fafhrd was vying for it. Very swiftly the two comrades became rivals, contesting as to who should be the first to offer Ahura assistance on those rare occasions when she needed it, striving to top each other's brazenly boastful accounts of incredible adventures, constantly on the alert lest the other steal a moment alone. Such a spate of gallantry had never before been known on their adventurings. They remained good friends—and they were aware of that—but very surly friends—and they were aware of that too. And Ahura's shy, or sly, silence encouraged them both.

They forded the Euphrates south of the ruins of Carchemish, and struck out for the headwaters of the Tigris, intersecting but swinging east away from the route of Xenophon and the Ten Thousand. It was then that their surliness came to a head. Ahura had roamed off a little, letting her horse crop the dry herbage, while the two sat on a boulder and expostulated in whispers, Fafhrd proposing that they both agree to cease paying court to the girl until their quest was over, the Mouser doggedly advancing his prior claim. Their whispers became so heated that they did not notice a white pigeon swooping toward them until it landed with a downward beat of wings on an arm Fafhrd had flung wide to emphasize his willingness to renounce the girl temporarily—if only the Mouser would.

Fafhrd blinked, then detached a scrap of parchment from the pigeon's leg, and read, "There is danger in the girl. You must both forgo her."

The tiny seal was an impression of seven tangled eyes.

"Just *seven* eyes," remarked the Mouser. "Pah, he is modest." And for a moment he was silent, trying to picture the gigantic web of unknown strands by which the Gossiper gathered his information and conducted his business.

But this unsuspected seconding of Fafhrd's argument finally won from him a sulky consent, and they solemnly pledged not to lay hand on the girl, or each in any way to further his cause, until they had found and dealt with the adept.

They were now in townless land that caravans avoided, a land like Xenophon's, full of chill misty mornings, dazzling noons, and treacherous twilights, with hints of shy, murderous, mountain-dwelling tribes recalling the omnipresent legends of "little people" as unlike men as cats are unlike dogs. Ahura seemed unaware of the sudden cessation of the attentions paid her, remaining as provocatively shy and indefinite as ever.

The Mouser's attitude toward Ahura, however, began to undergo a gradual but profound change. Whether it was the souring of his inhibited passion, or the shrewder insight of a mind no longer a-bubble with the fashioning of compliments and witticisms, he began to feel more and more that the Ahura he loved was only a faint spark almost lost in the darkness of a stranger who daily became more riddlesome, dubious, and even, in the end, repellent. He remembered the other name Chloe had given Ahura and found himself brooding oddly over the legend of Hermaphroditus bathing in the Carian fountain and becoming joined in one body with the nymph Salmacis. Now when he looked at Ahura he could see only the avid eyes that peered secretly at the world through a crevice. He began to think of her chuckling soundlessly at night at the mortifying spell that had been laid upon himself and Fafhrd. He became obsessed with Ahura in a very different way and took to spying on her and studying her expression when she was not looking, as if hoping in that way to penetrate her mystery.

Fafhrd noticed it and instantly suspected that the Mouser was contemplating going back on his pledge. He restrained his indignation with difficulty and took to watching the Mouser as closely as the Mouser watched Ahura. No longer when it became necessary to procure provisions was either

willing to hunt alone. The easy amicability of their friendship
deteriorated. Then, late one afternoon while they were
traversing a shadowy ravine east of Armenia, a hawk dove
suddenly and sank its talons in Fafhrd's shoulder. The Northerner
killed the creature in a flurry of reddish feathers before he noticed
that it too carried a message.

"Watch out for the Mouser," was all it said, but coupled
with the smart of the talon-pricks, that was quite enough for
Fafhrd. Drawing up beside the Mouser while Ahura's horse
pranced skittishly away from the disturbance, he told the
Mouser his full suspicions and warned him that any violation
of their agreement would at once end their friendship and
bring them into deadly collision.

The Mouser listened like a man in a dream, still moodily
watching Ahura. He would have liked to have told Fafhrd
his real motives but was doubtful whether he could make
them intelligible. Moreover, he was piqued at being
misjudged. So when Fafhrd's direful outburst was finished,
he made no comment. Fafhrd interpreted this as an admission
of guilt and cantered on in a rage.

They were now nearing that rugged vantage-land from
which the Medes and the Persians had swooped down on
Assyria and Chaldea, and where, if they could believe
Ningauble's geography, they would find the forgotten lair of
the Lord of Eternal Evil. At first the archaic map on the
shroud of Ahriman proved more maddening than helpful, but
after a while, clarified in part by a curiously erudite suggestion
of Ahura, it began to make disturbing sense, showing them
a deep gorge where the foregoing terrain led one to expect a
saddle-backed crest, and a valley where ought to have been
a mountain. If the map held true, they would reach the Lost
City in a very few days.

All the while, the Mouser's obsession deepened and at last
took definite and startling form. He believed that Ahura was
a man.

It was very strange that the intimacy of camp life and the Mouser's own zealous spying should not long ago have turned up concrete proof or disproof of this clear-cut supposition. Nevertheless, as the Mouser wonderingly realized on reviewing events, they had not. Granted, Ahura's form and movements, all her least little actions were those of a woman, but he recalled painted and padded minions, sweet not simpering, who had aped femininity almost as well. Preposterous—but there it was. From that moment his obsessive curiosity became a compulsive sweat and he redoubled his moody peering, much to the anger of Fafhrd, who took to slapping his sword hilt at unexpected intervals, though without ever startling the Mouser into looking away. Each in his way stayed as surly-sullen as the camel that displayed a more and more dour balkiness at this preposterous excursion from the healthy desert.

Those were nightmare days for the Gray One, as they advanced ever closer through gloomy gorges and over craggy crests toward Ahriman's primeval shrine. Fafhrd seemed an ominous, white-faced giant reminding him of someone he had known in waking life, and their whole quest a blind treading of the more subterranean routes of dream. He still wanted to tell the giant his suspicions but could not bring himself to it because of their monstrousness and because the giant loved Ahura. And all the while Ahura eluded him, a phantom fluttering just beyond reach; though, when he forced his mind to make the comparison, he realized that her behavior had in no way altered, except for an intensification of the urge to press onward, like a vessel nearing its home port.

Finally there came a night when he could bear his torturing curiosity no longer. He writhed from under a mountain of oppressive unremembered dreams and, propped on an elbow, looked around him, quiet as the creature for which he was named.

It would have been cold if it had not been so still. The fuel had burned to embers. It was rather the moonlight that showed him Fafhrd's tousled head and elbow outthrust from shaggy bearskin cloak. And it was the moonlight that struck full on Ahura stretched beyond the embers, her lidded, tranquil face fixed on the zenith, seeming hardly to breathe.

He waited a long time. Then, without making a sound, he laid back his gray cloak, picked up his sword, went around the fire, and kneeled beside her. Then, for another space, he dispassionately scrutinized her face. But it remained the hermaphroditic mask that had tormented his waking hours—if he were still sure of the distinction between waking and dream. Suddenly his hands grasped at her—and as abruptly checked. Again he stayed motionless for a long time. Then, with movements as deliberate and rehearsed-seeming as a sleepwalker's, but more silent, he drew back her woolen cloak, took a small knife from his pouch, lifted her gown at the neck, careful not to touch her skin, and slit it to her knee, treating her chiton the same.

The breasts, white as ivory, that he had known would not be there, were there. And yet, instead of his nightmare lifting, it deepened.

It was something too profound for surprise, this wholly unexpected further insight. For as he knelt there, somberly studying, he knew for a certainty that this ivory flesh too was a mask, as cunningly fashioned as the face and for as frighteningly incomprehensible a purpose. The ivory eyelids did not flicker, but the edges of the teeth showed in what he fancied was a deliberate, flickery smile.

He was never more certain than at this moment that Ahura was a man.

The embers crunched behind him.

Turning, the Mouser saw only the streak of gleaming steel poised above Fafhrd's head, motionless for a moment, as if with superhuman forbearance a god should give his creature a chance before loosing the thunderbolt.

The Mouser ripped out his own slim sword in time to ward the titan blow. From hilt to point, the two blades screamed.

And in answer to that scream, melting into, continuing, and augmenting it, there came from the absolute calm of the west a gargantuan gust of wind that sent the Mouser staggering forward and Fafhrd reeling back, and rolled Ahura across the place where the embers had been.

Almost as suddenly the gale died. As it died, something whipped batlike toward the Mouser's face and he grabbed at it. But it was not a bat, or even a large leaf. It felt like papyrus.

The embers, blown into a clump of dry grass, had perversely started a blaze. To its flaring light he held the thin scrap that had fluttered out of the infinite west.

He motioned frantically to Fafhrd, who was clawing his way out of a scrub pine.

There was squid-black writing on the scrap, in large characters, above the tangled seal.

"By whatever gods you revere, give up this quarrel. Press onward at once. Follow the woman."

They became aware that Ahura was peering over their abutting shoulders. The moon came gleamingly from behind the small black tatter of cloud that had briefly obscured it. She looked at them, pulled together chiton and gown, belted them with her cloak. They collected their horses, extricated the fallen camel from the cluster of thorn bushes in which it was satisfiedly tormenting itself, and set out.

After that the Lost City was found almost too quickly; it seemed like a trap or the work of an illusionist. One moment Ahura was pointing out to them a boulder-studded crag; the next, they were looking down a narrow valley choked with crazily-leaning, moonsilvered monoliths and their accomplice shadows.

From the first it was obvious that "city" was a misnomer.

Surely men had never dwelt in those massive stone tents and huts, though they may have worshipped there. It was a habitation for Egyptian colossi, for stone automata. But Fafhrd and the Mouser had little time to survey its entirety, for without warning Ahura sent her horse clattering and sliding down the slope.

Thereafter it was a harebrained, drunken gallop, their horses plunging shadows, the camel a lurching ghost, through forests of crude-hewn pillars, past teetering single slabs big enough for palace walls, under lintels made for elephants, always following the elusive hoofbeat, never catching it, until they suddenly emerged into clear moonlight and drew up in an open space between a great sarcophaguslike block or box with steps leading up to it and a huge, crudely man-shaped monolith.

But they had hardly begun to puzzle out the things around them before they became aware that Ahura was gesturing impatiently. They recalled Ningauble's instructions and realized that it was almost dawn. So they unloaded various bundles and boxes from the shivering, snapping camel, and Fafhrd unfolded the dark, cobwebby shroud of Ahriman and wrapped it around Ahura as she stood wordlessly facing the tomb, her face a marble portrait of eagerness, as if she sprang from the stone around her.

While Fafhrd busied himself with other things, the Mouser opened the ebony chest they had stolen from the False Laodice. A fey mood came upon him and, dancing cumbrously in imitation of a eunuch serving man, he tastefully arrayed a flat stone with all the little jugs and jars and tiny amphorae that the chest contained. And in an appropriate falsetto he sang:

"I laid a board for the Great Seleuce,

I decked it pretty and abstruse;

And he must have been pleased,

For when stuffed, he wheezed,

'As punishment castrate the man.'

"You thee, Fafhrd," he lisped, "the man had been cathtwated ath a boy, and tho it wath no punithment at all. Becauthe of pweviouth cathtwathion."

"I'll castrate your wit-engorged top end," Fafhrd cried, raising the next implement of magic, but thought better of it.

Then Fafhrd handed him Socrates' cup and, still prancing and piping, the Mouser measured into it the mummy powder and added the wine and stirred them together and, dancing fantastically toward Ahura, offered it to her. When she made no movement, he held it to her lips and she greedily gulped it without taking her eyes from the tomb.

Then Fafhrd came with the sprig from the Babylonian Tree of Life, which still felt marvelously fresh and firm-leafed to his touch, as if the Mouser had only snipped it a moment ago. And he gently pried open her clenched fingers and placed the sprig inside them and folded them again.

Thus ready, they waited. The sky reddened at the edge and seemed for a moment to grow darker, the stars fading and the moon turning dull. The outspread aphrodisiacs chilled, refusing the night breeze their savor. And the woman continued to watch the tomb, and behind her, seeming to watch the tomb too, as if it were her fantastic shadow, loomed the man-shaped monolith, which the Mouser now and then scrutinized uneasily over his shoulder, being unable to tell whether it were of primevally crude workmanship or something that men had laboriously defaced because of its evil.

The sky paled until the Mouser could begin to make out some monstrous carvings on the side of the sarcophagus—of men like stone pillars and animals like mountains—and until Fafhrd could see the green of the leaves in Ahura's hand.

Then he saw something astounding. In an instant the leaves withered and the sprig became a curled and blackened stick. In the same instant Ahura trembled and grew paler still, snow pale, and to the Mouser it seemed that there was a tenuous black cloud forming around her head, that the riddlesome stranger he hated was pouring upward like a smoky jinni from her body, the bottle.

The thick stone cover of the sarcophagus groaned and began to rise.

Ahura began to move toward the sarcophagus. To the Mouser it seemed that the cloud was drawing her along like a black sail.

The cover was moving more swiftly, as if it were the upper jaw of a stone crocodile. The black cloud seemed to the Mouser to strain triumphantly toward the widening slit, dragging the white wisp behind it. The cover opened wide. Ahura reached the top and then either peered down inside or, as the Mouser saw it, was almost sucked in along with the black cloud. She shook violently. Then her body collapsed like an empty dress.

Fafhrd gritted his teeth, a joint cracked in the Mouser's wrist. The hilts of their swords, unconsciously drawn, bruised their palms.

Then, like an idler from a day of bowered rest, an Indian prince from the tedium of the court, a philosopher from quizzical discourse, a slim figure rose from the tomb. His limbs were clad in black, his body in silvery metal, his hair and beard raven and silky. But what first claimed the sight, like an ensign on a masked man's shield, was a chatoyant quality of his youthful olive skin, a silvery gleaming that turned one's thoughts to fishes' bellies and leprosy—that, and a certain familiarity.

For the face of this black and silver stranger bore an unmistakable resemblance to Ahura.

5: Anra Devadoris

Resting his long hands on the edge of the tomb, the newcomer surveyed them pleasantly and nodded as if they were intimates. Then he vaulted lightly over and came striding down the steps, treading on the shroud of Ahriman without so much as a glance at Ahura.

He eyed their swords. "You anticipate danger?" he asked, politely stroking the beard which, it seemed to the Mouser, could never have grown so bushily silky except in a tomb.

"You are an adept?" Fafhrd retorted, stumbling over the words a little.

The stranger disregarded the question and stopped to study amusedly the zany array of aphrodisiacs.

"Dear Ningauble," he murmured, "is surely the father of all seven-eyed Lechers. I suppose you know him well enough to guess that he had you fetch these toys because he wants them for himself. Even in his duel with me, he cannot resist the temptation of a profit on the side. But perhaps this time the old pander had curtsied to destiny unwittingly. At least, let us hope so."

And with that he unbuckled his sword belt and carelessly laid it by, along with the wondrously slim, silver-hilted sword. The Mouser shrugged and sheathed his own weapon, but Fafhrd only grunted.

"I do not like you," he said. "Are you the one who put the swine-curse on us?"

The stranger regarded him quizzically.

"You are looking for a cause," he said. "You wish to know the name of an agent you feel has injured you. You plan to unleash your rage as soon as you know. But behind every cause is another cause, and behind the last agent is yet another agent. An immortal could not slay a fraction of them. Believe me, who have followed that trail further than most and who have had some experience of the special obstacles that are placed in the way of one who seeks to live beyond the confines of his skull and the meager present—the traps that are set for him, the titanic enmities he awakens. I beseech you to wait a while before warring, as I shall wait before answering your second question. That I am an adept I freely admit."

At this last statement the Mouser felt another light-headed impulse to behave fantastically, this time in mimicry of a magician. Here was the rare creature on whom he could test the rune against adepts in his pouch! He wanted to hum a death spell between his teeth, to flap his arms in an incantational gesture, to spit at the adept and spin widdershins on his left heel thrice. But he too chose to wait.

"There is always a simple way of saying things," said Fafhrd ominously.

"But there is where I differ with you," returned the adept, almost animatedly. "There are no ways of saying certain things, and others are so difficult that a man pines and dies before the right words are found. One must borrow phrases from the sky, words from beyond the stars. Else were all an ignorant, imprisoning mockery."

The Mouser stared at the adept, suddenly conscious of a monstrous incongruity about him—as if one should glimpse a hint of double-dealing in the curl of Solon's lips, or cowardice in the eyes of Alexander, or imbecility in the face of Aristotle. For although the adept was obviously erudite, confident, and powerful, the Mouser could not help thinking of a child morbidly avid for experience, a timid, painfully curious small boy. And the Mouser had the further bewildering feeling that this was the secret for which he had spied so long on Ahura.

Fafhrd's sword-arm bulged, and he seemed about to make an even pithier rejoinder. But instead he sheathed his sword, walked over to the woman, held his fingers to her wrists for a moment, then tucked his bearskin cloak around her.

"Her ghost has gone only a little way," he said. "It will soon return. What did you do to her, you black and silver popinjay?"

"What matters what I've done to her or you, or me?" retorted the adept, almost peevishly. "You are here, and I have business with you." He paused. "This, in brief, is my proposal: that I make you adepts like myself, sharing with you all knowledge of which your minds are capable, on condition only that you continue to submit to such spells as I have put upon you and may put upon you in future, to further our knowledge. What do you say to that?"

"Wait, Fafhrd!" implored the Mouser, grabbing his comrade's arm. "Don't strike yet. Let's look at the statue from all sides. Why, magnanimous magician, have you chosen to make this offer to us, and why have you brought us out here to make it, instead of getting your yes or no in Tyre?"

"An adept," roared Fafhrd, dragging the Mouser along, "offers to make me an adept! And for that I should go on kissing swine! Go spit down Fenris' throat!"

"As to why I have brought you here," said the adept coolly, "there are certain limitations on my powers of movement, or at least on my powers of satisfactory communication. There is, moreover, a special reason, which I will reveal to you as soon as we have concluded our agreement—though I may tell you that, unknown to yourselves, you have already aided me."

"But why pick on *us*? Why?" persisted the Mouser, bracing himself against Fafhrd's tugging.

"Some whys, if you follow them far enough, lead over the rim of reality," replied the black and silver one. "I have sought knowledge beyond the dreams of ordinary men; I have ventured far into the darkness that encircles minds and stars. But now, midmost of the pitchy windings of that fearsome labyrinth, I find myself suddenly at my skein's end. The tyrant powers who ignorantly guard the secret of the universe without knowing what it is, have scented me. Those vile wardens of whom Ningauble is the merest agent and even Ormadz a cloudy symbol, have laid their traps and built their barricades. And my best torches have snuffed out, or proved too flickery-feeble. I need new avenues of knowledge."

He turned upon them eyes that seemed to be changing to twin holes in a curtain. "There is something in the inmost core of you, something that you, or others before you, have close-guarded down the ages. Something that lets you laugh in a way that only the Elder Gods ever laughed. Something that makes you see a kind of jest in horror and disillusionment and death. There is much wisdom to be gained by the unraveling of that something."

"Do you think us pretty woven scarves for your slick fingers to fray," snarled Fafhrd. "So you can piece out that rope you're at the end of, and climb all the way down to Niflheim?"

"Each adept must fray himself, before he may fray others," the stranger intoned unsmilingly. "You do not know the treasure you keep virgin and useless within you, or spill in senseless laughter. There is much richness in it, many complexities, destiny-threads that lead beyond the sky to realms undreamt." His voice became swift and invoking.

"Have you no itch to understand, no urge for greater adventuring than schoolboy rambles? I'll give you gods for foes, stars for your treasure-trove, if only you will do as I command. All men will be your animals; the best, your hunting pack. Kiss snails and swine? That's but an overture. Greater than Pan, you'll frighten nations, rape the world. The universe will tremble at your lust, but you will master it and force it down. That ancient laughter will give you the might—"

"Filth-spewing pimp! Scabby-lipped pander! Cease!" bellowed Fafhrd.

"Only submit to me and to my will," the adept continued rapturously, his lips working so that his black beard twitched rhythmically. "All things we'll twist and torture, know their cause. The lechery of gods will pave the way we'll tramp through windy darkness 'til we find the one who lurks in senseless Odin's skull twitching the strings that move your lives and mine. All knowledge will be ours, all for us three. Only give up your wills, submit to me!"

For a moment the Mouser was hypnotized by the glint of ghastly wonders. Then he felt Fafhrd's biceps, which had slackened under his grasp—as if the Northerner were yielding too—suddenly tighten, and from his own lips he heard words projected coldly into the echoing silence.

"Do you think a rhyme is enough to win us over to your nauseous titillations? Do you think we care a jot for your high-flown muck-peering? Fafhrd, this slobberer offends me, past ills that he has done us aside. It only remains to determine which one of us disposes of him. I long to unravel him, beginning with the ribs."

"Do you not understand what I have offered you, the magnitude of the boon? Have we no common ground?"

"Only to fight on. Call up your demons, sorcerer, or else look to your weapon."

An unearthly lust receded, rippling from the adept's eyes, leaving behind only a deadliness. Fafhrd snatched up the cup of Socrates and dropped it for a lot, swore as it rolled toward the Mouser, whose cat-quick hand went softly to the hilt of the slim sword called Scalpel. Stooping, the adept groped blindly behind him and regained his belt and scabbard, drawing from it a blade that looked as delicate and responsive as a needle. He stood, a lank and icy indolence, in the red of the risen sun, the black anthropomorphic monolith looming behind him for his second.

The Mouser drew Scalpel silently from its sheath, ran a finger caressingly down the side of the blade, and in so doing noticed an inscription in black crayon which read, "I do not approve of this step you are taking. Ningauble." With a hiss of annoyance the Mouser wiped it off on his thigh and concentrated his gaze on the adept—so preoccupiedly that he did not observe the eyes of the fallen Ahura quiver open.

"And now, Dead Sorcerer," said the Gray One lightly, "my name is the Gray Mouser."

"And mine is Anra Devadoris."

Instantly the Mouser put into action his carefully weighed plan: to take two rapid skips forward and launch his blade-tipped body at the adept's sword, which was to be deflected, and at the adept's throat, which was to be sliced. He was already seeing the blood spurt when, in the middle of the second skip, he saw, whirring like an arrow toward his eyes, the adept's blade. With a belly-contorted effort he twisted to one side and parried blindly. The adept's blade whipped in greedily around Scalpel, but only far enough to snag and tear the skin at the side of the Mouser's neck. The Mouser recovered balance crouching, his guard wide open, and only a backward leap saved him from Anra Devadoris' second serpentlike strike. As he gathered himself to meet the next attack, he gaped amazedly, for never before in his life had he been faced by superior speed. Fafhrd's face was white. Ahura, however, her head raised a little from the furry cloak, smiled with a weak and incredulous, but evil joy—a frankly vicious joy wholly unlike her former sly, intangible intimations of cruelty.

But Anra Devadoris smiled wider and nodded with a patronizing gratefulness at the Mouser, before gliding in. And now it was the blade Needle that darted in unhurried lightning attack, and Scalpel that whirred in frenzied defense. The Mouser retreated in jerky, circling stages, his face sweaty, his throat hot, but his heart exulting, for never before had he fought this well—not even on that stifling morning when, his head in a sack, he had disposed of a whimsically cruel Egyptian kidnapper.

Inexplicably, he had the feeling that his days spent in spying on Ahura were now paying off.

Needle came slipping in, and for the moment the Mouser could not tell upon which side of Scalpel it skirred and so sprang backward, but not swiftly enough to escape a prick in the side. He cut viciously at the adept's withdrawing arm— and barely managed to jerk his own arm out of the way of a stop thrust.

In a nasty voice so low that Fafhrd hardly heard her, and the Mouser heard her not at all, Ahura called, "The spiders tickled your flesh ever so lightly as they ran, Anra."

Perhaps the adept hesitated almost imperceptibly, or perhaps it was only that his eyes grew a shade emptier. At all events, the Mouser was not given that opportunity, for which he was desperately searching, to initiate a counterattack and escape the deadly whirligig of his circling retreat. No matter how intently he peered, he could spy no gap in the sword-woven steel net his adversary was tirelessly casting toward him, nor could he discern in the face behind the net any betraying grimace, any flicker of eye hinting at the next point of attack, any flaring of nostrils or distention of lips telling of gasping fatigue similar to his own. It was inhuman, unalive, the mask of a machine built by some Daedalus, or of a leprously silver automaton stepped out of myth. And like a machine, Devadoris seemed to be gaining strength and speed from the very rhythm that was sapping his own.

The Mouser realized that he must interrupt that rhythm by a counterattack, any counterattack, or fall victim to a swiftness become blinding.

And then he further realized that the proper opportunity for that counterattack would never come, that he would wait in vain for any faltering in his adversary's attack, that he must risk everything on a guess.

His throat burned, his heart pounded on his ribs for air, a stinging, numbing poison seeped through his limbs.

Devadoris started a feint, or a deadly thrust, at his face.

Simultaneously, the Mouser heard Ahura jeer, "They hung their webs on your beard and the worms knew your secret parts, Anra."

He guessed—and cut at the adept's knee.

Either he guessed right, or else something halted the adept's deadly thrust.

The adept easily parried the Mouser's cut, but the rhythm was broken and his speed slackened.

Again he developed speed, again at the last possible moment the Mouser guessed. Again Ahura eerily jeered, "The maggots made you a necklace, and each marching beetle paused to peer into your eye, Anra."

Over and over it happened, speed, guess, macabre jeer, but each time the Mouser gained only momentary respite, never the opportunity to start an extended counterattack. His circling retreat continued so uninterruptedly that he felt as if he had been caught in a whirlpool. With each revolution, certain fixed landmarks swept into view: Fafhrd's blanched agonized face; the hulking tomb; Ahura's hate-contorted, mocking visage; the red stab of the risen sun; the gouged, black, somber monolith, with its attendant stony soldiers and their gigantic stone tents; Fafhrd again....

And now the Mouser knew his strength was failing for good and all. Each guessed counterattack brought him less respite, was less of a check to the adept's speed. The landmarks whirled dizzily, darkened. It was as if he had been sucked to the maelstrom's center, as if the black cloud which he had fancied pouring from Ahura were enveloping him vampirously, choking off his breath.

He knew that he would be able to make only one more counter-cut, and must therefore stake all on a thrust at the heart.

He readied himself.

But he had waited too long. He could not gather the necessary strength, summon the speed.

He saw the adept preparing the lightning death-stroke.

His own thrust was like the gesture of a paralyzed man seeking to rise from his bed.

Then Ahura began to laugh.

It was a horrible, hysterical laugh; a giggling, snickering laugh; a laugh that made him dully wonder why she should find such joy in his death; and yet, for all the difference, a laugh that sounded like a shrill, distorted echo of Fafhrd's or his own.

Puzzledly, he noted that Needle had not yet transfixed him, that Devadoris' lightning thrust was slowing, slowing, as if the hateful laughter were falling in cumbering swathes around the adept, as if each horrid peal dropped a chain around his limbs.

The Mouser leaned on his own sword and collapsed, rather than lunged, forward.

He heard Fafhrd's shuddering sigh.

Then he realized that he was trying to pull Scalpel from the adept's chest and that it was an almost insuperably difficult task, although the blade had gone in as easily as if Anra Devadoris had been a hollow man. Again he tugged, and Scalpel came clear, fell from his nerveless fingers. His knees shook, his head sagged, and darkness flooded everything.

Fafhrd, sweat-drenched, watched the adept. Anra Devadoris' rigid body teetered like a stone pillar, slim cousin to the monolith behind him. His lips were fixed in a frozen, foreknowing smile. The teetering increased, yet for a while, as if he were an incarnation of death's ghastly pendulum, he did not fall. Then he swayed too far forward and fell like a pillar, without collapse. There was a horrid, hollow crash as his head struck the black pavement.

Ahura's hysterical laughter burst out afresh.

Fafhrd ran forward calling to the Mouser, anxiously shook the slumped form. Snores answered him. Like some spent

Theban phalanx-man drowsing over his pike in the twilight of the battle, the Mouser was sleeping the sleep of complete exhaustion. Fafhrd found the Mouser's gray cloak, wrapped it around him, and gently laid him down.

Ahura was shaking convulsively.

Fafhrd looked at the fallen adept, lying there so formally outstretched, like a tomb-statue rolled over. Devadoris' lankness was skeletal. He had bled hardly at all from the wound given him by Scalpel, but his forehead was crushed like an eggshell. Fafhrd touched him. The skin was cold, the muscles hard as stone.

Fafhrd had seen men go rigid immediately upon death— Macedonians who had fought too desperately and too long. But they had become weak and staggering toward the end. Anra Devadoris had maintained the appearance of ease and perfect control up to the last moment, despite the poisons that must have been coursing through his veins almost to the exclusion of blood. All through the duel, his chest had hardly heaved.

"By Odin crucified!" Fafhrd muttered. "He was something of a man, even though he was an adept."

A hand was laid on his arm. He jerked around. It was Ahura come behind him. The whites showed around her eyes. She smiled at him crookedly, then lifted a knowing eyebrow, put her finger to her lips, and dropped suddenly to her knees beside the adept's corpse. Gingerly she touched the satin-smooth surface of the tiny blood-clot on the adept's breast. Fafhrd, noting afresh the resemblance between the dead and the crazy face, sucked in his breath. Ahura scurried off like a startled cat.

Suddenly she froze like a dancer and looked back at him, and a gloating, transcendent vindictiveness came into her face. She beckoned to Fafhrd. Then she ran lightly up the steps to the tomb and pointed into it and beckoned again. Doubtfully the Northerner approached, his eyes on her strained and unearthly face, beautiful as an efreet's. Slowly he mounted the steps.

Then he looked down.

Looked down to feel that the wholesome world was only a film on primary abominations. He realized that what Ahura was showing him had somehow been her ultimate degradation and the ultimate degradation of the thing that had named itself Anra Devadoris. He remembered the bizarre taunts that Ahura had thrown at the adept during the duel. He remembered her laughter, and his mind eddied along the edge of suspicions of pit-spawned improprieties and obscene intimacies. He hardly noticed that Ahura had slumped over the wall of the tomb, her white arms hanging down as if pointing all ten slender fingers in limp horror. He did not know that the blackly puzzled eyes of the suddenly awakened Mouser were peering up at him.

Thinking back, he realized that Devadoris' fastidiousness and exquisitely groomed appearance had made him think of the tomb as an eccentric entrance to some luxurious underground palace.

But now he saw that there were no doors in that cramping cell into which he peered, nor cracks indicating where hidden doors might be. Whatever had come from there, had lived there, where the dry corners were thick with webs and the floor swarmed with maggots, dung beetles, and furry black spiders.

6: *The Mountain*

Perhaps some chuckling demon, or Ningauble himself, planned it that way. At all events, as Fafhrd stepped down from the tomb, he got his feet tangled in the shroud of Ahriman and bellowed wildly (the Mouser called it "bleating") before he noticed the cause, which was by that time ripped to tatters.

Next Ahura, aroused by the tumult, set them into a brief panic by screaming that the black monolith and its soldiery were marching toward them to grind them under stony feet.

Almost immediately afterwards the cup of Socrates momentarily froze their blood by rolling around in a semicircle, as if its learned owner were invisibly pawing for it, perhaps to wet his throat after a spell of dusty disputation in the underworld. Of the withered sprig from the Tree of Life there was no sign, although the Mouser jumped as far and as skittishly as one of his namesakes when he saw a large black walking-stick insect crawling away from where the sprig might have fallen.

But it was the camel that caused the biggest commotion, by suddenly beginning to prance about clumsily in a most uncharacteristically ecstatic fashion, finally cavorting up eagerly on two legs to the mare, which fled in squealing dismay. Afterwards it became apparent that the camel must have gotten into the aphrodisiacs, for one of the bottles was pashed as if by a hoof, with only a scummy licked patch showing where its leaked contents had been, and two of the small clay jars were vanished entirely. Fafhrd set out after the two beasts on one of the remaining horses, hallooing crazily.

The Mouser, left alone with Ahura, found his glibness put to the test in saving her sanity by a barrage of small talk, mostly well-spiced Tyrian gossip, but including a wholly apocryphal tale of how he and Fafhrd and five small Ethiopian boys once played Maypole with the eyestalks of a drunken Ningauble, leaving him peering about in the oddest directions. (The Mouser was wondering why they had not heard from their seven-eyed mentor. After victories Ningauble was always particularly prompt in getting in his demands for payment; and very exacting too—he would insist on a strict accounting for the three missing aphrodisiac containers.)

The Mouser might have been expected to take advantage

of this opportunity to press his suit with Ahura, and if possible assure himself that he was now wholly free of the snail curse. But, her hysterical condition aside, he felt strangely shy with her, as if, although this was the Ahura he loved, he were now meeting her for the first time. Certainly this was a wholly different Ahura from the one with whom they had journeyed to the Lost City, and the memory of how he had treated that other Ahura put a restraint on him. So he cajoled and comforted her as he might have some lonely Tyrian waif, finally bringing two funny little hand-puppets from his pouch and letting them amuse her for him.

And Ahura sobbed and stared and shivered, and hardly seemed to hear what nonsense the Mouser was saying, yet grew quiet and sane-eyed and appeared to be comforted.

When Fafhrd eventually returned with the still-giddy camel and the outraged mare, he did not interrupt, but listened gravely, his gaze occasionally straying to the dead adept, the black monolith, the stone city, or the valley's downward slope to the north. High over their heads a flock of birds was flying in the same direction. Suddenly they scattered wildly, as if an eagle had dropped among them. Fafhrd frowned. A moment later he heard a whirring in the air. The Mouser and Ahura looked up too, momentarily glimpsed something slim hurtling downward. They cringed. There was a thud as a long whitish arrow buried itself in a crack in the pavement hardly a foot from Fafhrd and stuck there vibrating.

After a moment Fafhrd touched it with shaking hand. The shaft was crusted with ice, the feathers stiff, as if, incredibly, it had sped for a long time through frigid supramundane air. There was something tied snugly around the shaft. He detached and unrolled an ice-brittle sheet of papyrus, which softened under his touch, and read, "You must go farther. Your quest is not ended. Trust in omens. Ningauble."

Still trembling, Fafhrd began to curse thunderously. He

crumpled the papyrus, jerked up the arrow, broke it in two, threw the parts blindly away. "Misbegotten spawn of a eunuch, an owl, and an octopus!" he finished. "First he tries to skewer us from the skies, then he tells us our quest is not ended—when we've just ended it!"

The Mouser, well knowing these rages into which Fafhrd was apt to fall after battle, especially a battle in which he had not been able to participate, started to comment coolly. Then he saw the anger abruptly drain from Fafhrd's eyes, leaving a wild twinkle which he did not like.

"Mouser!" said Fafhrd eagerly. "Which way did I throw the arrow?"

"Why, north," said the Mouser without thinking.

"Yes, and the birds were flying north, and the arrow was coated with ice!" The wild twinkle in Fafhrd's eyes became a berserk brilliance. "Omens, he said? We'll trust in omens all right! We'll go north, north, and still north!"

The Mouser's heart sank. Now would be a particularly difficult time to combat Fafhrd's long-standing desire to take him to "that wondrously cold land where only brawny, hot-blooded men may live and they but by the killing of fierce, furry animals"—a prospect poignantly disheartening to a lover of hot baths, the sun, and southern nights.

"This is the chance of all chances," Fafhrd continued, intoning like a skald. "Ah, to rub one's naked hide with snow, to plunge like walrus into ice-garnished water. Around the Caspian and over greater mountains than these goes a way that men of my race have taken. Thor's gut, but you will love it! No wine, only hot mead and savory smoking carcasses, skin-toughening furs to wear, cold air at night to keep dreams clear and sharp, and great strong-hipped women. Then to raise sail on a winter ship and laugh at the frozen spray. Why have we so long delayed? Come! By the icy member that begot Odin, we must start at once!"

The Mouser stifled a groan. "Ah, blood-brother," he

intoned, not a whit less brazen-voiced, "my heart leaps even more than yours at the thought of nerve-quickening snow and all the other niceties of the manly life I have long yearned to taste. But"—here his voice broke sadly—"we forget this good woman, whom in any case, even if we disregard Ningauble's injunction, we must take safely back to Tyre."

He smiled inwardly.

"But I don't want to go back to Tyre," interrupted Ahura, looking up from the puppets with an impishness so like a child's that the Mouser cursed himself for ever having treated her as one. "This lonely spot seems equally far from all builded places. North is as good a way as any."

"Flesh of Freya!" bellowed Fafhrd, throwing his arms wide. "Do you hear what she says, Mouser? By Idun, that was spoken like a true snow-land woman! Not one moment must be wasted now. We shall smell mead before a year is out. By Frigg, a woman! Mouser, you are good for one so small, did you not notice the pretty way she put it?"

So it was bustle about and pack and (for the present, at least, the Mouser conceded) no way out of it. The chest of aphrodisiacs, the cup, and the tattered shroud were bundled back onto the camel, which was still busy ogling the mare and smacking its great leathery lips. And Fafhrd leaped and shouted and clapped the Mouser's back as if there were not an eon-old dead stone city around them and a lifeless adept warming in the sun.

In a matter of moments they were jogging off down the valley, with Fafhrd singing tales of snowstorms and hunting and monsters big as icebergs and giants as tall as frost mountains, and the Mouser dourly amusing himself by picturing his own death at the hands of some overly affectionate "great strong-hipped" woman.

Soon the way became less barren. Scrub trees and the valley's downward trend hid the city behind them. A surge of relief which the Mouser hardly noticed went through him as the last stony sentinel dipped out of sight, particularly the black monolith left to brood over the adept. He turned his attention to what lay ahead—a conical mountain barring the valley's mouth and wearing a high cap of mist, a lonely thunderhead which his imagination shaped into incredible towers and spires.

Suddenly his sleepy thoughts snapped awake. Fafhrd and Ahura had stopped and were staring at something wholly unexpected—a low wooden windowless house pressed back among the scrubby trees, with a couple of tilled fields behind it. The rudely carved guardian spirits at the four corners of the roof and topping the kingposts seemed Persian, but Persian purged of all southern influence—ancient Persian.

And ancient Persian too appeared the thin features, straight nose, and black-streaked beard of the aged man watching them circumspectly from the low doorway. It seemed to be Ahura's face he scanned most intently—or tried to scan, since Fafhrd mostly hid her.

"Greetings, Father," called the Mouser. "Is this not a merry day for riding, and yours good lands to pass?"

"Yes," replied the aged man dubiously, using a rusty dialect. "Though there are none, or few, who pass."

"Just as well to be far from the evil stinking cities," Fafhrd interjected heartily. "Do you know the mountain ahead, Father? Is there an easy way past it that leads north?"

At the word "mountain" the aged man cringed. He did not answer.

"Is there something wrong about the path we are taking?" the Mouser asked quickly. "Or something evil about that misty mountain?"

The aged man started to shrug his shoulders, held them contracted, looked again at the travelers. Friendliness seemed to fight with fear in his face, and to win, for he leaned forward and said hurriedly, "I warn you, sons, not to venture farther. What is the steel of your swords, the speed of your steeds, against—but remember"—he raised his voice—"I accuse no one." He looked quickly from side to side. "I have nothing at all to complain of. To me the mountain is a great benefit. My fathers returned here because the land is shunned by thief and honest man alike. There are no taxes on this land—no money taxes. I question nothing."

"Oh, well, Father, I don't think we'll go farther," sighed the Mouser wilily. "We're but idle fellows who follow our noses across the world. And sometimes we smell a strange tale. And that reminds me of a matter in which you may be able to give us generous lads some help." He chinked the coins in his pouch. "We have heard a tale of a demon that inhabits here—a young demon dressed in black and silver, pale, with a black beard."

As the Mouser was saying these things the aged man was edging backward and at the finish he dodged inside and slammed the door, though not before they saw someone pluck at his sleeve. Instantly there came muffled angry expostulation in a girl's voice.

The door burst open. They heard the aged man say "...bring it down upon us all." Then a girl of about fifteen came running toward them. Her face was flushed, her eyes anxious and scared.

"You must turn back!" she called to them as she ran. "None but wicked things go to the mountain—or the doomed. And the mist hides a great horrible castle. And powerful, lonely demons live there. And one of them—"

She clutched at Fafhrd's stirrup. But just as her fingers were about to close on it, she looked beyond him straight at Ahura. An expression of abysmal terror came into her face. She screamed, "He! The black beard!" and crumpled to the ground.

The door slammed, and they heard a bar drop into place.

They dismounted. Ahura quickly knelt by the girl, signed to them after a moment that she had only fainted. Fafhrd approached the barred door, but it would not open to any knocking, pleas, or threats. He finally solved the riddle by kicking it down. Inside he saw: the aged man cowering in a dark corner; a woman attempting to conceal a young child in a pile of straw; a very old woman sitting on a stool, obviously blind, but frightenedly peering about just the same; and a young man holding an ax in trembling hands. The family resemblance was very marked.

Fafhrd stepped out of the way of the young man's feeble ax-blow and gently took the weapon from him.

The Mouser and Ahura brought the girl inside. At sight of Ahura there were further horrified shrinkings.

They laid the girl on the straw, and Ahura fetched water and began to bathe her head.

Meanwhile, the Mouser, by playing on her family's terror and practically identifying himself as a mountain demon, got them to answer his questions. First he asked about the stone city. It was a place of ancient devil-worship, they said, a place to be shunned. Yes, they had seen the black monolith of Ahriman, but only from a distance. No, they did not worship Ahriman—see the fire-shrine they kept for his adversary Ormadz? But they dreaded Ahriman, and the stones of the devil-city had a life of their own.

Then he asked about the misty mountain and found it harder to get satisfactory answers. The cloud always shrouded its peak, they insisted. Though once toward sunset, the young man admitted, he thought he had glimpsed crazily leaning green towers and twisted minarets. But there was danger up there, horrible danger. What danger? He could not say.

The Mouser turned to the aged man. "You told me," he said harshly, "that my brother demons exact no money tax from you for this land. What kind of tax, then, do they exact?"

"Lives," whispered the aged man, his eyes showing more white.

"Lives eh? How many? And when do they come for them?"

"They never come. We go. Maybe every ten years, maybe every five, there comes a yellow-green light on the mountaintop at night, and a powerful calling in the air. Sometimes after such a night one of us is gone—who was too far from the house when the green light came. To be in the house with others helps resist the calling. I never saw the light except from our door, with a fire burning bright at my back and someone holding me. My brother went when I was a boy. Then for many years afterwards the light never came, so that even I began to wonder whether it was not a boyhood legend or illusion.

"But seven years ago," he continued quaveringly, staring at the Mouser, "there came riding late one afternoon, on two gaunt and death-wearied horses, a young man and an old— or rather the semblances of a young man and an old, for I knew without being told, knew as I crouched trembling inside the door, peering through the crack, that the masters were returning to the Castle Called Mist. The old man was bald as a vulture and had no beard. The young man had the beginnings of a silky black one. He was dressed in black and silver, and his face was very pale. His features were like—" Here his gaze flickered fearfully toward Ahura. "He rode stiffly, his lanky body rocking from side to side. He looked as if he were dead.

"They rode on toward the mountain without a sideward glance. But ever since that time the greenish-yellow light has glowed almost nightly from the mountaintop, and many of our animals have answered the call—and the wild ones too, to judge from their diminishing numbers. We have been careful, always staying near the house. It was not until three years ago that my eldest son went. He strayed too far in hunting and let darkness overtake him.

"And we have seen the black-bearded young man many times, usually at a distance, treading along the skyline or standing with head bowed upon some crag. Though once when my daughter was washing at the stream she looked up from her clothes-pounding and saw his dead eyes peering through the reeds. And once my eldest son, chasing a wounded snow-leopard into a thicket, found him talking with the beast. And once, rising early on a harvest morning, I saw him sitting by the well, staring at our doorway, although he did not seem to see me emerge. The old man we have seen too, though not so often. And for the last two years we have seen little or nothing of either, until—" And once again his gaze flickered helplessly toward Ahura.

Meanwhile the girl had come to her senses. This time her terror of Ahura was not so extreme. She could add nothing to the aged man's tale.

They prepared to depart. The Mouser noted a certain veiled vindictiveness toward the girl, especially in the eyes of the woman with the child, for having tried to warn them. So turning in the doorway he said, "If you harm one hair of the girl's head, we will return, and the black-bearded one with us, and the green light to guide us by and wreak terrible vengeance."

He tossed a few gold coins on the floor and departed.

(And so, although, or rather because her family looked upon her as an ally of demons, the girl from then on led a pampered life, and came to consider her blood as superior to theirs, and played shamelessly on their fear of the Mouser and Fafhrd and Black-beard, and finally made them give her all the golden coins, and with them purchased seductive garments after fortunate passage to a faraway city, where by clever stratagem she became the wife of a satrap and lived sumptuously ever afterwards—something that is often the fate of romantic people, if only they are romantic enough.)

Emerging from the house, the Mouser found Fafhrd making a brave attempt to recapture his former berserk mood. "Hurry up, you little apprentice-demon!" he welcomed. "We've a tryst with the good land of snow and cannot lag on the way!"

As they rode off, the Mouser rejoined good-naturedly, "But what about the camel, Fafhrd? You can't very well take it to the ice country. It'll die of phlegm."

"There's no reason why snow shouldn't be as good for camels as it is for men," Fafhrd retorted. Then, rising in his saddle and turning back, he waved toward the house and shouted, "Lad! You that held the ax! When in years to come your bones feel a strange yearning, turn your face to the north. There you will find a land where you can become a man indeed."

But in their hearts both knew that this talk was a pretense, that other planets now loomed in their horoscope—in particular one that shone with a greenish-yellow light. As they pressed on up the valley, its silence and the absence of animal and insect life now made sinister, they felt mysteries hovering all around. Some, they knew, were locked in Ahura, but both refrained from questioning her, moved by vague apprehensions of terrifying upheavals her mind had undergone.

Finally the Mouser voiced what was in the thoughts of both of them. "Yes, I am much afraid that Anra Devadoris, who sought to make us his apprentices, was only an apprentice himself and apt, apprentice-wise, to take credit for his master's work. Black-beard is gone, but the beardless one remains. What was it Ningauble said?...no simple creature, but a mystery?...no single identity, but a mirage?"

"Well, by all the fleas that bite the Great Antiochus, and all the lice that tickle his wife!" remarked a shrill, insolent voice behind them. "You doomed gentlemen already know what's in this letter I have for you."

They whirled around. Standing beside the camel—he might conceivably have been hidden, it is true, behind a nearly boulder—was a pertly grinning brown urchin, so typically Alexandrian that he might have stepped this minute out of Rakotis with a skinny mongrel sniffing at his heels.

(The Mouser half expected such a dog to appear at the next moment.)

"Who sent you, boy?" Fafhrd demanded. "How did you get here?"

"Now who and how would you expect?" replied the urchin. "Catch." He tossed the Mouser a wax tablet. "Say, you two, take my advice and get out while the getting's good. I think so far as your expedition's concerned, Ningauble's pulling up his tent pegs and scuttling home. Always a friend in need, my dear employer."

The Mouser ripped the cords, unfolded the tablet, and read:

"Greetings, my brave adventurers. You have done well, but the best remains to be done. Hark to the calling. Follow the green light. But be very cautious afterwards. I wish I could be of more assistance. Send the shroud, the cup, and the chest back with the boy as first payment."

"Loki-brat! Regin-spawn!" burst out Fafhrd. The Mouser looked up to see the urchin lurching and bobbing back toward the Lost City on the back of the eagerly fugitive camel. His impudent laughter returned shrill and faint.

"There," said the Mouser, "rides off the generosity of poor, penurious Ningauble. Now we know what to do with the camel."

"Zutt!" said Fafhrd. "Let him have the brute and the toys. Good riddance to his gossiping!"

"Not a very high mountain," said the Mouser an hour later, "but high enough. I wonder who carved this neat little path and who keeps it clear?"

As he spoke, he was winding loosely over his shoulder a long thin rope of the sort used by mountain climbers, ending in a hook.

It was sunset, with twilight creeping at their heels. The little path, which had grown out of nothing, only gradually revealing itself, now led them sinuously around great boulders and along the crests of ever-steeper rock-strewn slopes.

Conversation, which was only a film on wariness, had played with the methods of Ningauble and his agents—whether they communicated with one another directly, from mind to mind, or by tiny whistles that emitted a note too high for human ears to hear, but capable of producing a tremor in any brother whistle or in the ear of the bat.

It was a moment when the whole universe seemed to pause. A spectral greenish light gleamed from the cloudy top ahead—but that was surely only the sun's sky-reflected afterglow. There was a hint of all-pervading sound in the air, a mighty susurrus just below the threshold of hearing, as if an army of unseen insects were tuning up their instruments. These sensations were as intangible as the force that drew them onward, a force so feeble that they knew they could break it like a single spider-strand, yet did not choose to try.

As if in response to some unspoken word, both Fafhrd and the Mouser turned toward Ahura. Under their gaze she seemed to be changing momently, opening like a night flower, becoming ever more childlike, as if some master hypnotist were stripping away the outer, later petals of her mind, leaving only a small limpid pool, from whose unknown depths, however, dark bubbles were dimly rising.

They felt their infatuation pulse anew, but with a shy restraint on it. And their hearts fell silent as the hooded heights above, as she said, "Anra Devadoris was my twin brother."

7: Ahura Devadoris

"I never knew my father. He died before we were born. In one of her rare fits of communicativeness my mother told me, 'Your father was a Greek, Ahura. A very kind and learned man. He laughed a great deal.' I remember how stern she looked as she said that, rather than how beautiful, the sunlight glinting from her ringleted, black-dyed hair.

"But it seemed to me that she had slightly emphasized the word 'Your.' You see, even then I wondered about Anra. So I asked Old Berenice the housekeeper about it. She told me she had seen Mother bear us, both on the same night.

"Old Berenice went on to tell me how my father had died. Almost nine months before we were born, he was found one morning beaten to death in the street just outside the door. A gang of Egyptian longshoremen who were raping and robbing by night were supposed to have done it, although they were never brought to justice—that was back when the Ptolemies had Tyre. It was a horrible death. He was almost pashed to a pulp against the cobbles.

"At another time Old Berenice told me something about my mother, after making me swear by Athena and by Set and by Moloch, who would eat me if I did, never to tell. She said that Mother came from a Persian family whose five daughters in the old times were all priestesses, dedicated from birth to be the wives of an evil Persian god, forbidden the embraces of mortals, doomed to spend their nights alone with the stone image of the god in a lonely temple 'halfway across the world,' she said. Mother was away that day, and Old Berenice dragged me down into a little basement under Mother's bedroom and pointed out three ragged gray stones set among the bricks and told me they came from the temple. Old Berenice liked to frighten me, although she was deathly afraid of Mother.

"Of course I instantly went and told Anra, as I always did."

The little path was leading sharply upward now, along the spine of a crest. Their horses went at a walk, first Fafhrd's, then Ahura's, last the Mouser's. The lines were smoothed in Fafhrd's face, although he was still very watchful, and the Mouser looked almost like a quaint child.

Ahura continued, "It is hard to make you understand my relationship with Anra, because it was so close that even the word 'relationship' spoils it. There was a game we would play in the garden. He would close his eyes and guess what I was looking at. In other games we would change sides, but never in this one.

"He invented all sorts of versions of the game and didn't want to play any others. Sometimes I would climb up by the olive tree onto the tiled roof—Anra couldn't make it—and watch for an hour. Then I'd come down and tell him what I'd seen—some dyers spreading out wet green cloth for the sun to turn it purple, a procession of priests around the Temple of Melkarth, a galley from Pergamum setting sail, a Greek official impatiently explaining something to his Egyptian scribe, two henna-handed ladies giggling at some kilted sailors, a mysterious and lonely Jew—and he would tell me what kind of people they were and what they had been thinking and what they were planning to do. It was a very special kind of imagination, for afterwards when I began to go outside I found out that he was usually right. At the time I remember thinking that it was as if he were looking at the pictures in my mind and seeing more than I could. I liked it. It was such a gentle feeling.

"Of course our closeness was partly because Mother, especially after she changed her way of life, wouldn't let us go out at all or mix with other children. There was more reason for that than just her strictness. Anra was very delicate. He once broke his wrist, and it was a long time healing. Mother had a slave come in who was skilled in such things, and he told Mother he was afraid that Anra's bones were becoming too brittle. He told about children whose muscles and sinews gradually turned to stone, so that they became living statues. Mother struck him in the face and drove him from the house—an action that cost her a dear friend, because he was an important slave.

"And even if Anra had been allowed to go out, he couldn't have. Once after I had begun to go outside I persuaded him to come with me. He didn't want to, but I laughed at him, and he could never stand laughter. As soon as we climbed over the garden wall he fell down in a faint, and I couldn't rouse him from it, though I tried and tried. Finally I climbed back so I could open the door and drag him in, and Old Berenice spotted me, and I had to tell her what had happened. She helped me carry him in, but afterwards she whipped me because she knew I'd never dare tell Mother I'd taken him outside. Anra came to his senses while she was whipping me, but he was sick for a week afterwards. I don't think I ever laughed at him after that, until today.

"Cooped up in the house, Anra spent most of his time studying. While I watched from the roof or wheedled stories from Old Berenice and the other slaves, or later on went out to gather information for him, he would stay in Father's library, reading, or learning some new language from Father's grammars and translations. Mother taught both of us to read Greek, and I picked up a speaking knowledge of Aramaic and scraps of other tongues from the slaves and passed them on to him. But Anra was far cleverer than I at reading. He loved letters as passionately as I did the outside. For him, they were alive. I remember him showing me some Egyptian hieroglyphs and telling me that they were all animals and insects. And then he showed me some Egyptian hieratics and demotics and told me those were the same animals in disguise. But Hebrew, he said, was best of all, for each letter was a magic charm. That was before he learned Old Persian. Sometimes it was years before we found out how to pronounce the languages he learned. That was one of my most important jobs when I started to go outside for him.

"Father's library had been kept just as it was when he died. Neatly stacked in canisters were all the renowned philosophers, historians, poets, rhetoricians, and grammarians. But tossed in a corner along with potsherds and papyrus scraps like so much trash, were rolls of a very different sort. Across the back of one of them my father had scribbled, derisively I'm sure, in his big impulsive hand,

'Secret Wisdom!' It was those that from the first captured Anra's curiosity. He would read the respectable books in the canisters, but chiefly so he could go back and take a brittle roll from the corner, blow off the dust, and puzzle out a little more.

"They were very strange books that frightened and disgusted me and made me want to giggle all at once. Many of them were written in a cheap and ignorant style. Some of them told what dreams meant and gave directions for working magic—all sorts of nasty things to be cooked together. Others—Jewish rolls in Aramaic—were about the end of the world and wild adventures of evil spirits and mixed-up, messy monsters—things with ten heads and jeweled cartwheels for feet, things like that. Then there were Chaldean star-books that told how all the lights in the sky were alive and their names and what they did to you. And one jerky, half illiterate roll in Greek told about something horrible, which for a long while I couldn't understand, connected with an ear of corn and six pomegranate seeds. It was in another of those sensational Greek rolls that Anra first found out about Ahriman and his eternal empire of evil, and after that he couldn't wait until he'd mastered Old Persian. But none of the few Old Persian rolls in Father's library were about Ahriman, so he had to wait until I could steal such things for him outside.

"My going outside was after Mother changed her way of life. That happened when I was seven. She was always a very moody and frightening woman, though sometimes she'd be very affectionate toward me for a little while, and she always spoiled and pampered Anra, though from a distance, through slaves, almost as if she were afraid of him.

"Now her moods became blacker and blacker. Sometimes I'd surprise her looking in horror at nothing, or beating her forehead while her eyes were closed and her beautiful face was all taut, as if she were going mad. I had the feeling she'd been backed up to the end of some underground tunnel and must find a door leading out, or lose her mind.

"Then one afternoon I peeked into her bedroom and saw her looking into her silver mirror. For a long, long while she studied her face in it, and I watched her without making a sound. I knew that something important was happening. Finally she seemed to make some sort of difficult inward effort, and the lines of anxiety and sternness and fear disappeared from her face, leaving it smooth and beautiful as a mask. Then she unlocked a drawer I'd never seen into before and took out all sorts of little pots and vials and brushes. With these she colored and whitened her face and carefully smeared a dark, shining powder around her eyes and painted her lips reddish-orange. All this time my heart was pounding and my throat was choking up, I didn't know why. Then she laid down her brushes and dropped her chiton and felt of her throat and breasts in a thoughtful way and took up the mirror and looked at herself with a cold satisfaction. She was very beautiful, but it was a beauty that terrified me. Until now I'd always thought of her as hard and stern outside, but soft and loving within, if only you could manage to creep into that core. But now she was all turned inside out. Strangling my sobs, I ran to tell Anra and find out what it meant. But this time his cleverness failed him. He was as puzzled and disturbed as I.

"It was right afterwards that she became even stricter with me, and although she continued to spoil Anra from a distance, kept us shut up from the world more than ever. I wasn't even allowed to speak to the new slave she'd bought, an ugly, smirking, skinny-legged girl named Phryne who used to massage her and sometimes play the flute. There were all sorts of visitors coming to the house now at night, but Anra and I were always locked in our little bedroom high up by the garden. We'd hear them yelling through the wall and sometimes screaming and bumping around the inner court to the sound of Phryne's flute. Sometimes I'd lie staring at the darkness in an inexplicable sick terror all night long. I tried every way to get Old Berenice to tell me what was happening, but for once her fear of Mother's anger was too great. She'd only leer at me.

"Finally Anra worked out a plan for finding out. When he first told me about it, I refused. It terrified me. That was when I discovered the power he had over me. Up until that time the things I had done for him had been part of a game I enjoyed as much as he. I had never thought of myself as a slave obeying commands. But now when I rebelled, I found out not only that my twin had an obscure power over my limbs, so that I could hardly move them at all, or imagined I couldn't, if he were unwilling, but also that I couldn't bear the thought of him being unhappy or frustrated.

"I realize now that he had reached the first of those crises in his life when his way was blocked and he pitilessly sacrificed his dearest helper to the urgings of his insatiable curiosity.

"Night came. As soon as we were locked in I let a knotted cord out the little high window and wriggled out and climbed down. Then I climbed the olive tree to the roof. I crept over the tiles down to the square skylight of the inner court and managed to squirm over the edge—I almost fell—into a narrow, cobwebby space between the ceiling and the tiles. There was a faint murmur of talk from the dining room, but the court was empty. I lay still as a mouse and waited."

Fafhrd uttered a smothered exclamation and stopped his horse. The others did likewise. A pebble rattled down the slope, but they hardly heard it. Seeming to come from the heights above them and yet to fill the whole darkening sky was something that was not entirely a sound, something that tugged at them like the Sirens' voices at fettered Odysseus. For a while they listened incredulously, then Fafhrd shrugged and started forward again, the others following.

Ahura continued, "For a long time nothing happened, except occasionally slaves hurried in and out with full and empty dishes, and there was some laughter, and I heard Phryne's flute. Then suddenly the laughter grew louder and changed to singing, and there was the sound of couches pushed back and the patter of footsteps, and there swept into the court a Dionysiac rout.

"Phryne, naked, piped the way. My mother followed, laughing, her arms linked with those of two dancing young men, but clutching to her bosom a large silver wine-bowl. The wine sloshed over and stained purple her white silk chiton around her breasts, but she only laughed and reeled more wildly. After those came many others, men and women, young and old, all singing and dancing. One limber young man skipped high, clapping his heels, and one fat old grinning fellow panted and had to be pulled by girls, but they kept it up three times around the court before they threw themselves down on the couches and cushions. Then while they chattered and laughed and kissed and embraced and played pranks and watched a naked girl prettier than Phryne dance, my mother offered the bowl around for them to dip their wine cups.

"I was astounded—and entranced. I had been almost dead with fear, expecting I don't know what cruelties and horrors. Instead, what I saw was wholly lovely and natural. The revelation burst on me, 'So this is the wonderful and important thing that people do.' My mother no longer frightened me. Though she still wore her new face, there was no longer any hardness about her, inside or out, only joy and beauty. The young men were so witty and gay I had to put my fist in my mouth to keep from screaming with laughter. Even Phryne, squatting on her heels like a skinny boy as she piped, seemed for once unmalicious and likable. I couldn't wait to tell Anra.

"There was only one disturbing note, and that was so slight I hardly noticed it. Two of the men who took the lead in the joking, a young red-haired fellow and an older chap with a face like a lean satyr, seemed to have something up their sleeves. I saw them whisper to some of the others. And once the younger grinned at Mother and shouted, 'I know something about you from way back!' And once the older called at her mockingly, 'I know something about your great-grandmother, you old Persian you!' Each time Mother laughed and waved her hand derisively, but I could see that she was bothered underneath. And each time some of the others paused momentarily, as if they had an inkling of something, but didn't want to let on. Eventually the two men drifted out, and from then on there was nothing to mar the fun.

"The dancing became wilder and staggering, the laughter louder, more wine was spilled than drank. Then Phryne threw away her flute and ran and landed in the fat man's lap with a jounce that almost knocked the wind out of him. Four or five of the others tumbled down.

"Just at that moment there came a crashing and a loud rending of wood, as if a door were being broken in. Instantly everyone was as still as death. Someone jerked around, and a lamp snuffed out, throwing half the court into shadow.

"Then loud, shaking footsteps, like two paving blocks walking, sounded through the house, coming nearer and nearer.

"Everyone was frozen, staring at the doorway. Phryne still had her arm around the fat man's neck. But it was in Mother's face that the truly unbearable terror showed. She had retreated to the remaining lamp and dropped to her knees there. The whites showed around her eyes. She began to utter short, rapid screams, like a trapped dog.

"Then through the doorway clomped a great ragged-edged, square-limbed, naked stone man fully seven feet high. His face was just expressionless black gashes in a flat surface, and before him was thrust a mortary stone member. I couldn't bear to look at him, but I had to. He tramped echoingly across the room to Mother, jerked her up, still screaming, by the hair, and with the other hand ripped down her wine-stained chiton. I fainted.

"But it must have ended about there, for when I came to, sick with terror, it was to hear everyone laughing uproariously. Several of them were bending over Mother, at once reassuring and mocking her, the two men who had gone out among them, and to one side was a jumbled heap of cloth and thin boards, both crusted with mortar. From what they said I understood that the red-haired one had worn the horrible disguise, while satyr-face had made the footsteps by rhythmically clomping on the floor with a brick, and had simulated the breaking door by jumping on a propped-up board.

" 'Now tell us your great-grandmother wasn't married to a stupid old stone demon back in Persia!' he jeered pleasantly, wagging his finger.

"Then came something that tortured me like a rusty dagger and terrified me, in a very quiet way, as much as the image. Although she was white as milk and barely able to totter, Mother did her best to pretend that the loathsome trick they'd played on her was just a clever joke. I knew why. She was horribly afraid of losing their friendship and would have done anything rather than be left alone.

"Her pretense worked. Although some of them left, the rest yielded to her laughing entreaties. They drank until they sprawled out snoring. I waited until almost dawn, then summoned all my courage, made my stiff muscles pull me onto the tiles, cold and slippery with dew, and with what seemed the last of my strength, dragged myself back to our room.

"But not to sleep. Anra was awake and avid to hear what had happened. I begged him not to make me, but he insisted. I had to tell him everything. The pictures of what I'd seen kept bobbing up in my wretchedly tired mind so vividly that it seemed to be happening all over again. He asked all sorts of questions, wouldn't let me miss a single detail. I had to relive that first thrilling revelation of joy, tainted now by the knowledge that the people were mostly sly and cruel.

"When I got to the part about the stone image, Anra became terribly excited. But when I told him about it all being a nasty joke, he seemed disappointed. He became angry, as if he suspected me of lying.

"Finally he let me sleep.

"The next night I went back to my cubbyhole under the tiles."

Again Fafhrd stopped his horse. The mist masking the mountaintop had suddenly begun to glow, as if a green moon were rising, or as if it were a volcano spouting green flames. The hue tinged their upturned faces. It lured like some vast cloudy jewel. Fafhrd and the Mouser exchanged a glance of fatalistic wonder. Then all three proceeded up the narrowing ridge.

Ahura continued, "I'd sworn by all the gods I'd never do it. I'd told myself I'd rather die. But...Anra made me.

"Daytimes I wandered around like a stupefied little ghost slave. Old Berenice was puzzled and suspicious, and once or twice I thought Phryne grimaced knowingly. Finally even Mother noticed and questioned me and had a physician in.

"I think I would have gotten really sick and died, or gone mad, except that then, in desperation at last, I started to go outside, and a whole new world opened to me."

As she spoke on, her voice rising in hushed excitement at the memory of it, there was painted in the minds of Fafhrd and the Mouser a picture of the magic city that Tyre must have seemed to the child—the waterfront, the riches, the bustle of trade, the hum of gossip and laughter, the ships and strangers from foreign lands.

"Those people I had watched from the roof—I could touch almost anywhere. Every person I met seemed a wonderful mystery, something to be smiled and chattered at. I dressed as a slave-child, and all sorts of folk got to know me and expect my coming—other slaves, tavern wenches and sellers of sweetmeats, street merchants and scribes, errand boys and boatmen, seamstresses and cooks. I made myself useful, ran errands myself, listened delightedly to their endless talk, passed on gossip I'd heard, gave away bits of food I'd stolen at home, became a favorite. It seemed to me I could never get enough of Tyre. I scampered from morning to night. It was generally twilight before I climbed back over the garden wall.

"I couldn't fool Old Berenice, but after a while I found a way to escape her whippings. I threatened to tell Mother it was she who had told red-hair and satyr-face about the stone image. I don't know if I guessed right or not, but the threat worked. After that, she would only mumble venomously whenever I sneaked in after sunset. As for Mother, she was getting farther away from us all the time, alive only by night, lost by day in frightened brooding.

"Then, each evening, came another delight. I would tell Anra everything I had heard and seen, each new adventure, each little triumph. Like a magpie I repeated for him all the bright colors, sounds, and odors. Like a magpie I repeated for him the babble of strange languages I'd heard, the scraps of learned talk I'd caught from priests and scholars. I forgot what he'd done to me. We were playing the game again, the most wonderful version of all. Often he helped me, suggesting new places to go, new things to watch for, and once he even saved me from being kidnapped by a couple of ingratiating Alexandrian slave-dealers whom anyone but I would have suspected.

"It was odd how that happened. The two had made much of me, were promising me sweetmeats if I would go somewhere nearby with them, when I thought I heard Anra's voice whisper 'Don't.' I became cold with terror and darted down an alley.

"It seemed as though Anra were now able sometimes to see the pictures in my mind even when I was away from him. I felt ever so close to him.

"I was wild for him to come out with me, but I've told you what happened the one time he tried. And as the years passed, he seemed to become tied even tighter to the house. Once when Mother vaguely talked of moving to Antioch, he fell ill and did not recover until she had promised we would never, never go.

"Meanwhile he was growing up into a slim and darkly handsome youth. Phryne began to make eyes at him and sought excuses to go to his room. But he was frightened and rebuffed her. However, he coaxed me to make friends with her, to be near her, even share her bed those nights when Mother did not want her. He seemed to like that.

"You know the restlessness that comes to a maturing child, when he seeks love, or adventure, or the gods, or all three. That restlessness had come to Anra, but his only gods were in those dusty, dubious rolls my father had labeled 'Secret Wisdom!' I hardly knew what he did by day any more except that there were odd ceremonies and experiments mixed with his studies. Some of them he conducted in the little basement where the three gray stones were. At such times he had me keep watch. He no longer told me what he was reading or thinking, and I was so busy in my new world that I hardly noticed the difference.

"And yet I could see the restlessness growing. He sent me on longer and more difficult missions, had me inquire after books the scribes had never heard of, seek out all manner of astrologers and wise-women, required me to steal or buy stranger and stranger ingredients from the herb doctors. And when I did win such treasures for him, he would only snatch them from me unjoyfully and be twice as gloomy the evening after. Gone were such days of rejoicing as when I had brought him the first Persian rolls about Ahriman, the first lodestone, or repeated every syllable I had overheard of the words of a famous philosopher from Athens. He was beyond all that now. He sometimes hardly listened to my detailed reports, as if he had already glanced through them and knew they contained nothing to interest him.

"He grew haggard and sick. His restlessness took the form of a frantic pacing. I was reminded of my mother trapped in that blocked-off, underground corridor. It made my heart hurt to watch him. I longed to help him, to share with him my new exciting life, to give him the thing he so desperately wanted.

"But it was not my help he needed. He had embarked on a dark, mysterious quest I did not understand, and he had reached a bitter, corroding impasse where of his own experience he could go no farther.

"He needed a teacher."

8: *The Old Man Without a Beard*

"I was fifteen when I met the Old Man Without a Beard. I called him that then and I still call him that, for there is no other distinguishing characteristic my mind can seize and hold. Whenever I think of him, even whenever I look at him, his face melts into the mob. It is as if a master actor, after portraying every sort of character in the world, should have hit on the simplest and most perfect of disguises.

"As to what lies behind that too-ordinary face—the something you can sometimes sense but hardly grasp—all I can say is a satiety and an emptiness that are not of this world."

Fafhrd caught his breath. They had reached the end of the ridge. The leftward slope had suddenly tilted upward, become the core of the mountain, while the rightward slope had swung downward and out of sight, leaving an unfathomable black abyss. Between, the path continued upward, a stony strip only a few feet wide. The Mouser touched reassuringly the coil of rope over his shoulder. For a moment their horses hung back. Then, as if the faint green glow and the ceaseless murmuring that bathed them were an intangible net, they were drawn on.

"I was in a wine shop. I had just carried a message to one of the men-friends of the Greek girl Chloe, hardly older than myself, when I noticed him sitting in a corner. I asked Chloe about him. She said he was a Greek chorister and commercial poet down on his luck, or, no, that he was an Egyptian fortune-teller, changed her mind again, tried to remember what a Samian pander had told her about him, gave him a quick puzzled look, decided that she didn't really know him at all and that it didn't matter.

"But his very emptiness intrigued me. Here was a new kind of mystery. After I had been watching him for some time, he turned around and looked at me. I had the impression that he had been aware of my inquiring gaze from the beginning, but had ignored it as a sleepy man a buzzing fly.

"After that one glance he slumped back into his former position, but when I left the shop he walked at my side.

"'You're not the only one who looks through your eyes, are you?' he said quietly.

"I was so startled by his question that I didn't know how to reply, but he didn't require me to. His face brightened without becoming any more individualized, and he immediately began to talk to me in the most charming and humorous way, though his words gave no clue as to who he was or what he did.

"However, I gathered from hints he let fall that he possessed some knowledge of those odd sorts of things that always interested Anra and so I followed him willingly, my hand in his.

"But not for long. Our way led up a narrow twisting alley, and I saw a sideways glint in his eye, and felt his hand tighten on mine in a way I did not like. I became somewhat frightened and expected at any minute the danger warning from Anra.

"We passed a lowering tenement and stopped at a rickety three-story shack leaning against it. He said his dwelling was at the top. He was drawing me toward the ladder that served for stairs, and still the danger warning did not come.

"Then his hand crept toward my wrist and I did not wait any longer, but jerked away and ran, my fear growing greater with every step.

"When I reached home, Anra was pacing like a leopard. I was eager to tell him all about my narrow escape, but he kept interrupting me to demand details of the Old Man and angrily flirting his head because I could tell him so little. Then, when I came to the part about my running away, an astounding look of tortured betrayal contorted his features, he raised his hands as if to strike me, then threw himself down on the couch, sobbing.

"But as I leaned over him anxiously, his sobs stopped. He looked around at me, over his shoulder, his face white but composed, and said, 'Ahura, I must know everything about him.'

"In that one moment I realized all that I had overlooked for years—that my delightful airy freedom was a sham—that it was not Anra, but I, that was tethered—that the game was not a game, but a bondage—that while I had gone about so open and eager, intent only on sound and color, form and movement, he had been developing the side I had no time for, the intellect, the purpose, the will—that I was only a tool to him, a slave to be sent on errands, an unfeeling extension of his own body, a tentacle he could lose and grow again, like an octopus—that even my misery at his frantic disappointment, my willingness to do anything to please him, was only another lever to be coldly used against me—that our very closeness, so that we were only two halves of one mind, was to him only another tactical advantage.

"He had reached the second great crisis of his life, and again he unhesitatingly sacrificed his nearest.

"There was something uglier to it even than that, as I could see in his eyes as soon as he was sure he had me. We were like brother and sister kings in Alexandria or Antioch, playmates from infancy, destined for each other but unknowingly, and the boy crippled and impotent—and now, too soon and horridly had come the bridal night.

"The end was that I went back to the narrow alley, the lowering tenement, the rickety shack, the ladder, the third story, and the Old Man Without a Beard.

"I didn't give in without a struggle. Once I was out of the house I fought every inch of the way. Up until now, even in the cubbyhole under the tiles, I had only to spy and observe for Anra. I had not to do things.

"But in the end it was the same. I dragged myself up the last rung and knocked on the warped door. It swung open at my touch. Inside, across a fumy room, behind a large empty table, by the light of a single ill-burning lamp, his eyes as unwinking as a fish's, and upon me, sat the Old Man Without a Beard."

Ahura paused, and Fafhrd and the Mouser felt a clamminess descend upon their skins. Looking up, they saw uncoiling downward from dizzy heights, like the ghosts of constrictive snakes or jungle vines, thin tendrils of green mist.

"Yes," said Ahura, "there is always mist or smokiness of some sort where he is.

"Three days later I returned to Anra and told him everything—a corpse giving testimony as to its murderer. But in this instance the judge relished the testimony, and when I told him of a certain plan the Old Man had in mind, an unearthly joy shimmered on his face.

"The Old Man was to be hired as a tutor and physician for Anra. This was easily arranged, as Mother always acceded to Anra's wishes and perhaps still had some hope of seeing him stirred from his seclusion. Moreover, the Old Man had a mixture of unobtrusiveness and power that I am sure would have won him entry everywhere. Within a matter of weeks he had quietly established a mastery over everyone in the house—some, like Mother, merely to be ignored; others, like Phryne, ultimately to be used.

"I will always remember Anra on the day the Old Man came. This was to be his first contact with the reality beyond the garden wall, and I could see that he was terribly frightened. As the hours of waiting passed, he retreated to his room, and I think it was mainly pride that kept him from calling the whole thing off. We did not hear the Old Man coming—only Old Berenice, who was counting the silver outside, stopped her muttering. Anra threw himself back on the couch in the farthest corner of the room, his hands gripping its edge, his eyes fixed on the doorway. A shadow lurched into sight there, grew darker and more definite. Then the Old Man put down on the threshold the two bags he was carrying and looked beyond me at Anra. A moment later my twin's painful gasps died in a faint hiss of expired breath. He had fainted.

"That evening his new education began. Everything that had happened was, as it were, repeated on a deeper, stranger level. There were languages to be learned, but not any languages to be found in human books; rituals to be intoned, but not to any gods that ordinary men have worshipped; magic to be brewed, but not with herbs that I could buy or steal. Daily Anra was instructed in the ways of inner darkness, the sicknesses and unknown powers of the mind, the eon-buried emotions that must be due to insidious impurities the gods overlooked in the earth from which they made man. By silent stages our home became a temple of the abominable, a monastery of the unclean.

"Yet there was nothing of tainted orgy, of vicious excess about their actions. Whatever they did, was done with strict self-discipline and mystic concentration. There was no looseness anywhere about them. They aimed at a knowledge and a power, born of darkness, true, but one which they were willing to make any self-sacrifice to obtain. They were religious, with this difference: their ritual was degradation, their aim a world chaos played upon like a broken lyre by their master minds, their god the quintessence of evil, Ahriman, the ultimate pit.

"As if performed by sleepwalkers, the ordinary routine of our home went on. Indeed, I sometimes felt that we were all of us, except Anra, merely dreams behind the Old Man's empty eyes—actors in a deliberate nightmare where men portrayed beasts; beasts, worms; worms, slime.

"Each morning I went out and made my customary way through Tyre, chattering and laughing as before, but emptily, knowing that I was no more free than if visible chains leashed me to the house, a puppet dangled over the garden wall. Only at the periphery of my masters' intentions did I dare oppose them even passively—once I smuggled the girl Chloe a protective amulet because I fancied they were considering her as a subject for such experiments as they had tried on Phryne. And daily the periphery of their intentions widened—indeed, they would long since have left the house themselves, except for Anra's bondage to it.

"It was to the problem of breaking that bondage that they now devoted themselves. I was not told how they hoped to manage it, but I soon realized that I was to play a part.

"They would shine glittering lights into my eyes and Anra would chant until I slept. Hours or even days later I would awake to find that I had gone unconsciously about my daily business, my body a slave to Anra's commands. At other times Anra would wear a thin leather mask which covered all his features, so that he could only see, if at all, through my eyes. My sense of oneness with my twin grew steadily with my fear of him.

"Then came a period in which I was kept closely pent up, as if in some savage prelude to maturity or death or birth, or all three. The Old Man said something about 'not to see the sun or touch the earth.' Again I crouched for hours in the cubbyhole under the tiles or on reed mats in the little basement. And now it was my eyes and ears that were covered rather than Anra's. For hours I, whom sights and sounds had nourished more than food, could see nothing but fragmentary memories of the child-Anra sick, or the Old Man across the fumy room, or Phryne writhing on her belly and hissing like a snake. But worst of all was my separation from Anra. For the first time since our birth I could not see his face, hear his voice, feel his mind. I withered like a tree from which the sap is withdrawn, an animal in which the nerves have been killed.

"Finally came a day or night, I know not which, when the Old Man loosened the mask from my face. There could hardly have been more than a glimmer of light, but my long-blindfolded eyes made out every detail of the little basement with a painful clarity. The three gray stones had been dug out of the pavement. Supine beside them lay Anra, emaciated, pale, hardly breathing, looking as though he were about to die."

The three climbers stopped, confronted by a ghostly green wall. The narrow path had emerged onto what must be the mountain's tablelike top. Ahead stretched a level expanse of dark rock, mist-masked after the first few yards. Without a word they dismounted and led their trembling horses forward into a moist realm which, save that the water was weightless, most resembled a faintly phosphorescent sea bottom.

"My heart leaped out toward my twin in pity and horror. I realized that despite all tyranny and torment I still loved him more than anything in the world, loved him as a slave loves the weak, cruel master who depends for everything on that slave, loved him as the ill-used body loves the despot mind.

And I felt more closely linked to him, our lives and deaths interdependent, than if we had been linked by bonds of flesh and blood, as some rare twins are.

"The Old Man told me I could save him from death if I chose. For the present I must merely talk to him in my usual fashion. This I did, with an eagerness born of days without him. Save for an occasional faint fluttering of his sallow eyelids, Anra did not move, yet I felt that never before had he listened as intently, never before had he understood me as well. It seemed to me that all my previous speech with him had been crude by contrast. Now I remembered and told him all sorts of things that had escaped my memory or seemed too subtle for language. I talked on and on, haphazardly, chaotically, ranging swiftly from local gossip to world history, delving into myriad experiences and feelings, not all of them my own.

"Hours, perhaps days passed—the Old Man may have put some spell of slumber or deafness on the other inmates of the house to guard against interruption. At times my throat grew dry and he gave me drink, but I hardly dared pause for that, since I was appalled at the slight but unremitting change for the worse that was taking place in my twin and I had become possessed with the idea that my talking was the cord between life and Anra, that it created a channel between our bodies, across which my strength could flow to revive him.

"My eyes swam and blurred, my body shook, my voice ran the gamut of hoarseness down to an almost inaudible whisper. Despite my resolve I would have fainted, save that the Old Man held to my face burning aromatic herbs which caused me to come shudderingly awake.

"Finally I could no longer speak, but that was no release, as I continued to twitch my cracked lips and think on and on in a rushing feverish stream. It was as if I jerked and flung from the depths of my mind scraps of ideas from which Anra sucked the tiny life that remained to him.

"There was one persistent image—of a dying Hermaphroditus approaching Salmacis' pool, in which he would become one with the nymph.

"Farther and farther I ventured out along the talk-created channel between us, nearer and nearer I came to Anra's pale, delicate, cadaverous face, until, as with a despairing burst of effort I hurled my last strength to him, it loomed large as a green-shadowed ivory cliff falling to engulf me—"

Ahura's words broke off in a gasp of horror. All three stood still and stared ahead. For rearing up before them in the thickening mist, so near that they felt they had been ambushed, was a great chaotic structure of whitish, faintly yellowed stone, through whose narrow windows and wide open door streamed a baleful greenish light, source of the mist's phosphorescent glow. Fafhrd and the Mouser thought of Karnak and its obelisks, of the Pharos lighthouse, of the Acropolis, of the Ishtar Gate in Babylon, of the ruins of Khatti, of the Lost City of Ahriman, of those doomful mirage-towers that seamen see where are Scylla and Charybdis. Of a truth, the architecture of the strange structure varied so swiftly and to such unearthly extremes that it was lifted into an insane stylistic realm all its own. Mist-magnified, its twisted ramps and pinnacles, like a fluid face in a nightmare, pushed upward toward where the stars should have been.

9: *The Castle Called Mist*

"What happened next was so strange that I felt sure I had plunged from feverish consciousness into the cool retreat of a fanciful dream," Ahura continued as, having tethered their horses, they mounted a wide stairway toward that open door which mocked alike sudden rush and cautious reconnoitering. Her story went on with as calm and drugged a fatalism as their step-by-step advance. "I was lying on my back beside the three stones and watching my body move around the little basement. I was terribly weak, I could not stir a muscle, and yet I felt delightfully refreshed—all the dry burning and aching in my throat was gone. Idly, as one will in a dream, I studied my face. It seemed to be smiling in triumph, very foolishly I thought. But as I continued to study it, fear began to intrude into my pleasant dream. The face was mine, but there were unfamiliar quirks of expression. Then, becoming aware of my gaze, it grimaced contemptuously and turned and said something to the Old Man, who nodded matter-of-factly. The intruding fear engulfed me. With a tremendous effort I managed to roll my eyes downward and look at my real body, the one lying on the floor.

"It was Anra's."

They entered the doorway and found themselves in a huge, many-nooked and niched stone room—though seemingly no nearer the ultimate source of the green glow, except that here the misty air was bright with it. There were stone tables and benches and chairs scattered about, but the chief feature of the place was the mighty archway ahead, from which stone groinings curved upward in baffling profusion. Fafhrd's and the Mouser's eyes momentarily sought the keystone of the arch, both because of its great size and because there was an odd dark recess toward its top.

The silence was portentous, making them feel uneasily for their swords. It was not merely that the luring music had ceased—here in the Castle Called Mist there was literally no sound, save what rippled out futilely from their own beating hearts. There was instead a fog-bound concentration that froze into the senses, as though they were inside the mind of a titanic thinker, or as if the stones themselves were entranced.

Then, since it seemed as unthinkable to wait in that silence as for lost hunters to stand motionless in deep winter cold, they passed under the archway and took at random an upward-leading ramp.

Ahura continued, "Helplessly I watched them make certain preparations. While Anra gathered some small bundles of manuscripts and clothing, the Old Man lashed together the three mortar-crusted stones.

"It may have been that in the moment of victory he relaxed habitual precautions. At all events, while he was still bending over the stones, my mother entered the room. Crying out, 'What have you done to him?' she threw herself down beside me and felt at me anxiously. But that was not to the Old Man's liking. He grabbed her shoulders and roughly jerked her back. She lay huddled against the wall, her eyes wide, her teeth chattering—especially when she saw Anra, in my body, grotesquely lift the lashed stones. Meanwhile the Old Man hoisted me, in my new, wasted form, to his shoulder, picked up the bundles, and ascended the short stair.

"We walked through the inner court, rose-strewn and filled with Mother's perfumed, wine-splashed friends, who stared at us in befuddled astonishment, and so out of the house. It was night. Five slaves waited with a curtained litter in which the Old Man placed me. My last glimpse was of Mother's face, its paint tracked by tears, peering horrifiedly through the half open door."

The ramp issued onto an upper level, and they found themselves wandering aimlessly through a mazy series of rooms. Of little use to record here the things they thought they saw through shadowy doorways, or thought they heard through metal doors with massy complex bolts whose drawing they dared not fathom. There was a disordered, high-shelved library, certain of the rolls seeming to smoke and fume as though they held in their papyrus and ink the seeds of a holocaust; the corners were piled with sealed canisters of greenish stone and age-verdigrised brass tablets. There were instruments that Fafhrd did not even bother to warn the Mouser against touching. Another room exuded a fearful animal stench; upon its slippery floor they noted a sprinkling of short, incredibly thick black bristles. But the only living creature they saw at any time was a little hairless thing that looked as if it had once sought to become a bear cub; when Fafhrd stooped to pet it, it flopped away whimpering. There was a door that was thrice as broad as it was high, and its height hardly that of a man's knee. There was a window that let upon a blackness that was neither of mist nor of night, and yet seemed infinite; peering in, Fafhrd could faintly see rusted iron handholds leading upward. The Mouser uncoiled his climbing rope to its full length and swung it around inside the window, without the hook striking anything.

Yet the strangest impression this ominously empty stronghold begot in them was also the subtlest, and one which each new room or twisting corridor heightened—a feeling of architectural inadequacy. It seemed impossible that the supports were equal to the vast weights of the great stone floors and ceilings, so impossible that they almost became convinced that there were buttresses and retaining walls they could not see, either invisible or existing in some other world altogether, as if the Castle Called Mist had only partially emerged from some unthinkable outside. That certain bolted doors seemed to lead where no space could be, added to this hinting.

They wandered through passages so distorted that, though they retained a precise memory of landmarks, they lost all sense of direction.

Finally Fafhrd said, "This gets us nowhere. Whatever we seek, whomever we wait for—Old Man or demon—it might as well be in that first room of the great archway."

The Mouser nodded as they turned back, and Ahura said, "At least we'll be at no greater disadvantage there. Ishtar, but the Old Man's rhyme is true! 'Each chamber is a slavering maw, each arch a toothy jaw.' I always greatly feared this place, but never thought to find a mazy den that sure as death has stony mind and stony claws.

"They never chose to bring me here, you see, and from the night I left our home in Anra's body, I was a living corpse, to be left or taken where they wished. They would have killed me, I think, at least there came a time when Anra would, except it was necessary that Anra's body have an occupant— or my rightful body when he was out of it, for Anra was able to reenter his own body and walk about in it in this region of Ahriman. At such times I was kept drugged and helpless at the Lost City. I believe that something was done to his body at that time—the Old Man talked of making it invulnerable—for after I returned to it, I found it seeming both emptier and stonier than before."

Starting back down the ramp, the Mouser thought he heard from somewhere ahead, against the terrible silence, the faintest of windy groans.

"I grew to know my twin's body very well, for I was in it most of seven years in the tomb. Somewhere during that black period all fear and horror vanished—I had become habituated to death. For the first time in my life my will, my cold intelligence, had time to grow. Physically fettered, existing almost without sensation, I gained inward power. I began to see what I could never see before—Anra's weaknesses.

"For he could never cut me wholly off from him. The chain he had forged between our minds was too strong for that. No matter how far away he went, no matter what screens he raised up, I could always see into some sector of his mind, dimly, like a scene at the end of a long, narrow, shadowy corridor.

"I saw his pride—a silver-armored wound. I watched his ambition stalk among the stars as if they were jewels set on black velvet in his treasure house to be. I felt, almost as if it were my own, his choking hatred of the bland, miserly gods— almighty fathers who lock up the secrets of the universe, smile at our pleas, frown, shake their heads, forbid, chastise; and

FRITZ LEIBER   213 his groaning rage at the bonds of space and time, as if each cubit he could not see and tread upon were a silver manacle on his wrist, as if each moment before or after his own life were a silver crucifying nail. I walked through the gale-blown halls of his loneliness and glimpsed the beauty that he cherished—shadowy, glittering forms that cut the soul like knives—and once I came upon the dungeon of his love, where no light came to show it was corpses that were fondled and bones kissed. I grew familiar with his desires, which demanded a universe of miracles peopled by unveiled gods. And his lust, which quivered at the world as at a woman, frantic to know each hidden part.

"Happily, for I was learning at long last to hate him, I noted how, though he possessed my body, he could not use it easily and bravely as I had. He could not laugh, or love, or dare. He must instead hang back, peer, purse his lips, withdraw."

More than halfway down the ramp, it seemed to the Mouser that the groan was repeated, louder, more whistlingly.

"He and the Old Man started on a new cycle of study and experience that took them, I think, to all corners of the world and that they were confident, I'm sure, would open to them those black realms wherein their powers would become infinite. Anxiously from my cramped vantage-point I watched their quest ripen and then, to my delight, rot. Their outstretched fingers just missed the next handhold in the dark. There was something that both of them lacked. Anra became bitter, blamed the Old Man for their lack of success. They quarreled.

"When I saw Anra's failure become final, I mocked him with my laughter, not of lips but of mind. From here to the stars he could not have escaped it—it was then he would have killed me. But he dared not while I was in his own body, and I now had the power to bar him from that.

"Perhaps it was my faint thought-laughter that turned his desperate mind to you and to the secret of the laughter of the Elder Gods—that, and his need of magical aid in regaining his body. For a while then I almost feared he had found a new avenue of escape—or advance—until this morning before the tomb, with sheer cruel joy, I saw you spit on his offers, challenge, and, helped by my laughter, kill him. Now there is only the Old Man to fear."

Passing again under the massive multiple archway with its oddly recessed keystone, they heard the whistling groan once more repeated, and this time there was no mistaking its reality, its nearness, its direction. Hastening to a shadowy and particularly misty corner of the chamber, they made out an inner window set level with the floor, and in that window they saw a face that seemed to float bodiless on the thick fog. Its features defied recognition—it might have been a distillation of all the ancient, disillusioned faces in the world. There was no beard below the sunken cheeks.

Coming close as they dared, they saw that it was perhaps not entirely bodiless or without support. There was the ghostly suggestion of tatters of clothing or flesh trailing off, a pulsating sack that might have been a lung, and silver chains with hooks or claws.

Then the one eye remaining to that shameful fragment opened and fixed upon Ahura, and the shrunken lips twisted themselves into the caricature of a smile.

"Like you, Ahura," the fragment murmured in the highest of falsettos, "he sent me on an errand I did not want to run."

As one, moved by a fear they dared not formulate, Fafhrd and the Mouser and Ahura half turned round and peered over their shoulders at the mist-clogged doorway leading outside. For three, four heartbeats they peered. Then, faintly, they heard one of the horses whinny. Whereupon they turned fully round, but not before a dagger, sped by the yet unshaking hand of Fafhrd, had buried itself in the open eye of the tortured thing in the inner window.

Side by side they stood, Fafhrd wild-eyed, the Mouser taut,

Ahura with the look of someone who, having successfully climbed a precipice, slips at the very summit.

A slim shadowy bulk mounted into the glow outside the doorway.

"Laugh!" Fafhrd hoarsely commanded Ahura. "Laugh!" He shook her, repeating the command.

Her head flopped from side to side, the cords in her neck jerked, her lips twitched, but from them came only a dry croaking. She grimaced despairingly.

"Yes," remarked a voice they all recognized, "there are times and places where laughter is an easily-blunted weapon—as harmless as the sword which this morning pierced me through."

Death-pale as always, the tiny blood-clot over his heart, his forehead crumbled in, his black garb travel-dusted, Anra Devadoris faced them.

"And so we come back to the beginning," he said slowly, "but now a wider circle looms ahead."

Fafhrd tried to speak, to laugh, but the words and laughter choked in his throat.

"Now you have learned something of my history and my power, as I intended you should," the adept continued. "You have had time to weigh and reconsider. I still await your answer."

This time it was the Mouser who sought to speak or laugh and failed.

For a moment the adept continued to regard them, smiling confidently. Then his gaze wandered beyond them. He frowned suddenly and strode forward, pushed past them, knelt by the inner window.

As soon as his back was turned Ahura tugged at the Mouser's sleeve, tried to whisper something—with no more success than one deaf and dumb.

They heard the adept sob, "He was my nicest."

The Mouser drew a dagger, prepared to steal on him from

behind, but Ahura dragged him back, pointing in a very different direction.

The adept whirled on them. "Fools!" he cried, "have you no inner eye for the wonders of darkness, no sense of the grandeur of horror, no feeling for a quest beside which all other adventurings fade in nothingness, that you should destroy my greatest miracle—slay my dearest oracle? I let you come here to Mist, confident its mighty music and glorious vistas would win you to my view—and thus I am repaid. The jealous, ignorant powers ring me round—you are my great hope fallen. There were unfavorable portents as I walked from the Lost City. The white, idiot glow of Ormadz faintly dirtied the black sky. I heard in the wind the senile clucking of the Elder Gods. There was a fumbling abroad, as if even incompetent Ningauble, last and stupidest of the hunting pack, were catching up. I had a charm in reserve to thwart them, but it needed the Old Man to carry it. Now they close in for the kill. But there are still some moments of power left me, and I am not wholly yet without allies. Though I am doomed, there are still those bound to me by such ties that they must answer me if I call upon them. You shall not see the end, if end there be." With that he lifted his voice in a great eerie shout: "Father! Father!"

The echoes had not died before Fafhrd rushed at him, his great sword swinging.

The Mouser would have followed suit except that, just as he shook Ahura off, he realized at what she was so insistently pointing.

The recess in the keystone above the mighty archway.

Without hesitation he unslipped his climbing rope, and running lightly across the chamber, made a whistling cast.

The hook caught in the recess.

Hand over hand he climbed up.

Behind him he heard the desperate skirl of swords, heard also another sound, far more distant and profound.

His hand gripped the lip of the recess, he pulled himself up and thrust in head and shoulders, steadying himself on hip and elbow. After a moment, with his free hand, he whipped out his dagger.

Inside, the recess was hollowed like a bowl. It was filled with a foul greenish liquid and encrusted with glowing minerals. At the bottom, covered by the liquid, were several objects—three of them rectangular, the others irregularly round and rhythmically pulsating.

He raised his dagger, but for the moment did not, could not, strike. There was too crushing a weight of things to be realized and remembered—what Ahura had told about the ritual marriage in her mother's family—her suspicion that, although she and Anra were born together, they were not children of the same father—how her Greek father had died (and now the Mouser guessed at the hands of what)—the strange affinity for stone the slave-physician had noted in Anra's body—what she had said about an operation performed on him—why a heart-thrust had not killed him—why his skull had cracked so hollowly and egg-shell easy—how he had never seemed to breathe—old legends of other sorcerers who had made themselves invulnerable by hiding their hearts—above all, the deep kinship all of them had sensed between Anra and this half-living castle—the black, man-shaped monolith in the Lost City—

He saw Anra Devadoris, spitted on Fafhrd's blade, hurling himself closer along it, and Fafhrd desperately warding off Needle with a dagger.

As if pinioned by a nightmare, he helplessly heard the clash of swords rise toward a climax, heard it blotted out by the other sound—a gargantuan stony clomping that seemed to be following their course up the mountain, like a pursuing earthquake—

The Castle Called Mist began to tremble, and still he could not strike—

Then, as if surging across infinity from that utmost rim beyond which the Elder Gods had retreated, relinquishing the world to younger deities, he heard a mighty, star-shaking laughter that laughed at all things, even at this; and there was power in the laughter, and he knew the power was his to use.

With a downward sweep of his arm he sent his dagger plunging into the green liquid and tearing through the stone-crusted heart and brain and lungs and guts of Anra Devadoris.

The liquid foamed and boiled, the castle rocked until he was almost shaken from the niche, the laughter and stony clomping rose to a pandemonium.

Then, in an instant it seemed, all sound and movement ceased. The Mouser's muscles went weak. He half fell, half slid, to the floor. Looking about dazedly, making no attempt to rise, he saw Fafhrd wrench his sword from the fallen adept and totter back until his groping hand found the support of a table-edge, saw Ahura, still gasping from the laughter that had possessed her, go up and kneel beside her brother and cradle his crushed head on her knees.

No word was spoken. Time passed. The green mist seemed to be slowly thinning.

Then a small black shape swooped into the room through a high window, and the Mouser grinned.

"Hugin," he called luringly.

The shape swooped obediently to his sleeve and clung there, head down. He detached from the bat's leg a tiny parchment.

"Fancy, Fafhrd, it's from the commander of our rear guard," he announced gaily. "Listen:

"'To my agents Fafhrd and the Gray Mouser, funeral greetings! I have regretfully given up all hope for you, and yet—token of my great affection—I risk my own dear Hugin in order to get this last message through. Incidentally, Hugin, if given opportunity, will return to me from Mist—something

I am afraid you will not be able to do. So if, before you die, you see anything interesting—and I am sure you will—kindly scribble me a memorandum. Remember the proverb: Knowledge takes precedence over death. Farewell for two thousand years, dearest friends. Ningauble.'"

"That demands drink," said Fafhrd, and walked out into the darkness. The Mouser yawned and stretched himself, Ahura stirred, printed a kiss on the waxen face of her brother, lifted the trifling weight of his head from her lap, and laid it gently on the stone floor. From somewhere in the upper reaches of the castle they heard a faint crackling.

Presently Fafhrd returned, striding more briskly, with two jars of wine under his arm.

"Friends," he announced, "the moon's come out, and by its light this castle begins to look remarkably small. I think the mist must have been dusted with some green drug that made us see sizes wrong. We must have been drugged, I'll swear, for we never saw something that's standing plain as day at the bottom of the stairs with its foot on the first step— a black statue that's twin brother to the one in the Lost City."

The Mouser lifted his eyebrows. "And if we went back to the Lost City…?" he asked.

"Why," said Fafhrd, "we might find that those fool Persian farmers, who admitted hating the thing, had knocked down the statue there, and broken it up, and hidden the pieces." He was silent for a moment. Then, "Here's wine," he rumbled, "to sluice the green drug from our throats."

The Mouser smiled. He knew that hereafter Fafhrd would refer to their present adventure as "the time we were drugged on a mountaintop."

They all three sat on a table-edge and passed the two jars endlessly round. The green mist faded to such a degree that Fafhrd, ignoring his claims about the drug, began to argue that even it was an illusion. The crackling from above increased in volume; the Mouser guessed that the impious rolls in the library, no longer shielded by the damp, were bursting into flame. Some proof of this was given when the abortive bear cub, which they had completely forgotten, came waddling frightenedly down the ramp. A trace of decorous down was already sprouting from its naked hide. Fafhrd dribbled some wine on its snout and held it up to the Mouser.

"It wants to be kissed," he rumbled.

"Kiss it yourself, in memory of pig-trickery," replied the Mouser.

This talk of kissing turned their thoughts to Ahura. Their rivalry forgotten, at least for the present, they persuaded her to help them determine whether her brother's spells were altogether broken. A moderate number of hugs demonstrated this clearly.

"Which reminds me," said the Mouser brightly, "now that our business here is over, isn't it time we started, Fafhrd, for your lusty Northland and all that bracing snow?"

Fafhrd drained one jar dry and picked up the other.

"The Northland?" he ruminated. "What is it but a stamping ground of petty, frost-whiskered kinglets who know not the amenities of life. That's why I left the place. Go back? By Thor's smelly jerkin, not now!"

The Mouser smiled knowingly and sipped from the remaining jar. Then, noticing the bat still clinging to his sleeve, he took stylus, ink, and a scrap of parchment from his pouch, and, with Ahura giggling over his shoulder, wrote:

"To my aged brother in petty abominations, greetings! It is with the deepest regret that I must report the outrageously lucky and completely unforeseen escape of two rude and unsympathetic fellows from the Castle Called Mist. Before leaving, they expressed to me the intention of returning to someone called Ningauble—you are Ningauble, master, are you not?—and lopping off six of his seven eyes for souvenirs. So I think it only fair to warn you. Believe me, I am your friend. One of the fellows was very tall and at times his bellowings seemed to resemble speech. Do you know him? The other fancied a gray garb and was of extreme wit and personal beauty, given to…"

Had any of them been watching the corpse of Anra Devadoris at this moment, they would have seen a slight twitching of the lower jaw. At last the mouth came open, and out leaped a tiny black mouse. The cublike creature, to whom Fafhrd's fondling and the wine had imparted the seeds of self-confidence, lurched drunkenly at it, and the mouse began a squeaking scurry toward the wall. A wine jar, hurled by Fafhrd, shattered on the crack into which it shot; Fafhrd had seen, or thought he had seen, the untoward place from which the mouse had come.

"Mice in his mouth," he hiccuped. "What dirty habits for a pleasant young man! A nasty, degrading business, this thinking oneself an adept."

"I am reminded," said the Mouser, "of what a witch told me about adepts. She said that, if an adept chances to die, his soul is reincarnated in a mouse. If, as a mouse, he managed to kill a rat, his soul passes over into a rat. As a rat, he must kill a cat; as a cat, a wolf; as a wolf, a panther; and, as a panther, a man. Then he can recommence his adeptry. Of course, it seldom happens that anyone gets all the way through the sequence and in any case it takes a very long time. Trying to kill a rat is enough to satisfy a mouse with mousedom."

Fafhrd solemnly denied the possibility of any such foolery, and Ahura cried until she decided that being a mouse would interest rather than dishearten her peculiar brother. More wine was drunk from the remaining jar. The crackling from the rooms above had become a roar, and a bright red glow consumed the dark shadows. The three adventurers prepared to leave the place.

Meantime the mouse, or another very much like it, thrust its head from the crack and began to lick the wine damp shards, keeping a fearful eye upon those in the great room, but especially upon the strutting little would-be bear.

The Mouser said, "Our quest's done. I'm for Tyre."

Fafhrd said, "I'm for Ning's Gate and Lankhmar. Or is that a dream?"

The Mouser shrugged, "Mayhap Tyre's the dream. Lankhmar sounds as good."

Ahura said, "Could a girl go?"

A great blast of wind, cold and pure, blew away the last lingering of Mist. As they went through the doorway they saw, outspread above them, the self-consistent stars.

FRITZ LEIBER'S
LANKhMAR

BOOK IV
SWORDS AGAINST WIZARDRY

This book is dedicated to
HARRY OTTO FISCHER
who first explored Quarmall
and who wrote ten thousand of these words,
here unchanged,
about that subterranean kingdom.

Additionally, Part Two of this novel —
Stardock — is dedicated to
those two hardy cragsmen,
Poul Anderson and Paul Turner.

CONTENTS BOOK IV

FRITZ LEIBER'S
LANKHMAR

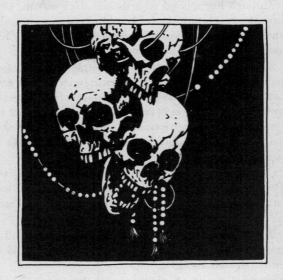

IN THE WITCH'S TENT

1

The hag bent over the brazier. Its upward-seeking gray fumes interwove with strands of her downward-dangling, tangled black hair. Its glow showed her face to be as dark, jagged-featured, and dirty as the new-dug root-clump of a blackapple tree. A half century of brazier heat and smoke had cured it as black, crinkly, and hard as Mingol bacon.

Through her splayed nostrils and slack mouth, which showed a few brown teeth like old tree stumps irregularly fencing the gray field of her tongue, she garglingly inhaled and bubblingly expelled the fumes.

Such of them as escaped her greedy lungs tortuously found their way to the tent's saggy roof, resting on seven ribs down-curving from the central pole, and deposited on the ancient rawhide their tiny dole of resin and soot. It is said that such a tent, boiled out after decades or preferably centuries of use, yields a nauseous liquid which gives a man strange and dangerous visions.

Outside the tent's drooping walls radiated the dark, twisty alleys of Illik-Ving, an overgrown and rudely boisterous town, which is the eighth and smallest metropolis of the Land of the Eight Cities.

While overhead there shivered in the chill wind the strange stars of the World of Nehwon, which is so like and unlike our own world.

Inside the tent, two barbarian-clad men watched the crouching witch across the brazier. The big man, who had red-blond hair, stared somber-eyed and intently. The little man, who was dressed all in gray, drooped his eyelids, stifled a yawn, and wrinkled his nose.

"I don't know which stinks worse, she or the brazier," he murmured. "Or maybe it's the whole tent, or this alley muck we must sit in. Or perchance her familiar is a skunk. Look, Fafhrd, if we must consult a sorcerous personage, we should have sought out Sheelba or Ningauble before ever we sailed north from Lankhmar across the Inner Sea."

"They weren't available," the big man answered in a clipped whisper. "Shh, Gray Mouser, I think she's gone into trance."

"Asleep, you mean," the little man retorted irreverently.

The hag's gargling breath began to sound more like a death rattle. Her eyelids fluttered, showing two white lines. Wind stirred the tent's dark wall — or it might be unseen presences fumbling and fingering.

The little man was unimpressed. He said, "I don't see why we have to consult anyone. It isn't as if we were going outside Nehwon altogether, as we did in our last adventure. We've got the papers — the scrap of ramskin parchment, I mean — and we know where we're going. Or at least you say you do."

"Shh!" the big man commanded, then added hoarsely, "Before embarking on any great enterprise, it's customary to consult a warlock or witch."

The little man, now whispering likewise, countered with, "Then why couldn't we have consulted a civilized one? — any member in good standing of the Lankhmar Sorcerers Guild. He'd at least have had a comely naked girl or two around, to rest your eyes on when they began to water from scanning his crabbed hieroglyphs and horoscopes."

"A good earthy witch is more honest than some city rogue tricked out in black cone-hat and robe of stars," the big man argued. "Besides, this one is nearer our icy goal and its influences. You and your townsman's lust for luxuries! You'd turn a wizard's workroom into a brothel."

"Why not?" the little man wanted to know. "Both species of glamour at once!" Then, jerking his thumb at the hag, "Earthy, you said? Dungy describes her better."

"Shh, Mouser, you'll break her trance."

"Trance?" The little man reinspected the hag. Her mouth had shut and she was breathing wheezingly through her beaky nose alone, the fume-sooty tip of which sought to meet her jutting chin. There was a faint high wailing, as of distant wolves, or nearby ghosts, or perhaps just an odd overtone of the hag's wheezes.

The little man sneered his upper lip and shook his head. His hands shook a little too, but he hid that. "No, she's only stoned out of her skull, I'd say," he commented judiciously. "You shouldn't have given her so much poppy gum."

"But that's the entire intent of trance," the big man protested. "To lash, stone, and otherwise drive the spirit out of the skull and whip it up mystic mountains, so that from their peaks it can spy out the lands of past and future, and mayhaps other-world."

"I wish the mountains ahead of *us* were merely mystic," the little man muttered. "Look, Fafhrd, I'm willing to squat here all night — at any rate for fifty more stinking breaths or two hundred bored heartbeats — to pleasure your whim. But has it occurred to you that we're in danger in this tent? And I don't mean solely from spirits. There are other rogues than ourselves in Illik-Ving, some perhaps on the same quest as ours, who'd dearly love to scupper us. And here in this blind leather hut we're deer on a skyline — or sitting ducks."

Just then the wind came back with its fumblings and fingerings, and in addition a scrabbling that might be that of wind-swayed branch tips or of dead men's long fingernails a-scratch. There were faint growlings and wailings too, and with them stealthy footfalls. Both men thought of the Mouser's last warning. Fafhrd and he looked toward the tent's night-slitted skin door and loosened their swords in their scabbards.

At that instant the hag's noisy breathing stopped and with it all other sound. Her eyes opened, showing only whites — milky ovals infinitely eerie in the dark root-tangle of her sharp features and stringy hair. The gray tip of her tongue traveled like a large maggot around her lips.

The Mouser made to comment, but the out-thrust palm-side of Fafhrd's spread-fingered hand was more compelling than any *shh*.

In a voice low but remarkably clear, almost a girl's voice, the hag intoned:

"For reasons sorcerous and dim
You travel toward the world's frost rim...."

"Dim" is the key word there, the Mouser thought. *Typical witchy say-nothing. She clearly knows naught about us except that we're headed north, which she could get from any gossipy mouth.*

"You north, north, north, and north must go
Through dagger-ice and powder-snow...."

More of the same, was the Mouser's inward comment. *But must she rub it in, even the snow? Brr!*

"And many a rival, envy-eyed,
Will dog your steps until you've died...."

Aha, the inevitable fright-thrust, without which no fortune-tale is complete!

"But after peril's cleansing fire
You'll meet at last your hearts' desire...."

And now pat the happy ending! Gods, but the stupidest palm-reading prostitute of Ilthmar could —

"And then you'll find — "

Something silvery gray flashed across the Mouser's eyes, so close its form was blurred. Without a thought he ducked back and drew Scalpel.

The razor-sharp spear-blade, driven through the tent's side as if it were paper, stopped inches from Fafhrd's head and was dragged back.

A javelin hurtled out of the hide wall. This the Mouser struck aside with his sword.

Now a storm of cries rose outside. The burden of some was, "Death to the strangers!" Of others, "Come out, dogs, and be killed!"

The Mouser faced the skin door, his gaze darting.

Fafhrd, almost as quick to react as the Mouser, hit on a somewhat irregular solution to their knotty tactical problem: that of men besieged in a fortress whose walls neither protect them nor permit outward viewing. At first step, he leaped to the tent's central pole and with a great heave drew it from the earth.

The witch, likewise reacting with good solid sense, threw herself flat on the dirt.

"We decamp!" Fafhrd cried. "Mouser, guard our front and guide me!"

And with that he charged toward the door, carrying the whole tent with him. There was a rapid series of little explosions as the somewhat brittle old thongs that tied its rawhide sides to its pegs snapped. The brazier tumbled over, scattering coals. The hag was overpassed. The Mouser, running ahead of Fafhrd, threw wide the door-slit. He had to use Scalpel at once, to parry a sword thrust out of the dark, but with his other hand he kept the door spread.

The opposing swordsman was bowled over, perhaps a bit startled at being attacked by the tent. The Mouser trod on him. He thought he heard ribs snap as Fafhrd did the same, which seemed a nice if brutal touch. Then he was crying out, "Veer left now, Fafhrd! Now to the right a little! There's an alley coming up on our left. Be ready to turn sharp into it when I give the word. Now!" And grasping the door's hide edges, the Mouser helped swing the tent as Fafhrd pivoted.

From behind came cries of rage and wonder, also a screeching that sounded like the hag, enraged at the theft of her home.

The alley was so narrow that the tent's sides dragged against buildings and fences. At the first sign of a soft spot in the dirt underfoot, Fafhrd drove the tent-pole into it, and they both dashed out of the tent, leaving it blocking the alley.

The cries behind them grew suddenly louder as their pursuers turned into the alley, but Fafhrd and the Mouser did not run off over-swiftly. It seemed certain their attackers would spend considerable time scouting and assaulting the empty tent.

They loped together through the outskirts of the sleeping city toward their own well-hidden camp outside it. Their nostrils sucked in the chill, bracing air funneling down from the best pass through the Trollstep Mountains, a craggy chain which walled off the Land of the Eight Cities from the vast plateau of the Cold Waste to the north.

Fafhrd remarked, "It's unfortunate the old lady was interrupted just when she was about to tell us something important."

The Mouser snorted. "She'd already sung her song, the sum of which was zero."

"I wonder who those rude fellows were and what were their motives!" Fafhrd asked. "I thought I recognized the voice of that ale-swiller Gnarfi, who has an aversion to bear-meat."

"Scoundrels behaving as stupidly as we were," the Mouser

answered. "Motives? — as soon impute 'em to sheep! Ten dolts following an idiot leader."

"Still, it appears that someone doesn't like us," Fafhrd opined.

"Was that ever news!" the Gray Mouser retorted.

FRITZ LEIBER'S LANKHMAR

STARDOCK

II

Early one evening, weeks later, the sky's gray cloud-armor blew away south, smashed and dissolving as if by blows of an acid-dipped mace. The same mighty northeast wind contemptuously puffed down the hitherto impregnable cloud wall to the east, revealing a grimly majestic mountain range running north to south and springing abruptly from the plateau, two leagues high, of the Cold Waste—like a dragon fifty leagues long heaving up its spike-crested spine from icy entombment.

Fafhrd, no stranger to the Cold Waste, born at the foot of these same mountains and childhood climber of their lower slopes, named them off to the Gray Mouser as the two men stood together on the crunchy hoarfrosted eastern rim of the hollow that held their camp. The sun, set for the camp, still shone from behind their backs onto the western faces of the major peaks as he named them—but it shone not with any romanticizing rosy glow, but rather with a clear, cold, detail-pinning light fitting the peaks' dire aloofness.

"Travel your eye to the first great northerly upthrust," he told the Mouser, "that phalanx of heaven-menacing ice-spears shafted with dark rock and gleaming green—that's the Ripsaw. Then, dwarfing them, a single ivory-icy tooth, unscalable by any sane appraisal—the Tusk, he's called. Another unscalable then, still higher and with south wall a sheer precipice shooting up a league and curving outward toward the needletop: he is White Fang, where my father died—the canine of the Mountains of the Giants.

"Now begin again with the first snow dome at the south of the chain," continued the tall fur-cloaked man, copper-bearded and copper-maned, his head otherwise bare to the frigid air, which was as quiet at ground level as sea-deep beneath storm. "The Hint, she's named, or the Come On. Little enough she looks, yet men have frozen nighting on her slopes and been whirled to death by her whimsical queenly avalanches. Then a far vaster snow dome, true queen to the Hint's princess, a hemisphere of purest white, grand enough to roof the council hall of all the gods that ever were or will be—she is Gran Hanack, whom my father was first of men to mount and master. Our town of tents was pitched *there* near her base. No mark of it now, I'll guess, not even a midden.

"After Gran Hanack and nearest to us of them all, a huge flat-topped pillar, a pedestal for the sky almost, looking to be of green-shot snow but in truth all snow-pale granite scoured by the storms: Obelisk Polaris.

"Lastly," Fafhrd continued, sinking his voice and gripping his smaller comrade's shoulder, "let your gaze travel up the snow-tressed, dark-rocked, snowcapped peak between the Obelisk and White Fang, her glittering skirt somewhat masked by the former, but taller than they as they are taller than the Waste. Even now she hides behind her the mounting moon. She is Stardock, our quest's goal."

"A pretty enough, tall, slender wart on this frostbit patch of Nehwon's face," the Gray Mouser conceded, writhing his shoulder from Fafhrd's grip. "And now at last tell me, friend, why you never climbed this Stardock in your youth and seized the treasure there, but must wait until we get a clue to it in a dusty, hot, scorpion-patrolled desert tower a quarter world away—and waste half a year getting here."

Fafhrd's voice grew a shade unsure as he answered, "My father never climbed her; how should I? Also, there were no legends of a treasure on Stardock's top in my father's clan...though there was a storm of other legends about Stardock, each forbidding her ascent. They called my father the Legend Breaker and shrugged wisely when he died on White Fang.... Truly, my memory's not so good for those days, Mouser—I got many a mind-shattering knock on my head before I learned to deal all knocks first...and then I was hardly a boy when the clan left the Cold Waste—though the rough hard walls of Obelisk Polaris had been my upended playground...."

The Mouser nodded doubtfully. In the stillness they heard their tethered ponies munching the ice-crisped grass of the hollow, then a faint unangry growl from Hrissa the ice-cat, curled between the tiny fire and the piled baggage—likely one of the ponies had come cropping too close. On the great icy plain around them, nothing moved—or almost nothing.

The Mouser dipped gray lambskin-gloved fingers into the bottom of his pouch and from the pocket there withdrew a tiny oblong of parchment and read from it, more by memory than sight:

"Who mounts white Stardock, the Moon Tree,
"Past worm and gnome and unseen bars,
"Will win the key to luxury:
"The Heart of Light, a pouch of stars."

Fafhrd said dreamily, "They say the gods once dwelt and had their smithies on Stardock and from thence, amid jetting fire and showering sparks, launched all the stars; hence her name. They say diamonds, rubies, smaragds—all great gems— are the tiny pilot models the gods made of the stars...and then threw carelessly away across the world when their great work was done."

"You never told me that before," the Mouser said, looking at him sharply.

Fafhrd blinked his eyes and frowned puzzledly. "I am beginning to remember childhood things."

The Mouser smiled thinly before returning the parchment to its deep pocket. "The guess that a pouch of stars might be a bag of gems," he listed, "the story that Nehwon's biggest diamond is called the Heart of Light, a few words on a ramskin scrap in the topmost room of a desert tower locked and sealed for centuries—small hints, those, to draw two men across this murdering, monotonous Cold Waste. Tell me, Old

Horse, were you just homesick for the miserable white meadows of your birth to pretend to believe 'em?"

"Those small hints," Fafhrd said, gazing now toward White Fang, "drew other men north across Nehwon. There must have been other ramskin scraps, though why they should be discovered at the same time, I cannot guess."

"We left all such fellows behind at Illik-Ving, or Lankhmar even, before we ever mounted the Trollsteps," the Mouser asserted with complete confidence. "Weak sisters, they were, smelling loot but quailing at hardship."

Fafhrd gave a small headshake and pointed. Between them and White Fang rose the tiniest thread of black smoke.

"Did Gnarfi and Kranarch seem weak sisters?—to name but two of the other seekers," he asked when the Mouser finally saw and nodded.

"It could be," the Mouser agreed gloomily. "Though aren't there any ordinary travelers of this Waste? Not that we've seen a man-shaped soul since the Mingol."

Fafhrd said thoughtfully, "It might be an encampment of the ice gnomes...though they seldom leave their caves except at High Summer, now a month gone...." He broke off, frowning puzzledly. "Now how did I know that?"

"Another childhood memory bobbing to the top of the black pot?" the Mouser hazarded. Fafhrd shrugged doubtfully.

"So, for choice, Kranarch and Gnarfi," the Mouser concluded. "Two strong brothers, I'll concede. Perhaps we should have picked a fight with 'em at Illik-Ving," he suggested. "Or perhaps even now...a swift march by night...a sudden swoop—"

Fafhrd shook his head. "Now we're climbers, not killers," he said. "A man must be all climber to dare Stardock." He directed the Mouser's gaze back toward the tallest mountain. "Let's rather study her west wall while the light holds.

"Begin first at her feet," he said. "That glimmering skirt falling from her snowy hips, which are almost as high as the

Obelisk—that's the White Waterfall, where no man may live.

"Now to her head again. From her flat tilted snowcap hang two great swelling braids of snow, streaming almost perpetually with avalanches, as if she combed 'em day and night—the Tresses, those are called. Between them's a wide ladder of dark rock, marked at three points by ledges. The topmost of the three ledge-banks is the Face—d'you note the darker ledges marking eyes and lips? The midmost of the three is called the Roosts; the lowermost—level with Obelisk's wide summit—the Lairs."

"What lairs and roosts there?" the Mouser wanted to know.

"None may say, for none have climbed the Ladder," Fafhrd replied. "Now as to our route up her—it's most simple. We scale Obelisk Polaris—a trustworthy mountain if there ever was one—then cross by a dippling snow-saddle (there's the danger-stretch of our ascent!) to Stardock and climb the Ladder to her top."

"How do we climb the Ladder in the long blank stretches between the ledges?" the Mouser asked with childlike innocence, almost. "That is, if the Lairers and Roosters will honor our passports and permit us to try."

Fafhrd shrugged. "There'll be a way, rock being rock."

"Why's there no snow on the Ladder?"

"Too steep."

"And supposing we climb it to the top," the Mouser finally asked, "how do we lift our black-and-blue skeletonized bodies over the brim of Stardock's snowy hat, which seems to outcurve and downcurve most stylishly?"

"There's a triangular hole in it somewhere called the Needle's Eye," Fafhrd answered negligently. "Or so I've heard. But never you fret, Mouser, we'll find it."

"Of course we will," the Mouser agreed with an airy certainty that almost sounded sincere, "we who hop-skip across shaking snow bridges and dance the fantastic up vertical walls without ever touching hand to granite. Remind me to bring a longish knife to carve our initials on the sky when we celebrate the end of our little upward sortie."

His gaze wandered slightly northward. In another voice he continued, "The dark north wall of Stardock now—that looks steep enough, to be sure, but free of snow to the very top. Why isn't that our route—rock, as you say with such unanswerable profundity, being rock."

Fafhrd laughed unmockingly. "Mouser," he said, "do you mark against the darkening sky that long white streamer waving south from Stardock's top? Yes, and below it a lesser streamer—can you distinguish that? That second one comes through the Needle's Eye! Well, those streamers from Stardock's hat are called the Grand and Petty Pennons. They're powdered snow blasted off Stardock by the northeast gale, which blows at least seven days out of eight, never predictably. That gale would pluck the stoutest climber off the north wall as easily as you or I might puff dandelion down from its darkening stem. Stardock's self shields the Ladder from the gale."

"Does the gale never shift around to strike the Ladder?" the Mouser inquired lightly.

"Only occasionally," Fafhrd reassured him.

"Oh, that's great," the Mouser responded with quite overpowering sincerity and would have returned to the fire, except just then the darkness began swiftly to climb the Mountains of the Giants, as the sun took his final dive far to the west, and the gray-clad man stayed to watch the grand spectacle.

It was like a black blanket being pulled up. First the glittering skirt of the White Waterfall was hidden, then the Lairs on the Ladder and then the Roosts. Now all the other peaks were gone, even the Tusk's and White Fang's gleaming cruel tips, even the greenish-white roof of Obelisk Polaris. Now only Stardock's snow hat was left and below it the Face between the silvery Tresses. For a moment the ledges called the Eyes gleamed, or seemed to. Then all was night.

Yet there was a pale afterglow about. It was profoundly silent and the air utterly unmoving. Around them, the Cold Waste seemed to stretch north, west, and south to infinity.

And in that space of silence something went whisper-gliding through the still air, with the faint rushy sound of a great sail in a moderate breeze. Fafhrd and the Mouser both stared all around wildly. Nothing. Beyond the little fire, Hrissa the ice-cat sprang up hissing. Still nothing. Then the sound, whatever had made it, died away.

Very softly, Fafhrd began, "There is a legend…." A long pause. Then with a sudden headshake, in a more natural voice: "The memory slips away, Mouser. All my mind-fingers couldn't clutch it. Let's patrol once around the camp and so to bed."

From first sleep the Mouser woke so softly that even Hrissa, back pressed against him from his knees to his chest on the side toward the fire, did not rouse.

Emerging from behind Stardock, her light glittering on the southern Tress, hung the swelling moon, truly a proper fruit of the Moon Tree. Strange, the Mouser thought, how small the moon was and how big Stardock, silhouetted against the moon-pale sky.

Then, just below the flat top of Stardock's hat, he saw a bright, pale blue twinkling. He recalled that Ashsha, pale blue and brightest of Nehwon's stars, was near the moon tonight, and he wondered if he were seeing her by rare chance through the Needle's Eye, proving the latter's existence. He wondered too what great sapphire or blue diamond—perhaps the Heart of Light?—had been the gods' pilot model for Ashsha, smiling drowsily the while at himself for entertaining such a silly, lovely myth. And then, embracing the myth entirely, he asked himself whether the gods had left any of their full-scale stars, unlaunched, on Stardock. Then Ashsha, if it were she, winked out.

The Mouser felt cozy in his cloak lined with sheep's-wool and now thong-laced into a bag by the horn hooks around its hem. He stared long and dreamily at Stardock until the moon broke loose from her and a blue jewel twinkled on top of her hat and broke loose too—now Ashsha surely. He wondered unfearfully about the windy rushing he and Fafhrd had heard in the still air—perhaps only a long tongue of a storm licking down briefly. If the storm lasted, they would climb up into it.

Hrissa stretched in her sleep. Fafhrd grumbled low in a dream, wrapped in his own great thong-laced cloak stuffed with eiderdown.

The Mouser dropped his gaze to the ghostly flames of the dying fire, seeking sleep himself. The flames made girl-bodies, then girl-faces. Next a ghostly pale green girl-face—perhaps an afterimage, he thought at first—appeared beyond the fire, staring at him through close-slitted eyes across the flame tops. It grew more distinct as he gazed at it, but there was no trace of hair or body about it—it hung against the dark like a mask.

Yet it was weirdly beautiful: narrow chin, high-arched cheeks, wine-dark short lips slightly pouted, straight nose that went up without a dip into the broad, somewhat low forehead—and then the mystery of those fully lidded eyes seeming to peer at him through wine-dark lashes. And all, save lashes and lips, of palest green, like jade.

The Mouser did not speak or stir a muscle, simply because the face was very beautiful to him—just as any man might hope for the moment never to end when his naked mistress unconsciously or by secret design assumes a particularly charming attitude.

Also, in the dismal Cold Waste, any man treasures illusions, though knowing them almost certainly to be such.

Suddenly the eyes parted wide, showing only the darkness

behind, as if the face were a mask indeed. The Mouser did start then, but still not enough to wake Hrissa.

Then the eyes closed, the lips puckered with taunting invitation; then the face began swiftly to dissolve as if it were being literally wiped away. First the right side went, then the left, then the center, last of all the dark lips and the eyes. For a moment the Mouser fancied he caught a winy odor; then all was gone.

He contemplated waking Fafhrd and almost laughed at the thought of his comrade's surly reactions. He wondered if the face had been a sign from the gods, or a sending from some black magician castled on Stardock, or Stardock's very soul perhaps—though then where had she left her glittering tresses and hat and her Ashsha eye?—or only a random creation of his own most clever brain, stimulated by sexual privation and tonight by beauteous if devilishly dangerous mountains. Rather quickly he decided on the last explanation and he slumbered.

Two evenings later, at the same hour, Fafhrd and the Gray Mouser stood scarcely a knife cast from the west wall of Obelisk Polaris, building a cairn from pale greenish rock-shards fallen over the millennia. Among this scanty scree were some bones, many broken, of sheep or goats.

As before, the air was still though very cold, the Waste empty, the set sun bright on the mountain faces.

From this closest vantage point the Obelisk was foreshortened into a pyramid that seemed to taper up forever, vertically. Encouragingly, his rock felt diamond-hard while the lowest reaches of the wall at any rate were thick with bumpy handholds and footholds, like pebbled leather.

To the south, Gran Hanack and the Hint were hidden.

To the north White Fang towered monstrously, yellowish white in the sunlight, as if ready to rip a hole in the graying sky. Bane of Fafhrd's father, the Mouser recalled.

Of Stardock, there could be seen the dark beginning of the wind-blasted north wall and the north end of the deadly White Waterfall. All else of Stardock the Obelisk hid.

Save for one touch: almost straight overhead, seeming now to come from Obelisk Polaris, the ghostly Grand Pennon streamed southwest.

From behind Fafhrd and the Mouser as they worked came the tantalizing odor of two snow hares roasting by the fire, while before it Hrissa tore flesh slowly and savoringly from the carcass of a third she'd coursed down. The ice-cat was about the size and shape of a cheetah, though with long tufty white hair. The Mouser had bought her from a far-ranging Mingol trapper just north of the Trollsteps.

Beyond the fire the ponies eagerly chomped the last of the grain, strengthening stuff they'd not tasted for a week.

Fafhrd wrapped his sheathed longsword Graywand in oiled silk and laid it in the cairn, then held out a big hand to the Mouser.

"Scalpel?"

"I'm taking my sword with me," the Mouser stated, then added justifyingly, "it's but a feather to yours."

"Tomorrow you'll find what a feather weighs," Fafhrd foretold. The big man shrugged and placed by Graywand his helmet, a bear's hide, a folded tent, shovel and pickax, gold bracelets from his wrists and arms, quills, ink, papyrus, a large copper pot, and some books and scrolls. The Mouser added various empty and near-empty bags, two hunting spears, skis, an unstrung bow with a quiver of arrows, tiny jars of oily paint and squares of parchment, and all the harness of the ponies, many of the items wrapped against damp like Graywand.

Then, their appetites quickening from the roast-fumes, the two comrades swiftly built two top courses, roofing the cairn.

Just as they turned toward supper, facing the raggedly gilt-edged flat western horizon, they heard in the silence the rushy sail-like noise again, fainter this time but twice: once in the air to the north and, almost simultaneously, to the south.

Again they stared around swiftly but searchingly, yet there was nothing anywhere to be seen except—again Fafhrd saw it first—a thread of black smoke very near White Fang, rising from a point on the glacier between that mountain and Stardock.

"Gnarfi and Kranarch, if it be they, have chosen the rocky north wall for their ascent," the Mouser observed.

"And it will be their bane," Fafhrd predicted, up-jerking his thumb at the Pennon.

The Mouser nodded with less certainty, then demanded, "Fafhrd, what *was* that sound? You've lived here."

Fafhrd's brow crinkled and his eyes almost shut. "Some legend of great birds…" he muttered questioningly, "…or of great fish—no, that couldn't be right."

"Memory pot still seething all black?" the Mouser asked. Fafhrd nodded.

Before he left the cairn, the Northerner laid beside it a slab of salt. "That," he said, "along with the ice-filmed pool and herbage we just passed, should hold the ponies here for a week. If we don't return, well, at least we showed 'em the way between here and Illik-Ving."

Hrissa smiled up from her bloody tidbit, as if to say, "No need to worry about me or my rations."

Again the Mouser woke as soon as sleep had gripped him tight, this time with a surge of pleasure, as one who remembers a rendezvous. And again, this time without any preliminary star-staring or flame-gazing, the living mask faced him across the sinking fire: every same expression-quirk and feature—short lips, nose and forehead one straight line— except that tonight it was ivory pale with greenish lips and lids and lashes.

The Mouser was considerably startled, for last night he had stayed awake, waiting for the phantom girl-face—and even trying to make it come again—until the swelling moon had risen three handbreadths above Stardock...without any success whatever. His mind had known that the face had been an hallucination on the first occasion, but his feelings had insisted otherwise—to his considerable disgust and the loss of a quarter night's sleep.

And by day he had secretly consulted the last of the four short stanzas on the parchment scrap in his pouch's deepest pocket:

Who scales the Snow King's citadel
Shall father his two daughters' sons;
Though he must face foes fierce and fell,
His seed shall live while time still runs.

Yesterday that had seemed rather promising—at least the fathering and daughters part—though today, after his lost sleep, the merest mockery.

But now the living mask was there again and going through all the same teasing antics, including the shuddersome yet somehow thrilling trick of opening wide its lids to show not eyes but a dark backing like the rest of the night. The Mouser was enchanted in a shivery way, but unlike the first night he was full-mindedly alert, and he tested for illusions by blinking and squinting his own eyes and silently shifting his head about in his hood—with no effect whatever on the living mask. Then he quietly unlaced the thong from the top hooks of his cloak—Hrissa was sleeping against Fafhrd tonight—and slowly reached out his hand and picked up a pebble and flicked it across the pale flames at a point somewhat below the mask.

Although he knew there wasn't anything beyond the fire but scattered scree and ringingly hard earth, there wasn't the faintest sound of the pebble striking anywhere. He might have thrown it off Nehwon.

At almost the same instant, the mask smiled tauntingly.

The Mouser was very swiftly out of his cloak and on his feet.

But even more swiftly the mask dissolved away—this time in one swift stroke from forehead to chin.

He quickly stepped, almost lunged, around the fire to the spot where the mask had seemed to hang, and there he stared around searchingly. Nothing—except a fleeting breath of wine or spirits of wine. He stirred the fire and stared around again. Still nothing. Except that Hrissa woke beside Fafhrd and bristled her moustache and gazed solemnly, perhaps scornfully, at the Mouser, who was beginning to feel rather like a fool. He wondered if his mind and his desires were playing a silly game against each other.

Then he trod on something. His pebble, he thought, but when he picked it up, he saw it was a tiny jar. It could have been one of his own pigment jars, but it was too small, hardly bigger than a joint of his thumb, and made not of hollowed stone but some kind of ivory or other tooth.

He knelt by the fire and peered into it, then dipped in his little finger and gingerly rubbed the tip against the rather hard grease inside. It came out ivory-hued. The grease had an oily, not winy odor.

The Mouser pondered by the fire for some time. Then with a glance at Hrissa, who had closed her eyes and laid back her moustache again, and at Fafhrd, who was snoring softly, he returned to his cloak and to sleep.

He had not told Fafhrd a word about his earlier vision of the living mask. His surface reason was that Fafhrd would laugh at such calf-brained nonsense of smoke-faces; his deeper reason the one which keeps any man from mentioning a pretty new girl even to his dearest friend.

So perhaps it was the same reason which next morning

kept Fafhrd from telling his dearest friend what happened to him late that same night. Fafhrd dreamed he was feeling out the exact shape of a girl's face in absolute darkness while her slender hands caressed his body. She had a rounded forehead, very long-lashed eyes, in-dipping nose bridge, apple cheeks, an impudent snub nose—*it felt* impudent!— and long lips whose grin his big gentle fingers could trace clearly.

He woke to the moon glaring down at him aslant from the south. It silvered the Obelisk's interminable wall, turning rock-knobs to black shadow bars. He also woke to acute disappointment that a dream had been only a dream. Then he would have sworn that he felt fingertips briefly brush his face and that he heard a faint silvery chuckle which receded swiftly. He sat up like a mummy in his laced cloak and stared around. The fire had sunk to a few red ember-eyes, but the moonlight was bright, and by it he could see nothing at all.

Hrissa growled at him reproachfully for a silly sleep-breaker. He damned himself for mistaking the afterimage of a dream for reality. He damned the whole girl-less, girl-vision-breeding Cold Waste. A bit of the night's growing chill spilled down his neck. He told himself he should be fast asleep like the wise Mouser over there, gathering strength for tomorrow's great effort. He lay back, and after some time he slumbered.

Next morning the Mouser and Fafhrd woke at the first gray of dawn, the moon still bright as a snowball in the west, and quickly breakfasted and readied themselves and stood facing Obelisk Polaris in the stinging cold, all girls forgotten, their manhood directed solely at the mountain.

Fafhrd stood in high-laced boots with newly-sharpened thick hobnails. He wore a wolfskin tunic, fur turned in but open now from neck to belly. His lower arms and legs were bare. Short-wristed rawhide gloves covered his hands. A rather small pack, wrapped in his cloak, rode high on his back.

Clipped to it was a large coil of black hempen rope. On his stout unstudded belt, his sheathed ax on his right side balanced on the other a knife, a small waterskin, and a bag of iron spikes headed by rings.

The Mouser wore his ramskin hood, pulled close around his face now by its drawstring, and on his body a tunic of gray silk, triple layered. His gloves were longer than Fafhrd's and fur-lined. So were his slender boots, which were footed with crinkly behemoth hide. On *his* belt, his dagger Cat's Claw and his waterskin balanced his sword Scalpel, its scabbard thonged loosely to his thigh. While to this cloak-wrapped pack was secured a curiously thick, short, black bamboo rod headed with a spike at one end and at the other a spike and large hook, somewhat like that of a shepherd's crook.

Both men were deeply tanned and leanly muscular, in best trim for climbing, hardened by the Trollsteps and the Cold Waste, their chests a shade larger than ordinary from weeks of subsisting on the latter's thin air.

No need to search about for the best-looking ascent—Fafhrd had done that yesterday as they'd approached the Obelisk.

The ponies were cropping again, and one had found the salt and was licking it with his thick tongue. The Mouser looked around for Hrissa to cuff her cheek in farewell, but the ice-cat was sniffing out a spoor beyond the campsite, her ears a-prick.

"She makes a cat-parting," Fafhrd said. "Good."

A faint shade of rose touched the heavens and the glacier by White Fang. Scanning toward the latter, the Mouser drew in his breath and squinted hard, while Fafhrd gazed narrowly from under the roof of his palm.

"Brownish figures," the Mouser said at last. "Kranarch and Gnarfi always dressed in brown leather, I recall. But I make them more than two."

"I make them four," Fafhrd said. "Two strangely shaggy—clad in brown fur suits, I guess. And all four mounting from the glacier up the rock wall."

"Where the gale will—" the Mouser began, then looked up. So did Fafhrd.

The Grand Pennon was gone.

"You said that sometimes—" the Mouser started.

"Forget the gale and those two and their rough-edged reinforcements," Fafhrd said curtly. He faced around again at Obelisk Polaris. So did the Mouser.

Squinting up the greenish-white slope, head bent sharply back, the Mouser said, "This morning he seems somewhat steeper than even that north wall and rather extensive upward."

"Pah!" Fafhrd retorted. "As a child I would climb him before breakfast. Often." He raised his clenched right rawhide glove as if it held a baton, and cried, "We go!"

With that he strode forward and without a break began to walk up the knobby face—or so it seemed, for although he used handholds he kept his body far out from the rock, as a good climber should.

The Mouser followed in Fafhrd's steps and holds, stretching his legs farther and keeping somewhat closer to the cliff.

Midmorning and they were still climbing without a break. The Mouser ached or stung in every part. His pack was like a fat man on his back, Scalpel a sizable boy clinging to his belt. And his ears had popped five times.

Just above, Fafhrd's boots clashed rock-knobs and into rock-holes with an unhesitating mechanistic rhythm the Mouser had begun to hate. Yet he kept his eyes resolutely fixed on them. Once he had looked down between his own legs and decided not to do that again.

It is not good to see the blue of distance, or even the gray-blue of middle distance, below one.

So he was taken by surprise when a small white bearded face, bloodily encumbered, came bobbing up alongside and past him.

Hrissa halted on a ledgelet by Fafhrd and took great whistling breaths, her tufted belly-skin pressing up against her spine with each exhalation. She breathed only through her pinkish nostrils because her jaws were full of two snow hares, packed side by side, with dead heads and hindquarters a-dangle.

Fafhrd took them from her and dropped them in his pouch and laced it shut.

Then he said, just a shade grandiloquently, "She has proved her endurance and skill, and she has paid her way. She is one of us."

It had not occurred to the Mouser to doubt any of that. It seemed to him simply that there were three comrades now climbing Obelisk Polaris. Besides, he was most grateful to Hrissa for the halt she had brought. Partly to prolong it, he carefully pressed a handful of water from his bag and stretched it to her to lap: Then he and Fafhrd drank a little too.

All the long summer day they climbed the west wall of the cruel but reliable Obelisk. Fafhrd seemed tireless. The Mouser got his second wind, lost it, and never quite got his third. His whole body was one great leaden ache, beginning deep in his bones and filtering outward, like refined poison, through his flesh. His vision became a bobbing welter of real and remembered rock-knobs, while the necessity of never missing one single grip or foot-placement seemed the ruling of an insane schoolmaster god. He silently cursed the whole maniacal Stardock project, cackling in his brain at the idea that the luring stanzas on the parchment could mean anything but pipe dreams. Yet he would not cry quits or seek again to prolong the brief breathers they took.

He marveled dully at Hrissa's leaping and hunching up

beside them. But by midafternoon he noted she was limping, and once he saw a light blood-print of two pads where she'd set a paw.

They made camp at last almost two hours before sunset, because they'd found a rather wide ledge—and because a very light snowfall had begun, the tiny flakes sifting silently down like meal.

They made a fire of resin-pellets in the tiny claw-footed brazier Fafhrd packed, and they heated over it water for herb tea in their single narrow high pot. The water was a long time getting even lukewarm. With Cat's Claw the Mouser stirred two dollops of honey into it.

The ledge was as long as three men stretched out and as deep as one. On the sheer face of Obelisk Polaris that much space seemed an acre, at least.

Hrissa stretched slackly behind the tiny fire. Fafhrd and the Mouser huddled to either side of it, their cloaks drawn around them, too tired to look around, talk, or even think.

The snowfall grew a little thicker, enough to hide the Cold Waste far below.

After his second swallow of sweetened tea, Fafhrd asserted they'd come at least two-thirds of the way up the Obelisk.

The Mouser couldn't understand how Fafhrd could pretend to know that, any more than a man could tell by looking at the shoreless waters of the Outer Sea how far he'd sailed across it. To the Mouser they were simply in the exact center of a dizzily tip-tilted plain of pale granite, green-tinged and now snow-sprinkled. He was still too weary to outline this concept to Fafhrd, but he managed to make himself say, "As a child you would climb up and down the Obelisk before breakfast?"

"We had rather late breakfasts then," Fafhrd explained gruffly.

"Doubtless on the afternoon of the fifth day," the Mouser concluded.

After the tea was drunk, they heated more water and left the hacked and disjointed bits of one of the snow hares in the fluid until they turned gray, then slowly chewed them and drank the dull soup. At about the same time Hrissa became a little interested in the flayed carcass of the other hare set before her nose—by the brazier to keep it from freezing.

Enough interested to begin to haggle it with her fangs and slowly chew and swallow.

The Mouser very gently examined the pads of the ice-cat's paws. They were worn silk-thin, there were two or three cuts in them, and the white fur between them was stained deep pink. Using a feather touch, the Mouser rubbed salve into them, shaking his head the while. Then he nodded once and took from his pouch a large needle, a spool of thin thong, and a small rolled hide of thin, tough leather.

From the last he cut with Cat's Claw a shape rather like a very fat pear and stitched from it a boot for Hrissa.

When he tried it on the ice-cat's hind paw, she let it be for a little, then began to bite at it rather gently, looking up queerly at the Mouser. He thought, then very carefully bored holes in it for the ice-cat's non-retracting claws, then drew the boot up the leg snugly until the claws protruded fully and tied it there with the drawstring he'd run through slits at the top.

Hrissa no longer bothered the boot. The Mouser made others, and Fafhrd joined in and cut and stitched one too.

When Hrissa was fully shod in her four clawed paw-mittens, she smelled each, then stood up and paced back and forth the length of the ledge a few times, and finally settled herself by the still-warm brazier and the Mouser, chin on his ankle.

The tiny grains of snow were still falling ruler-straight, frosting the ledge and Fafhrd's coppery hair. He and the Mouser began to pull up their hoods and lace their cloaks about them for the night. The sun still shone through the snowfall, but its light was filtered white and brought not an atom of warmth.

Obelisk Polaris was not a noisy mountain, as many are— a-drip with glacial water, rattling with rock slides, and even with rock strata a-creak from uneven loss or gain of heat. The silence was profound.

The Mouser felt an impulse to tell Fafhrd about the living girl-mask or illusion he'd seen by night, while simultaneously Fafhrd considered recounting to the Mouser his own erotic dream.

At that moment there came again, without prelude, the rushing in the silent air and they saw, clearly outlined by the falling snow, a great flat undulating shape.

It came swooping past them, rather slowly, about two spear-lengths out from the ledge.

There was nothing at all to be seen except the flat, flakeless space the thing made in the airborne snow and the eddies it raised; it in no way obscured the snow beyond. Yet they felt the gust of its passage.

The shape of this invisible thing was most like that of a giant skate or stingray four yards long and three wide; there was even the suggestion of a vertical fin and a long, lashing tail.

"Great invisible fish!" the Mouser hissed, thrusting his hand down in his half-laced cloak and managing to draw Scalpel in a single sweep. "Your mind was most right, Fafhrd, when you thought it wrong!"

As the snow-sketched apparition glided out of sight around the buttress ending the ledge to the south, there came from it a mocking rippling laughter in two voices, one alto, one soprano.

"A sightless fish that laughs like girls—most monstrous!" Fafhrd commented shakenly, hefting his ax, which he'd got out swiftly too, though it was still attached to his belt by a long thong.

They crouched there then for a while, scrambled out of their cloaks, and with weapons ready, awaited the invisible monster's return, Hrissa standing between them with fur bristling. But after a while they began to shake from the cold and so they perforce got back into their cloaks and laced them, though still gripping their weapons and prepared to throw off the upper lacings in a flash. Then they briefly discussed the weirdness just witnessed, insofar as they could, each now confessing his earlier visions or dreams of girls.

Finally the Mouser said, "The girls might have been riding the invisible thing, lying along its back—and invisible too! Yet, what *was* the thing?"

This touched a small spot in Fafhrd's memory. Rather unwillingly he said, "I remember waking once as a child in the night and hearing my father say to my mother, '…like great thick quivering sails, but the ones you can't see are the worst.' They stopped speaking then, I think because they heard me stir."

The Mouser asked, "Did your father ever speak of seeing girls in the high mountains—flesh, apparition, or witch, which is a mixture of the two; visible or invisible?"

"He wouldn't have mentioned 'em if he had," Fafhrd replied. "My mother was a very jealous woman and a devil with a chopper."

The whiteness they'd been scanning turned swiftly to darkest gray. The sun had set. They could no longer see the falling snow. They pulled up their hoods and laced their cloaks tight and huddled together at the back of the ledge with Hrissa close between them.

Trouble came early the next day. They roused with first light, feeling battered and nightmare-ridden, and uncramped themselves with difficulty while the morning ration of strong herb tea and powdered meat and snow were stewed in the same pot to a barely uncold aromatic gruel. Hrissa gnawed her rewarmed hare's bones and accepted a little bear's fat and water from the Mouser.

The snow had stopped during the night, but the Obelisk was powdered with it on every step and hold, while under the snow was ice—the first-fallen snow melted by yesterday afternoon's meager warmth on the rock and quickly refroze.

So Fafhrd and the Mouser roped together, and the Mouser swiftly fashioned a harness for Hrissa by cutting two holes in the long side of an oblong of leather. Hrissa protested somewhat when her forelegs were thrust through the holes and the ends of the oblong double-stitched together snugly over her shoulders. But when an end of Fafhrd's black hempen rope was tied around her harness where the stitching was, she simply lay down flat on the ledge, on the warm spot where the brazier had stood, as if to say, "This debasing tether I will not accept, though humans may."

But when Fafhrd slowly started up the wall and the Mouser followed and the rope tightened on Hrissa, and when she had looked up and seen them still roped like herself, she followed sulkily after. A little later she slipped off a bulge—her boots, snug as they were, must have been clumsy to her after naked pads—and swung scrabbling back and forth several long moments before she was supporting her own weight again. Fortunately the Mouser had a firm stance at the time.

After that, Hrissa came on more cheerily, sometimes even climbing to the side ahead of the Mouser and smiling back at him—rather sardonically, the Mouser fancied.

The climbing was a shade steeper than yesterday with an even greater insistence that each hand- and foothold be perfect. Gloved fingers must grip stone, not ice; spikes must clash through the brittle stuff to rock. Fafhrd roped his ax to his right wrist and used its hammer to tap away treacherous thin platelets and curves of the glassy frozen water.

And the climbing was more wearing because it was harder to avoid tenseness. Even looking sideways at the steepness of the wall tightened the Mouser's groin with fear. He wondered *what if the wind should blow?*—and fought the impulse to cling flat to the cliff. Yet at the same time sweat began to trickle down his face and chest, so that he had to throw back his hood and loosen his tunic to his belly to keep his clothes from sogging.

But there was worse to come. It had looked as though the slope above were gentling, but now, drawing nearer, they perceived a bulge jutting out a full two yards some seven yards above them. The under-slope was pocked here and there— fine handholds, except that they opened down. The bulge extended as far as they could see to either side, at most points looking worse.

They found themselves the best and highest holds they could, close together, and stared up at their problem. Even Hrissa, a-cling by the Mouser, seemed subdued.

Fafhrd said softly, "I mind me now they used to say there was an out-jutting around the Obelisk's top. His Crown, I think my father called it. I wonder…"

"Don't you know?" the Mouser demanded, a shade harshly. Standing rigid on his holds, his arms and legs were aching worse than ever.

"O Mouser," Fafhrd confessed, "in my youth I never climbed Obelisk Polaris farther than halfway to last night's camp. I only boasted to raise our spirits."

There being nothing to say to that, the Mouser shut his lips, though somewhat thinly. Fafhrd began to whistle a tuneless tune and carefully fished a small grapnel with five dagger-sharp flukes from his pouch and tied it securely to the long end of their black rope still coiled on his back. Then stretching his right arm as far out as he might from the cliff, he whirled the grapnel in a smallish circle, faster and faster, and finally hurled it upward. They heard it clash against rock somewhere above the bulge, but it did not catch on any crack or hump and instantly came sliding and then dropping down, missing the Mouser by hardly a handbreadth, it seemed to him.

Fafhrd drew up the grapnel—with some delays, since it tended to catch on every crack or hump below them—and whirled and hurled it again. And again and again and again, each time without success. Once it stayed up, but Fafhrd's first careful tug on the rope brought it down.

Fafhrd's sixth cast was his first really bad one. The grapnel never went out of sight at all. As it reached the top of the throw, it glinted for an instant.

"Sunlight!" Fafhrd hissed happily. "We're almost to the summit!"

"That 'almost' is a whopper, though," the Mouser commented, but even he couldn't keep a cheerful note out of his voice.

By the time Fafhrd had failed on seven more casts, all cheerfulness was gone from the Mouser again. His aches were horrible, his hands and feet were numbing in the cold, and his brain was numbing too, so that the next time Fafhrd cast and missed, he was so unwise as to follow the grapnel with his gaze as it fell.

For the first time today he really looked out and down.

The Cold Waste was a pale blue expanse almost like the sky—and seeming even more distant—all its copses and mounds and tiny tarns having long since become pinpoints and vanished. Many leagues to the west, almost at the horizon, a jagged pale gold band showed where the shadows of the mountains ended. Midway in the band was a blue gap—Stardock's shadow continuing over the edge of the world.

Giddily the Mouser snatched his gaze back to Obelisk Polaris...and although he could still see the granite, it didn't seem to count anymore—only four insecure holds on a kind of pale green nothingness, with Fafhrd and Hrissa somehow suspended beside him. His mind could no longer accept the Obelisk's steepness.

As the urge to hurl himself down swelled in him, he somehow transformed it into a sardonic snort, and he heard himself say with daggerish contempt, "Leave off your foolish fishing, Fafhrd! I'll show you now how Lankhmarian mountain science deals with a trifling problem such as this which has baffled all your barbarian whirling and casting!"

And with that he unclipped from his pack with reckless speed the thick black bamboo pike or crook and began cursingly with numb fingers to draw out and let snap into place its telescoping sections until it was four times its original length.

This tool of technical climbing, which indeed the Mouser had brought all the way from Lankhmar, had been a matter of dispute between them the whole trip, Fafhrd asserting it was a tricksy toy not worth the packing.

Now, however, Fafhrd made no comment, but merely coiled up his grapnel and thrust his hands into his wolfskin jerkin against his sides to warm them and, mild-eyed, watched the Mouser's furious activity. Hrissa shifted to a perch closer to Fafhrd and crouched stoically.

But when the Mouser shakily thrust the narrower end of his black tool toward the bulge above, Fafhrd reached out a hand to help him steady it, yet could not refrain from saying, "If you think to get a good enough hold with the crook on the rim to shinny up that stick—"

"Quiet, you loutish kibitzer!" the Mouser snarled and with Fafhrd's help thrust pike-end into a pock in the rock hardly a finger's length from the rim. Then he seated the spiked foot of the pole in a small, deep hollow just above his head. Next he snapped out two short recessed lever-arms from the base of the pole and began to rotate them. It soon became clear that they controlled a great screw hidden in the pole, for the latter lengthened until it stood firmly between the two pocks in the rock, while the stiff black shaft itself bent a little.

At that instant a sliver of rock, being pressed by the pole, broke off from the rim. The pole thrummed as it straightened and the Mouser, screaming a curse, slipped off his holds and fell.

It was good then that the rope between the two comrades was short and that the spikes of Fafhrd's boots were seated firmly, like so many demon-forged dagger-points, in the rock of his footholds—for as the strain came suddenly on Fafhrd's belt and on his rope-gripping left hand, he took it without plummeting after the Mouser, only bending his knees a little and grunting softly, while his right hand snatched hold of the vibrating pole and saved it.

The Mouser had not even fallen far enough to drag Hrissa from her perch, though the rope almost straightened between them. The ice-cat, her tufted neck bent sharply between foreleg and chest, peered down with great curiosity at the dangling man.

His face was ashen. Fafhrd made no mark of that, but simply handed him the black pole, saying, "It's a good tool. I've screwed it back short. Seat it in another pock and try again."

Soon the pole stood firm between the hollow by the Mouser's head and a pock a hand's width from the rim. The bowlike bend in the pole faced downward. Then they put the Mouser first on the rope, and he went climbing up and out along the pole, hanging from it back downward, his boot-edges finding tiny holds on the pole's section-shoulders—out into and over the vast, pale blue-gray space which had so lately dizzied him.

The pole began to bend a little more with the Mouser's weight, the pike-end slipping a finger's span in the upper pock with a horrible tiny grating sound, but Fafhrd gave the screw another turn, and the pole held firm.

Fafhrd and Hrissa watched the Mouser reach its end, where he paused briefly. Then they saw him reach up his left arm until it was out of sight to the elbow above the rim, meanwhile gripping with his right hand the crook and twining his legs around the shaft. He appeared to feel about with his left hand and find something. Then he moved out and up still further and very slowly his head and after it, in a sudden swift sweep, his right arm went out of sight above the rim.

For several long moments they saw only the bottom half of the bent Mouser, his dark crinkly-soled boots twined securely to the end of the pole. Then, rather slowly, like a gray snail, and with a final push of one boot against the top of the crook, he went entirely out of sight.

Fafhrd slowly paid out rope after him.

After some time the Mouser's voice, quite ghostly yet clear, came down to them: "Hola! I've got the rope anchored around a boss big as a tree stump. Send up Hrissa."

So Fafhrd put Hrissa on the rope ahead of him, knotting it to her harness with a sheepshank.

Hrissa fought desperately for a moment against being swung into space, but as soon as it was done hung deathly still. Then as she was drawn slowly up, Fafhrd's knot began to slip. The ice-cat swiftly snatched at the rope with her teeth and gripped it far back between her jaws. The moment she came near the rim, her clawed mittens were ready, and she scrabbled and was dragged out of sight.

Soon word came down from the Mouser that Hrissa was safe and Fafhrd might follow. He frowningly tightened the screw another half turn, though the pole creaked ominously, and then very gently climbed out along it. The Mouser now kept the rope taut from above, but for the first stretch it could hardly take more than a few pounds of Fafhrd's weight off the pole.

The upper spike once again grated horribly a bit in its pock, but it still held firm. Helped more by the rope now, Fafhrd got his hands and head over the rim.

What he saw was a smooth, gentle rock slope, which could be climbed by friction, and at the top of it the Mouser and Hrissa standing backgrounded by blue sky and gilded by sunlight.

Soon he stood beside them.

The Mouser said, "Fafhrd, when we get back to Lankhmar remind me to give Glinthi the Artificer thirteen diamonds from the pouch of them we'll find on Stardock's hat: one for each section and joint of my climbing pole, one each for the spikes at the ends and two for each screw."

"Are there two screws?" Fafhrd asked respectfully.

"Yes, one at each end," the Mouser told him and then made Fafhrd brace the rope for him so that he could climb down the slope and, bending all his upper body down over the rim, shorten the pole by rotating its upper screw until he was able to drag it triumphantly back over the top with him.

As the Mouser telescoped its sections together again, Fafhrd said to him seriously, "You must thong it to your belt as I do my ax. We must not chance losing Glinthi's help on the rest of this journey."

Throwing back their hoods and opening their tunics wide to the hot sun, Fafhrd and the Mouser looked around, while Hrissa luxuriously stretched and worked her slim limbs and neck and body, the white fur of which hid her bruises. Both men were somewhat exalted by the thin air and filled brain-high with the ease of mind and spirit that comes with a great danger skillfully conquered.

Rather to their amazement, the southward swinging sun

had climbed barely halfway to noon. Perils which had seemed demihours long had lasted minutes only.

The summit of Obelisk Polaris was a great rolling field of pale rock too big to measure by Lankhmar acres. They had arrived near the southwest corner, and the gray-tinted stone meadow seemed to stretch east and north almost indefinitely. Here and there were hummocks and hollows, but they swelled and dipped most gently. There were a few scattered large boulders, not many, while off to the east were darker indistinct shapes which might be bushes and small trees footed in cracks filled with blown dirt.

"What lies east of the mountain chain?" the Mouser asked. "More Cold Waste?"

"Our clan never journeyed there," Fafhrd answered. He frowned. "Some taboo on the whole area, I think. Mist always masked the east on my father's great climbs, or so he told us."

"We could have a look now," the Mouser suggested.

Fafhrd shook his head. "Our course lies there," he said, pointing northeast, where Stardock rose like a giantess standing tall but asleep, or feigning sleep, looking seven times as big and high at least as she had before the Obelisk hid her top two days ago.

The Mouser said, a shade dolefully, "All our brave work scaling the Obelisk has only made Stardock higher. Are you sure there's not another peak, perhaps invisible, on top of her?"

Fafhrd nodded without taking his eyes off her, who was empress without consort of the Mountains of the Giants. Her Tresses had grown to great swelling rivers of snow, and now the two adventurers could see faint stirrings in them— avalanches slipping and tumbling.

The Southern Tress came down in a great dipping double curve toward the northwest corner of the mighty rock summit on which they stood.

At the top, Stardock's corniced snow hat, its upper rim glittering with sunlight as if it were edged around with diamonds, seemed to nod toward them a trifle more than it ever had before, and the demurely-eyed Face with it, like a great lady hinting at possible favors.

But the gauzy, long pale veils of the Grand and Petty Pennons no longer streamed from her Hat. The air atop Stardock must be as still at the moment as it was where they stood upon the Obelisk.

"What devil's luck that Kranarch and Gnarfi should tackle the north wall the one day in eight the gale fails!" Fafhrd cursed. "But 'twill be their destruction yet—yes, and of their two shaggy-clad henchmen too. This calm can't hold."

"I recall now," the Mouser remarked, "that when we caroused with 'em in Illik-Ving, Gnarfi, drunken, claimed he could whistle up winds—had learned the trick from his grandmother—and could whistle 'em down too, which is more to the point."

"The more reason for us to hasten!" Fafhrd cried, upping his pack and slipping his big arms through the wide shoulder straps. "On, Mouser! Up, Hrissa! We'll have a bite and sup before the snow ridge."

"You mean we must tackle that freezing, treacherous problem today?" demurred the Mouser, who would dearly have loved to strip and bake in the sun.

"Before noon!" Fafhrd decreed. And with that he set them a stiff walking pace straight north, keeping close to the summit's west edge, as if to countermand from the start any curiosity the Mouser might have about a peek to the east. The latter followed with only minor further protests; Hrissa came on limpingly, lagging at first far behind, but catching up as her limp went and her cat-zest for newness grew.

And so they marched across the great, strange rolling granite plain of Obelisk's top, patched here and there with limestone stretches white as marble. Its sun-drenched silence and uniformity became eerie after a bit. The shallowness of its hollows was deceptive: Fafhrd noted several in which battalions of armed men might have hidden a-crouch, unseen until one came within a spear's cast.

The longer they strode along, the more closely Fafhrd studied the rock his hobnails clashed. Finally he paused to point out a strangely rippled stretch.

"I'd swear that once was seabottom," he said softly.

The Mouser's eyes narrowed. Thinking of the great invisible fishlike flier they had seen last evening, its raylike form undulating through the snowfall, he felt gooseflesh crawling on him.

Hrissa slunk past them, head a-weave.

Soon they passed the last boulder, a huge one, and saw, scarcely a bowshot ahead, the glitter of snow.

The Mouser said, "The worst thing about mountain climbing is that the easy parts go so quickly."

"Hist!" warned Fafhrd, sprawling down suddenly like a great four-legged water beetle and putting his cheek to the rock. "Do you hear it, Mouser!"

Hrissa snarled, staring about, and her white fur bristled.

The Mouser started to stoop, but realized he wouldn't have to, so fast the sound was coming on: a general high-pitched drumming, as of five hundred fiends rippling their giant thick fingernails on a great stone drumhead.

Then, without pause, there came surging straight toward them over the nearest rock swelling to the southeast, a great wide-fronted stampede of goats, so packed together and their fur so glossy white that they seemed for a flash like an onrushing of living snow. Even the great curving horns of their leaders were ivory-hued. The Mouser noted that a stretch of the sunny air just above their center shimmered and wavered as it will above a fire. Then he and Fafhrd were racing back toward the last boulder with Hrissa bounding ahead.

Behind them the devil's tattoo of the stampede grew louder and louder.

They reached the boulder and vaulted atop it, where Hrissa already crouched, hardly a pounding heartbeat before the white horde. And well it was that Fafhrd had his ax out the instant they won there, for the midmost of the great billies sprang high, forelegs tucked up and head bowed to present his creamy horns—so close Fafhrd could see their splintered tips. But in that same instant Fafhrd got him in his snowy shoulder with a great swashing deep-cleaving blow so heavy that the beast was carried past them to the side and crashed on the short slope leading down to the rim of the west wall.

Then the white stampede was splitting around the great boulder, the animals so near and packed that there was no longer room for leaping, and the din of their hooves and the gasping and now the frightened bleating was horrendous, and the caprid stench was stifling, while the boulder rocked with their passage.

In the worst of the bruit there was a momentary downrushing of air, briefly dispelling the stench, as something passed close above their heads, rippling the sky like a long flapping blanket of fluid glass, while through the clangor could be heard for a moment a harsh, hateful laughter.

The lesser tongue of the stampede passed between the boulder and the rim, and of these goats many went tumbling over the edge with bleats like screams of the damned, carrying with them the body of the great billy Fafhrd had maimed.

Then as sudden in its departure as a snow squall that dismasts a ship in the Frozen Sea, the stampede was past them and pounding south, swinging east somewhat from the deadly rim, with the last few of the goats, chiefly nannies and kids, bounding madly after.

Pointing his arm toward the sun as if for a sword-thrust, the Mouser cried furiously, "See there, where the beams twist all askew above the herd! It's the same flier as just now overpassed us and last night we saw in the snowfall—the flier who raised the stampede and whose riders guided it against us! Oh, damn the two deceitful ghostly bitches, luring us on to a goaty destruction stinking worse than a temple orgy in the City of Ghouls!"

"I thought this laughter was far deeper," Fafhrd objected. "It was not the girls."

"So they have a deep-throated pimp—does that improve them in your eyes? Or your great flapping love-struck ears?" the Mouser demanded angrily.

The drumming of the stampede had died away even swifter than it had come, and in the new-fallen silence they heard now a happy half-obstructed growling. Hrissa, springing off the boulder at stampede-end, had struck down a fat kid and was tearing at its bloodied white neck.

"Ah, I can smell it broiling now!" the Mouser cried with a great smile, his preoccupations altering in less than an instant. "Good Hrissa! Fafhrd, if those be treelets and bushes and grass to the east—and they must be that, for what else feeds these goats?—there's sure to be dead wood—why, there may even be mint!—and we can…"

"You'll eat the flesh raw for lunch or not at all!" Fafhrd decreed fiercely. "Are we to risk the stampede again? Or give the sniggering flier a chance to marshal against us some snow lions?—which are sure to be here too, to prey on the goats. And are we to present Kranarch and Gnarfi the summit of Stardock on a diamond-studded silver platter?—if this devil's lull holds tomorrow too and they be industrious strong climbers, not nice-bellied sluggards like one I could name!"

So, with only a gripe or two more from the Mouser, the kid was swiftly bled, gutted and skinned, and some of its spine-meat and haunches wrapped and packed for supper. Hrissa drank some more blood and ate half the liver and then followed the Mouser and Fafhrd as they set off north toward the snow ridge. The two men were chewing thin-sliced peppered collops of raw kid, but striding swiftly and keeping a wary eye behind for another stampede.

The Mouser expected now at last to get a view of the eastern depths, by peering east along the north wall of Obelisk Polaris, but here again he was foiled by the first great swell of the snow-saddle.

However, the northern view was fearsomely majestic. A full half league below them now and seen almost vertically on, the White Waterfall went showering down mysteriously, twinkling even in the shadow.

The ridge by which they must travel first curved up a score of yards, then dipped smoothly down to a long snow-saddle another score of yards below them, then slowly curved up into the South Tress, down which they could now plainly see avalanches trickling and tumbling.

It was easy to see how the northeast gale, blowing almost continually but missing the Ladder, would greatly pile up snow between the taller mountain and the Obelisk—but whether the rocky connection between the two mountains underlay the snow by only a few yards or by as much as a quarter league was impossible to know.

"We must rope again," Fafhrd decreed. "I'll go first and cut steps for us across the west slope."

"What need we steps in this calm!" the Mouser demanded. "Or to go by the west slope? You just don't want me to see the east, do you? The top of the ridge is broad enough to drive two carts across abreast."

"The ridge-top in the wind's path almost certainly over-hangs emptiness to the east and would break away," Fafhrd explained. "Look you, Mouser; do I know more about snow and ice or do you?"

"I once crossed the Bones of the Old Ones with you," the Mouser retorted, shrugging. "There was snow there, I recall."

"Pooh, the mere spillings of a lady's powderbox compared to this. No, Mouser, on this stretch my word is law."

"Very well," the Mouser agreed.

So they roped up rather close—in order, Fafhrd, Mouser, and Hrissa—and without more ado Fafhrd donned his gloves and thonged his ax to his wrist and began cutting steps for them around the shoulder of the snow swell.

It was rather slow work, for under a dusting of powder snow the stuff was hard, and for each step Fafhrd must make at least two cuts—first an in-chopping backhand one to make the step, then a down-chop to clear it. And as the slope grew steeper, he must make the steps somewhat closer together. The steps he made were rather small, at least for his great boots, but they were sure.

Soon the ridge and the Obelisk cut off the sun. It grew very chill. The Mouser closed his tunic and drew his hood around his face, while Hrissa, between her short leaps from step to step, performed a kind of tiny cat-jig on them, to keep her gloved paws from freezing. The Mouser reminded himself to stuff them a bit with lamb's wool when he renewed the salve. He had his pike out now, telescoped short and thonged to his wrist.

They passed the shoulder of the swell and came opposite the beginning of the snow-saddle, but Fafhrd did not cut steps up toward it. Rather, the steps he now was cutting descended at a sharper angle than the saddle dipped, though the slope they were crossing was becoming quite steep.

"Fafhrd," the Mouser protested quietly, "we're heading for Stardock's top, not the White Waterfall."

"You said, 'Very well,'" Fafhrd retorted between chops. "Besides, who does the work?" His ax rang as it bit into ice.

"Look, Fafhrd," the Mouser said, "there are two goats crossing to Stardock along the saddletop. No, three."

"We should trust goats? Ask yourself why they've been sent." Again Fafhrd's ax rang.

The sun swung into view as it coursed southward, sending their three shadows ranging far ahead of them.

The pale gray of the snow turned glittery white. The Mouser unhooded to the yellow rays. For a while the enjoyment of their warmth on the back of his head helped him keep his mouth shut, but then the slope grew steeper yet, as Fafhrd continued remorselessly to cut steps downward.

"I seem to recall that our purpose was to *climb* Stardock, but my memory must be disordered," the Mouser observed. "Fafhrd, I'll take your word we must keep away from the top of the ridge, but do we have to keep away so *far*? And the three goats have all skipped across."

Still, "'Very well,' you said," was all Fafhrd would answer, and this time there was a snarl in his voice.

The Mouser shrugged. Now he was bracing himself with his pike continuously, while Hrissa would pause studyingly before each leap.

Their shadows went less than a spear's cast ahead of them now, while the hot sun had begun to melt the surface snow, sending down trickles of ice water to wet their gloves and make their footing unsure.

Yet still Fafhrd kept cutting steps downward. And now of a sudden he began to cut them downward more steeply still, adding with taps of his ax a tiny handhold above each step— and these handholds were needed!

"Fafhrd," the Mouser said dreamily, "perhaps an ice-sprite has whispered to you the secret of levitation, so that from this fine takeoff you can dive, level out, and then go spring to Stardock's top. In that case I wish you'd teach myself and Hrissa how to grow wings in an instant."

"Hist!" Fafhrd spoke softly yet sharply at that instant. "I have a feeling. Something comes. Brace yourself and watch behind us."

The Mouser drove his pike in deep and rotated his head. As he did, Hrissa leaped from the last step behind to the one on which the Mouser stood, landing half on his boot and clinging to his knee—yet this done so dexterously the Mouser was not dislodged.

"I see nothing," the Mouser reported, staring almost sunward. Then, words suddenly clipped: "Again the beams twist like a spinning lantern! The glints on the ice ripple and wave. 'Tis the flier come again! Cling!"

There came the rushing sound, louder than ever before and swiftly mounting, then a great sea-wave of air, as of a great body passing swiftly only spans away; it whipped their clothes and Hrissa's fur and forced them to cling fiercely to their holds, though Fafhrd made a full-armed swipe with his ax. Hrissa snarled. Fafhrd almost louted forward off his holds with the momentum of his blow.

"I'll swear I scored on him, Mouser," he snarled, recovering. "My ax touched something besides air."

"You harebrained fool!" the Mouser cried. "Your scratches will anger him and bring him back." He let go of the chopped ice-hold with his hand and, steadying himself by his pike, he searched the sun-bright air ahead and around for ripples.

"More like I've scared him off," Fafhrd asserted, doing the same. The rushy sound faded and did not return; the air became quiet, and the steep slope grew very still; even the water-drip faded.

Turning back to the wall with a grunt of relief, the Mouser touched emptiness. He grew still as death himself. Turning his eyes only he saw that upward from a point level with his knees the whole snow ridge had vanished—the whole saddle and a section of the swell to either side of it—as if some great god had reached down while the Mouser's back was turned and removed that block of reality.

Giddily he clung to his pike. He was standing atop a newly created snow-saddle now. Beyond and below its raw, fresh-fractured white eastern slope, the silently departed great snow-cornice was falling faster and faster, still in one hill-size chunk.

Behind them the steps Fafhrd had cut mounted to the new snow rim, then vanished.

"See, I chopped us down far enough only in the nick," Fafhrd grumbled. "My judgment was faulty."

The falling cornice was snatched downward out of sight so that the Mouser and Fafhrd at last could see what lay east of the Mountains of the Giants: a rolling expanse of dark green that might be treetops except that from here even giant trees would be tinier than grass blades—an expanse even farther below them than the Cold Waste at their backs. Beyond the green-carpeted depression, another mountain range loomed like the ghost of one.

"I have heard legends of the Great Rift Valley," Fafhrd murmured. "A mountainsided cup for sunlight, its warm floor a league below the Waste."

Their eyes searched.

"Look," the Mouser said, "how trees climb the eastern face of Obelisk almost to his top. Now the goats don't seem so strange."

They could see nothing, however, of the east face of Stardock.

"Come on!" Fafhrd commanded. "If we linger, the invisible growl-laughtered flier may gather courage to return despite my ax-nick."

And without further word he began resolutely to cut steps onward...and still a little down.

Hrissa continued to peer over the rim, her bearded chin almost resting on it, her nostrils a-twitch as if she faintly scented gossamer threads of meat-odor mounting from the leagues' distant dark green, but when the rope tightened on her harness, she followed.

Perils came thick now. They reached the dark rock of the Ladder only by chopping their way along a nearly vertical ice wall in the twinkly gloom under a close-arching waterfall of snow that shot out from an icy boss above them—perhaps

a miniature version of the White Waterfall that was
Stardock's skirt.

When they stepped at last, numb with cold and hardly
daring to believe they'd made it, onto a wide dark ledge, they
saw a jumble of bloody goat tracks in the snow around.

Without more warning than that, a long snowbank
between that step and the next above reared up its nearest
white end a dozen feet and hissed fearsomely, showing it to
be a huge serpent with head a big as an elk's, all covered with
shaggy snow-white fur. Its great violet eyes glared like those
of a mad horse and its jaw gaped to show slashing-teeth like
a shark's and two great fangs jetting a mist of pale ichor.

The furred serpent hesitated for two sways between the
nearer, taller man with flashing ax and the farther, smaller
one with thick black stick. In that pause Hrissa, with snarling
hisses of her own, sprang forward past the Mouser on the
downslope side and the furred serpent struck at this newest
and most active foe.

Fafhrd got a blast of its hot acrid breath, and the vapor
trail from its nearer fang bathed his left elbow.

The Mouser's attention was fixed on a fur-wisped violet
eye as big as a girl's fist.

Hrissa looked down the monster's gaping dark red gullet
rimmed by slaver-swimming ivory knives and the two ichor-
jetting fangs.

Then the jaws clashed shut, but in the intervening instant
Hrissa had leaped back more swiftly even than she'd
advanced.

The Mouser plunged the pike-end of his climbing pole into
the glaring violet eye.

Swinging his ax two-handed, Fafhrd slashed at the furry
neck just back of the horselike skull, and there gushed out
red blood which steamed as it struck the snow.

Then the three climbers were scrambling upward, while

the monster writhed in convulsions which shook the rock and spattered with red alike the snow and its snow-white fur.

At what they hoped was a safe distance above it, the climbers watched it dying, though not without frequent glances about for creatures like it or other perilous beasts.

Fafhrd said, "A hot-blooded serpent, a snake with fur—it goes against experience. My father never spoke of such; I doubt he ever met 'em."

The Mouser answered, "I'll wager they find their prey on the east slope of Stardock and come here only to lair or breed. Perhaps the invisible flier drove the three goats over the snow-saddle to lure this one." His voice grew dreamy. "Or perhaps there's a secret world inside Stardock."

Fafhrd shook his head, as if to clear it of such imagination-snaring visions. "Our way lies upward," he said. "We'd best be well above the Lairs before nightfall. Give me a dollop of honey when I drink," he added, loosening his water bag as he turned and scanned up the Ladder.

From its base the Ladder was a dark narrow triangle climbing to the blue sky between the snowy, ever-tumbling Tresses. First there were the ledges on which they stood, easy at first, but swiftly growing steeper and narrower. Next an almost blank stretch, etched here and there with shadows and ripplings hinting at part-way climbing routes, but none of them connected. Then another band of ledges, the Roosts. Then a stretch still blanker than the first. Finally another ledge-band, narrower and shorter—the Face—and atop all what seemed a tiny pen-stroke of white ink: the brim of Stardock's pennonless snowy hat.

All the Mouser's aches and weariness came back as he squinted up the Ladder while feeling in his pouch for the honey jar. Never, he was sure, had he seen so much distance compressed into so little space by vertical foreshortening. It was as if the gods had built a ladder to reach the sky, and after using it had kicked most of the steps away. But he clenched his teeth and prepared to follow Fafhrd.

All their previous climbing began to seem book-simple compared to what they now straggled through, step by straining step, all the long summer afternoon. Where Obelisk Polaris had been a stern schoolmaster, Stardock was a mad queen, tireless in preparing her shocks and surprises, unpredictable in her wild caprices.

The ledges of the Lairs were built of rock that sometimes broke away at a touch, and they were piled with loose gravel. Also, the climbers made acquaintance with Stardock's rocky avalanches, which brought stones whizzing and spattering down around them without warning, so that they had to press close to the walls and Fafhrd regretted leaving his helmet in the cairn. Hrissa first snarled at each pelting pebble which hit near her, but when at last struck in the side by a small one, showed fear and slunk close to the Mouser, trying until rebuked to push between the wall and his legs.

And once they saw a cousin of the white worm they had slain rear up man-high and glare at them from a distant ledge, but it did not attack.

They had to work their way to the northernmost point of the topmost ledge before they found, at the very edge of the Northern Tress, almost underlying its streaming snow, a scree-choked gully which narrowed upward to a wide vertical groove—or chimney, as Fafhrd called it.

And when the treacherous scree was at last surmounted, the Mouser discovered that the next stretch of the ascent was indeed very like climbing up the inside of a rectangular chimney of varying width and with one of the four walls missing—that facing outward to the air. Its rock was sounder than that of the Lairs, but that was all that could be said for it.

Here all tricks of climbing were required and the utmost

of main strength into the bargain. Sometimes they hoisted themselves by cracks wide enough for finger- and toeholds; if a crack they needed was too narrow, Fafhrd would tap into it one of his spikes to make a hold, and this spike must, if possible, be unwedged after use and recovered. Sometimes the chimney narrowed so that they could walk up it laboriously with shoulders to one wall and boot soles to the other. Twice it widened and became so smooth-walled that the Mouser's extensible climbing-pike had to be braced between wall and wall to give them a necessary step.

And five times the chimney was blocked by a huge rock or chockstone which in falling had wedged itself fast, and these fearsome obstructions had to be climbed around on the outside, generally with the aid of one or more of Fafhrd's spikes driven between chockstone and wall, or his grapnel tossed over it.

"Stardock has wept millstones in her day," the Mouser said of these gigantic barriers, jerking his body aside from a whizzing rock for a period to his sentence.

This climbing was generally beyond Hrissa, and she often had to be carried on the Mouser's back, or left on a chockstone or one of the rare paw-wide ledges and hoisted up when opportunity offered. They were strongly tempted, especially after they grew death-weary, to abandon her but could not forget how her brave feint had saved them from the white worm's first stroke.

All this, particularly the passing of the chockstones, must be done under the pelting of Stardock's rocky avalanches— so that each new chockstone above them was welcomed as a roof, until it had to be surmounted. Also, snow sometimes gushed into the chimney, overspilling from one of the snowy avalanches forever whispering down the North Tress—one more danger to guard against. Ice water runneled too from time to time down the chimney, drenching boots and gloves and making all holds unsure.

In addition, there was less nourishment in the air, so that they had more often to halt and gasp deeply until their lungs were satisfied. And Fafhrd's left arm began to swell where the venomous mist from the worm's fang had blown around it, until he could hardly bend its swollen fingers to grip crack or rope. Besides, it itched and stung. He plunged it again and again into snow to no avail.

Their only allies on this most punishing ascent were the hot sun, heartening them by its glow and offsetting the growing frigidity of the thin still air, and the very difficulty and variety of the climb itself, which at least kept their minds off the emptiness around and beneath them—the latter a farther drop than they'd ever stood over on the Obelisk. The Cold Waste seemed like another world, poised separate from Stardock in space.

Once they forced themselves to eat a bite and several times sipped water. And once the Mouser was seized with mountain sickness, ending only when he had retched himself weary.

The only incident of the climb unrelated to Stardock's mad self occurred when they were climbing out around the fifth chockstone, slowly, like two large slugs, the Mouser first this time and bearing Hrissa, with Fafhrd close behind. At this point the North Tress narrowed so that a hump of the North Wall was visible across the snow stream.

There was a whirring unlike that of any rock. Another whirring then, closer and ending in a *thunk*. When Fafhrd scrambled atop the chockstone and into the shelter of the walls, he had a cruelly barbed arrow through his pack.

At cost of a third arrow whirring close by his head, the Mouser peeped out north with Fafhrd clinging to his heels and swiftly dragging him back.

"'Twas Kranarch all right; I saw him twang his bow," the Mouser reported. "No sight of Gnarfi, but one of their new comrades clad in brown fur crouched behind Kranarch, braced on the same boss. I couldn't see his face, but 'tis a most burly fellow, short of leg."

"They keep apace of us," Fafhrd grunted.

"Also, they scruple not to mix climbing with killing," the Mouser observed as he broke off the tail of the arrow piercing Fafhrd's pack and yanked out the shaft. "Oh, comrade, I fear your sleeping cloak is sixteen times holed. And that little bladder of pine liniment—it got holed too. Ah, what fragrance!"

"I'm beginning to think those two men of Illik-Ving aren't sportsmen," Fafhrd asserted. "So…up and on!"

They were all dog-weary, even cat-Hrissa, and the sun was barely ten fingerbreadths (at the end of an outstretched arm) above the flat horizon of the Waste; and something in the air had turned Sol white as silver—he no longer sent warmth to combat the cold. But the ledges of the Roosts were close above now, and it was possible to hope they would offer a better campsite than the chimney.

So although every man and cat muscle protested against it, they obeyed Fafhrd's command.

Halfway to the Roosts it began to snow, powdery grains falling arrow-straight like last night, but thicker.

This silent snowfall gave a sense of serenity and security which was most false, since it masked the rockfalls which still came firing down the chimney like the artillery of the God of Chance.

Five yards from the top a fist-size chunk struck Fafhrd glancingly on the right shoulder, so that his good arm went numb and hung useless, but the little climbing that remained was so easy he could make it with boots and puffed-up, barely-usable left hand.

He peeped cautiously out of the chimney's top, but the Tress here had thickened up again, so that there was no sight of the North Wall. Also the first ledge was blessedly wide and so overhung with rock that not even snow had fallen on its inner half, let alone stones. He scrambled up eagerly, followed by the Mouser and Hrissa.

But even as they cast themselves down to rest at the back of the ledge, the Mouser wriggling out of his heavy pack and unthonging his climbing-pike from his wrist—for even *that* had become a torturesome burden—they heard a now-familiar rushing in the air, and there came a great flat shape swooping slowly through the sun-silvered snow which outlined it. Straight at the ledge it came, and this time it did not go past, but halted and hung there, like a giant devil fish nuzzling the sea's rim, while ten narrow marks, each of suckers in line, appeared in the snow on the ledge's edge, as of ten short tentacles gripping there.

From the center of this monstrous invisibility rose a smaller snow-outlined invisibility of the height and thickness of a man. Midway up this shape was one visible thing: a slim sword of dark gray blade and silvery hilt, pointed straight at the Mouser's breast.

Suddenly the sword shot forward, almost as fast as if hurled, but not quite, and after it, as swiftly, the man-size pillar, which now laughed harshly from its top.

The Mouser snatched up one-handed his unthonged climbing pike and thrust at the snow-sketched figure behind the sword.

The gray sword snaked around the pike and with a sudden sharp twist swept it from the Mouser's fatigue-slack fingers.

The black tool, on which Glinthi the Artificer had expended all the evenings of the Month of the Weasel three years past, vanished into the silvery snowfall and space.

Hrissa backed against the wall frothing and snarling, a-tremble in every limb.

Fafhrd fumbled frantically for his ax, but his swollen fingers could not even unsnap the sheath binding its head to his belt.

The Mouser, enraged at the loss of his precious pike to the point where he cared not a whit whether his foe was invisible or not, drew Scalpel from its sheath and fiercely parried the gray sword as it came streaking in again.

A dozen parries he had to make and was pinked twice in the arm and pressed back against the wall almost like Hrissa, before he could take the measure of his foe, now out of the snowfall and wholly invisible, and go himself on the attack.

Then, glaring at a point a foot above the gray sword—a point where he judged his foe's eyes to be (if his foe carried his eyes in his head)—he went stamping forward, beating at the gray blade, slipping Scalpel around it with the tiniest disengages, seeking to bind it with his own sword, and ever thrusting impetuously at invisible arm and trunk.

Three times he felt his blade strike flesh, and once it bent briefly against invisible bone.

His foe leaped back onto the invisible flier, making narrow footprints in the slush gathered there. The flier rocked.

In his fighting rage the Mouser almost followed his foe onto that invisible, living, pulsating platform, yet prudently stopped at the brink.

And well it was he did so, for the flier dropped away like a skate in flight from a shark, shaking its slush into the snowfall. There came a last burst of laughter more like a wail, fading off and down in the silvery murk.

The Mouser began to laugh himself, a shade hysterically, and retreated to the wall. There he wiped off his blade and felt the stickiness of invisible blood, and laughed a wild high laugh again.

Hrissa's fur was still on end—and was a long time flattening.

Fafhrd quit trying to fumble out his ax and said seriously, "The girls couldn't have been with him—we'd have seen their forms or footprints on the slush-backed flier. I think he's jealous of us and works against 'em."

The Mouser laughed—only foolishly now—for a third time.

The murk turned dark gray. They set about firing the brazier and making ready for night. Despite their hurts and supreme weariness, the shock and fright of the last encounter had excited new energy from them and raised their spirits and given them appetites. They feasted well on thin collops of kid frizzled in the resin-flames or cooked pale gray in water that, strangely, could be sipped without hurt almost while it boiled.

"Must be nearing the realm of the Gods," Fafhrd muttered. "It's said they joyously drink boiling wine—and walk hurtlessly through flames."

"Fire is just as hot here, though," the Mouser said dully.

"Yet the air seems to have less nourishment. On what do you suppose the Gods subsist?"

"They are ethereal and require neither air nor food," Fafhrd suggested after a long frown of thinking.

"Yet you just now said they drink wine."

"Everybody drinks wine," Fafhrd asserted with a yawn, killing the discussion and also the Mouser's dim, unspoken speculation as to whether the feebler air, pressing less strongly on heating liquid, let its bubbles escape more easily.

Power of movement began to return to Fafhrd's right arm and his left was swelling no more. The Mouser salved and bandaged his own small wounds, then remembered to salve Hrissa's pads and tuck into her boots a little pine-scented eiderdown tweaked from the arrow-holes in Fafhrd's cloak.

When they were half laced up in their cloaks, Hrissa snuggled between them—and a few more precious resin-pellets dropped in the brazier as a bedtime luxury—Fafhrd got out a tiny jar of strong wine of Ilthmar, and they each took a sip of it, imagining those sunny vineyards and that hot, rich soil so far south.

A momentary flare from the brazier showed them the snow

falling yet. A few rocks crashed nearby and a snowy avalanche hissed, then Stardock grew still in the frigid grip of night. The climbers' aerie seemed most strange to them, set above every other peak in the Mountains of the Giants—and likely all Nehwon—yet walled with darkness like a tiny room.

The Mouser said softly, "Now we know what roosts in the Roosts. Do you suppose there are dozens of those invisible mantas carpeting around us on ledges like this, or a-hang from them? Why don't they freeze? Or does someone stable them? And the invisible folk, what of them? No more can you call 'em mirage—you saw the sword, and I fought the man-thing at the other end of it. Yet invisible! How's that possible?"

Fafhrd shrugged and then winced because it hurt both shoulders cruelly. "Made of some stuff like water or glass," he hazarded. "Yet pliant and twisting the light less—and with no surface shimmer. You've seen sand and ashes made transparent by firing. Perhaps there's some heatless way of firing monsters and men until they are invisible."

"But how light enough to fly?" the Mouser asked.

"Thin beasts to match thin air," Fafhrd guessed sleepily.

The Mouser said, "And then those deadly worms—and the Fiend knows what perils above." He paused. "And yet we must still climb Stardock to the top, mustn't we? Why?"

Fafhrd nodded. "To beat out Kranarch and Gnarfi…" he muttered. "To beat out my father…the mystery of it…the girls…O Mouser, could you stop here any more than you could stop after touching half of a woman?"

"You don't mention diamonds anymore," the Mouser noted. "Don't you think we'll find them?"

Fafhrd started another shrug and mumbled a curse that turned into a yawn.

The Mouser dug in his pouch to the bottom pocket and brought out the parchment and blowing on the brazier read it all by the resin's last flaming:

Who mounts white Stardock, the Moon Tree,
Past worm and gnome and unseen bars,
Will win the key to luxury:
The Heart of Light, a pouch of stars.
The gods who once ruled all the world
Have made that peak their citadel,
From whence the stars were one time hurled
And paths lead on to Heav'n and Hell.
Come, heroes, past the Trollstep rocks.
Come, best of men, across the Waste.
For you, glory each door unlocks.
Delay not, up, and come in haste.
Who scales the Snow King's citadel
Shall father his two daughters' sons;
Though he must face foes fierce and fell,
His seed shall live while time still runs.

The resin burnt out. The Mouser said, "Well, we've met a
worm and one unseen fellow who sought to bar our way—
and two sightless witches who might be Snow King's
daughters for all I know. Gnomes now—they would be a
change, wouldn't they? You said something about ice gnomes,
Fafhrd. What was it?"

He waited with an unnatural anxiety for Fafhrd's answer.
After a bit he began to hear it: soft regular snores.

The Mouser snarled soundlessly, his demon of restlessness
now become a fury despite all his aches. He shouldn't have
thought of girls—or rather of one girl who was nothing but
a taunting mask with pouting lips and eyes of black mystery
seen across a fire.

Suddenly he felt stifled. He quickly unhooked his cloak
and despite Hrissa's questioning mew felt his way south
along the ledge. Soon snow, sifting like ice needles on his

flushed face, told him he was beyond the overhang. Then the snow stopped. Another overhang, he thought—but he had not moved. He strained his eyes upward, and there was the black expanse of Stardock's topmost quarter silhouetted against a band of sky pale with the hidden moon and specked by a few faint stars. Behind him to the west, the snowstorm still obscured the sky.

He blinked his eyes and then he swore softly, for now the black cliff they must climb tomorrow was a-glow with soft scattered lights of violet and rose and palest green and amber. The nearest, which were still far above, looked tinily rectangular, like gleam-spilling windows seen from below.

It was as if Stardock were a great hostelry.

Then freezing flakes pinked his face again, and the band of sky narrowed to nothing. The snowfall had moved back against Stardock once more, hiding all stars and other lights.

The Mouser's fury drained from him. Suddenly he felt very small and foolhardy and very, very cold. The mysterious vision of the lights remained in his mind, but muted, as if part of a dream. Most cautiously he crept back the way he had come, feeling the radiant warmth of Fafhrd and Hrissa and the burnt-out brazier just before he touched his cloak. He laced it around him and lay for a long time doubled up like a baby, his mind empty of everything except frigid blackness. At last he slumbered.

Next day started gloomy. The two men chafed and wrestled each other as they lay, to get the stiffness a little out of them and enough warmth in them to rise. Hrissa withdrew from between them limping and sullen.

At any rate, Fafhrd's arms were recovered from their swelling and numbing, while the Mouser was hardly aware of his own arm's little wounds.

They breakfasted on herb tea and honey and began climbing the Roosts in a light snowfall. This last pest stayed with them all morning except when gusty breezes blew it back from Stardock. On these occasions they could see the great smooth cliff separating the Roosts from the ultimate ledges of the Face. By the glimpses they got, the cliff looked to be without any climbing routes whatever, or any marks at all— so that Fafhrd laughed at the Mouser for a dreamer with his tale of windows spilling colored light—but finally as they neared the cliff's base they began to distinguish what seemed to be a narrow crack—a hairline to vision—mounting its center.

They met none of the invisible flat fliers, either a-wing or a-perch, though whenever gusts blew strange gaps into the snowfall, the two adventurers would firm themselves on their perches and grip for their weapons, and Hrissa would snarl.

The wind slowed them little though chilling them much, for the rock of the Roosts was true.

And they still had to watch out for stony peltings, though these were fewer than yesterday, perhaps because so much of Stardock now lay below them.

They reached the base of the great cliff at the point where the crack began, which was a good thing since the snowfall had grown so heavy that a hunt for it would have been difficult.

To their joy, the crack proved to be another chimney, scarcely a yard across and not much more deep, and as knobbly inside with footholds as the cliff outside was smooth. Unlike yesterday's chimney, it appeared to extend upward indefinitely without change of width, and as far as they could see there were no chockstones. In many ways it was like a rock ladder half sheltered from the snow. Even Hrissa could climb here, as on Obelisk Polaris.

They lunched on food warmed against their skins. They were afire with eagerness, yet forced themselves to take time to chew and sip. As they entered the chimney, Fafhrd going first, there came three faint growling booms—thunder perhaps and certainly ominous, yet the Mouser laughed.

With never-failing footholds and opposite wall for back-brace, the climbing was easy, except for the drain on main strength, which required rather frequent halts to gulp down fresh stores of the thin air. Only twice did the chimney narrow so that Fafhrd had to climb for a short stretch with his body outside it; the Mouser, slighter framed, could stay inside.

It was an intoxicating experience, almost. Even as the day grew darker from the thickening snowfall and as the crackling booms returned sharper and stronger—thunder now for sure, since they were heralded by brief palings up and down the chimney—snow-muted lightning flashes—the Mouser and Fafhrd felt as merry as children mounting a mysterious twisty stairway in a haunted castle. They even wasted a little breath in joking calls which went echoing faintly up and down the rugged shaft as it paled and gloomed with the lightning.

But then the shaft grew by degrees almost as smooth as the outer cliff and at the same time it began gradually to widen, first a handbreadth, then another, then a finger more, so that they had to mount more perilously, bracing shoulders against one wall and boots against the other and so "walking" up with pushes and heaves. The Mouser drew up Hrissa, and the ice-cat crouched on his pitching, rocking chest—no inconsiderable burden. Yet both men still felt quite jolly—so that the Mouser began to wonder if there might not be some actual intoxicant in air near Heaven.

Being a head or two taller than the Mouser, Fafhrd was better equipped for this sort of climbing and was still able to go on at the moment when the Mouser realized that his body was stretched almost straight between shoulders and boot soles—with Hrissa a-crouch on him like a traveler on a little bridge. He could mount no farther—and was hazy about how he had managed to come this far.

Fafhrd came down like a great spider at the Mouser's call

and seemed not much impressed by the latter's plight—in fact, a lightning flash showed his great bearded face all a-grin.

"Abide you here a bit," he said. "'Tis not so far to the top. I think I glimpsed it the last flash but one. I'll mount and draw you up, putting all the rope between you and me. There's a crack by your head—I'll knock in a spike for safety's sake. Meanwhile, rest."

Whereupon Fafhrd did all of these things so swiftly and was on his upward way again so soon that the Mouser forebore to utter any of the sardonic remarks churning inside his rigid belly.

Successive lightning flashes showed the Northerner's long-limbed form growing smaller at a gratifyingly rapid rate until he looked hardly bigger than a trap spider at the end of his tube. Another flash and he was gone, but whether because he had reached the top or passed a bend in the chimney the Mouser couldn't be sure.

The rope kept paying upward, however, until there was only a small loop below the Mouser. He was aching abominably now and was also very cold, but gritted his teeth against the pain. Hrissa chose this moment to prowl up and down her small human bridge, restlessly. There was a blinding lightning flash and a crash of thunder that shook Stardock. Hrissa cringed.

The rope grew taut, tugging at the belt of the Mouser, who started to put his weight on it, holding Hrissa to his chest, but then decided to wait for Fafhrd's call. This was a good decision on his part, for just then the rope went slack and began to fall on the Mouser's belly like a stream of black water. Hrissa crouched away from it on his face. It came pelting endlessly, but finally its upper end hit the Mouser under the breastbone with a snap. The only good thing was that Fafhrd didn't come hurtling down with it. Another blinding mountain-shaking crash showed the upper chimney utterly empty.

"Fafhrd!" the Mouser called. *"Fafhrd!"* There came back only the echo.

The Mouser thought for a bit, then reached up and felt by his ear for the spike Fafhrd had struck in with a single offhand slap of his ax-hammer. Whatever had happened to Fafhrd, nothing seemed to remain to do but tie rope to spike and descend by it to where the chimney was easier.

The spike came out at the first touch and went clattering shrilly down the chimney until a new thunderblast drowned the small sound.

The Mouser decided to "walk" down the chimney. After all, he'd come up that way the last few score of yards.

The first attempt to move a leg told him his muscles were knotted by cramp. He'd never be able to bend his leg and straighten it again without losing his purchase and falling.

The Mouser thought of Glinthi's pike, lost in white space, and he slew that thought.

Hrissa crouched on his chest and gazed down into his face with an expression the next levin-glare showed to be sad yet critical, as if to ask, "Where is this vaunted human ingenuity?"

Fafhrd had barely eased himself out of the chimney onto the wide, deep rock-roofed ledge at its top, when a door two yards high, a yard wide, and two spans thick had silently opened in the rock at the back of the ledge.

The contrast was most remarkable between the roughness of that rock and the ruler-flat smoothness of the dark stone forming the thick sides of the door and the lintel, jambs, and threshold of the doorway.

Soft pink light spilled out and with it a perfume whose heavy fumes were cargoed with dreams of pleasure barges afloat in a rippling sunset sea.

Those musky narcotic fumes, along with the alcoholic headiness of the thin air, almost made Fafhrd forget his purpose, but touching the black rope was like touching Hrissa and the Mouser at its other end. He unknotted it from his belt and prepared to secure it around a stout rock pillar beside the open door. To get enough rope to make a good knot he had to draw it up quite tight.

But the dream-freighted fumes grew thicker, and he no longer felt the Mouser and Hrissa in the rope. Indeed, he began to forget his two comrades altogether.

And then a silvery voice—a voice he knew well from having heard it laugh once and once chuckle—called, "Come in, barbarian. Come in to me."

The end of the black rope slipped from his fingers unnoticed and hissed softly across the rock and down the chimney.

Stooping a little, he went through the doorway which silently closed behind him just in time to shut out the Mouser's desperate call.

He was in a room lit by pink globes hanging at the level of his head. Their soft warm radiance colored the hangings and rugs of the room, but especially the pale spread of the great bed that was its only furniture.

Beside the bed stood a slim woman whose black silk robe concealed all of her except her face, yet did not disguise her body's sleek curves. A black lace mask hid the rest of her.

She looked at Fafhrd for seven thudding heartbeats, then sat down on the bed. A slender arm and hand clothed all in black lace came from under her robe and patted the spread beside her and rested there. Her mask never wavered from Fafhrd's face.

He shouldered out of his pack and unbuckled his ax belt.

The Mouser finished pounding all the thin blade of his dagger into the crack by his ear, using the firestone from his pouch for hammer, so that sparks showered from every cramped stroke of stone against pommel—small lightning flashes to match the greater flares still chasing up and down the chimney, while their thunder crashed an obbligato to the Mouser's taps. Hrissa crouched on his ankles, and from time to time the Mouser glared at her, as if to say, "Well, cat?"

A gust of snow-freighted wind roaring up the chimney momentarily lifted the lean shaggy beast a span above him and almost blew the Mouser loose, but he tightened his pushing muscles still more and the bridge, arching upward a trifle, held firm.

He had just finished knotting an end of the black rope around the dagger's crossguard and grip—and his fingers and forearms were almost useless with fatigue—when a window two feet high and five wide silently opened in the back of the chimney, its thick rock shutter sliding aside, not a span away from the Mouser's inward shoulder.

A red glow sprang from the window and somewhat illuminated four faces with piggy black eyes and with low hairless domes above.

The Mouser considered them. They were all four of extreme ugliness, he decided dispassionately. Only their wide white teeth, showing between their grinning lips which almost joined ear to swinish ear, had any claim to beauty.

Hrissa sprang at once through the red window and disappeared. The two faces between which she jumped did not flicker a black button-eye.

Then eight short brawny arms came out and easily pried the Mouser out and lifted him inside. He screamed faintly from a sudden increase in the agony of his cramps. He was aware of thick dwarfish bodies clad in hairy black jerkins and breeks—and one in a black hairy skirt—but all with thick-nailed splay-feet bare. Then he fainted.

When he came to, it was because he was being punishingly massaged on a hard table, his body naked and slick with warm oil. He was in a low, ill-lit chamber and still closely surrounded by the four dwarves, as he could tell from the eight horny hands squeezing and thumping his muscles before he ever opened his eyes.

The dwarf kneading his right shoulder and banging the top of his spine crinkled his warty eyelids and bared his beautiful white teeth bigger than a giant's in what might be intended for a friendly grin. Then he said in an atrocious Mingol patois, "I am Bonecracker. This is my wife Gibberfat. Cosseting your body on the larboard side are my brothers Legcruncher and Breakskull. Now drink this wine and follow me."

The wine stung, yet dispelled the Mouser's dizziness, and it was certainly a blessing to be free of the murderous massage—and also apparently of the cramp-lumps in his muscles.

Bonecracker and Gibberfat helped him off the slab while Legcruncher and Breakskull rubbed him quickly down with rough towels. The warm low-ceilinged room rocked dizzily for a moment; then he felt wondrous fine.

Bonecracker waddled off into the dimness beyond the smoky torches. With never a question the Mouser followed the dwarf. Or were these Fafhrd's ice gnomes? he wondered.

Bonecracker pulled aside heavy drapes in the dark. Amber light fanned out. The Mouser stepped from rock-roughness onto down-softness. The drapes swished to behind him.

He was alone in a chamber mellowly lit by hanging globes like great topazes—yet he guessed they would bounce aside like puffballs if touched. There was a large wide couch and beyond it a low table against the arras-hung wall with an ivory stool set before it. Above the table was a great silver mirror, while on it were fantastic small bottles and many tiny ivory jars.

No, the room was not altogether empty. Hrissa, sleekly groomed, lay curled in a far corner. She was not watching the Mouser, however, but a point above the stool.

The Mouser felt a shiver creeping on him, yet not altogether one of fear.

A dab of palest green leaped from one of the jars to the point Hrissa was watching and vanished there. But then he saw a streak of reflected green appear in the mirror. The riddlesome maneuver was repeated, and soon in the mirror's silver there hung a green mask, somewhat clouded by the silver's dullness.

Then the mask vanished from the mirror and simultaneously reappeared unblurred hanging in the air above the ivory stool. It was the mask the Mouser knew achingly well—narrow chin, high-arched cheeks, straight nose and forehead.

The pouty wine-dark lips opened a little and a soft throaty voice asked, "Does my visage displease you, man of Lankhmar?"

"You jest cruelly, O Princess," the Mouser replied, drawing on all his aplomb and sketching a courtier's bow, "for you are Beauty's self."

Slim fingers, half outlined now in pale green, dipped into the unguent jar and took up a more generous dab.

The soft throaty voice, that so well matched half the laughter he had once heard in a snowfall, now said, "You shall judge all of me."

Fafhrd woke in the dark and touched the girl beside him. As soon as he knew she was awake too, he grasped her by the hips. When he felt her body stiffen, he lifted her into the air and held her above him as he lay flat on his back.

She was wondrous light, as if made of pastry or eiderdown, yet when he laid her beside him again, her flesh felt as firm as any, though smoother than most.

"Let us have a light, Hirriwi, I beg you," he said.

"That were unwise, Faffy," she answered in a voice like a

curtain of tiny silver bells lightly brushed. "Have you forgotten that now I am wholly invisible?—which might tickle some men, yet you, I think…"

"You're right, you're right, I like you real," he answered, gripping her fiercely by the shoulders to emphasize his feelings, then guiltily jerking away his hands as he thought of how delicate she must be.

The silver bells clashed in full laughter, as if the curtain of them had been struck a great swipe. "Have no fears," she told him. "My airy bones are grown of matter stronger than steel. It is a riddle beyond your philosophers and relates to the invisibility of my race and of the animals from which it sprang. Think how strong tempered glass can be, yet light goes through it. My cursed brother Faroomfar has the strength of a bear for all his slimness while my father Oomforafor is a very lion despite his centuries. Your friend's encounter with Faroomfar was no final test—but oh how it made him howl— Father raged at him—and then there are the cousins. Soon as this night be ended—which is not soon, my dear; the moon still climbs—you must return down Stardock. Promise me that. My heart grows cold at the thought of the dangers you've already faced—and was like ice I know not how many times this last three-day."

"Yet you never warned us," he mused. "You lured me on."

"Can you doubt why?" she asked. He was feeling her snub nose then and her apple cheeks, and so he felt her smile too. "Or perhaps you resent it that I let you risk your life a little to win here to this bed?"

He implanted a fervent kiss on her wide lips to show her how little true that was, but she thrust him back after a moment.

"Wait, Faffy dear," she said. "No, wait, I say! I know you're greedy and impetuous, but you can at least wait while the moon creeps the width of a star. I asked you to promise me you would descend Stardock at dawn."

There was a rather long silence in the dark.

"Well?" she prompted. "What shuts your mouth?" she queried impatiently. "You've shown no such indecision in certain other matters. Time wastes, the moon sails."

"Hirriwi," Fafhrd said softly, "I must climb Stardock."

"Why?" she demanded ringingly. "The poem has been fulfilled. You have your reward. Go on, and only frigid fruitless perils await you. Return, and I'll guard you from the air—yes, and your companion too—to the very Waste." Her sweet voice faltered a little. "O Faffy, am I not enough to make you forego the conquest of a cruel mountain? In addition to all else, I love you—if I understand rightly how mortals use that word."

"No," he answered her solemnly in the dark. "You are wondrous, more wondrous than any wench I've known—and I love you, which is not a word I bandy—yet you only make me hotter to conquer Stardock. Can you understand that?"

Now there was silence for a while in the other direction.

"Well," she said at length, "you are masterful and will do what you will do. And I have warned you. I could tell you more, show you reasons counter, argue further, but in the end I know I would not break your stubbornness—and time gallops. We must mount our own steeds and catch up with the moon. Kiss me again. Slowly. So."

The Mouser lay across the foot of the bed under the amber globes and contemplated Keyaira, who lay lengthwise with her slender apple-green shoulders and tranquil sleeping face propped by many pillows.

He took up the corner of a sheet and moistened it with wine from a cup set against his knee and with it rubbed Keyaira's slim right ankle so gently that there was no change in her narrow bosom's slow-paced rise and fall. Presently he had cleared away all the greenish unguent from a patch as big as half his palm. He peered down at his handiwork. This time he expected surely to see flesh, or at least the green cosmetic on the underside of her ankle, but no, he saw through the irregular little rectangle he'd wiped only the bed's tufted coverlet reflecting the amber light from above. It was a most fascinating and somewhat unnerving mystery.

He glanced questioningly over at Hrissa who now lay on an end of the low table, the thin-glassed, fantastic perfume bottles standing around her, while she contemplated the occupants of the bed, her white tufted chin set on her folded paws. It seemed to the Mouser that she was looking at him with disapproval, so he hastily smoothed back unguent from other parts of Keyaira's leg until the peephole was once more greenly covered.

There was a low laugh. Keyaira, propped on her elbows now, was gazing at him through slitted heavy-lashed eyelids.

"We invisibles," she said in a humorous voice truly or feignedly heavy with sleep, "show only the outward side of any cosmetic or raiment on us. It is a mystery beyond our seers."

"You are Mystery's queenly self a-walk through the stars," the Mouser pronounced, lightly caressing her green toes. "And I the most fortunate of men. I fear it's a dream and I'll wake on Stardock's frigid ledges. How is it I am here?"

"Our race is dying out," she said. "Our men have become sterile. Hirriwi and I are the only princesses left. Our brother Faroomfar hotly wished to be our consort—he still boasts his virility—'twas he you dueled with—but our father Oomforafor said, 'It must be new blood—the blood of heroes.' So the cousins and Faroomfar, he much against his will, must fly hither and yon and leave those little rhymed lures written on ramskin in perilous, lonely spots apt to tempt heroes."

"But how can visibles and invisibles mate?" he asked.

She laughed with delight. "Is your memory *that* short, Mouse?"

"I mean, have progeny," he corrected himself, a little irked, but not much, that she had hit on his boyhood nickname. "Besides, wouldn't such offspring be cloudy, a mix of seen and unseen?"

Keyaira's green mask swung a little from side to side.

"My father thinks such mating will be fertile and that the children will breed true to invisibility—that being dominant over visibility—yet profit greatly in other ways from the admixture of hot, heroic blood."

"Then your father commanded you to mate with me?" the Mouser asked, a little disappointed.

"By no means, Mouse," she assured him. "He would be furious if he dreamt you were here, and Faroomfar would go mad. No, I took a fancy to you, as Hirriwi did to your comrade, when first I spied on you on the Waste—very fortunate that was for you, since my father would have got your seed, if you had won to Stardock's top, in quite a different fashion. Which reminds me, Mouse, you must promise me to descend Stardock at dawn."

"That is not so easy a promise to give," the Mouser said. "Fafhrd will be stubborn, I know. And then there's that other matter of a bag of diamonds, if that's what a pouch of stars means—oh, it's but a trifle, I know, compared to the embraces of a glorious girl...still..."

"But if I say I love you?—which is only truth..."

"Oh Princess," the Mouser sighed, gliding his hand to her knee. "How can I leave you at dawn? Only one night..."

"Why, Mouse," Keyaira broke in, smiling roguishly and twisting her green form a little, "do you not know that every night is an eternity? Has not any girl taught you that yet, Mouse? I am astonished. Think, we have half an eternity left us yet—which is also an eternity, as your geometer, whether white-bearded or dainty-breasted, should have taught you."

"But if I am to sire many children—" the Mouser began.

"Hirriwi and I are somewhat like queen bees," Keyaira

explained, "but think not of that. We have eternity tonight, 'tis true, but only if we make it so. Come closer."

A little later, plagiarizing himself somewhat, the Mouser said softly, "The sole fault of mountain climbing is that the best parts go so swiftly."

"They can last an eternity," Keyaira breathed in his ear. "Make them last, Mouse."

Fafhrd woke shaking with cold. The pink globes were gray and tossing in icy gusts from the open door. Snow had blown in on his clothes and gear scattered across the floor and was piled inches deep on the threshold, across which came also the only illumination—leaden daylight.

A great joy in him fought all these grim gray sights and conquered them.

Nevertheless he was naked and shivering. He sprang up and beat his clothes against the bed and thrust his limbs into their icy stiffness.

As he was buckling his ax belt, he remembered the Mouser down in the chimney, helpless. Somehow all night, even when he'd spoken to Hirriwi of the Mouser, he'd never thought of that.

He snatched up his pack and sprang out on the ledge.

From the corner of his eye he caught something moving behind him. It was the massive door closing.

A titan gust of snow-fisted wind struck him. He grabbed the rough rock pillar to which he'd last night planned to tie the rope and hugged it tight. The gods help the Mouser below! Someone came sliding and blowing along the ledge in the wind and snow and hugged the pillar lower down.

The gust passed. Fafhrd looked for the door. There was no sign of it. All the piled snow was redrifted. Keeping close hold of pillar and pack with one hand, he felt over the rough wall with the other. Fingernails no more than eyes could discover the slightest crack.

"So you got tossed out too?" a familiar voice said gaily. "*I* was tossed out by ice gnomes, I'll have you know.

"Mouser!" Fafhrd cried. "Then you weren't—? I thought—"

"You never thought of me once all night, if I know you," the Mouser said. "Keyaira assured me you were safe and somewhat more than that. Hirriwi would have told you the same of me if you'd asked her. But of course you didn't."

"Then you too—?" Fafhrd demanded, grinning with delight.

"Yes, Prince Brother-in-Law," the Mouser answered him, grinning back.

They pommeled each other around the pillar a bit—to battle chill, but in sheer high spirits too.

"Hrissa?" Fafhrd asked.

"Warm inside, the wise one. They don't put out the cat here, only the man. I wonder, though…. Do you suppose Hrissa was Keyaira's to begin with and that she foresaw and planned…" His voice trailed off.

No more gusts had come. The snowfall was so light they could see almost a league—up to the Hat above the snow-streaked ledges of the Face and down to where the Ladder faded out.

Once again their minds were filled, almost overpowered by the vastness of Stardock and by their own Predicament: two half-frozen mites precariously poised on a frozen vertical world only distantly linked with Nehwon.

To the south here was a pale silver disk in the sky—the sun. They'd been abed till noon.

"Easier to fashion an eternity out of an eighteen-hour night," the Mouser observed.

"We galloped the moon deep under the sea," Fafhrd mused.

"Your girl promise to make you go down?" the Mouser asked suddenly.

Fafhrd nodded his head. "She tried."

"Mine too. And not a bad idea. The summit smells, by her account. But the chimney looks stuffed with snow. Hold my ankles while I peer over. Yes, packed solid all the way down. So—?"

"Mouser," Fafhrd said, almost gloomily, "whether there's a way down or no, I must climb Stardock."

"You know," the Mouser answered, "I am beginning to find something in that madness myself. Besides, the east wall of Stardock may hold an easy route to that lush-looking Rift Valley. So let's do what we can with the bare seven hours of light left us. Daytime's no stuff to fashion eternities."

Mounting the ledges of the Face was both the easiest and hardest climbing they'd had yet to do. The ledges were wide, but some of them sloped outward and were footed with rotten shale that went skidding away into space at a touch, and now and again there were brief traverses which had to be done by narrow cracks and main strength, sometimes swinging by their hands alone.

And weariness and chill and even dizzying faintness came far quicker at this height. They had to halt often to drink air and chafe themselves. While in the back of one deep ledge— Stardock's right eye, they judged—they were forced to spend time firing the brazier with all the remaining resin-pellets, partly to warm food and drink, but chiefly to warm themselves.

Last night's exertions had weakened them too, they sometimes thought, but then the memories of those exertions would return to strengthen them.

And then there were the sudden treacherous wind gusts and the constant yet variable snowfall, which sometimes hid the summit and sometimes let them see it clear against the silvery sky, with the great white out-curving brim of the Hat now poised threateningly above them—a cornice like that of the snow-saddle, only now they were on the wrong side.

The illusion grew stronger that Stardock was a separate world from Nehwon in snow-filled space.

Finally the sky turned blue, and they felt the sun on their backs—they had climbed above the snowfall at last—and Fafhrd pointed at a tiny nick of blue deep in the brim of the Hat—a nick just visible above the next snow-streaked rock bulge—and he cried, "The apex of the Needle's Eye!"

At that, something dropped into a snowbank beside them, and there was a muffled clash of metal on rock, while from snow a notched and feathered arrow-end stuck straight up.

They dodged under the protective roof of a bigger bulge as a second arrow and a third clashed against the naked rock on which they'd stood.

"Gnarfi and Kranarch have beaten us, curse 'em," Fafhrd hissed, "and set an ambush for us at the Eye, the obvious spot. We must go roundabout and get above 'em."

"Won't they expect that?"

"They were fools to spring their ambush too soon. Besides, we have no other tactic."

So they began to climb south, though still upward, always keeping rock or snow between them and where they judged the Needle's Eye to be. At last, when the sun was dropping swiftly toward the western horizon, they came swinging back north again and still upward, stamping out steps now in the steepening bank of snow that reversed its curve above them to make the brim of the Hat that now roofed them ominously, covering two-thirds of the sky. They sweated and shook by turns and fought off almost continuous bouts of giddy faintness, yet still strove to move as silently and warily as they might.

At last they rounded one more snow bulge and found themselves looking down a slope at the great bare stretch of rock normally swept by the gale that came through the Needle's Eye to make the Petty Pennon.

On the outward lip of the exposed rock were two men,

both clad in suits of brown leather, much scuffed and here and there ripped, showing the inward-turned fur. Lank, black-bearded, elk-faced Kranarch stood whipping his arms against his chest for warmth. Beside him lay his strung bow and some arrows. Stocky boar-faced Gnarfi knelt peeping over the rim. Fafhrd wondered where their two brown-clad bulky servitors were.

The Mouser dug into his pouch. At the same moment Kranarch saw them and snatched up his weapon though rather more slowly than he would have in thicker air. With a similar slowness the Mouser drew out the fist-size rock he had picked up several ledges below for just such a moment as this.

Kranarch's arrow whistled between his and Fafhrd's heads. A moment later the Mouser's rock struck Kranarch full on his bow-shoulder. The weapon fell from his hand, and that arm dangled. Then Fafhrd and the Mouser charged recklessly down the snow slope, the former brandishing his unthonged ax, the latter drawing Scalpel.

Kranarch and Gnarfi received them with their own swords, and Gnarfi with a dagger in his left hand as well. The battle that followed had the same dreamlike slowness as the exchange of missiles. First Fafhrd's and the Mouser's rush gave them the advantage. Then Kranarch's and Gnarfi's great strength—or restedness, rather—told, and they almost drove their enemy off the rim. Fafhrd took a slash in the ribs which bit through his tough wolfskin tunic, slicing flesh and jarring bone.

But then skill told, as it generally will, and the two brown-clad men received wounds and suddenly turned and ran through the great white pointy-topped triangular archway of the Needle's Eye. As he ran Gnarfi screeched, "Graah! Kruk!"

"Doubtless calling for their shaggy-clad servants or bearers," the Mouser gasped in surmise, resting sword arm on knee, almost spent. "Farmerish fat country fellows those looked, hardly trained to weapons. We need not fear 'em greatly, I think, even if they come to Gnarfi's call." Fafhrd nodded, gasping himself. "Yet they climbed Stardock," he added dubiously.

Just then there came galloping through the snowy archway on their hind legs with their nails clashing the windswept rock and their fang-edged slavering red mouths open wide and their great-clawed arms widespread—two huge brown bears.

With a speed which their human opponents had been unable to sting from them, the Mouser snatched up Kranarch's bow and sent two arrows speeding, while Fafhrd swung his ax in a gleaming circle and cast it. Then the two comrades sprang swiftly to either side, the Mouser wielding Scalpel and Fafhrd drawing his knife.

But there was no need for further fighting. The Mouser's first arrow took the leading bear in the neck, his second straight in its red mouth-roof and brain, while Fafhrd's ax sank to its helve between two ribs on the trailing bear's left side. The great animals pitched forward in their blood and death throes and rolled twice over and went tumbling ponderously off the rim.

"Doubtless both shes," the Mouser remarked as he watched them fall. "Oh those bestial men of Illik-Ving! Still, to charm or train such beasts to carry packs and climb and even give up their poor lives…"

"Kranarch and Gnarfi are no sportsmen, that's for certain now," Fafhrd pronounced. "Don't praise their tricks." As he stuffed a rag into his tunic over his wound, he grimaced and swore so angrily that the Mouser didn't speak his quip: *Well, bears are only shortened bearers. I'm always right.*

Then the two comrades trudged slowly under the high tentlike arch of snow to survey the domain, highest on all Nehwon, of which they had made themselves masters—

refusing from light-headed weariness to think, in that moment of triumph, of the invisible beings who were Stardock's lords. They went warily, yet not too much so, because Gnarfi and Kranarch had run scared and were wounded not trivially—and the latter had lost his bow.

Stardock's top behind the great toppling snow wave of the Hat was almost as extensive north to south as that of Obelisk Polaris, yet the east rim looked little more than a long bowshot away. Snow with a thick crust beneath a softer layer covered it all except for the north end and stretches of the east rim, where bare dark rock showed.

The surface, both snow and rock, was flatter even than that of the Obelisk and sloped somewhat from north to south. There were no structures or beings visible, nor signs of hollows where either might hide. Truth to tell, neither the Mouser nor Fafhrd could recall ever having seen a lonelier or barer place.

The only oddity they noticed at first were three holes in the snow a little to the south, each about as big as a hogshead but having the form of an equilateral triangle and apparently going down through the snow to the rock. The three were arranged as the apex of another equilateral triangle.

The Mouser squinted around closely, then shrugged. "But a pouch of stars could be a rather small thing, I suppose," he said. "While a heart of light—no guessing its size."

The whole summit was in bluish shadow except for the northernmost end and for a great pathway of golden light from the setting sun leading from the Needle's Eye all the way across the wind-leveled snow to the east rim.

Down the center of this sunroad went Kranarch's and Gnarfi's running footsteps, the snow flecked here and there with blood. Otherwise the snow ahead was printless. Fafhrd and the Mouser followed those tracks, walking east up their long shadows.

"No sign of 'em ahead," the Mouser said. "Looks like

there is some route down the east wall, and they've taken it—at least far enough to set another ambush."

As they neared the east rim, Fafhrd said, "I see other prints making north—a spear's cast that way. Perhaps they turned."

"But where to?" the Mouser asked.

A few steps more and the mystery was solved horribly. They reached the end of the snow, and there on the dark bloodied rock, hidden until now by the wind-piled margin of the snow, sprawled the carcasses of Gnarfi and Kranarch, their middle clothes ripped away, their bodies obscenely mutilated.

Even as the Mouser's gorge rose, he remembered Keyaira's lightly-spoken words: "If you had won to Stardock's top, my father would have got your seed in quite a different fashion."

Shaking his head and glaring fiercely, Fafhrd walked around the bodies to the east rim and peered down.

He recoiled a step, then knelt and once more peered.

The Mouser's hopeful theory was prodigiously disproved. Never in his life had Fafhrd looked straight down half such a distance.

A few yards below, the east wall vanished inward. No telling how far the east rim jutted out from Stardock's heart-rock.

From this point the fall was straight to the greenish gloom of the Great Rift Valley— five Lankhmar leagues, at least. Perhaps more.

He heard the Mouser say over his shoulder, "A path for birds or suicides. Naught else."

Suddenly the green below grew bright, though without showing the slightest feature except for a silvery hair, which might be a great river, running down its center. Looking up again, they saw that the sky had gone all golden with a mighty afterglow. They faced around and gasped in wonder.

The last sunrays coming through the Needle's Eye, swinging southward and a little up, glancingly illuminated a transparent, solid symmetric shape big as the biggest oak tree and resting exactly over the three triangular holes in the snow. It might only be described as a sharp-edged solid star of about eighteen points, resting by three of those on Stardock and built of purest diamond or some like substance.

Both had the same thought: that this must be a star the gods had failed to launch. The sunlight had touched the fire in its heart and made it shine, but for a moment only and feebly, not incandescently and forever, as it would have in the sky.

A piercingly shrill, silvery trumpet call broke the silence of the summit.

They swung their gaze north. Outlined by the same deep golden sunlight, ghostlier than the star, yet still clearly to be seen in some of its parts against the yellow sky, a tall slender castle lifted transparent walls and towers from the stony end of the summit. Its topmost spires seemed to go out of sight upward rather than end.

Another sound then—a wailing snarl. A pale animal bounded toward them across the snow from the northwest. Leaping aside with another snarl from the sprawled bodies, Hrissa rushed past them south with a third snarl tossed at them.

Almost too late they saw the peril against which she had tried to warn them.

Advancing toward them from west and north across the unmarked snow were a score of sets of footprints. There were no feet in those prints, nor bodies above them, yet they came on—right print, left print, appearing in succession—and ever more rapidly. And now they saw what they had missed at first because viewed end-on above each paired set of prints— a narrow-shafted, narrow-bladed spear, pointed straight toward them, coming on as swiftly as the prints.

They ran south with Hrissa, Fafhrd in the lead. After a

half dozen sprinting steps the Northerner heard a cry behind him. He stopped and then swiftly spun around.

The Mouser had slipped in the blood of their late foes and fallen. When he got to his feet, the gray spear points were around him on all sides save the rim. He made two wild defensive slashes with Scalpel, but the gray spear points came in relentlessly. Now they were in a close semicircle around him and hardly a span apart, and he was standing on the rim. They advanced another thrust, and the Mouser perforce sprang back from them—and down he fell.

There was a rushing sound, and chill air sluiced Fafhrd from behind, and something sleekly hairy brushed his calves. As he braced himself to rush forward with his knife and slay an invisible or two for his friend, slender unseen arms clasped him from behind and he heard Hirriwi's silvery voice say in his ear, "Trust us," and a coppery-golden sister voice say, "We'll after him," and then he found himself pulled down onto a great invisible pulsing shaggy bed three spans above the snow, and they told him "Cling!" and he clung to the long thick unseen hair, and then suddenly the living bed shot forward across the snow and off the rim and there tilted vertically so his feet pointed at the sky and his face at the Great Rift Valley— and then the bed plunged straight down.

The thin air roared past, and his beard and mane were whipped back by the speed of that plunge, but he tightened his grip on the handfuls of invisible hair, and a slender arm pressed him down from either side, so that he felt through the fur the throbbing heartbeat of the great invisible carpetlike creature they rode. And he became aware that somehow Hrissa had got under his arm, for there was the small feline face beside his, with slitted eyes and with beard-tuft and ears blown back. And he felt the two invisible girls' bodies alongside his.

He realized that mortal eyes, could such have watched, would have seen only a large man clasping a large white cat and falling headfirst through empty space—but he would be falling much faster than any man should fall, even from such a vast height.

Beside him Hirriwi laughed, as if she had caught his thought, but then that laughter broke off suddenly and the roaring of the wind died almost to utter silence. He guessed it was because the swiftly thickening air had deafened him.

The great dark cliffs flashing upward a dozen yards away were a blur. Yet below him the Great Rift Valley was still featureless green—no, the larger details were beginning to show now: forests and glades and curling hair-thin streams and little lakes like dewdrops.

Between him and the green below he saw a dark speck. It grew in size. It was the Mouser!—rather characteristically falling headfirst, straight as an arrow, with hands locked ahead of him and legs pressed together behind, probably in the faint hope that he might hit deep water.

The creature they rode matched the Mouser's speed and then gradually swung its plunge toward him, flattening out more and more from the vertical, so that the Mouser was pressed against them. Arms visible and invisible clasped him then, pulling him closer, so that all five of the plungers were crowded together on that one great sentient bed.

The creature's dive flattened still more then, halting its fall—there was a long moment while they were all pressed stomach-surgingly tight against the hairy back, while the trees still rushed up at them—and then they were coasting above those same treetops and spiraling down into a large glade.

What happened next to Fafhrd and the Mouser went all in a great tumbling rush, much too swiftly: the feel of springy turf under their feet and balmy air sluicing their bodies, quick kisses exchanged, laughing, shouted congratulations that still sounded all muffled like ghost voices, something hard and irregular yet soft-covered pressed into the Mouser's hands, a last kiss—and then Hirriwi and Keyaira had broken away and a great burst of air flattened the grass and the great invisible flier was gone and the girls with it.

They could watch its upward spiraling flight for a little, however, because Hrissa had gone away on it too. The ice-cat seemed to be peering down at them in farewell. Then she too vanished as the golden afterglow swiftly died in the darkening sky overhead.

They stood leaning together for support in the twilight. Then they straightened themselves, yawning prodigiously, and their hearing came back. They heard the gurgling of a brook and the twittering of birds and a small, faint rustle of dry leaves going away from them and the tiny buzz of a spiraling gnat.

The Mouser opened the invisible pouch in his hands.

"The gems seem to be invisible too," he said, "though I can feel 'em well enough. We'll have a hard time selling them—unless we can find a blind jeweler."

The darkness deepened. Tiny cold fires began to glow in his palms: ruby, emerald, sapphire, amethyst, and pure white.

"No, by Issek!" the Gray Mouser said. "We'll only need to sell them by night—which is unquestionably the best time for trade in gems."

The new-risen moon, herself invisible beyond the lesser mountains walling the Rift Valley to the east, painted palely now the upper half of the great slender column of Stardock's east wall.

Gazing up at that queenly sight, Fafhrd said, "Gallant ladies, all four."

FRITZ LEIBER'S
LANKhMAR

The TWO BEST Thieves
IN LANKhMAR

III

Through the Mazy avenues and alleys of the great city of Lankhmar, Night was a-slink, though not yet grown tall enough to whirl her black star-studded cloak across the sky, which still showed pale, towering wraiths of sunset.

The hawkers of drugs and strong drinks forbidden by day had not yet taken up their bell-tinklings and thin, enticing cries. The pleasure girls had not lit their red lanterns and sauntered insolently forth. Bravos, desperadoes, procurers, spies, pimps, conmen, and other malfeasors yawned and rubbed drowsy sleep from eyes yet thick-lidded. In fact, most of the Night People were still at breakfast, while most of the Day People were at supper. Which made for an emptiness and hush in the streets, suitable to Night's slippered tread. And which created a large bare stretch of dark, thick, unpierced wall at the intersection of Silver Street with the Street of the Gods, a crossing-point where there habitually foregathered the junior executives and star operatives of the Thieves Guild; also meeting there were the few freelance thieves bold and resourceful enough to defy the Guild and the few thieves of aristocratic birth, sometimes most brilliant amateurs, whom the Guild tolerated and even toadied to, on account of their noble ancestry, which dignified a very old but most disreputable profession.

Midway along the bare stretch of wall, where none might conceivably overhear, a very tall and a somewhat short thief drifted together. After a while they began to converse in prison-yard whispers.

A distance had grown between Fafhrd and the Gray Mouser during their long and uneventful trek south from the Great Rift Valley. It was due simply to too much of each other and to an ever more bickering disagreement as to how the invisible jewels, gift of Hirriwi and Keyaira, might most advantageously be disposed of — a dispute which had finally grown so acrimonious that they had divided the jewels, each carrying his share. When they finally reached Lankhmar, they had lodged apart and each made his own contact with jeweler, fence or private buyer. This separation had made their relationship quite scratchy, but in no way diminished their absolute trust in each other.

"Greetings, Little Man," Fafhrd prison-growled. "So you've come to sell your share to Ogo the Blind, or at least give him a viewing? — if such expression may be used of a sightless man."

"How did you know that?" the Mouser whispered sharply.

"It was the obvious thing to do," Fafhrd answered somewhat condescendingly. "Sell the jewels to a dealer who could note neither their night-glow nor daytime invisibility. A dealer who must judge them by weight, feel, and what they can scratch or be scratched by. Besides, we stand just across from the door to Ogo's den. It's very well guarded, by the by — at fewest, ten Mingol swordsmen."

"At least give me credit for such trifles of common knowledge," the Mouser answered sardonically. "Well, you guessed right; it appears that by long association with me you've gained some knowledge of how my wit works, though I doubt that it's sharpened your own a whit. Yes, I've already had one conference with Ogo, and tonight we conclude the deal."

Fafhrd asked equably, "Is it true that Ogo conducts all his interviews in pitchy dark?"

"Ho! So there are some few things you admit not knowing! Yes, it's quite true, which makes any interview with Ogo risky work. By insisting on absolute darkness, Ogo the Blind cancels at a stroke the interviewer's advantage — indeed, the advantage passes to Ogo, since he is used by a lifetime of it to utter darkness — a long lifetime, since he's an ancient one, to judge by his speech. Nay, Ogo knows not what darkness is, since it's all he's ever known. However, I've a device to trick him there if need be. In my thick, tightly drawstringed pouch I carry fragments of brightest glow-wood, and can spill them out in a trice."

Fafhrd nodded admiringly and then asked, "And what's in that flat case you carry so tightly under your elbow? An elaborate false history of each of the jewels embossed in ancient parchment for Ogo's fingers to read?"

"There your guess fails! No, it's the jewels themselves, guarded in clever wise so that they cannot be filched. Here, take a peek." And after glancing quickly to either side and overhead, the Mouser opened the case a handbreadth on its hinges.

Fafhrd saw the rainbow-twinkling jewels firmly affixed in artistic pattern to a bed of black velvet, but all closely covered by an inner top consisting of a mesh of stout iron wire.

The Mouser clapped the case shut. "On our first meeting, I took two of the smallest of the jewels from their spots in the box and let Ogo feel and otherwise test them. He may dream of filching them all, but my box and the mesh thwart that."

"Unless he steals from you the box itself," Fafhrd agreed. "As for myself, I keep my share of the jewels chained to me."

And after such precautionary glances as the Mouser had made, he thrust back his loose left sleeve, showing a stout browned-iron bracelet snapped around his wrist. From the bracelet hung a short chain which both supported and kept tightly shut a small, bulging pouch. The leather of the pouch was everywhere sewed across with fine brown wire. He unclicked the bracelet, which opened on a hinge, then clicked it fast again.

"The browned-iron wire's to foil any cutpurse," Fafhrd explained offhandedly, pulling down his sleeve.

The Mouser's eyebrows rose. Then his gaze followed them as it went from Fafhrd's wrist to his face, while the small man's expression changed from mild approval to bland inquiry. He asked, "And you trust such devices to guard your half of the gems from Nemia of the Dusk?"

"How did you know my dealings were with Nemia?" Fafhrd asked in tones just the slightest surprised.

"Because she's Lankhmar's only woman fence, of course. All know you favor women when possible, in business as well as erotic matters. Which is one of your greatest failings, if I may say so. Also, Nemia's door lies next to Ogo's, though that's a trivial clue. You know, I presume, that seven Kleshite stranglers protect her somewhat overripe person? Well, at least then you know the sort of trap you're rushing into. Deal with a woman! — surest route to disaster. By the by, you mentioned 'dealings.' Does that plural mean this is not your first interview with her?"

Fafhrd nodded. "As you with Ogo.... Incidentally, am I to understand that you trust men simply because they're men? That were a greater failing than the one you impute to me. Anyhow, as you with Ogo, I go to Nemia of the Dusk a second time, to complete our deal. The first time I showed her the gems in a twilit chamber, where they appeared to greatest advantage, twinkling just enough to seem utterly real. Did you know, in passing, that she always works in twilight or soft gloom? — which accounts for the second half of her name. At all events, as soon as she glimpsed them, Nemia greatly desired the gems — her breath actually caught in her throat — and she agreed at once to my price, which is not low, as basis for further bargaining. However, it happens that she invariably follows the rule — which I myself consider a sound one — of never completing a transaction of any sort with a member of the opposite sex without first testing them in amorous commerce. Hence this second meeting. If the member be old or otherwise ugly, Nemia deputes the task to one of her maids, but in my case, of course..." Fafhrd coughed modestly. "One more point I'd like to make: 'overripe' is the wrong expression. 'Full-bloomed' or 'the acme of maturity' is what you're looking for."

"Believe me, I'm sure Nemia is in fullest bloom — a late August flower. Such women always prefer twilight for the display of their 'perfectly matured' charms," the Mouser answered somewhat stifledly. He had for some time been hard put to restrain laughter, and now it appeared in quiet little bursts as he said, "Oh, you great fool! And you've actually agreed to go to bed with her? And expect not to be parted from your jewels (including family jewels?), let alone not strangled, while at that disadvantage? Oh, this is worse than I thought."

"I'm not always at such a disadvantage in bed as some people may think," Fafhrd answered with quiet modesty. "With me, amorous play sharpens instead of dulls the senses. I trust you have as much luck with a man in ebon darkness as I with a woman in soft gloom. Incidentally, why must you have two conferences with Ogo? Not Nemia's reason, surely?"

The Mouser's grin faded and he lightly bit his lip. With elaborate casualness he said, "Oh, the jewels must be inspected by the Eyes of Ogo — *his* invariable rule. But whatever test is tried, I'm prepared to out-trick it."

Fafhrd pondered, then asked, "And what, or who are, or is, the Eyes of Ogo? Does he keep a pair of them in his pouch?"

"Is," the Mouser said. Then with even more elaborate casualness, "Oh, some chit of a girl, I believe. Supposed to have an intuitive faculty where gems are concerned. Interesting, isn't it, that a man as clever as Ogo should believe such superstitious nonsense? Or depend on the soft sex in any fashion. Truly, a mere formality."

"'Chit of a girl,'" Fafhrd mused, nodding his head again and yet again and yet again. "That describes to a red dot on each of her immature nipples the sort of female you've come to favor in recent years. But of course the amorous is not at all involved in this deal of yours, I'm sure," he added, rather too solemnly.

"In no way whatever," the Mouser replied, rather too sharply. Looking around, he remarked, "We're getting a bit of company, despite the early hour. There's Dickon of the Thieves Guild, that old pen-pusher and drawer of the floor plans of houses to be robbed — I don't believe he's actually worked on a job since the Year of the Snake. And there's fat

Grom, their subtreasurer, another armchair thief. Who comes so dramatically a-slither? — by the Black Bones, it's Snarve, our overlord Glipkerio's nephew! Who's that he speaks to? — oh, only Tork the Cutpurse."

"And there now appears," Fafhrd took up, "Vlek, said to be the Guild's star operative these days. Note his smirk and hear how his shoes creak faintly. And there's that gray-eyed, black-haired amateur, Alyx the Picklock — well, at least her boots don't squeak, and I rather admire her courage in adventuring here, where the Guild's animosity toward freelance females is as ill a byword as that of the Pimps Guild. And, just now turning from the Street of the Gods, who have we but Countess Kronia of the Seventy-seven Secret Pockets, who steals by madness, not method. There's one bone-bag I'd never trust, despite her emaciated charms and the weakness you lay to me."

Nodding, the Mouser pronounced, "And such as these are called the aristocracy of thiefdom! In all honesty I must say that notwithstanding your weaknesses — which I'm glad you admit — one of the two best thieves in Lankhmar now stands beside me. While the other, needless to say, occupies my ratskin boots."

Fafhrd nodded back, though carefully crossing two fingers.

Stilling a yawn, the Mouser said, "By the by, have you yet any thought about what you'll be doing after those gems are stolen from your wrist, or — though unlikely — sold and paid for? I've been approached about — or at any rate been considering a wander toward — in the general direction of the Eastern Lands."

"Where it's hotter even than in this sultry Lankhmar? Such a stroll hardly appeals to me," Fafhrd replied, then casually added, "In any case, I've been thinking of taking ship — er — northward."

"Toward that abominable Cold Waste once more? No, thank you!" the Mouser answered. Then, glancing south along Silver Street, where a pale star shone close to the horizon, he went on still more briskly, "Well, it's time for my interview with Ogo — and his silly girl Eyes. Take your sword to bed with you, I advise, and look to it that neither Graywand nor your more vital blade are filched from you in Nemia's dusk."

"Oh, so first twinkle of the Whale Star is the time set for your appointment too?" Fafhrd remarked, himself stirring from the wall. "Tell me, is the true appearance of Ogo known to anyone? Somehow the name makes me think of a fat, old, and overlarge spider."

"Curb your imagination, if you please," the Mouser answered sharply. "Or keep it for your own business, where I'll remind you that the only dangerous spider is the female. No, Ogo's true appearance is unknown. But perhaps tonight I'll discover it!"

"I'd like you to ponder that your besetting fault is overcuriosity," said Fafhrd, "and that you can't trust even the stupidest girl to be always silly."

The Mouser turned impulsively and said, "However tonight's interviews fall out, let's rendezvous after. The Silver Eel?"

Fafhrd nodded, and they gripped hands together. Then each rogue sauntered toward his fateful door.

The Mouser crouched a little, every sense a-quiver, in space utterly dark. On a surface before him — a table, he had felt it out to be — lay his jewel box, closed. His left hand touched the box. His right gripped Cat's Claw and with that weapon nervously threatened the inky darkness all around.

A voice which was at once dry and thick croaked from behind him, "Open the box!"

The Mouser's skin crawled at the horror of that voice. Nevertheless, he complied with the direction. The rainbow light of the meshed jewels spilled upward, dimly showing the room to be low-ceilinged and rather large. It appeared to be empty except for the table and, indistinct in the far left corner behind him, a dark low shape which the Mouser did not like. It might be a hassock or a fat, round, black pillow. Or it might be... The Mouser wished Fafhrd hadn't made his last suggestion.

From ahead of him a rippling, silvery voice quite unlike the first called, "Your jewels, like no others I have ever seen, gleam in the absence of all light."

Scanning piercingly across the table and box, the Mouser could see no sign of the second caller. Evening out his own voice, so it was not breathy with apprehension, but bland with confidence, he said, to the emptiness, "My gems are like no others in the world. In fact, they come not from the world, being of the same substance as the stars. Yet you know by your test that one of them is harder than diamond."

"They are truly unearthly and most beautiful jewels," the sourless silvery voice answered. "My mind pierces them through and through, and they are what you say they are. I shall advise Ogo to pay your asking price."

At that instant the Mouser heard behind him a little cough and a dry, rapid scuttling. He whirled around, dirk poised to strike. There was nothing to be seen or sensed, except for the hassock or whatever, which had not moved. The scuttling was no longer to be heard.

He swiftly turned back, and there across the table from him, her front illumined by the twinkling jewels, stood a slim naked girl with pale straight hair, somewhat darker skin, and overlarge eyes staring entrancedly from a child's tiny-chinned, pouty-lipped face.

Satisfying himself by a rapid glance that the jewels were in their proper pattern under their mesh and none missing, he swiftly advanced Cat's Claw so that its needle point touched the taut skin between the small yet jutting breasts.

"Do not seek to startle me so again!" he hissed. "Men — aye, and girls — have died for less."

The girl did not stir by so much as the breadth of a fine hair; neither did her expression nor her dreamy yet concentrated gaze change, except that her short lips smiled, then parted to say honey-voiced, "So you are the Gray Mouser. I had expected a crouchy, sear-faced rogue, and I find...a prince." The very jewels seemed to twinkle more wildly because of her sweet voice and sweeter presence, striking opalescent glimmers from her pale irises.

"Neither seek to flatter me!" the Mouser commanded, catching up his box and holding it open against his side. "I am inured, I'll have you know, to the ensorcelments of all the world's minxes and nymphs."

"I speak truth only, as I did of your jewels," she answered guilelessly. Her lips had stayed parted a little, and she spoke without moving them.

"Are you the Eyes of Ogo?" the Mouser demanded harshly, yet drawing Cat's Claw back from her bosom. It bothered him a little, yet only a little, that the tiniest stream of blood, like a black thread, led down for a few inches from the prick his dirk had made.

Utterly unmindful of the tiny wound, the girl nodded. "And I can see through you, as through your jewels, and I discover naught in you but what is noble and fine, save for certain small subtle impulses of violence and cruelty, which a girl like myself might find delightful."

"There your all-piercing eyes err wholly, for I am a great villain," the Mouser answered scornfully, though he felt a pulse of fond satisfaction within him.

The girl's eyes widened as she looked over his shoulder somewhat apprehensively, and from behind the Mouser the dry and thick voice croaked once more, "Keep to business! Yes, I will pay you in gold your offering price, a sum it will take me some hours to assemble. Return at the same time tomorrow night and we will close the deal. Now shut the box."

The Mouser had turned around, still clutching his box, when Ogo began to speak. Again he could not distinguish the source of the voice, though he scanned minutely. It seemed to come from the whole wall.

Now he turned back. Somewhat to his disappointment, the naked girl had vanished. He peered under the table, but there was nothing there. Doubtless some trapdoor or hypnotic device…

Still suspicious as a snake, he returned the way he had come. On close approach, the black hassock appeared to be only that. Then as the door to the outside slid open noiselessly, he swiftly obeyed Ogo's last injunction, snapping shut the box, and departed.

Fafhrd gazed tenderly at Nemia lying beside him in perfumed twilight, while keeping the edge of his vision on his brawny wrist and the pouch pendant from it, both of which his companion was now idly fondling.

To do Nemia justice, even at the risk of imputing a certain cattiness to the Mouser, her charms were neither overblown, nor even ample, but only…sufficient.

From just behind Fafhrd's shoulder came a spitting hiss. He quickly turned his head and found himself looking into the crossed blue eyes of a white cat standing on the small bedside table beside a bowl of bronze chrysanthemums.

"Ixy!" Nemia called remonstratingly yet languorously.

Despite her voice, Fafhrd heard behind him, in rapid succession, the click of a bracelet opening and the slightly louder click of one closing.

He turned back instantly, to discover only that Nemia had meanwhile clasped on his wrist, beside the browned-iron bracelet, a golden one around which sapphires and rubies marched alternately in single file.

Gazing at him from betwixt the strands of her long dark hair, she said huskily, "It is only a small token which I give to those who please me...greatly."

Fafhrd drew his wrist closer to his eyes to admire his prize, but mostly to palpate his pouch with the fingers of his other hand, to assure himself that it bulged as tightly as ever.

It did, and in a burst of generous feeling he said, "Let me give you one of my gems in precisely the same spirit," and made to undo his pouch.

Nemia's long-fingered hand glided out to prevent. "No," she breathed. "Let never the gems of business be mixed with the jewels of pleasure. Now if you should choose to bring me some small gift tomorrow night, when at the same hour we exchange your jewels for my gold and my letters of credit on Glipkerio, underwritten by Hisvin the Grain Merchant..."

"Right," Fafhrd said briefly, concealing the relief he felt. He'd been an idiot to think of giving Nemia one of the gems — and with it a day's opportunity to discover its abnormalities.

"Until tomorrow," Nemia said, opening her arms to him.

"Until tomorrow, then," Fafhrd agreed, embracing her fervently, yet keeping his pouch clutched in the hand to which it was chained — and already eager to be gone.

The Silver Eel was far less than half filled, its candles few, its cupbearers torpid, as Fafhrd and the Gray Mouser entered simultaneously by different doors and made for one of the many empty booths.

The only eye to watch them at all closely was a gray one above a narrow section of pale cheek bordered by dark hair, peering past the curtain of the backmost booth.

When their thick table-candles had been lit and cups set before them and a jug of fortified wine, and fresh charcoal tumbled into the red-seeded brazier at table's end, the Mouser placed his flat box on the table and, grinning, said, "All's set. The jewels passed the test of the Eyes — a toothsome wenchlet; more of her later. I get the cash tomorrow night — all my offering price! But you, friend, I hardly thought to see you back alive. Drink we up! I take it you escaped from Nemia's divan whole and sound in organs and limbs — as far as you yet know. But the jewels?"

"They came through too," Fafhrd answered, swinging the pouch lightly out of his sleeve and then back in again. "And I get my money tomorrow night…the full amount of my asking price, just like you."

As he named those coincidences, his eyes went thoughtful.

They stayed that way while he took two large swallows of wine. The Mouser watched him curiously.

"At one point," Fafhrd finally mused, "I thought she was trying the old trick of substituting for mine an identical but worthlessly filled pouch. Since she'd seen the pouch at our first meeting, she could have had a similar one made up, complete with chain and bracelet."

"But was she—?" the Mouser asked.

"Oh no, it turned out to be something entirely different," Fafhrd said lightly, though some thought kept two slight vertical furrows in his forehead. "That's odd," the Mouser remarked. "At one point — just one, mind you — the Eyes of Ogo, if she'd been extremely swift, deft, and silent, might have been able to switch boxes on me."

Fafhrd lifted his eyebrows.

The Mouser went on rapidly, "That is, if my box had been closed. But it was open, in darkness, and there'd have been no way to reproduce the varicolored twinkling of the gems. Phosphorus or glow-wood? Too dim. Hot coals? No, I'd have felt the heat. Besides, how get that way a diamond's pure white glow? Quite impossible."

Fafhrd nodded agreement but continued to gaze over the Mouser's shoulder.

The Mouser started to reach toward his box, but instead

with a small self-contemptuous chuckle picked up the jug and began to pour himself another drink in a careful small stream.

Fafhrd shrugged at last, used the back of his fingers to push over his own pewter cup for a refill, and yawned mightily, leaning back a little and at the same time pushing his spread-fingered hands to either side across the table, as if pushing away from him all small doubts and wonderings.

The fingers of his left hand touched the Mouser's box.

His face went blank. He looked down his arm at the box.

Then to the great puzzlement of the Mouser, who had just begun to fill Fafhrd's cup, the Northerner leaned forward and placed his head ear-down on the box.

"Mouser," he said in a small voice, "your box is buzzing."

Fafhrd's cup was full, but the Mouser kept on pouring.

Heavily fragrant wine puddled and began to run toward the glowing brazier.

"When I touched the box, I felt vibration," Fafhrd went on bemusedly. "It's buzzing. It's still buzzing."

With a low snarl, the Mouser slammed down the jug and snatched the box from under Fafhrd's ear. The wine reached the brazier's hot bottom and hissed. He tore the box open, opened also its mesh top, and he and Fafhrd peered in.

The candlelight dammed, but by no means extinguished the yellow, violet, reddish, and white twinkling glows rising from various points on the black velvet bottom.

But the candlelight was quite bright enough also to show, at each such point, matching the colors listed, a firebeetle, glowwasp, nightbee, or diamondfly, each insect alive but delicately affixed to the floor of the box with fine silver wire. From time to time the wings or wingcases of some buzzed.

Without hesitation, Fafhrd unclasped the browned-iron bracelet from his wrist, unchained the pouch, and dumped it on the table.

Jewels of various sizes, all beautifully cut, made a fair heap.

But they were all dead black.

Fafhrd picked up a big one, tried it with his fingernail, then whipped out his hunting knife and with its edge easily scored the gem.

He carefully dropped it in the brazier's glowing center. After a bit it flamed up yellow and blue.

"Coal," Fafhrd said.

The Mouser clawed his hands over his faintly twinkling box, as if about to pick it up and hurl it through the wall and across the Inner Sea.

Instead he unclawed his hands and hung them decorously at his sides.

"I am going away," he announced quietly, but very clearly, and did so.

Fafhrd did not look up. He was dropping a second black gem in the brazier.

He did take off the bracelet Nemia had given him; he brought it close to his eyes, said, "Brass...glass," and spread his fingers to let it drop in the spilled wine. After the Mouser was gone, Fafhrd drained his brimming cup, drained the Mouser's and filled it again, then went on supping from it as he continued to drop the black jewels one by one in the brazier.

Nemia and the Eyes of Ogo sat cozily side by side on a luxurious divan. They had put on negligees. A few candles made a yellowish dusk.

On a low, gleaming table were set delicate flagons of wines and liqueurs, slim-stemmed crystal goblets, golden plates of sweetmeats and savories, and in the center two equal heaps of rainbow-glowing gems.

"What a quaint bore barbarians are," Nemia remarked, delicately stifling a yawn, "though good for one's sensuous self, once in a great while. This one had a little more brains than most. I think he might have caught on, except that I made the two clicks come so exactly together when I snapped back on his wrist the bracelet with the false pouch and at the same time my brass keepsake. It's amazing how barbarians are hypnotized by brass along with any odd bits of glass colored like rubies and sapphires — I think the three primary colors paralyze their primitive brains."

"Clever, *clever* Nemia," the Eyes of Ogo cooed with a tender caress. "My little fellow almost caught on too when I made the switch, but then he got interested in threatening me with his knife. Actually jabbed me between the breasts. I think he has a dirty mind."

"Let me kiss the blood away, darling Eyes," Nemia suggested. "Oh, dreadful...dreadful."

While shivering under her treatment — Nemia had a slightly bristly tongue — Eyes said, "For some reason he was quite nervous about Ogo." She made her face blank, her pouty mouth hanging slightly open.

The richly draped wall opposite her made a scuttling sound and then croaked in a dry, thick voice, "Open your box, Gray Mouser. Now close it. Girls, girls! Cease your lascivious play!"

Nemia and Eyes clung to each other laughing. Eyes said in her natural voice, if she had one, "And he went away still thinking there was a real Ogo. I'm quite certain of that. My, they both must be in a froth by now."

Sitting back, Nemia said, "I suppose we'll have to take some special precautions against their raiding us to get their jewels back."

Eyes shrugged. "I have my five Mingol swordsmen."

Nemia said. "And I have my three and a half Kleshite stranglers."

"Half?" Eyes asked.

"I was counting Ixy. No, but seriously."

Eyes frowned for half a heartbeat, then shook her head

decisively. "I don't think we need worry about Fafhrd and the Gray Mouser raiding us back. Because we're girls, their pride will be hurt, and they'll sulk a while and then run away to the ends of the earth on one of those adventures of theirs."

"Adventures!" said Nemia, as one who says, "Cesspools and privies!"

"You see, they're really weaklings," Eyes went on, warming to her topic. "They have no drive whatever, no ambition, no true passion for money. For instance, if they did — and if they didn't spend so much time in dismal spots away from Lankhmar — they'd have known that the King of Ilthmar has developed a mania for gems that are invisible by day, but glow by night, and has offered half his kingdom for a sack of star-jewels. And then they'd never have had even to consider such an idiotic thing as coming to us."

"What do you suppose he'll do with them? The King, I mean."

Eyes shrugged. "I don't know. Build a planetarium. Or eat them." She thought a moment. "All things considered, it might be as well if we got away from here for a few weeks. We deserve a vacation."

Nemia nodded, closing her eyes. "It should be absolutely the opposite sort of place to the one in which the Mouser and Fafhrd will have their next — ugh! — adventure."

Eyes nodded too and said dreamily, "Blue skies and rippling water, spotless beach, a tepid wind, flowers and slim slavegirls everywhere…"

Nemia said, "I've always wished for a place that has no weather, only perfection. Do you know which half of Ilthmar's kingdom has the least weather?"

"Precious Nemia," Eyes murmured, "you're so civilized. And so very, very clever. Next to one other, you're certainly the best thief in Lankhmar."

"Who's the other?" Nemia was eager to know.

"Myself, of course," Eyes answered modestly.

Nemia reached up and tweaked her companion's ear — not too painfully, but enough.

"If there were the least money depending on that," she said quietly but firmly, "I'd teach you differently. But since it's only conversation…"

"Dearest Nemia."

"Sweetest Eyes."

The two girls gently embraced and kissed each other fondly.

The Mouser glared thin-lipped across a table in a curtained booth in the Golden Lamprey, a tavern not unlike the Silver Eel.

He rapped the teak before him with his fingertip, and the perfumed stale air with his voice, saying, "Double those twenty gold pieces and I'll make the trip and hear Prince Gwaay's proposal."

The very pale man opposite him, who squinted as if even the candlelight were a glare, answered softly, "Twenty-five — and you serve him for one day after arrival."

"What sort of ass do you take me for?" the Mouser demanded dangerously. "I might be able to settle all his troubles in one day — I usually can — and what then? No, no preagreed service; I hear his proposal only. And…thirty-five gold pieces in advance."

"Very well, thirty gold pieces — twenty to be refunded if you refuse to serve my master, which would be a risky step, I warn you."

"Risk is my bedmate," the Mouser snapped. "Ten only to be refunded."

The other nodded and began slowly to count rilks onto the teak. "Ten *now*," he said. "Ten when you join our caravan tomorrow morning at the Grain Gate. And ten when we reach Quarmall."

"When we first glimpse the spires of Quarmall," the Mouser insisted.

The other nodded.

The Mouser moodily snatched the golden coins and stood up. They felt very few in his fist. For a moment he thought of returning to Fafhrd and with him devising plans against Ogo and Nemia.

No, never! He realized he couldn't in his misery and self-rage bear the thought of even looking at Fafhrd.

Besides, the Northerner would certainly be drunk.

And two, or at most three, rilks would buy him certain tolerable and even interesting pleasures to fill the hours before dawn brought him release from this hateful city.

Fafhrd was indeed drunk, being on his third jug. He had burnt up all the black jewels and was now with the greatest delicacy and most careful use of the needle point of his knife, releasing unharmed each of the silver-wired firebeetles, glowwasps, nightbees, and diamondflies. They buzzed about erratically.

Two cupbearers and the chucker-out had come to protest, and now Slevyas himself joined them, rubbing the back of his thick neck. He had been stung and a customer too. Fafhrd had himself been stung twice, but hadn't seemed to notice. Nor did he now pay the slightest attention to the four haranguing him.

The last nightbee was released. It careened off noisily past Slevyas' neck, who dodged his head with a curse. Fafhrd sat back, suddenly looking very wretched. With varying shrugs the master of the Silver Eel and his three servitors made off, one cupbearer making swipes at the air.

Fafhrd tossed up his knife. It came down almost point first, but didn't quite stick in the teak. He laboriously scabbarded it, then forced himself to take a small sip of wine.

As if someone were about to emerge from the backmost booth, there was a stirring of its heavy curtains, which like all the others had stitched to them heavy chain and squares of metal, so that one guest couldn't stab another through them, except with luck and the slimmest stilettos.

But at that moment a very pale man, who held up his cloak to shield his eyes from the candlelight, entered by the side door and made to Fafhrd's table.

"I've come for my answer, Northerner," he said in a voice soft yet sinister. He glanced at the toppled jugs and spilled wine. "That is, if you remember my proposition."

"Sit down," Fafhrd said. "Have a drink. Watch out for the glowwasps — they're vicious." Then, scornfully, "Remember! Prince Hasjarl of Marquall — Quarmall. Passage by ship. A mountain of gold rilks. Remember!"

Keeping on his feet, the other amended, "Twenty-five rilks. Provided you take ship with me at once and promise to render a day's service to my prince. Thereafter by what further agreement you and he arrive at."

He placed on the table a small golden tower of precounted coins.

"Munificent!" Fafhrd said, grabbing it up and reeling to his feet. He placed five of the coins on the table and shoved the rest in his pouch, except for three more, which scattered dulcetly across the floor. He corked and pouched the third wine jug. Coming out from behind the table, he said, "Lead the way, comrade," gave the squinty-eyed man a mighty shove toward the side door, and went weaving after him.

In the backmost booth, Alyx the Picklock pursed her lips and shook her head disapprovingly.

FRITZ LEIBER'S
LANKHMAR

THE LORDS OF
QUARMALL

IV

The room was dim, almost maddeningly dim to one who loved sharp detail and the burning sun. The few wall-set torches that provided the sole illumination flamed palely and thinly, more like will-o'-the-wisps than true fire, although they released a pleasant incense. One got the feeling that the dwellers of this region resented light and only tolerated a thin mist of it for the benefit of strangers.

Despite its vast size, the room was carved all in somber solid rock—smooth floor, polished curving walls, and domed ceiling—either a natural cave finished by man or else chipped out and burnished entirely by human effort, although the thought of that latter amount of work was nearly intolerable. From numerous deep niches between the torches, metal statuettes and masks and jeweled objects gleamed darkly.

Through the room, bending the feeble bluish flames, came a perpetual cool draft bringing acid odors of damp ground and moist rock which the sweet spicy scent of the torches never quite masked.

The only sounds were the occasional rutch of rock on wood from the other end of the long table, where a game was being played with black and white stone counters—that and, from beyond the room, the ponderous sighing of the great fans that sucked down the fresh air on its last stage of passage from the distant world above and drove it through this region…and the perpetual soft thudding of the naked feet of the slaves on the heavy leather tread-belts that drove those great wooden fans…and the very faint mechanic gasping of those slaves.

After one had been in this region for a few days, or only a few hours, the sighing of the fans and the soft thudding of the feet and the faint gaspings of the tortured lungs seemed to drone out only the name of this region, over and over.

"Quarmall…" they seemed to chant. "Quarmall…Quarmall is all…"

The Gray Mouser, upon whose senses and through whose mind these sensations and fancies had been flooding and flitting, was a small man strongly muscled. Clad in gray silks irregularly woven, with tiny thread-tufts here and there, he looked restless as a lynx and as dangerous.

From a great tray of strangely hued and shaped mushrooms set before him like sweetmeats, the Mouser disdainfully selected and nibbled cautiously at the most normal looking, a gray one. Its perfumy savor masking bitterness offended him, and he spat it surreptitiously into his palm and dropped that hand under the table and flicked the wet chewed fragments to the floor. Then, while he sucked his cheek sourly, the fingers of both his hands began to play as slowly and nervously with the hilts of his sword Scalpel and his dagger Cat's Claw as his mind played with his boredoms and murky wonderings.

Along each side of the long narrow table, in great high-backed chairs widely spaced, sat six scrawny old men, bald or shaven of dome and chin, and chicken-fluted of jowl, and each clad only in a neat white loincloth. Eleven of these stared intently at nothing and perpetually tensed their meager muscles until even their ears seemed to stiffen, as though concentrating mightily in realms unseen. The twelfth had his chair half turned and was playing across a far corner of the table the board-game that made the occasional tiny rutching noises. He was playing it with the Mouser's employer Gwaay, ruler of the Lower Levels of Quarmall and younger son to Quarmal, Lord of Quarmall.

Although the Mouser had been three days in Quarmall's depths he had come no closer to Gwaay than he was now, so that he knew him only as a pallid, handsome, soft-spoken youth, no realer to the Mouser, because of the eternal dimness and the invariable distance between them, than a ghost.

The game was one the Mouser had never seen before and quite tricky in several respects.

The board looked green, though it was impossible to be

certain of colors in the unending twilight of the torches, and it had no perceptible squares or tracks on it, except for a phosphorescent line midway between the opponents, dividing the board into two equal fields.

Each contestant started the game with twelve flat circular counters set along his edge of the board. Gwaay's counters were obsidian-black, his ancient opponent's marble-white, so the Mouser was able to distinguish them despite the dimness.

The object of the game seemed to be to move the pieces randomly forward over uneven distances and get at least seven of them into your opponent's field first.

Here the trickiness was that one moved the pieces not with the fingers but only by looking at them intently. Apparently, if one gazed only at a single piece, one could move it quite swiftly. If one gazed at several, one could move them all together in a line or cluster, but more sluggishly.

The Mouser was not yet wholly convinced that he was witnessing a display of thought-power. He still suspected threads, soundless air-puffings, surreptitious joggings of the board from below, powerful beetles under the counters, and hidden magnets—for Gwaay's pieces at least could by their color be some sort of lodestone.

At the present moment Gwaay's black counters and the ancient's white ones were massed at the central line, shifting only a little now and then as the push-of-war went first a nail's breadth one way, then the other. Suddenly Gwaay's rearmost counter circled swiftly back and darted toward an open space at the board's edge. Two of the ancient's counters formed a wedge and thrust across the midline through the weak point thus created. As the ancient's two detached counters returned to oppose them, Gwaay's end-running counter sped across. The game was over—Gwaay gave no sign of this, but the ancient began fumblingly to return the pieces to their starting positions with his fingers.

"Ho, Gwaay, that was easily won!" the Mouser called out

cockily. "Why not take on two of them together? The oldster must be a sorcerer of the Second Rank to play so weakly—or even a doddering apprentice of the Third."

The ancient shot the Mouser a venomous gaze. "We are, all twelve of us, sorcerers of the First Rank and have been from our youth," he proclaimed portentously. "As you should swiftly learn were one of us to point but a little finger against you."

"You have heard what he says," Gwaay called softly to the Mouser without looking at him.

The Mouser, daunted no whit, at least outwardly, called back, "I still think you could beat two of them together, or seven—or the whole decrepit dozen! If they are of First Rank, you must be of Zero or Negative Magnitude."

The ancient's lips worked speechlessly and bubbled with froth at that affront, but Gwaay only called pleasantly, "Were but three of my faithful magi to cease their sorcerous concentrations, my brother Hasjarl's sendings would burst through from the Upper Levels and I would be stricken with all the diseases in the evil compendium, and a few others that exist in Hasjarl's putrescent imagination alone—or perchance I should be erased entirely from this life."

"If nine out of twelve must be forever a-guarding you, they can't get much sleep," the Mouser observed, calling back.

"Times are not always so troublous," Gwaay replied tranquilly. "Sometimes custom or my father enjoins a truce. Sometimes the dark inward sea quiets. But today I know by certain signs that a major assault is being made on the liver and lights and blood and bones and rest of me. Dear Hasjarl has a double coven of sorcerers hardly inferior to my own—Second Rank, but High Second—and he whips them on. And I am as distasteful to Hasjarl, oh Gray Mouser, as the simple fruits of our manure beds are to your lips. Tonight, furthermore, my father Quarmal casts his horoscope in the tower of the Keep, high above Hasjarl's Upper Levels, so it befits I keep all rat-holes closely watched."

"If it's magical helpings you lack," the Mouser retorted boldly, "I have a spell or two that would frizzle your elder brother's witches and warlocks!" And truth to tell the Mouser had parchment-crackling in his pouch one spell—though one spell only—which he dearly wanted to test. It had been given him by his own wizardly mentor and master Sheelba of the Eyeless Face.

Gwaay replied, more softly than ever, so that the Mouser felt that if there had been a yard more between them he would not have heard, "It is your work to ward from my physical body Hasjarl's sword-sendings, in particular those of this great champion he is reputed to have hired. My sorcerers of the First Rank will shield off Hasjarl's sorcerous *billets-doux*. Each to his proper occupation." He lightly clapped his hands together. A slim slavegirl appeared noiselessly in the dark archway beyond him. Without looking once at her, Gwaay softly commanded, "Strong wine for our warrior." She vanished.

The ancient had at last laboriously shuffled the black-and-white counters into their starting positions, and Gwaay regarded his thoughtfully. But before making a move, he called to the Mouser, "If time still hangs heavy on your hands, devote some of it to selecting the reward you will take when your work is done. And in your search overlook not the maiden who brings you the wine. Her name is Ivivis."

At that the Mouser shut up. He had already chosen more than a dozen expensive be-charming objects from Gwaay's drawers and niches and locked them in a disused closet he had discovered two levels down. If this should be discovered, he would explain that he was merely making an innocent preselection pending final choice, but Gwaay might not view it that way and Gwaay was sharp, judging from the way he'd noted the rejected mushroom and other things.

It had not occurred to the Mouser to preempt a girl or two by locking her in the closet also, though it was admittedly an attractive idea.

The ancient cleared his throat and said chucklingly across the board, "Lord Gwaay, let this ambitious sworder try his sorcerous tricks. Let him try them on me!"

The Mouser's spirits rose, but Gwaay only raised palm and shook his head slightly and pointed a finger at the board; the ancient began obediently to think a piece forward.

The Mouser's spirits fell. He was beginning to feel very much alone in this dim underworld where all spoke and moved in whispers. True, when Gwaay's emissary had approached him in Lankhmar, the Mouser had been happy to take on this solo job. It would teach his loud-voiced swordmate Fafhrd a lesson if his small gray comrade (and brain!) should disappear one night without a word…and then return perchance a year later with a brimful treasure chest and a mocking smile.

The Mouser had even been happy all the long caravan trip from Lankhmar south to Quarmall, along the Hlal River and past the Lakes of Pleea and through the Mountains of Hunger. It had been a positive pleasure to loll on a swaying camel beyond reach of Fafhrd's hugeness and disputatious talk and boisterous ways, while the nights grew ever bluer and warmer and strange jewel-fiery stars came peering over the southern horizon.

But now he had been three nights in Quarmall since his secret coming to the Lower Levels—three nights and days, or rather one hundred and forty-four interminable demi-hours of buried twilight—and he was already beginning in his secretest mind to wish that Fafhrd were here, instead of half a continent away in Lankhmar—or even farther than that if he'd carried out his misty plans to revisit his northern homeland. Someone to drink with, at any rate—and even a roaring quarrel would be positively refreshing after seventy-two hours of nothing but silent servitors, tranced sorcerers, stewed mushrooms, and Gwaay's unbreakable soft-tongued equanimity.

Besides, it appeared that all Gwaay wanted was a mighty sworder to nullify the threat of this champion Hasjarl was supposed to have hired as secretly as Gwaay had smuggled in the Mouser. If Fafhrd were here, he could be Gwaay's sworder, while the Mouser would have better opportunity to peddle Gwaay his magical talents. The one spell he had in his pouch—he had got it from Sheelba in return for the tale of the Perversions of Clutho—would forever establish his reputation as an archimage of deadly might, he was sure.

The Mouser came out of his musings to realize that the slavegirl Ivivis was kneeling before him—for how long she had been there he could not say—and proffering an ebony tray on which stood a squat stone jug and a copper cup.

She knelt with one leg doubled, the other thrust behind her as in a fencing lunge, stretching the short skirt of her green tunic, while her arms reached the tray forward.

Her slim body was most supple—she held the difficult pose effortlessly. Her fine straight hair was pale as her skin—both a sort of ghost color. It occurred to the Mouser that she would look very well in his closet, perhaps cherishing against her bosom the necklace of large black pearls he had discovered piled behind a pewter statuette in one of Gwaay's niches.

However, she was kneeling as far away from him as she could and still stretch him the tray, and her eyes were most modestly downcast, nor would she even flicker up their lids to his gracious murmurings—which were all the approach he thought suitable at this moment.

He seized the jug and cup. Ivivis drooped her head still lower in acknowledgment, then flirted silently away.

The Mouser poured a finger of blood-red, blood-thick wine and sipped. Its flavor was darkly sweet, but with a bitter undertaste. He wondered if it were fermented from scarlet toadstools.

The black-and-white counters skittered rutchingly in obedience to Gwaay's and the ancient's peerings. The pale torch flames bent to the unceasing cool breeze, while the fan-slaves and their splayed bare feet on the leather belts and the great unseen fans themselves on their ponderous axles muttered unendingly, "Quarmall…Quarmall is downward tall…Quarmall…Quarmall is all…"

In an equally vast room many levels higher yet still underground—a windowless room where torches flared redder and brighter, but their brightness nullified by an acrid haze of incense smoke, so that here too the final effect was exasperating dimness—Fafhrd sat at the table's foot.

Fafhrd was ordinarily a monstrously calm man, but now he was restlessly drumming fist on thumb-root, on the verge of admitting to himself that he wished the Gray Mouser were here, instead of back in Lankhmar or perchance off on some ramble in the desert-patched Eastern Lands.

The Mouser, Fafhrd thought, might have more patience to unriddle the mystifications and crooked behavior-ways of these burrowing Quarmallians. The Mouser might find it easier to endure Hasjarl's loathsome taste for torture, and at least the little gray fool would be someone human to drink with!

Fafhrd had been very glad to be parted from the Mouser and from his vanities and tricksiness and chatter when Hasjarl's agent had contacted him in Lankhmar, promising large pay in return for Fafhrd's instant, secret, and solitary coming. Fafhrd had even dropped a hint to the small fellow that he might take ship with some of his Northerner countrymen who had sailed down across the Inner Sea.

What he had not explained to the Mouser was that, as soon as Fafhrd was aboard her, the longship had sailed not north but south, coasting through the vast Outer Sea along Lankhmar's western seaboard.

It had been an idyllic journey, that—pirating a little now and then, despite the sour objections of Hasjarl's agent, battling great storms and also the giant cuttlefish, rays, and serpents which swarmed ever thicker in the Outer Sea as one sailed south. At the recollection Fafhrd's fist slowed its drumming and his lips almost formed a long smile.

But now this Quarmall! This endless stinking sorcery! This torture-besotted Hasjarl! Fafhrd's fist drummed fiercely again.

Rules!—he mustn't explore downward, for that led to the Lower Levels and the enemy. Nor must he explore upward— that way was to Father Quarmal's apartments, sacrosanct. None must know of Fafhrd's presence. He must satisfy himself with such drink and inferior wenches as were available in Hasjarl's limited Upper Levels. (They called these dim labyrinths and crypts *upper!*)

Delays!—they mustn't muster their forces and march down and smash brother-enemy Gwaay; that was unthinkable rashness. They mustn't even shut off the huge treadmill-driven fans whose perpetual creaking troubled Fafhrd's ears and which sent the life-giving air on the first stages of its journey to Gwaay's underworld, and through other rock-driven wells sucked out the stale—no, those fans must never be stopped, for Father Quarmal would frown on any battle-tactic which suffocated valuable slaves; and from anything Father Quarmal frowned on, his sons shrank shuddering.

Instead, Hasjarl's war-council must plot years-long campaigns weaponed chiefly with sorcery and envisioning the conquest of Gwaay's Lower Levels a quarter tunnel—or a quarter mushroom field—at a time.

Mystifications!—mushrooms must be served at all meals but never eaten or so much as tasted. Roast rat, on the other hand, was a delicacy to be crowed over. Tonight Father Quarmal would cast his own horoscope and for some reason that superstitious starsighting and scribbling would be of incalculable cryptic consequence. All maids must scream loudly twice when familiarities were suggested to them, no matter what their subsequent behavior. Fafhrd must never get closer to Hasjarl than a long dagger's cast—a rule which gave Fafhrd no chance to discover how Hasjarl managed never to miss a detail of what went on around him while keeping his eyes fully closed almost all the time.

Perhaps Hasjarl had a sort of short-range second sight, or perhaps the slave nearest him ceaselessly whispered an account of all that transpired, or perhaps—well, Fafhrd had no way of knowing.

But somehow Hasjarl could see things with his eyes shut.

This paltry trick of Hasjarl's evidently saved his eyes from the irritation of the incense smoke, which kept those of Hasjarl's sorcerers and of Fafhrd himself red and watering. However, since Hasjarl was otherwise a most energetic and restless prince—his bandy-legged misshapen body and mismated arms forever a-twitch, his ugly face always grimacing—the detail of eyes tranquilly shut was peculiarly jarring and shiversome.

All in all, Fafhrd was heartily sick of the Upper Levels of Quarmall though scarcely a week in them. He had even toyed with the notion of double-crossing Hasjarl and hiring out to his brother or turning informer for his father—although they might, as employers, be no improvement whatever.

But mostly he simply wanted to meet in combat this champion of Gwaay's he kept hearing so much of—meet him and slay him and then shoulder his reward (preferably a shapely maiden with a bag of gold in her either hand) and turn his back forever on the accursed dim-tunneled whisper-haunted hill of Quarmall!

In an excess of exasperation he clapped his hand to the hilt of his longsword Graywand.

Hasjarl saw that, although Hasjarl's eyes were closed, for he quickly pointed his gnarly face down the long table at Fafhrd, between the ranks of the twenty-four heavily-robed, thickly-bearded sorcerers crowded shoulder to shoulder. Then, his eyelids still shut, Hasjarl commenced to twitch his

mouth as a preamble to speech and with a twitter-tremble as
overture called, "Ha, hot for battle, eh, Fafhrd boy? Keep him
in the sheath! Yet tell me, what manner of man do you think
this warrior—the one you protect me against—Gwaay's grim
man-slayer? He is said to be mightier than an elephant in
strength, and more guileful than the very Zobolds." With a
final spasm Hasjarl managed, still without opening his eyes,
to look expectantly at Fafhrd.

Fafhrd had heard all this sort of worrying time and time
again during the past week, so he merely answered with a
snort:

"Zutt! They all say that about anybody. I know. But unless
you get me some action and keep these old flea-bitten beards
out of my sight—"

Catching himself up short, Fafhrd tossed off his wine and
beat with his pewter mug on the table for more. For although
Hasjarl might have the demeanor of an idiot and the
disposition of a ocelot, he served excellent ferment of grape
ripened on the hot brown southern slopes of Quarmall
hill…and there was no profit in goading him.

Nor did Hasjarl appear to take offense—or if he did, he
took it out on his bearded sorcerers, for he instantly began
to instruct one to enunciate his runes more clearly, questioned
another as to whether his herbs were sufficiently pounded,
reminded a third that it was time to tinkle a certain silver
bell thrice, and in general treated the whole two dozen as if
they were a roomful of schoolboys and he their eagle-eyed
pedagogue—though Fafhrd had been given to understand
that they were all magi of the First Rank.

The double coven of sorcerers in turn began to bustle more
nervously, each with his particular spell—touching off more
stinks, jiggling black drops out of more dirty vials, waving
more wands, pin-stabbing more figurines, finger-tracing
eldritch symbols more swiftly in the air, mounding up each
in front of him from his bag more noisome fetishes, and so
on.

From his hours of sitting at the foot of the table, Fafhrd had learned that most of the spells were designed to inflict a noisome disease upon Gwaay: the Black Plague, the Red Plague, the Boneless Death, the Hairless Decline, the Slow Rot, the Fast Rot, the Green Rot, the Bloody Cough, the Belly Melts, the Ague, the Runs, and even the footling Nose Drip. Gwaay's own sorcerers, he gathered, kept warding off these malefic spells with counter-charms, but the idea was to keep on sending them in hopes that the opposition would some day drop their guard, if only for a few moments.

Fafhrd rather wished Gwaay's gang were able to reflect back the disease-spells on their dark-robed senders. He had become weary even of the abstruse astrologic signs stitched in gold and silver on those robes, and of the ribbons and precious wires knotted cabalistically in their heavy beards.

Hasjarl, his magicians disciplined into a state of furious busyness, opened wide his eyes for a change and with only a preliminary lip-writhe called to Fafhrd, "So you want action, eh, Fafhrd boy?"

Fafhrd, mightily irked at the last epithet, planted an elbow on the table and wagged that hand at Hasjarl and called back, "I do. My muscles cry to bulge. You've strong-looking arms, Lord Hasjarl. What say you we play the wrist game?"

Hasjarl tittered evilly and cried, "I go but now to play another sort of wrist game with a maid suspected of commerce with one of Gwaay's pages. She never screamed even once...then. Wouldst accompany me and watch the action, Fafhrd?" And he suddenly shut his eyes again with the effect of putting on two tiny masks of skin—yet shut them so firmly there could be no question of his peering through the lashes.

Fafhrd shrank back in his chair, flushing a little. Hasjarl had divined Fafhrd's distaste for torture on the Northerner's first night in Quarmall's Upper Levels and since then had never missed an opportunity to play on what Hasjarl must view as Fafhrd's weakness.

To cover his embarrassment, Fafhrd drew from under his tunic a tiny book of stitched parchment pages. The Northerner would have sworn that Hasjarl's eyelids had not flickered once since closing, yet now the villain cried, "The sigil on the cover of that packet tells me it is something of Ningauble of the Seven Eyes. What is it, Fafhrd?"

"Private matters," the latter retorted firmly. Truth to tell, he was somewhat alarmed. The contents of the packet were such as he dared not permit Hasjarl see. And just as the villain somehow knew, there was indeed on the top parchment the bold black figure of a seven-fingered hand, each finger bearing an eye for a nail—one of the many signs of Fafhrd's wizardly patron.

Hasjarl coughed hackingly. "No servant of Hasjarl has private matters," he pronounced. "However, we will speak of that at another time. Duty calls me." He bounded up from his chair and fiercely eyeing his sorcerers cried at them barkingly, "If I find one of you dozing over his spells when I return, it were better for him—aye, and for his mother too had he been born with slave's chains on his ankles!"

He paused, turning to go, and pointing his face at Fafhrd again, called rapidly yet cajolingly, "The girl is named Friska. She's but seventeen. I doubt not she will play the wrist game most adroitly and with many a charming exclamation. I will converse with her, at length. I will question her, as I twist the crank, very slowly. And she will answer, she will comment, she will describe her feelings, in sounds if not in words. Sure you won't come?" And trailing an evil titter behind him, Hasjarl strode rapidly from the room, red torches in the archway outlining his monstrous bandy-legged form in blood.

Fafhrd ground his teeth. There was nothing he could do at the moment. Hasjarl's torture chamber was also his guard barrack. Yet the Northerner chalked up in his mind an intention, or perhaps an obligation.

To keep his mind from nasty unmanning imaginings, he began carefully to reread the tiny parchment book which Ningauble had given him as a sort of reward for past services, or an assurance for future ones, on the night of the Northerner's departure from Lankhmar.

Fafhrd did not worry about Hasjarl's sorcerers overlooking what he read. After their master's last threat, they were all as furiously and elbow-jostlingly busy with their spells as so many bearded black ants.

Quarmall was first brought to my attention *(Fafhrd read in Ningauble's little handwritten, or tentacle-writ book)* by the report that certain passageways beneath it ran deep under the Sea and extended to certain caverns wherein might dwell some remnant of the Elder Ones. Naturally I dispatched agents to probe the truth of the report: two well-trained and valuable spies were sent (also two others to watch them) to find the facts and accumulate gossip. Neither pair returned, nor did they send messages or tokens in explanation, or indeed word of any sort. I was interested; but being unable at that time to spare valuable material on so uncertain and dangerous a quest, I bided my time until information should be placed at my disposal (as it usually is).

After twenty years my discretion was rewarded. *(So went the crabbed script as Fafhrd continued to read.)* An old man, horribly scarred and peculiarly pallid, was fetched to me. His name was Tamorg, and his tale interesting in spite of the teller's incoherence. He claimed to have been captured from a passing caravan when yet a small lad and carried into captivity within Quarmall. There he served as a slave on the Lower Levels, far below the ground. Here there was no natural light, and the only air was sucked down into the mazy caverns by means of large fans, treadmill-driven; hence his pallor and otherwise unusual appearance.

Tamorg was quite bitter about these fans, for he had been chained at one of those endless belts for a longer time than he cared to think about. (He really did not know exactly how long, since there was, by his own statement, no measure of time in the Lower Levels.) Finally he was released from his onerous walking, as nearly as I could glean from his garbled tale, by the invention or breeding of a specialized type of slave who better served the purpose.

From this I postulate that the Masters of Quarmall are sufficiently interested in the economics of their holdings to improve them: a rarity among overlords. Moreover, if these specialized slaves were bred, the life-span of these overlords must perforce be longer than ordinary; or else the cooperation between father and son is more perfect than any filial relationship I have yet noted.

Tamorg further related that he was put to more work digging, along with eight other slaves likewise taken from the treadmills. They were forced to enlarge and extend certain passages and chambers; so for another space of time he mined and buttressed. This time must have been long, for by close cross-questioning I found that Tamorg digged and walled, single-handed, a passage a thousand and twenty paces long. These slaves were not chained, unless maniacal, nor was it necessary to bind them so; for these Lower Levels seem to be a maze within a maze, and an unlucky slave once strayed from familiar paths stood small chance of retracing his steps. However, rumor has it, Tamorg said, that the Lords of Quarmall keep certain slaves who have memorized each a portion of the ever-extending labyrinth. By this means they are able to traverse with safety and communicate one level to the other.

Tamorg finally escaped by the simple expedient of accidentally breaking through the wall whereat he dug. He enlarged the opening with his mattock and stooped to peer. At that moment a fellow workman pushed against him, and Tamorg was thrust head-foremost into the opening he had made. Fortunately it led into a chasm at the bottom of which ran a swift but deep underground stream, into which Tamorg fell. As swimming is an art not easily forgotten, he managed to keep afloat until he reached the outer world. For several days he was blinded by the sun's rays and felt comfortable only by dim torchlight.

I questioned him in detail about the many interesting phenomena which must have been before him constantly, but he was very unsatisfactory, being ignorant of all observational methods. However I placed him as gatekeeper in the palace of D—whose coming and going I desired to check upon. So much for that source of information.

My interest in Quarmall was aroused (*Ningauble's book went on*) and my appetite whetted by this scanty meal of facts, so I applied myself toward getting more information. Through my connection with Sheelba I made contact with Eeack, the Overlord of Rats; by holding out the lure of secret passages to the granaries of Lankhmar, he was persuaded to visit me. His visit proved both barren and embarrassing. Barren because it turned out that rats are eaten as a delicacy in Quarmall and hunted for culinary purposes by well-trained weasels. Naturally, under such circumstances, any rat within the walls of Quarmall stood little chance of doing liaison work except from the uncertain vantage of a pot. Eeack's personal cohort of countless rats, evil-smelling and famished, consumed all edibles within reach of their sharp teeth; and out of pity for the plight in which I was left Eeack favored me by cajoling Scraa to wake and speak with me.

Scraa (*Ningauble's notes continued*) is one of those eon-old roaches who existed contemporaneously with those monstrous reptiles which once ruled the world, and whose racial memories go back into the mistiness of time before the Elder Ones retreated from the surface. Scraa presented me the following short history of Quarmall neatly inscribed on a peculiar parchment composed of cleverly welded wingcases flattened and smoothed most subtly. I append his document and apologize for his somewhat dry and prosy style.

"The city-state of Quarmall houses a civilization almost unheard of in the sphere of anthropoid organization. Perhaps the closest analogy which might be made is to that of the slave-making ants. The domain of Quarmall is at the present day limited to the small mountain, or large hill, on which it stands; but like a radish the main portion of it lies buried beneath the surface. This was not always so.

"Once the Lords of Quarmall ruled over broad meadows and vast seas; their ships swam between all known ports, and their caravans marched the routes from sea to sea. Slowly from the fertile valleys and barren cliffs, from the desert spots and the open sea the grip of Quarmall loosened; not willingly but ever forced did the Lords of Quarmall retreat. Inexorably they were driven, year by year, generation by generation, from all their possessions and rights; until finally they were confined to that last and staunchest stronghold, the impregnable castle of Quarmall. The cause of this driving is lost in the dimness of fable; but it was probably due to those most gruesome practices which even to this day persuade the surrounding countryside that Quarmall is unclean and cursed.

"As the Lords of Quarmall were pushed back, driven in spite of their sorceries and valor, they burrowed under that last, vast stronghold ever deeper and ever broader. Each succeeding Lord dug more deeply into the bowels of the small mount on which sat the Keep of Quarmall. Eventually the memory of past glories faded and was forgotten and the Lords of Quarmall concentrated on their mazy tunneling to the exclusion of the outer world. They would have forgotten the outer world entirely but for their constant and ever-increasing need of slaves and of sustenance for those slaves.

"The Lords of Quarmall are magicians of great repute and adepts in the practice of the Art. It is said that by their skill they can charm men into bondage both of body and of soul."

So much did Scraa write. All in all it is a very unsatisfactory bit of gossip: hardly a word about those intriguing passageways which first aroused my interest; nothing about the conformation of the Land or its inhabitants; not even a map! But then poor ancient Scraa lives almost entirely in the past—the present will not become important to him for another eon or so.

However, I believe I know two fellows who might be persuaded to undertake a mission there.... (*Here Ningauble's notes ended, much to Fafhrd's irritation and suspicious puzzlement—and carking shamed discomfort too, for now he must think again of the unknown girl Hasjarl was torturing.*)

Outside the mount of Quarmall the sun was past meridian, and shadows had begun to grow. The great white oxen threw their weight against the yoke. It was not the first time nor would it be the last, they knew. Each month as they approached this mucky stretch of road the master whipped and slashed them frantically, attempting to goad them into a speed which they, by nature, were unable to attain. Straining until the harness creaked, they obliged as best they could: for they knew that when this spot was pulled the master would reward them with a bit of salt, a rough caress, and a brief respite from work. It was unfortunate that this particular piece of road stayed mucky long after the rains had ceased; almost from one season to the next. Unfortunate that it took a longer time to pass.

Their master had reason to lash them so. This spot was accounted accursed among his people. From this curved eminence the towers of Quarmall could be spied on; and more important these towers looked down upon the road, even as one looking up could see them. It was not healthy to look on the towers of Quarmall, or to be looked upon by them. There was sufficient reason for this feeling. The master of the oxen spat surreptitiously, made an obvious gesture with his fingers, and glanced fearfully over his shoulder at the skythrusting lacy-topped towers as the last mudhole was traversed. Even in this fleeting glance he caught the glimpse of a flash, a brilliant scintillation, from the tallest keep. Shuddering, he leaped into the welcome covert of the trees and thanked the gods he worshipped for his escape.

Tonight he would have much to speak of in the tavern. Men would buy him bowls of wine to swill, and bitter beer of herbs. He could lord it for an evening. Ah! but for his quickness he might even now be plodding soulless to the mighty gates of Quarmall; there to serve until his body was no more and even after. For tales were told of such charmings, and of other things, among the elders of the village: tales that bore no moral but which all men did heed. Was it not only last Serpent Eve that young Twelm went from the ken of men? Had he not jeered at these very tales and, drunken, braved the terraces of Quarmall? Sure, and this was so! And it was also true that his less brave companion had seen him swagger with bravado to the last, the highest terrace, almost to the moat; then when Twelm, alarmed at some unknown cause, turned to run, his twisted-arched body was pulled willy-nilly back into the darkness. Not even a scream was heard to mark the passing of Twelm from this earth and the ken of his fellowmen. Juln, that less brave or less foolhardy companion of Twelm, had spent his time thenceforth in a continual drunken stupor. Nor would he stir from under roofs at night.

All the way to the village the master of the oxen pondered. He tried to formulate in his dim peasant intellect a method by which he might present himself as a hero. But even as he painfully constructed a simple, self-aggrandizing tale, he bethought himself of the fate of that one who had dared to brag of robbing Quarmall's vineyards; the one whose name was spoken only in a hushed whisper, secretly. So the driver decided to confine himself to facts, simple as they were, and trust to the atmosphere of horror that he knew any manifestation of activity in Quarmall would arouse.

While the driver was still whipping his oxen, and the Mouser watching two shadow-men play a thought-game, and Fafhrd swilling wine to drown the thought of an unknown girl in pain—at that same time Quarmal, Lord of Quarmall, was casting his own horoscope for the coming year. In the highest tower of the Keep he labored, putting in order the huge astrolabe and the other massive instruments necessary for his accurate observations.

Through curtains of broidery the afternoon sun beat hotly into the small chamber; beams glanced from the polished surfaces and scintillated into rainbow hues as they reflected askew. It was warm, even for an old man lightly gowned, and Quarmal stepped to the windows opposite the sun and drew the broidery aside, letting the cool moor-breeze blow through his observatory.

He glanced idly out the deep-cut embrasures. In the distance down past the terraced slopes he could see the little, curved brown thread of road which led eventually to the village.

Like ants the small figures on it appeared: ants struggling through some sticky trap; and like ants, even as Quarmal watched, they persisted and finally disappeared. Quarmal sighed as he turned away from the windows. Sighed in a slight disappointment because he regretted not having looked a moment sooner. Slaves were always needed. Besides, it would have been an opportunity for trying out a recently invented instrument or two.

Yet it was never Quarmal's way to regret the past, so with a shrug he turned away.

For an old man Quarmal was not particularly hideous until his eyes were noticed. They were peculiar in their shape, and the ball was a rich ruby-red. The dead-white iris had that nauseous sheen of pearly iridescence found only in the sea dwellers among living creatures; this character he inherited from his mother, a mer-woman. The pupils, like specks of black crystal, sparkled with incredible malevolent intelligence. His baldness was accentuated by the long tufts of coarse black hair which grew symmetrically over each ear. Pale, pitted skin hung loosely on his jowls, but was tightly drawn over the high cheekbones. Thin as a sharpened blade, his long jutting nose gave him the appearance of an old hawk or kestrel.

If Quarmal's eyes were the most arresting feature in his countenance, his mouth was the most beautiful. The lips were full and ruddy, remarkable in so aged a man, and they had that peculiar mobility found in some elocutionists and orators and actors. Had it been possible for Quarmal to have known vanity, he might have been vain about the beauty of his mouth; as it was this perfectly molded mouth served only to accentuate the horror of his eyes.

He looked up veiledly now through the iron rondures of the astrolabe at the twin of his own face pushing forth from a windowless square of the opposite wall: it was his own waxen life-mask, taken within the year and most realistically tinted and blackly hair-tufted by his finest artist, save that the white-irised eyes were of necessity closed—though the mask still gave a feeling of peering. The mask was the last in several rows of such, each a little more age-darkened than the succeeding one. Though some were ugly and many were elderly-handsome, there was a strong family resemblance between the shut-eyed faces, for there had been few if any intrusions into the male lineage of Quarmall.

There were perhaps fewer masks than might have been expected, for most Lords of Quarmall lived very long and had sons late. Yet there were also a considerable many, since Quarmall was such an ancient rulership. The oldest masks were of a brown almost black and not wax at all but the cured and mummified face skins of those primeval autocrats. The arts of flaying and tanning had early been brought to an exquisite degree of perfection in Quarmall and were still practiced with jealously prideful skill.

Quarmal dropped his gaze from the mask to his lightly-robed body. He was a lean man, and his hips and shoulders still gave evidence that once he had hawked, hunted, and fenced with the best. His feet were high-arched, and his step was still light. Long and spatulate were his knob-knuckled fingers, while fleshy muscular palms gave witness to their dexterity and nimbleness, a necessary advantage to one of his calling. For Quarmal was a sorcerer, as were all the Lords of Quarmall from the eon-mighty past. From childhood up through manhood each male was trained into his calling, like some vines are coaxed to twist and thread a difficult terrace.

As Quarmal returned from the window to attend his duties he pondered on his training. It was unfortunate for the House of Quarmall that he possessed two instead of the usual single heir. Each of his sons was a creditable necromancer and well skilled in other sciences pertaining to the Art; both were exceedingly ambitious and filled with hatred. Hatred not only for one another but for Quarmal their father.

Quarmal pictured in his mind Hasjarl in his Upper Levels below the Keep and Gwaay below Hasjarl in his Lower Levels…Hasjarl cultivating his passions as if in some fiery circle of Hell, making energy and movement and logic carried to the ultimate the greatest goods, constantly threatening with whips and tortures and carrying through those threats, and now hiring a great brawling beast of a man to be his sworder…Gwaay nourishing restraint as if in Hell's frigidest circle, trying to reduce all life to art and intuitive thought, seeking by meditation to compel lifeless rock to do his bidding and constrain Death by the power of his will, and now hiring a small gray man like Death's younger brother to be his knifer.…Quarmal thought of Hasjarl and Gwaay, and for a moment a strange smile of fatherly pride bent his lips, and then he shook his head, and his smile became stranger still, and he shuddered very faintly.

It was well, thought Quarmal, that he was an old man, far past his prime, even as magicians counted years, for it would be unpleasant to cease living in the prime of life, or even in the twilight of life's day. And he knew that sooner or later, in spite of all protecting charms and precautions, Death would creep silently on him or spring suddenly from some unguarded moment. This very night his horoscope might signal Death's instant escapeless approach; and though men lived by lies, treating truth's very self as lie to be exploited, the stars remained the stars.

Each day Quarmal's sons, he knew, grew more clever and more subtle in their usage of the Art which he had taught them. Nor could Quarmal protect himself by slaying them. Brother might murder brother, or the son his sire, but it was forbidden from ancient times for the father to slay his son. There were no very good reasons for this custom, nor were any needed. Custom in the House of Quarmall stood unchallenged, and it was not lightly defied.

Quarmal bethought him of the babe sprouting in the womb of Kewissa, the childlike favorite concubine of his age. So far as his precautions and watchfulness might have enforced, that babe was surely his own—and Quarmal was the most watchful and cynically realistic of men. If that babe lived and proved a boy—as omens foretold it would be— and if Quarmal were given but twelve more years to train him, and if Hasjarl and Gwaay should be taken by the fates or each other...

Quarmal clipped off in his mind this line of speculation. To expect to live a dozen more years with Hasjarl and Gwaay growing daily more clever-subtle in their sorceries—or to hope for the dual extinguishment of two such cautious sprigs of his own flesh—were vanity and irrealism indeed!

He looked around him. The preliminaries for the casting were completed, the instruments prepared and aligned; now only the final observations and their interpretation were required. Lifting a small leaden hammer Quarmal lightly struck a brazen gong. Hardly had the resonance faded when the tall, richly appareled figure of a man appeared in the arched doorway.

Flindach was Master of the Magicians. His duties were many but not easily apparent. His power carefully concealed was second only to that of Quarmal. A wearied cruelty sat upon his dark visage, giving him an air of boredom which ill matched the consuming interest he took in the affairs of others. Flindach was not a comely man: a purple wine mark covered his left cheek, three large warts made an isosceles triangle on his right, while his nose and chin jutted like those of an old witch. Startlingly, with an effect of mocking irreverence, his eyes were ruby-whited and pearly-irised like those of his lord; he was a younger offspring of the same mer-woman who had birthed Quarmal—after Quarmal's father had done with her and, following one of Quarmal's bizarre customs, had given her to *his* Master of the Magicians.

Now those eyes of Flindach, large and hypnotically staring, shifted uneasily as Quarmal spoke: "Gwaay and Hasjarl, my sons, work today on their respective Levels. It would be well if they were called into the council room this night. For it is the night on which my doom is to be foretold. And I sense premonitorily that this casting will bear no good. Bid them dine together and permit them to amuse one another by plotting at my death—or by attempting each other's."

He shut his lips precisely as he finished and looked more evil than a man expecting Death should look. Flindach, used to terrors in the line of business, could scarcely repress a shudder at the glance bestowed on him; but remembering his position he made the sign of obeisance, and without a word or backward look departed.

The Gray Mouser did not once remove his gaze from Flindach as the latter strode across the domed dim sorcery

chamber of the Lower Levels until he reached Gwaay's side.
The Mouser was mightily intrigued by the warts and wine
mark on the cheeks of the richly-robed witch-faced man and
by his eerie red-whited eyes, and he instantly gave this
charming visage a place of honor in the large catalog of freak-
faces he stored in his memory vaults.

Although he strained his ears, he could not hear what
Flindach said to Gwaay or what Gwaay answered.

Gwaay finished the telekinetic game he was playing by
sending all his black counters across the midline in a great
rutching surge that knocked half his opponent's white
counters tumbling into his loinclothed lap. Then he rose
smoothly from his stool.

"I sup tonight with my beloved brother in my all-revered
father's apartments," he pronounced mellowly to all. "While
I am there and in the escort of great Flindach here, no
sorcerous spells may harm me. So you may rest for a space
from your protective concentrations, oh my gracious magi of
the First Rank." He turned to go.

The Mouser, inwardly leaping at the chance to glimpse the
sky again, if only by chilly night, rose springily too from his
chair and called out, "Ho, Prince Gwaay! Though safe from
spells, will you not want the warding of my blades at this
dinner party? There's many a great prince never made king
'cause he was served cold iron 'twixt the ribs between the
soup and the fish. I also juggle most prettily and do conjuring
tricks."

Gwaay half turned back. "Nor may steel harm me while
my sire's hand is stretched above," he called so softly that
the Mouser felt the words were being lobbed like feather balls
barely as far as his ear. "Stay here, Gray Mouser."

His tone was unmistakably rebuffing, nevertheless the
Mouser, dreading a dull evening, persisted, "There is also the
matter of that serious spell of mine of which I told you,
Prince—a spell most effective against magi of the *Second* Rank

and lower, such as a certain noxious brother employs. Now were a good time—"

"Let there be no sorcery tonight!" Gwaay cut him off sternly, though speaking hardly louder than before. "'Twere an insult to my sire and to his great servant Flindach here, a Master of Magicians, even to think of such! Bide quietly, swordsman, keep peace, and speak no more." His voice took on a pious note. "There will be time enough for sorcery and swords, if slaying there must be."

Flindach nodded solemnly at that, and they silently departed. The Mouser sat down. Rather to his surprise, he noted that the twelve aged sorcerers were already curled up like pillbugs on their sides on their great chairs and snoring away. He could not even while away time by challenging one of them to the thought-game, hoping to learn by playing, or to a bout at conventional chess. This promised to be a most glum evening indeed.

Then a thought brightened the Mouser's swarthy visage. He lifted his hands, cupping the palms, and clapped them lightly together as he had seen Gwaay do.

The slim slavegirl Ivivis instantly appeared in the far archway. When she saw that Gwaay was gone and his sorcerers slumbering, her eyes became bright as a kitten's. She scampered to the Mouser, her slender legs flashing, seated herself with a last bound on his lap, and clapped her lissome arms around him.

Fafhrd silently faded back into a dark side passage as Hasjarl came hurrying along the torchlit corridor beside a richly robed official with hideously warted and mottled face and red eyeballs, on whose other side strode a pallid comely youth with strangely ancient eyes. Fafhrd had never before met Flindach or, of course, Gwaay.

Hasjarl was clearly in a pet, for he was grimacing insanely and twisting his hands together furiously as though pitting one in murderous battle against the other. His eyes, however, were tightly shut. As he stamped swiftly part, Fafhrd thought he glimpsed a bit of tattooing on the nearest upper eyelid.

Fafhrd heard the red-eyeballed one say, "No need to run to your sire's banquet-board, Lord Hasjarl. We're in good time." Hasjarl answered only a snarl, but the pale youth said sweetly, "My brother is ever a baroque pearl of dutifulness."

Fafhrd moved forward, watched the three out of sight, then turned the other way and followed the scent of hot iron straight to Hasjarl's torture chamber.

It was a wide, low-vaulted room and the brightest Fafhrd had yet encountered in these murky, misnamed Upper Levels.

To the right was a low table around which crouched five squat brawny men more bandy-legged than Hasjarl and masked each to the upper lip. They were noisily gnawing bones snatched from a huge platter of them, and swilling ale from leather jacks. Four of the masks were black, one red.

Beyond them was a fire of coals in a circular brick tower half as high as a man. The iron grill above it glowed redly. The coals brightened almost to white, then grew more deeply red again, as a twisted half-bald hag in tatters slowly worked a bellows.

Along the walls to either side, there thickly stood or hung various metal and leather instruments which showed their foul purpose by their ghostly hand-and-glove resemblance to various outer surfaces and inward orifices of the human body: boots, collars, masks, iron maidens, funnels, and the like.

To the left a fair-haired pleasingly plump girl in white under tunic lay bound to a rack. Her right hand in an iron half-glove stretched out tautly toward a machine with a crank. Although her face was tear-streaked, she did not seem to be in present pain.

Fafhrd strode toward her, hurriedly slipping out of his pouch and onto the middle finger of his right hand the massy ring Hasjarl's emissary had given him in Lankhmar as token from his master. It was of silver, holding a large black seal on which was Hasjarl's sign: a clenched fist.

The girl's eyes widened with new fears as she saw Fafhrd coming.

Hardly looking at her as he paused by the rack, Fafhrd turned toward the table of masked messy feasters, who were staring at him gape-mouthed by now. Stretching out toward them the back of his right hand, he called harshly yet carelessly, "By authority of this sigil, release to me the girl Friska!" From mouth-corner he muttered to the girl, "Courage!"

The black-masked creature who came hurrying toward him like a terrier appeared either not to recognize at once Hasjarl's sign or else not to reason out its import, for he said only, wagging a greasy finger, "Begone, barbarian. This dainty morsel is not for you. Think not to quench your rough lusts here. Our Master—"

Fafhrd cried out, "If you will not accept the authority of the Clenched Fist one way, then you must take it the other."

Doubling up the hand with the ring on it, he smashed it against the torturer's suet-shining jaw so that he stretched himself out on the dark flags, skidded a foot, and lay quietly.

Fafhrd turned at once toward the half-risen feasters and slapping Graywand's hilt but not drawing it, he planted his knuckles on his hips and, addressing himself to the red mask he barked out rather like Hasjarl, "Our Master of the Fist had an afterthought and ordered me to fetch the girl Friska so that he might continue her entertainment at dinner for the amusement of those he goes to dine with. Would you have a new servant like myself report to Hasjarl your derelictions and delays? Loose her quickly and I'll say nothing." He stabbed a finger at the hag by the bellows, "You!—fetch her outer dress."

The masked ones sprang to obey quickly enough at that, their tucked-up masks falling over their mouths and chins.

There were mumblings of apology, which he ignored. Even the one he had slugged got groggily to his feet and tried to help.

The girl had been released from her wrist-twisting device, Fafhrd supervising, and she was sitting up on the side of the rack when the hag came with a dress and two slippers, the toe of one stuffed with oddments of ornament and such. The girl reached for them, but Fafhrd grabbed them instead and, seizing her by the left arm, dragged her roughly to her feet.

"No time for that now," he commanded. "We will let Hasjarl decide how he wants you trigged out for the sport," and without more ado he strode from the torture chamber, dragging her beside him, though again muttering from mouth-side, "Courage."

When they were around the first bend in the corridor and had reached a dark branching, he stopped and looked at her frowningly. Her eyes grew wide with fright; she shrank from him, but then firming her features she said fearful-boldly, "If you rape me, by the way, I'll tell Hasjarl."

"I don't mean to rape but rescue you, Friska," Fafhrd assured her rapidly. "That talk of Hasjarl sending to fetch you was but my trick. Where's a secret place I can hide you for a few days?—until we flee these musty crypts forever! I'll bring you food and drink."

At that Friska looked far more frightened. "You mean Hasjarl didn't order this? And that you dream of escaping from Quarmall? Oh stranger, Hasjarl would only have twisted my wrist a little longer, perhaps not maimed me much, only heaped a few more indignities, certainly spared my life. But if he so much as suspected that I had sought to escape from Quarmall...Take me back to the torture chamber!"

"That I will not," Fafhrd said irkedly, his gaze darting up and down the empty corridor. "Take heart, girl. Quarmall's not the wide world. Quarmall's not the stars and the sea. Where's a secret room?"

"Oh, it's hopeless," she faltered. "We could never escape. The stars are a myth. Take me back."

"And make myself out a fool? No," Fafhrd retorted harshly. "We're rescuing you from Hasjarl and from Quarmall too. Make up your mind to it, Friska, for I won't be budged. If you try to scream I'll stop your mouth. *Where's a secret room?*" In his exasperation he almost twisted her wrist, but remembered in time and only brought his face close to hers and rasped, *"Think!"* She had a scent like heather underlying the odor of sweat and tears.

Her eyes went distant then, and she said in a small voice, almost dreamlike, "Between the Upper and the Lower Levels there is a great hall with many small rooms adjoining. Once it was a busy and teeming part of Quarmall, they say, but now debated ground between Hasjarl and Gwaay. Both claim it, neither will maintain it, not even sweep its dust. It is called the Ghost Hall." Her voice went smaller still. "Gwaay's page once begged me meet him a little this side of there, but I did not dare."

"Ha, that's the very place," Fafhrd said with a grin. "Lead us to it."

"But I don't remember the way," Friska protested. "Gwaay's page told me, but I tried to forget…"

Fafhrd had spotted a spiral stair in the dark branchway.

Now he strode instantly toward it, drawing Friska along beside him.

"We know we have to start by going down," he said with rough cheer. "Your memory will improve with motion, Friska."

The Gray Mouser and Ivivis had solaced themselves with such kisses and caresses as seemed prudent in Gwaay's Hall of Sorcery, or rather now of Sleeping Sorcerers. Then, at first coaxed chiefly by Ivivis, it is true, they had visited a nearby kitchen, where the Mouse had readily wheedled from the lumpish cook three large thin slices of medium-rare unmistakable rib-beef, which he had devoured with great satisfaction.

At least one of his appetites mollified, the Mouser had consented that they continue their little ramble and even pause to view a mushroom field. Most strange it had been to see, betwixt the rough-finished pillars of rock, the rows of white button-fungi grow dim, narrow, and converge toward infinity in the ammonia-scented darkness.

At this point they had become teasing in their talk, he taxing Ivivis with having many lovers drawn by her pert beauty, she stoutly denying it, but finally admitting that there was a certain Klevis, page to Gwaay, for whom her heart had once or twice beat faster.

"And best, Gray Guest, you keep an eye open for him," she had warned, wagging a slim finger, "for certain he is the fiercest and most skillful of Gwaay's swordsmen."

Then to change this topic and to reward the Mouser for his patience in viewing the mushroom field, she had drawn him, they going hand in hand now, to a wine cellar. There she had prettily begged the aged and cranky butler for a great tankard of amber fluid for her companion. It had proved to the Mouser's delight to be purest and most potent essence of grape with no bitter admixture whatever.

Two of his appetites now satisfied, the third returned to the Mouser more hotly. Hand-holding became suddenly merely tantalizing and Ivivis' pale green tunic no more an object for admiration and for compliments to her, but only a barrier to be got rid of as swiftly as possible and with the smallest necessary modicum of decorousness.

Himself taking the lead, he drew her as directly as he could recall the route, and with little speech, toward the closet he had preempted for his loot, two levels below Gwaay's Hall of

Sorcery. At last he found the corridor he sought, one hung to either side with thick purple arras and lit by infrequent copper chandeliers which hung each from the rock ceiling on three copper chains and held three thick black candles.

This far Ivivis followed him with only the fewest flirtatious balkings and a minimum of wondering, innocent-eyed questions as to what he intended and why such haste was needful. But now her hesitations became convincing, her eyes began to show a genuine uneasiness, or even fearfulness, and when he stopped by the arras-slit before the door to his closet and with the courtliest of lecherous smirks he could manage indicated to her that they had reached their destination, she drew sharply back, stifling an exclamation with the flat of her hand.

"Gray Mouser," she whispered rapidly, her eyes at once frightened and beseeching, "there is a confession I should have made earlier and now must make at once. By one of those malign and mocking coincidences which haunt all Quarmall, you have chosen for your hidey hole the very chamber where—"

Well it was for the Gray Mouser then that he took seriously Ivivis' look and tone, that he was by nature sense-aware and distrustful, and in particular that his ankles now took note of a slight yet unaccustomed draft from under the arras. For without other warning a fist pointed with a dark dagger punched through the arras-slit at his throat.

With the edge of his left hand, which had been raised to indicate to Ivivis their bedding-place, the Mouser struck aside the black-sleeved arm.

The girl exclaimed, not loudly, "Klevis!"

With his right hand the Mouser caught hold of the wrist going by him and twisted it. With his spread left hand he simultaneously rammed his attacker in the armpit.

But the Mouser's grip, made by hurried snatch, was imperfect. Moreover, Klevis was not minded to resist and have his arm dislocated or broken in that fashion. Spinning with the Mouser's twist, he also went into a deliberate forward somersault.

The net result was that Klevis lost his cross-gripped dagger, which clattered dully on the thick-carpeted floor, but tore loose unhurt from the Mouser and after two more somersaults came lightly to his feet, at once turning and drawing rapier.

By then the Mouser had drawn Scalpel and his dirk Cat's Claw too, but held the latter behind him. He attacked cautiously, with probing feints. When Klevis counterattacked strongly, he retreated, parrying each fierce thrust at the last moment, so that again and again the enemy blade went whickering close by him.

Klevis lunged with especial fierceness. The Mouser parried, high this time and not retreating. In an instant they were pressed body to body, their rapiers strongly engaged near their hilts and above their heads.

By turning a little, the Mouser blocked Klevis' knee driven at his groin. While with the dirk Klevis had overlooked, he stabbed the other from below, Cat's Claw entering just under Klevis' breastbone to pierce his liver, gizzard, and heart.

Letting go his dirk, the Mouser nudged the body away from him and turned.

Ivivis was facing them, with Klevis' punching-dagger gripped ready for a thrust.

The body thudded to the floor.

"Which of us did you propose to skewer?" the Mouser asked.

"I don't know," the girl answered in a flat voice. "You, I suppose."

The Mouser nodded. "Just before this interruption, you were saying, 'The very chamber where—' What?"

"— where I often met Klevis, to be with him," she replied.

Again the Mouser nodded. "So you loved him and—"

"Shut up, you fool!" she interrupted. *"Is he dead?"* There were both deep concern and exasperation in her voice.

The Mouser backed along the body until he stood at the head of it. Looking down, he said, "As mutton. He was a handsome youth."

For a long moment they eyed each other like leopards across the corpse. Then, averting her face a little, Ivivis said, "Hide the body, you imbecile. It tears my heartstrings to see it."

Nodding, the Mouser stooped and rolled the corpse under the arras opposite the closet door. He tucked in Klevis' rapier beside him. Then he withdrew Cat's Claw from the body. Only a little dark blood followed. He cleaned his dirk on the arras, then let the hanging drop.

Standing up, he snatched the punching-dagger from the brooding girl and flipped it so that it too vanished under the arras.

With one hand he spread wide the slit in the arras. With the other he took hold of Ivivis' shoulder and pressed her toward the doorway which Klevis had left open to his undoing.

She instantly shook loose from his grip but walked through the doorway. The Mouser followed. The leopard look was still in both their eyes.

A single torch lit the closet. The Mouser shut the door and barred it.

Ivivis snarled at him, summing it up: "You owe me much, Gray Stranger."

The Mouser showed his teeth in an unhumorous grin. He did not stop to see whether his stolen trinkets had been disturbed. It did not even occur to him, then, to do so.

Fafhrd felt relief when Friska told him that the darker slit at the very end of the dark, long, straight corridor they'd just entered was the door to the Ghost Hall. It had been a hurrying, nervous trip, with many peerings around corners and dartings back into dark alcoves while someone passed, and a longer trip vertically downward than Fafhrd had anticipated. If they had now only reached the top of the Lower Levels, this Quarmall must be bottomless! Yet Friska's spirits had improved considerably. Now at times she almost skipped along in her white chemise cut low behind. Fafhrd strode purposefully, her dress and slippers in his left hand, his ax in his right.

The Northerner's relief in no wise diminished his wariness, so that when someone rushed from an inky tunnel-mouth they were passing, he stroked out almost negligently and he felt and heard his ax crunch halfway through a head.

He saw a comely blond youth, now most sadly dead and his comeliness rather spoiled by Fafhrd's ax, which still stood in the great wound it had made. A fair hand opened, and the sword it had held fell from it.

"Hovis!" he heard Friska cry. "O gods! O gods that are not here. Hovis!"

Lifting a booted foot, Fafhrd stamped it sideways at the youth's chest, at once freeing his ax and sending the corpse back into the tunneled dark from which the live man had so rashly hurtled.

After a swift look and listen all about, he turned toward Friska where she stood white-faced and staring.

"Who's this Hovis?" he demanded, shaking her lightly by the shoulder when she did not reply.

Twice her mouth opened and shut again, while her face remained as expressionless as that of a silly fish. Then with a little gasp she said, "I lied to you, barbarian. I have met Gwaay's page Hovis here. More than once."

"Then why didn't you warn me, wench!" Fafhrd demanded. "Did you think I would scold you for your morals, like some city graybeard? Or have you no regard at all for your men, Friska?"

"Oh, do not chide me," Friska begged miserably. "Please do not chide me."

Fafhrd patted her shoulder. "There, there," he said. "I forget you were shortly tortured and hardly of a mind to remember everything. Come on."

They had taken a dozen steps when Friska began to shudder and sob together in a swiftly mounting crescendo. She turned and ran back, crying, "Hovis! Hovis, forgive me!"

Fafhrd caught her before three steps. He shook her again, and when that did not stop her sobbing, he used his other hand to slap her twice, rocking her head a little.

She stared at him dumbly.

He said not fiercely but somberly, "Friska, I must tell you that Hovis is where your words and tears can never again reach him. He's dead. Beyond recall. Also, I killed him. That's beyond recall too. But you are still alive. You can hide from Hasjarl. Ultimately, whether you believe it or not, you can escape with me from Quarmall. Now come on with me, and no looking back."

She blindly obeyed, with only the faintest of moanings.

The Gray Mouser stretched luxuriously on the silver-tipped bearskin he'd thrown on the floor of his closet. Then he lifted on an elbow and, finding the black pearls he'd pilfered, tried them against Ivivis' bosom in the pale cool light of the single torch above. Just as he'd imagined, the pearls looked very well there. He started to fasten them around her neck.

"No, Mouser," she objected lazily. "It awakens an unpleasant memory."

He did not persist, but lying back again, said unguardedly, "Ah, but I'm a lucky man, Ivivis. I have you and I have an employer who, though somewhat boresome with his sorceries and his endless mild speaking, seems a harmless enough chap and certainly more endurable than his brother Hasjarl, if but half of what I hear of that one is true."

The voice of Ivivis briskened. "You think Gwaay harmless?—and kinder than Hasjarl? La, that's a quaint conceit. Why, but a week ago he summoned my late dearest friend, Divis, then his favorite concubine, and telling her it was a necklace of the same stones, hung around her neck an emerald adder, the sting of which is infallibly deadly."

The Mouser turned his head and stared at Ivivis. "Why did Gwaay do that?" he asked.

She stared back at him blankly. "Why, for nothing at all, to be sure," she said wonderingly. "As everyone knows, that is Gwaay's way."

The Mouser said, "You mean that, rather than say, 'I am wearied of you,' he killed her?"

Ivivis nodded. "I believe Gwaay can no more bear to hurt people's feelings by rejecting them than he can bear to shout."

"It is better to be slain than rejected?" the Mouser questioned ingenuously.

"No, but for Gwaay it is easier on his feelings to slay than to reject. Death is everywhere here in Quarmall."

The Mouser had a fleeting vision of Klevis' corpse stiffening behind the arras.

Ivivis continued, "Here in the Lower Levels we are buried before we are born. We live, love, and die buried. Even when we strip, we yet wear a garment of invisible mold."

The Mouser said, "I begin to understand why it is necessary to cultivate a certain callousness in Quarmall, to be able to enjoy at all any moments of pleasure snatched from life, or perhaps I mean from death."

"That is most true, Gray Mouser," Ivivis said very soberly, pressing herself against him.

Fafhrd started to brush aside the cobwebs joining the two dust-filled sides of the half open, high, nail-studded door, then checked himself and bending very low ducked under them.

"Do you stoop too," he told Friska. "It were best we leave no signs of our entry. Later I'll attend to our footprints in the dust, if that be needful."

They advanced a few paces, then stood hand in hand, waiting for their eyes to grow accustomed to the darkness. Fafhrd still clutched in his other hand Friska's dress and slippers.

"This is the Ghost Hall?" Fafhrd asked. "Aye," Friska whispered close to his ear, sounding fearful. "Some say that Gwaay and Hasjarl send their dead to battle here. Some say that demons owing allegiance to neither—"

"No more of that, girl," Fafhrd ordered gruffly. "If I must battle devils or liches, leave me my hearing and my courage."

They were silent a space then while the flame of the last torch twenty paces beyond the half shut door slowly revealed to them a vast chamber low-domed with huge, rough black blocks pale-mortared for a ceiling. It was set out with a few tatter-shrouded furnishings and showed many small closed doorways. To either side were wide rostra set a few feet above floor level, and toward the center there was, surprisingly, what looked like a dried-up fountain pool.

Friska whispered, "Some say the Ghost Hall was once the harem of the father lords of Quarmall during some centuries when they dwelt underground between Levels, ere this Quarmal's father coaxed by his sea-wife returned to the Keep. See, they left so suddenly that the new ceiling was neither finish-polished, nor final-cemented, nor embellished with drawings, if such were purposed."

Fafhrd nodded. He distrusted that unpillared ceiling and thought the whole place looked rather more primitive than Hasjarl's polished and leather-hung chambers. That gave him a thought.

"Tell me, Friska," he said. "How is it that Hasjarl can see with his eyes closed? Is it that—"

"Why, do you not know that?" she interrupted in surprise.

"Do you not know even the secret of his horrible peeping? He simply—"

A dim velvet shape that chittered almost inaudibly shrill swooped past their faces, and with a little shriek Friska hid her face in Fafhrd's chest and clung to him tightly.

In combing his fingers through her heather-scented hair to show her no flying mouse had found lodgment there and in smoothing his palms over her bare shoulders and back to demonstrate that no bat had landed there either, Fafhrd began to forget all about Hasjarl and the puzzle of his second sight—and his worries about the ceiling falling in on them too.

Following custom, Friska shrieked twice, very softly.

Gwaay languidly clapped his white, perfectly groomed hands and with a slight nod motioned for the waiting slaves to remove the platters from the low table. He leaned lazily into the deep-cushioned chair and through half-closed lids looked momentarily at his companion before he spoke. His brother across the table was not in a good humor. But then it was rare for Hasjarl to be other than in a pet, a temper, or more often merely sullen and vicious. This may have been due to the fact that Hasjarl was a very ugly man, and his nature had grown to conform to his body; or perhaps it was the other way around. Gwaay was indifferent to both theories; he merely knew that in one glance all his memory had told him of Hasjarl was verified; and he again realized the bitter magnitude of his hatred for his brother. However, Gwaay spoke gently in a low, pleasant voice:

"Well, how now, Brother, shall we play at chess, that demon game they say exists in every world? 'Twill give you a chance to lord it over me again. You always win at chess, you know, except when you resign. Shall I have the board set before us?" and then cajolingly, "I'll give you a pawn!" and he raised one hand slightly as if to clap again in order that his suggestion might be carried out.

With the lash he carried slung to his wrist Hasjarl slashed the face of the slave nearest him, and silently pointed at the massive and ornate chessboard across the room. This was quite characteristic of Hasjarl. He was a man of action and given to few words, at least away from his home territory.

Besides, Hasjarl was in a nasty humor. Flindach had torn him from his most interesting and exciting amusement: torture! And for what? thought Hasjarl: to play at chess with his priggish brother; to sit and look at his pretty brother's face; to eat food that would surely disagree with him; to wait the answer to the casting, which he already knew—had known for years; and finally to be forced to smile into the horrible blood-whited eyes of his father, unique in Quarmall save for those of Flindach, and toast the House of Quarmall for the ensuing year. All this was most distasteful to Hasjarl and he showed it plainly.

The slave, a bloody welt swift-swelling across his face, carefully slid the chessboard between the two. Gwaay smiled as another slave arranged the chessmen precisely on their squares; he had thought of a scheme to annoy his brother. He had chosen the black as usual, and he planned a gambit which he knew his avaricious opponent couldn't refuse; one Hasjarl would accept to his own undoing.

Hasjarl sat grimly back in his chair, arms folded. "I should have made you take white," he complained. "I know the paltry tricks you can do with black pebbles—I've seen you as a girl-pale child darting them through the air to startle the slaves' brats. How am I to know you will not cheat by fingerless shifting your pieces while I deep ponder?"

Gwaay answered gently, "My paltry powers, as you most justly appraise them, Brother, extend only to bits of basalt, trifles of obsidian and other volcanic rocks conformable to my nether level. While these chess pieces are jet, Brother, which in your great scholarship you surely know is only a kind of coal, vegetable stuff pressed black, not even in the

same realm as the very few materials subject to my small
magickings. Moreover, for you to miss the slightest trick with
those quaint slave-surgeried eyes of yours, Brother, were
matter for mighty wonder."

Hasjarl growled. Not until all was ready did he stir; then,
like an adder's strike, he plucked a black rook's pawn from
the board and with a sputtering giggle, snarled: "Remember,
Brother? It was a pawn you promised! Move!"

Gwaay motioned the waiting slave to advance his king's
pawn. In like manner Hasjarl replied. A moment's pause and
Gwaay offered his gambit: pawn to king-bishop's fourth!
Eagerly Hasjarl snatched the apparent advantage and the
game began in earnest. Gwaay, his face easy-smiling in repose,
seemed to be less interested in the game than in the shadow
play of the flickering lamps on the figured leather
upholsterings of calfskin, lambskin, snakeskin, and even
slave-skin and nobler human hide; seemed to move offhand,
without plan, yet confidently. Hasjarl, his lips compressed in
concentration, was intent on the board, each move a planned
action both mental and physical. His concentration made
him for the moment oblivious of his brother, oblivious of all
but the problem before him; for Hasjarl loved to win beyond
all computation.

It had always been this way; even as children the contrast
was apparent. Hasjarl was the elder; older by only a few
months which his appearance and demeanor lengthened to
years. His long, misshapen torso was ill-borne on short bandy
legs. His left arm was perceptibly longer than the right; and
his fingers, peculiarly webbed to the first knuckle, were
gnarled and stubby with brittle striated nails. It was as if
Hasjarl were a poorly reconstructed puzzle put together in
such fashion that all the pieces were mismated and awry.

This was particularly true of his features. He possessed his
sire's nose, though thickened and coarse-pored; but this was
contradicted by the thin-lipped, tightly compressed mouth

continually pursed until it had assumed a perpetual sphincterlike appearance. Hair, lank and lusterless, grew low on his forehead; and low, flattened cheekbones added yet another contradiction.

As a lad, led by some perverse whim, Hasjarl had bribed coaxed, or more probably browbeaten one of the slaves versed in surgery to perform a slight operation on his upper eyelids. It was a small enough thing in itself, yet its implications and results had affected the lives of many men unpleasantly, and never ceased to delight Hasjarl.

That merely the piercing of two small holes, centered over the pupil when the eyes were closed, could produce such qualms in other people was incredible; but it was so. Feather-weight grommets of sleekest gold, jade or—as now—ivory— kept the holes from growing shut.

When Hasjarl peered through these tiny apertures it gave the effect of an ambush and made the object of his gaze feel spied upon; but this was the least annoying of his many irritating habits.

Hasjarl did nothing easily, but he did all things well. Even in swordplay his constant practice and overly long left arm made him the equal of the athletic Gwaay. His administration of the Upper Levels over which he ruled was above all things economical and smooth; for woe betide the slave who failed in the slightest detail of his duties. Hasjarl saw and punished.

Hasjarl was well nigh the equal of his teacher in the practice of the Art; and he had gathered about him a band of magicians almost the caliber of Flindach himself. But he was not happy in his prowess so hardly won, for between the absolute power which he desired and the realization of that desire stood two obstacles: the Lord of Quarmall whom he feared above all things; and his brother Gwaay whom he hated with a hatred nourished on envy and fed by his own thwarted desires.

Gwaay, antithetically, was supple of limb, well-formed and

good to look upon. His eyes, wide-set and pale, were deceptively gentle and kindly; for they masked a will as strong and capable of action as coiled spring-steel. His continual residence in the Lower Levels over which he ruled gave to his pallid smooth skin a peculiar waxy luster.

Gwaay possessed that enviable ability to do all things well, with little exertion and less practice. In a way he was much worse than his brother: for while Hasjarl slew with tortures and slow pain and an obvious personal satisfaction, he at least attached some importance to life because he was so meticulous in its taking; whereas Gwaay smiling gently would slay, without reason, as if jesting. Even the group of sorcerers which he had gathered about him for protection and amusement was not safe from his fatal and swift humors.

Some thought that Gwaay was a stranger to fear, but this was not so. He feared the Lord of Quarmall and he feared his brother; or rather he feared that he would be slain by his brother before he could slay him. Yet so well were his fear and hatred concealed that he could sit relaxed, not two yards from Hasjarl, and smile amusedly, enjoying every moment of the evening. Gwaay flattered himself on his perfect control over all emotion.

The chess game had developed beyond the opening stage, the moves coming slower, and now Hasjarl rapped down a rook on the seventh rank.

Gwaay observed gently, "Your turreted warrior rushes deep into my territory, Brother. Rumor has it you've hired a brawny champion out of the north. With what purpose, I wonder, in our peace-wrapped cavern world? Could he be a sort of living rook?" He poised, hand unmoving, over one of his knights.

Hasjarl giggled. "And if his purpose is to slash pretty throats, what's that to you? I know naught of this rook-warrior, but 'tis said—slaves' chat, no doubt—that you yourself have had fetched a skilled sworder from Lankhmar. Should I call him a knight?"

"Aye, two can play at a game," Gwaay remarked with prosy philosophy and lifting his knight, softly but firmly planted it at his king's sixth.

"I'll not be drawn," Hasjarl snarled. "You shall not win by making my mind wander." And arching his head over the board, he cloaked himself again with his all-consuming calculations.

In the background slaves moved silently, tending the lamps and replenishing the founts with oil. Many lamps were needed to light the council room, for it was low-celled and massively beamed, and the arras-hung walls reflected little of the yellow rays and the mosaic floor was worn to a dull richness by countless footsteps in the past. From the living rock this room had been carved; long-forgotten hands had set the huge cypress beams and inlaid the floor so cunningly.

Those gay, time-faded tapestries had been hung by the slaves of some ancient Lord of Quarmall, who had pilfered them from a passing caravan, and so with all the rich adornments. The chessmen and the chairs, the chased lamp sconces and the oil which fed the wicks, and the slaves which tended them: all was loot. Loot from generations back when the Lords of Quarmall plundered far and wide and took their toll from every passing caravan.

High above that warm, luxuriously furnished chamber where Gwaay and Hasjarl played at chess, the Lord of Quarmall finished the final calculations which would complete his horoscope. Heavy leather hangings shut out the stars that had but now twinkled down their benisons and dooms. The only light in that instrument-filled room was the tiny flare of a single taper. By such scant illumination did custom bid the final casting be read, and Quarmal strained even his keen vision to see the Signs and Houses rightly.

As he rechecked the final results his supple lips writhed in a sneer, a grimace of displeasure. *Tonight or tomorrow*, he thought with an inward chill. *At most, late on the morrow.* Truly, he had little time.

Then, as if pleased by some subtle jest, he smiled and nodded, making his skinny shadow perform monstrous gyrations on the curtains and brasured wall.

Finally Quarmal laid aside his crayon and taking the single candle lighted by its flame seven larger tapers. With the aid of this better light he read once more the horoscope. This time he made no sign of pleasure or any other emotion. Slowly he rolled the intricately diagrammed and inscribed parchment into a slender tube, which he thrust in his belt; then rubbing together his lean hands he smiled again. At a nearby table were the ingredients which he needed for his scheme's success: powders, oils, tiny knives, and other materials and instruments.

The time was short. Swiftly he worked, his spatulate fingers performing miracles of dexterity. Once he went on an errand to the wall. The Lord of Quarmall made no mistakes, nor could he afford them.

It was not long before the task was completed to his satisfaction. After extinguishing the last-lit candles, Quarmal, Lord of Quarmall, relaxed into his chair and by the dim light of a single taper summoned Flindach, in order that his horoscope might be announced to those below.

As was his wont, Flindach appeared almost at once. He presented himself confronting his master with arms folded across his chest, and head bowed submissively. Flindach never presumed. His figure was illuminated only to the waist; above that shadow concealed whatever expression of interest or boredom his warted and wine-marked face might show.

In like manner the pitted yet sleeker countenance of Quarmal was obscured; only his pale irises gleamed phosphorescent from the shadows like two minute moons in a dark bloody sky.

As if he were measuring Flindach, or as if he saw him for

the first time, Quarmal slowly raised his glance from foot to forehead of the figure before him, and looking direct into the shaded eyes of Flindach so like his own, he spoke. "O Master of Magicians, it is within your power to grant me a boon this night."

He raised a hand as Flindach would have spoken and swiftly continued: "I have watched you grow from boy to youth and from youth to man; I have nurtured your knowledge of the Art until it is only second to my own. The same mother carried us, though I her firstborn and you the child of her last fertile year—that kinship helped. Your influence within Quarmall is almost equal to mine. So I feel that some reward is due your diligence and faithfulness."

Again Flindach would have spoken, but was dissuaded by a gesture. Quarmal spoke more slowly now and accompanied his words with staccato taps on the parchment roll. "We both well know, from hearsay and direct knowledge, that my sons plot my death. And it is also true that in some manner they must be thwarted, for neither of the twain is fit to become the Lord of Quarmall; nor does it seem probable that either will ever reach such wisdom. Under their warring, Quarmall would die of inanition and neglect, as has died the Ghost Hall. Furthermore, each of them, to buttress his sorceries, has secretly hired a sworded champion from afar—you've seen Gwaay's—and this is the beginning of the bringing of free mercenaries into Quarmall and the sure doom of our power." He stretched a hand toward the dark close-crowded rows of mummied and waxen masks and he asked rhetorically, "Did the Lords of Quarmall guard and preserve our hidden realm that its councils might be entered, crowded, and at last be captured by foreign captains?

"Now a far more secret matter," he continued, his voice sinking. "The concubine Kewissa carries my seed: male—growing, by all omens and oracles—though this is known only to Kewissa and myself, and now to you, Flindach. Should this unborn sprout reach but boyhood brotherless, I might die content, leaving to you his tutelage in all confidence and trust."

Quarmal paused and sat impassive as an effigy. "Yet to forestall Hasjarl and Gwaay becomes more difficult each day, for they increase in power and in scope. Their own innate wickedness gives them access to regions and demons heretofore but imagined by their predecessors. Even I, well versed in necromancy, am often appalled." He paused and quizzically looked at Flindach.

For the first time since he had entered, Flindach spoke. His voice was that of one traced in the recitation of incantations, deep and resonant. "Master, what you speak is true. Yet how will you encompass their plots? You know, as well as I, the custom that forbids what is perhaps the only means of thwarting them."

Flindach paused as if he would say more, but Quarmal quickly intervened. "I have concocted a scheme, which may or may not succeed. The success of it depends almost entirely upon your cooperation." He lowered his voice almost to a whisper, beckoning for Flindach to step closer. "The very stones may carry tales, O Flindach, and I would that this plan were kept entirely secret." Quarmal beckoned again, and Flindach stepped still nearer until he was within arm's reach of his master. Half stooping, he placed himself in such a position that his ear was close to Quarmal's mouth. This was closer than ever he remembered approaching Quarmal, and strange qualms filled his mind, recrudescences of childish old wives' tales. This ancient ageless man with eyes pearl-irised as his own seemed to Flindach not like half brother at all, but like some strange, merciless half father. His burgeoning terror was intensified when he felt the sinewy fingers of Quarmal close on his wrist and gently urge him closer, almost to his knees, beside the chair.

Quarmal's lips moved swiftly, and Flindach controlled his urge to rise and flee as the plan was unfolded to him. With a sibilant phrase, the final phrase, Quarmall finished, and Flindach realized the full enormity of that plan. Even as he comprehended it, the single taper guttered and was extinguished. There was darkness absolute.

The chess game progressed swiftly; the only sounds, except the ceaseless shuffle of naked feet and the hiss of lamp wicks, were the dull click of the chessmen and the staccato cough of Hasjarl. The low table off which the twain had eaten was placed opposite the broad arched door which was the only apparent entrance to the council chamber.

There was another entrance. It led to the Keep of Quarmall; and it was toward this arras-concealed door that Gwaay glanced most often. He was positive that the news of the casting would be as usual, but a certain curiosity whelmed him this evening; he felt a faint foreshadowing of some untoward event, even as wind blows gusty before a storm.

An omen had been vouchsafed Gwaay by the gods today; an omen that neither his necromancers nor his own skill could interpret to his complete satisfaction. So he felt that it would be wise to await the development of events prepared and expectant.

Even as he watched the tapestry behind which he knew was the door whence would step Flindach to announce the consequences of the casting, that hanging bellied and trembled as if some breeze blew on it, or some hand pushed against it lightly.

Hasjarl abruptly threw himself back in his chair and cried in his high-pitched voice, "Check with my rook to your king, and mate in three!" He dropped one eyelid evilly and peered triumphantly at Gwaay.

Gwaay, without removing his eyes from the still-swaying tapestry, said in precise, mellow words, "The knight interposes, Brother, discovering check. I mate in two. You are wrong again, my comrade."

But even as Hasjarl swept the men with a crash to the floor, the arras was more violently disturbed. It was parted by two slaves and the harsh gong-note, announcing the entrance of some high official, sounded.

Silently from betwixt the hanging stepped the tall lean form of Flindach. His shadowed face, despite the disfiguring wine mark and the treble mole, had a great and solemn dignity. And in its somber expressionlessness—an expressionlessness curiously mocked by a knowing glitter deep in the black pupils of the pearl-irised crimson-balled eyes— it seemed to forebode some evil tiding.

All motion ceased in that long low hall as Flindach, standing in the archway framed in rich tapestries, raised one arm in a gesticulation demanding silence. The attendant well-trained slaves stood at their posts, heads bowed submissively; Gwaay remained as he was, looking directly at Flindach; and Hasjarl, who had half-turned at the gong note, likewise awaited the announcement. In a moment, they knew, Quarmal their father would step from behind Flindach and smiling evilly would announce his horoscope. Always this had been the procedure; and always, since each could remember, Gwaay and Hasjarl had at this moment wished for Quarmal's death.

Flindach, arm lifted in dramatic gesture, began to speak.

"The casting of the horoscope has been completed and the finding has been made. Even as the Heavens foretell is the fate of man fulfilled. I bring this news to Hasjarl and Gwaay, the sons of Quarmal."

With a swift motion Flindach plucked a slender parchment tube from his belt and, breaking it with his hands, dropped it crumpled at his feet. In almost the same gesture he reached behind his left shoulder and stepping from the shadow of the arch drew a peaked cowl over his head.

Throwing wide both arms, Flindach spoke, his voice seeming to come from afar:

"Quarmal, Lord of Quarmall, rules no more. The casting is fulfilled. Let all within the walls of Quarmall mourn. For three days the place of the Lord of Quarmall will be vacant. So custom demands and so shall it be. On the morrow, when the sun enters his courtyard, that which remains of what was once a great and puissant lord will be given to the flames. Now I go to mourn my Master and oversee the obsequies and prepare myself with fasting and with prayer for his passing. Do you likewise."

Flindach slowly turned and disappeared into the darkness from which he had come.

For the space of ten full heartbeats Gwaay and Hasjarl sat motionless. The announcement came as a thunderclap to both. Gwaay for a second felt an impulse to giggle and smirk like a child who has unexpectedly escaped punishment and is instead rewarded; but in the back of his mind he was half-convinced that he had known all along the outcome of the casting. However, he controlled his childish glee and sat silent, staring.

On the other hand Hasjarl reacted as might be expected of him. He went through a series of outlandish grimaces and ended with an obscene half-smothered titter. Then he frowned, and turning said to Gwaay, "Heard you not what said Flindach? I must go and prepare myself!" and he lurched to his feet and paced silently across the room, out the broad-arched door.

Gwaay remained sitting for another few moments, frowning eyes narrowed in concentration, as if he were puzzling over some abstruse problem which required all his powers to solve. Suddenly he snapped his fingers and, motioning for his slaves to precede him, made ready for his return to the Lower Levels, whence he had come.

Fafhrd had barely left the Ghost Hall when he heard the faint rattle and clink of armed men moving cautiously. His bemusement with Friska's charms vanished as if he had been doused with ice water. He shrank into the deeper darkness and eavesdropped long enough to learn that these were pickets of Hasjarl, guarding against an invasion from Gwaay's Lower Levels—and not tracking down Friska and himself as he'd first feared. Then he made off swiftly for Hasjarl's Hall of Sorcery, grimly pleased that his memory for landmarks and turnings seemed to work as well for mazy tunnels as for forest trails and steep zigzag mountain escalades.

The bizarre sight that greeted him when he reached his goal stopped him on the stony threshold. Standing shin-deep and stark naked in a steaming marble tub shaped like a ridgy seashell, Hasjarl was berating and haranguing the great roomful around him. And every man jack of them—sorcerers, officers, overseers, pages bearing great fringy towels and dark red robes and other apparel—was standing quakingly still with cringing eyes, except for the three slaves soaping and laving their Lord with tremulous dexterity.

Fafhrd had to admit that Hasjarl naked was somehow more consistent—ugly everywhere—a kobold birthed from a hot-spring. And although his grotesque child-pink torso and mismated arms were a-writhe and a-twitch in a frenzy of apprehension, he had dignity of a sort.

He was snarling, "Speak, all of you, is there a precaution I have forgotten, a rite omitted, a rat-hole overlooked that Gwaay might creep through? Oh, that on this night when demons lurk and I must mind a thousand things and dress me for my father's obsequies, I should be served by wittols! Are you all deaf and dumb? Where's my great champion, who should ward me now? Where are my scarlet grommets? Less soap there, you—take that! You, Essem, are we guarded well above?—I don't trust Flindach. And Yissim, have we guards enough below?—Gwaay is a snake who'll strike through any gap. Dark Gods, defend me! Go to the barracks, Yissim, get more men, and reinforce our downward guards—and while you're there, I mind me now, bid them continue Friska's torture. Wring the truth from her! She's in Gwaay's plots—this night has made me certain. Gwaay knew my father's death was imminent and laid invasion plans long weeks agone. Any of you may be his purchased spies! Oh where's my champion? *Where are my scarlet grommets?*"

Fafhrd, who'd been striding forward, quickened his pace at mention of Friska. A simple inquiry at the torture chamber would reveal her escape and his part in it. He must create diversions. So he halted close in front of pink wet steaming Hasjarl and said boldly, "Here is your champion, Lord. And he counsels not sluggy defense, but some swift stroke at Gwaay! Surely your mighty mind has fashioned many a shrewd attacking stratagem. Launch you a thunderbolt!"

It was all Fafhrd could do to keep speaking forcefully to the end and not let his voice trail off as his attention became engrossed in the strange operation now going on. While Hasjarl crouched stock-still with head a-twist, an ashen-faced bath-slave had drawn out Hasjarl's left upper eyelid by its lashes and was inserting into the hole in it a tiny flanged scarlet ring or grommet no bigger than a lentil. The grommet was carried on the tip of an ivory wand as thin as a straw, and the whole deed was being done by the slave with the anxiety of a man refilling the poison pouches of an untethered rattlesnake—if such an action might be imagined for purposes of comparison.

However, the operation was quickly completed, and then on the right eye too—and evidently with perfect satisfaction, since Hasjarl did not slash the slave with the soapy wet lash still dangling from his wrist—and when Hasjarl straightened up he was grinning broadly at Fafhrd.

"You counsel me well, champion," he cried. "These other fools could do nothing but shake. There *is* a stroke long-planned that I'll try now, one that won't violate the obsequies. Essem, take slaves and fetch the dust—you know the stuff I

mean—and meet me at the vents! Girls, sluice these suds off
with tepid water. Boy, give me my slippers and my toweling
robe!—those other clothes can wait. Follow me, Fafhrd!

But just then his red-grommeted gaze lit on his four-and-
twenty bearded and hooded sorcerers standing apprehensive
by their chairs.

"Back to your charms at once, you ignoramuses!" he roared
at them. "I did not tell you to stop because I bathed! Back to
your charms and send your plagues at Gwaay—red, black and
green, nose drip and bloody rot—or I will burn your beards
off to the eyelashes as prelude to more dire torturings! Haste,
Essem! Come, Fafhrd!"

The Gray Mouser at that same moment was returning from
his closet with Ivivis when Gwaay, velvet-shod and followed
by barefoot slaves, came around a turn in the dim corridor
so swiftly there was no evading him.

The young Lord of the Lower Levels seemed preternaturally
calm and controlled, yet with the impression that under the
calm was naught but quivering excitement and darting
thought—so much so that it would hardly have surprised the
Mouser if there had shone forth from Gwaay an aura of Blue
Essence of Thunderbolt. Indeed, the Mouser felt his skin
begin to prickle and sting as if just such an influence were
invisibly streaming from his employer.

Gwaay scanned the Mouser and the pretty slavegirl in a
flicker and spoke, his voice dancing rapid and gaysome.

"Well, Mouser, I can see you've sampled your reward ahead
of time. Ah, youth and dim retreats and pillowed dreams and
amorous hostessings—what else gilds life or makes it worth the
guttering sooty candle? Was the girl skillful? Good! Ivivis, dear,
I must reward your zeal. I gave Divis a necklace—would you
one? Or I've a brooch shaped like a scorpion, ruby-eyed—"

The Mouser felt the girl's hand quiver and chill in his

and he cut in quickly with, "My demon speaks to me, Lord Gwaay, and tells me it's a night when the Fates walk."

Gwaay laughed. "Your demon has been listening behind the arras. He's heard tales of my father's swift departure." As he spoke a drop formed at the end of his nose, between his nostrils. Fascinated, the Mouser watched it grow. Gwaay started to lift the back of his hand to it, then shook it off instead. For an instant he frowned, then laughed again.

"Aye, the Fates trod on Quarmall Keep tonight," Gwaay said, only now his gay rapid voice was a shade hoarse.

"My demon whispers me further that there are dangerous powers abroad this night," the Mouser continued.

"Aye, brother love and such," Gwaay quipped in reply, but now his voice was a croak. A look of great startlement widened his eyes. He shivered as with a chill, and drops pattered from his nose. Three hairs came loose from his scalp and fell across his eyes. His slaves shrank back from him.

"My demon warns me we'd best use my Great Spell quickly against those powers," the Mouser went on, his mind returning as always to Sheelba's untested rune. "It destroys only sorcerers of the Second Rank and lower. Yours, being of the First Rank, will be untouched. But Hasjarl's will perish."

Gwaay opened his mouth to reply, but no words came forth, only a moaning nightmarish groan like that of a mute. Hectic spots shone forth high on his cheeks, and now it seemed to the Mouser that a reddish blotch was crawling up the right side of his chin, while on the left black spots were forming. A hideous stench became apparent. Gwaay staggered and his eyes brimmed with a greenish ichor. He lifted his hand to them, and its back was yellowish crusted and red-cracked. His slaves ran.

"Hasjarl's sendings!" the Mouser hissed. "Gwaay's sorcerers still sleep! I'll rouse 'em! Support him, Ivivis!" And turning he sped like the wind down corridor and up

ramp until he reached Gwaay's Hall of Sorcery. He entered
it, clapping and whistling harshly between his teeth, for
true enough the twelve scrawny loinclothed magi were still
curled snoring on their wide high-backed chairs. The
Mouser darted to each in turn, righting and shaking him
with no gentle hands and shouting in his ear, "To your
work! Anti-venom! Guard Gwaay!"

Eleven of the sorcerers roused quickly enough and were
soon staring wide-eyed at nothingness, though with their
bodies rocking and their heads bobbing for a while from the
Mouser's shaking—like eleven small ships just overpassed by
a squall.

He was having a little more trouble with the twelfth,
though this one was coming awake, soon would be doing his
share, when Gwaay appeared of a sudden in the archway with
Ivivis at his side, though not supporting him. The young
Lord's face gleamed as silvery clear in the dimness as the massy
silver mask of him that hung in the niche above the arch.

"Stand aside, Gray Mouser, I'll jog the sluggard," he cried
in a rippingly bright voice and snatching up a small obsidian
jar tossed it toward the drowsy sorcerer.

It should have fallen no more than halfway between them.
Did he mean to wake the ancient by its shattering? the
Mouser wondered. But then Gwaay stared at it in the air and
it quickened its speed fearfully. It was as if he had tossed up a
ball, then batted it. Shooting forward like a bolt fired point-
blank from a sinewy catapult it shattered the ancient's skull
and spattered the chair and the Mouser with his brains.

Gwaay laughed, a shade high-pitched, and cried lightly, "I
must curb my excitement! I must! I must! Sudden recovery
from two dozen deaths—or twenty-three and the Nose
Drip—is no reason for a philosopher to lose control. Oh, I'm
a giddy fellow!"

Ivivis cried suddenly, "The room swims! I see silver fish!"

The Mouser felt dizzy himself then and saw a

phosphorescent green hand reach through the archway toward Gwaay—reach out on a thin arm that lengthened to yards. He blinked hard and the hand was gone—but now there were swimmings of purple vapor.

He looked at Gwaay and that one, frowny-eyed now, was sniffling hard and then sniffling again, though no new drop could be seen to have formed on his nose-end.

Fafhrd stood three paces behind Hasjarl, who looked in his bunched and high-collared robe of earth-brown toweling rather like an ape.

Beyond Hasjarl on the right there trotted on a thick wide roller-riding leather belt three slaves of monstrous aspect: great splayed feet, legs like an elephant's, huge furnace-bellows chests, dwarfy arms, pinheads with wide toothy mouths and with nostrils bigger than their eyes or ears—creatures bred to run ponderously and nothing else. The moving belt disappeared with a half twist into a vertical cylinder of masonry five yards across and reemerged just below itself, but moving in the opposite direction, to pass under the rollers and complete its loop. From within the cylinder came the groaning of the great wooden fan which the belt whirled and which drove life-sustaining air downward to the Lower Levels.

Beyond Hasjarl on the left was a small door as high as Fafhrd's head in the cylinder. To it there mounted one by one, up four narrow masonry steps, a line of dusky, great-headed dwarves. Each bore on his shoulder a dark bag which when he reached the window he untied and emptied into the clamorous shaft, shaking it out most thoroughly while he held it inside, then folding it and leaping down to give place to the next bag-bearer.

Hasjarl leered over his shoulder at Fafhrd. "A nosegay for Gwaay!" he cried. "'Tis a king's ransom I strew on the downward gale: powder of poppy, dust of lotus and mandragora, crumble of hemp. A million lewdly pleasant dreams, and all for Gwaay! Three ways this conquers him: he'll sleep a day and miss my father's funeral, then Quarmall's mine by right of sole appearance yet with no bloodshed, which would mar the rites; his sorcerers will sleep and my infectious spells burst through and strike him down in stinking jellied death; his realm will sleep, each slave and cursed page, so we conquer all merely by marching down after the business of the funeral. Ho, swifter there!" And seizing a long whip from an overseer, he began to crack it over the squat cones of the tread-slaves' heads and sting their broad backs with it. Their trot changed to a ponderous gallop, the moan of the fan rose in pitch, and Fafhrd waited to hear it shatter cracklingly, or see the belt snap, or the rollers break on their axles.

The dwarf at the shaft-window took advantage of Hasjarl's attention being elsewhere to snatch a pinch of powder from his bag and bring it to his nostrils and sniff it down, leering ecstatically. But Hasjarl saw and whipped him about the legs most cruelly. The dwarf dutifully emptied his bag and shook it out while making little hops of agony. However he did not seem much chastened or troubled by his whipping, for as he left the chamber Fafhrd saw him pull his empty bag over his head and waddle off breathing deeply through it.

Hasjarl went on whip-cracking and calling, "Swifter, I say! For Gwaay a drugged hurricane!"

The officer Yissim raced into the room and darted to his master.

"The girl Friska's escaped!" he cried. "Your torturers say your champion came with your seal, telling them you had ordered her release—and snatched her off! All this occurred a quarter day ago."

"Guards!" Hasjarl squealed. "Seize the Northerner! Disarm and bind the traitor!"

But Fafhrd was gone.

The Mouser, in company with Ivivis, Gwaay and a colorful rabble of drug-induced hallucinations, reeled into a chamber similar to the one from which Fafhrd had just disappeared. Here the great cylindrical shaft ended in a half turn. The fan that sucked down the air and blew it out to refresh the Lower Levels was set vertically in the mouth of the shaft and was visible as it whirled.

By the shaft-mouth hung a large cage of white birds, all lying on its floor with their feet in the air. Besides these tell-tales, there was stretched on the floor of the chamber its overseer, also overcome by the drugs whirlwinding from Hasjarl.

By contrast, the three pillar-legged slaves ponderously trotting their belt seemed not affected at all. Presumably their tiny brains and monstrous bodies were beyond the reach of any drug, short of its lethal dose.

Gwaay staggered up to them, slapped each in turn, and commanded, "Stop!" Then he himself dropped to the floor.

The groaning of the fan died away, its seven wooden vanes became clearly visible as it stopped (though for the Mouser they were interwoven with scaly hallucinations), and the only real sound was the slow gasping of the tread-slaves.

Gwaay smiled weirdly at them from where he sprawled, and he raised an arm drunkenly and cried, "Reverse! About face!" Slowly the tread-slaves turned, taking a dozen tiny steps to do it, until they all three faced the opposite direction on the belt.

"Trot!" Gwaay commanded them quickly. Slowly they obeyed and slowly the fan took up again its groaning, but now it was blowing air up the shaft against Hasjarl's downward fanning.

Gwaay and Ivivis rested on the floor for a space, until their brains began to clear and the last hallucinations were chased from view. To the Mouser they seemed to be sucked up the shaft through the fan blades: a filmy horde of blue-and-purple wraiths armed with transparent saw-toothed spears and cutlasses.

Then Gwaay, smiling in highest excitement with his eyes, said softly and still a bit breathlessly, "My sorcerers…were not overcome…I think. Else I'd be dying…Hasjarl's two dozen deaths. Another moment…and I'll send across the level…to reverse the exhaust fan. We'll get fresh air through it. And put more slaves on this belt here—perchance I'll blow my brother's nightmares back to him. Then lave and robe me for my father's fiery funeral and mount to give Hasjarl a nasty shock. Ivivis, as soon as you can walk, rouse my bath girls. Bid them make all ready."

He reached across the floor and grasped the Mouser strongly at the elbow. "You, Gray One," he whispered, "prepare to work this mighty tune of yours which will smite down Hasjarl's warlocks. Gather your simples, pray your demonic prayers—consulting first with my twelve arch-magi…if you can rouse the twelfth from his dark hell. As soon as Quarmall's lich is in the flames, I'll send you word to speak your deadly spell." He paused, and his eyes gleamed with a witchy glare in the dimness. "The time has come for sorcery and swords!"

There was a tiny scrabbling as one of the white birds staggered to its feet on the cage-bottom. It gave a chirrup that was rather like a hiccup, yet still had a note of challenge in it.

All that night through, all Quarmall was awake. Into the Ordering Room of the Keep, a magician came crying, "Lord Flindach! The mind-casters have incontrovertible advertisements that the two brothers war against each other. Hasjarl sends sleepy resins down the shafts, while Gwaay blows them back."

The warty and purple-blotched face of the Master of Magicians looked up from where he sat busy at a table surrounded by a small host awaiting orders.

"Have they shed blood?" he asked.

"Not yet."

"It is well. Keep enchanted eyes on them."

Then, gazing sternly in turn from under his hood at those whom he addressed, the Master of Magicians gave his other orders:

To two magicians robed as his deputies: "Go on the instant to Hasjarl and Gwaay. Remind them of the obsequies and stay with them until they and their companies reach the funeral courtyard."

To a eunuch: "Hasten to your master Brilla. Learn if he requires further materials or assistance building the funeral pyre. Help will be furnished him at once and without stint."

To a captain of slingers: "Double the guard on the walls. Yourself make the rounds. Quarmall must be entirely secure from outward assaults and escapes from within on this coming morn."

To a richly-clad woman of middle years: "To Quarmal's harem. See that his concubines are perfectly groomed and clad, as if their Lord himself meant to visit them at dawn. Quiet their apprehensions. Send to me the Ilthmarix Kewissa."

In Hasjarl's Hall of Sorcery, that Lord let his slaves robe him for the obsequies, while not neglecting to direct the search for his traitorous champion Fafhrd, to instruct the shaft-watchers in the precautions they must take against Gwaay's attempts to return the poppy dust, perchance with interest, and to tutor his sorcerers in the exact spells they must use against Gwaay once Quarmal's body was devoured by the flame.

In the Ghost Hall, Fafhrd munched and drank with Friska a small feast he'd brought. He told her how he'd fallen into disfavor with Hasjarl, and he mulled plans for his escape with her from the realm of Quarmall.

In Gwaay's Hall of Sorcery, the Gray Mouser conferred in turn with the eleven skinny wizards in their white loincloths, telling them nothing of Sheelba's spell, but securing from each the firm assurance that he was a magus of the First Rank.

In the steam room of Gwaay's bath, that Lord recuperated his flesh and faculties shaken by disease spells and drugs. His girls, supervised by Ivivis, brought him fragrant oils and elixirs, and scrubbed and laved him as he directed languidly yet precisely. The slender forms, blurred and silvered by the clouds of steam, moved and posed as in a languorous ballet.

The huge pyre was finally completed, and Brilla heaved a sigh of relief and contentment with the knowledge of work well done. He relaxed his fat, massive frame onto a bench against the wall and spoke to one of his companions in a high-pitched feminine voice:

"Such short notice, and at such a time, but the gods are not to be denied, and no man can cheat his stars. It is shameful though, to think that Quarmal will go so poorly attended: only a half dozen Lankhmarts, an Ilthmarix, and three Mingols—and one of those blemished. I always told him he should keep a better harem. However the male slaves are in fine fettle and will perhaps make up for the rest. Ah! but it's a fine flame the Lord will have to light his way!" Brilla wagged his head dolefully and, snuffling, blinked a tear from his piggy eye; he was one of the few who really regretted the passing of Quarmal.

As High Eunuch to the Lord, Brilla's position was a sinecure and, besides, he had always been fond of Quarmal since he could remember. Once when a small chubby boy Brilla had been rescued from the torments of a group of larger, more virile slaves who had freed him at the mere passing-by of Quarmal. It was this small incident, unwotted or long forgotten by Quarmal, which had provoked a lifelong devotion in Brilla.

Now only the gods knew what the future held. Today the body of Quarmal would be burned, and what would happen after that was better left unpondered, even in the innermost thoughts of a man. Brilla looked once more at his handiwork, the funeral pyre. Achieving it in six short hours, even with hosts of slaves at his command, had taxed his powers. It towered in the center of the courtyard, even higher than the arch of the great gate thrice the stature of a tall man. It was built in the form of a square pyramid, truncated midway; and the inflammable woods that composed it were completely hidden by somber-hued drapes.

A runway was built from the ground across the vast courtyard to the topmost tier on each of the four sides; and at the top was a sizable square platform. It was here that the litter containing the body of Quarmal would be placed, and here the sacrificial victims be immolated. Only those slaves of proper age and talents were permitted to accompany their Lord on his long journey beyond the stars.

Brilla approved of what he saw and, rubbing his hands, looked about curiously. It was only on such occasions as this that one realized the immensity of Quarmall, and these occasions were rare; perhaps once in his life a man would see such an event. As far as Brilla could see small bands of slaves were lined, rank on rank, against the walls of the courtyard, even as was his own band of eunuchs and carpenters. There were the craftsmen from the Upper Levels, skilled workmen all in metal and in wood; there were the workers from the fields and vineyards all brown and gnarled from their labors; there were the slaves from the Lower Levels, blinking in the unaccustomed daylight, pallid and curiously deformed; and all the rest who served in the bowels of Quarmall, a representative group from each level.

The size of the turnout seemed to contradict the dawn's frightening rumors of secret war last night between the Levels, and Brilla felt reassured.

Most important and best placed were the two bands of henchmen of Hasjarl and Gwaay, one group on each side of the pyre. Only the sorcerers of the twain were absent, Brilla noted with a pang of unease, though refusing to speculate why.

High above all this mass of mixed humanity, atop the towering walls, were the ever-silent, ever-alert guards; standing quietly at their posts, slings dangling ready to hand. Never yet had the walls of Quarmall been stormed, and never had a slave once within those close-watched walls passed into the outer world alive.

Brilla was admirably placed to observe all that occurred. To his right, projecting from the wall of the courtyard, was the balcony from which Hasjarl and Gwaay would watch the consuming of their father's body; to his left, likewise projecting, was the platform from which Flindach would direct the rituals. Brilla sat almost next to the door whence the prepared and purified body of Quarmal would be borne for its final fiery cleansing. He wiped the sweat from his flabby jowls with the hem of his under tunic and wondered how much longer it would be before things started. The sun could not be far from the top of the wall now, and with its first beams the rites began.

Even as he wondered there came the tremendous, muffled vibration of the huge gong. There was a craning of necks and a rustling as many bodies shifted; then silence. On the left balcony the figure of Flindach appeared.

Flindach was cowled with the Cowl of Death and his garments were of heavy woven brocades, somber and dull. At his waist glittered the circular fan-bladed Golden Symbol of Power, which while the Chair of Quarmall was vacant, Flindach as High Steward must keep inviolate.

He lifted his arms toward the place where the sun would in a moment appear and intoned the Hymn of Greeting; even as he chanted, the first tawny rays struck into the eyes of those across the courtyard. Again that muffled vibration, which shook the very bones of those closest to it, and opposite Flindach, on the other balcony, appeared Gwaay and Hasjarl. Both were garbed alike but for their diadems and scepters. Hasjarl wore a sapphire-jeweled silver band on his forehead, and in his hand was the scepter of the Upper Levels, crested with a clenched fist; Gwaay wore a diadem inlaid with rubies, and in his hand was his scepter surmounted by a worm, dagger-transfixed. Otherwise the twain were dressed identically in ceremonial robes of darkest red, belted with broad leather girdles of black; they wore no weapons nor were any other ornaments permissible.

As they seated themselves upon the high stools provided, Flindach turned toward the gate nearest Brilla and began to chant. His sonorous voice was answered by a hidden chorus and reechoed by certain of the bands in the courtyard. For the third time the monstrous gong was sounded, and as the last echoes faded the body of Quarmal, litter-borne, appeared. It was carried by the six Lankhmar slavegirls and followed by the Mingols; this small band was all that remained of the many who had slept in the bed of Quarmal.

But where, Brilla asked himself with a heart-bounding start, was Kewissa the Ilthmarix, the old Lord's favorite? Brilla had ordered the marshaling of the girls himself. She could not—

Slowly through a lane of prostrate bodies the litter progressed toward the pyre. The carcass of Quarmal was propped in a sitting posture, and it swayed in a manner horribly suggestive of life as the slavewomen staggered under their unaccustomed load. He was garbed in robes of purple silk, and his brow bore the golden bands of Quarmall's Lord.

Those lean hands, once so active in the practice of necromancy and incantations, were folded stiffly over the Grammarie which had been his bible during life. On his wrist, hooded and chained, was a great gyrfalcon, and at the feet of its dead master lay his favorite coursing leopard, quiet in the quietness of death. Even as was the falcon hooded, so with waxlike lids were the once awesome eyes of Quarmal covered; those eyes which had seen so much of death were now forever dead.

Although Brilla's mind was still agitated about Kewissa, he spoke a word of encouragement to the other girls as they passed, and one of them flung him a wistful smile; they all knew it was an honor to accompany their master into the future, but none of them desired it particularly; however there was little they could do about it except follow directions. Brilla felt sorry for them all; they were so young, had such luscious bodies and were capable of giving so much pleasure to a man, for he had trained them well. But custom must be fulfilled. Yet how then had Kewissa—? Brilla shut off that speculation.

The litter moved on up the ramp. The chanting grew in volume and tempo as the top of the pyre was reached, and the rays of the sun, now shining full onto the dead countenance of Quarmal, as the litter turned toward it, reflected from the bright hair and white skin of the Lankhmar slavegirls, who had with their companions thrown themselves at the feet of Quarmal.

Suddenly Flindach dropped his arms and there was silence, a complete and total silence startling in its contrast to the measured chant and clashing gongs.

Gwaay and Hasjarl sat motionless, staring intently at the figure that had once been the Lord of Quarmall.

Flindach again raised his arms and from the gate opposite to that from whence had come the body of Quarmal, there leaped eight men. Each bore a flambeau and was naked but for a purple cowl which obscured his face. To the accompaniment of harsh gong notes they ran swiftly to the pyre, two on each side and, thrusting their torches into the prepared wood, cast themselves over the flames they created and clambering up the pyramid embraced the slavegirls wantonly.

Almost at once the flames ate into the resinous and oil-impregnated wood. For a moment through the thick smoke the interlocking writhing forms of the slaves could be perceived, and the lean figure of dead Quarmal staring through closed lids directly into the face of the sun. Then, incensed by the heat and acrid fumes, the great falcon screamed in vicious anger and wing-flapping rose from the wrist of its master. The chains held fast; but all could see the arm of Quarmal lifted high in a gesture of sublime dismissal before the smoke obscured. The chanting reached crescendo and abruptly ended as Flindach gave the sign that the rites were finished.

As the eager flames swiftly consumed the pyre and the burden it bore, Hasjarl broke the silence which custom had enjoined. He turned toward Gwaay and fingering the knuckly knob of his scepter and with an evil grin he spoke.

"Ha! Gwaay, it would have been a merry thing to have seen you leching in the flames. Almost as merry as to see our sire gesticulating after death. Go quickly, Brother! There's yet a chance to immolate yourself and so win fame and immortality." And he giggled, slobbering.

Gwaay had just made an unapparent sign to a page nearby, and the lad was hurrying away. The young Lord of the Lower Levels was in no manner amused by his brother's ill-timed jesting, but with a smile and shrug he replied sarcastically, "I choose to seek death in less painful paths. Yet the idea is a good one; I'll treasure it." Then suddenly in a deeper voice: "It had been better that we were both stillborn than to fritter our lives away in futile hatreds. I'll overlook your dream-dust and your poppy hurricanes, and e'en your noisome sorceries, and make a pact with you, O Hasjarl! By the somber gods who rule under Quarmall's Hill and by the Worm which is my sign I swear that from my hand your life is sacrosanct; with neither spells nor steel nor venoms will I slay thee!"

Gwaay rose to his feet as he finished and looked directly at Hasjarl.

Taken unaware, Hasjarl for a second sat in silence; a puzzled expression crossed his face; then a sneer distorted his thin lips and he spat at Gwaay:

"So! You fear me more even than I thought. Aye! And rightly so! Yet the blood of yon old cinder runs in both our bodies, and there is a tender spot within me for my brother. Yes, I'll pact with thee, Gwaay! By the Elder Ones who swim in lightless deeps and by the Fist that is my token, I'll swear your life is sacrosanct—until I crush it out!" And with a final evil titter Hasjarl, like a malformed stoat, slid from stool and out of sight.

Gwaay stood quietly listening, gazing at the space where Hasjarl had sat; then, sure his brother was well gone, he slapped his thighs mightily and, convulsed with silent laughter, gasped to no one in particular, "Even the wiliest hares are caught in simple snares," and still smiling he turned to watch the dancing flames.

Slowly the variegated groups were herded into the passageways whence they had come and the courtyard was cleared once again, except for those slaves and priests whose duties kept them there.

Gwaay remained watching for a time, then he too slipped off the balcony into the inner rooms. And a faint smile yet clung to his mouth corners as if some jest were lingering in his mind pleasantly.

"…And by the blood of that one whom it is death to look upon…"

So sonorously invoked the Mouser, as with eyes closed and arms outstretched he cast the rune given him by Sheelba of the Eyeless Face which would destroy all sorcerers of less than First Rank of an undetermined distance around the casting point—surely for a few miles, one might hope, so smiting Hasjarl's warlocks to dust.

Whether his Great Spell worked or not—and in his inmost heart he strongly mistrusted that it would—the Mouser was very pleased with the performance he was giving. He doubted Sheelba himself could have done better. What magnificent deep chest tones—even Fafhrd had never heard him declaim so.

He wished he could open his eyes for just a moment to note the effect his performance was having on Gwaay's magicians—they'd be staring open-mouthed for all their supercilious boasting, he was sure—but on this point Sheelba's instructions had been adamant: eyes tightly shut while the last sentences of the rune were being recited and the great forbidden words spoken; even the tiniest blink would nullify the Great Spell. Evidently magicians were supposed to be without vanity or curiosity—what a bore!

Of a sudden in the dark of his head, he felt contact with another and a larger darkness, a malefic and puissant darkness, of which light itself is only the absence. He shivered. His hair stirred. Cold sweat prickled his face. He almost stuttered midway through the word "slewerisophnak." But concentrating his will, he finished without flaw.

When the last echoing notes of his voice had ceased to rebound between the domed ceiling and floor, the Mouser slit open one eye and glanced surreptitiously around him.

One glance and the other eye flew open to fullness. He was too surprised to speak.

And whom he would have spoken to, had he not been too surprised, was also a question.

The long table at the foot of which he stood was empty of occupants. Where but moments before had sat eleven of the very greatest magicians of Quarmall—sorcerers of the First Rank, each had sworn on his black Grammarie—was only space.

The Mouser called softly. It was possible that these provincial fellows had been frightened at the majesty of his dark Lankhmarian delivery and had crawled under the table.

But there was no answer.

He spoke louder. Only the ceaseless groan of the fans could be sensed, though hardly more noticeable after four days hearing them than the coursing of his blood. With a shrug the Mouser relaxed into his chair. He murmured to himself, "If those slick-faced old fools run off, what next? Suppose all Gwaay's henchmen flee?"

As he began to plan out in his mind what strategy of airy nothing to adopt if that should come to pass, he glanced somberly at the wide high-backed chair nearest his place, where had sat the boldest-seeming of Gwaay's arch-magi. There was only a loosely crumpled white loincloth—but in it was what gave the Mouser pause. A small pile of flocculent gray dust was all.

The Mouser whistled softly between his teeth and raised himself the better to see the rest of the seats. On each of them was the same: a clean loincloth, somewhat crumpled as if it had been worn for a little while, and within the cloth that small heap of grayish powder.

At the other end of the long table, one of the black counters, which had been standing on its edge, slowly rolled off the board of the thought-game and struck the floor with a tiny *tick*. It sounded to the Mouser rather like the last noise in the world.

Very quietly he stood up and silently walked in his ratskin moccasins to the nearest archway, across which he had drawn thick curtains for the Great Spell. He was wondering just what the range of the spell had been, *where* it had stopped, if it had stopped at all. Suppose, for instance, that Sheelba had underestimated its power and it disintegrated not only sorcerers, but...

He paused in front of the curtain and gave one last over-the-shoulder glance. Then he shrugged, adjusted his swordbelt, and, grinning far more bravely than he felt, said to no one in particular, "But they assured me that they were the *very* greatest sorcerers."

As he reached toward the curtain, heavy with embroidery, it wavered and shook. He froze, his heart leaping wildly. Then the curtains parted a little and there was thrust in the saucy face of Ivivis, wide-eyed with excited curiosity.

"Did your Great Spell work, Mouser?" she asked him breathlessly.

He let out his own breath in a sigh of relief. "You survived it, at all events," he said and reaching out pulled her against him. Her slim body pressing his felt very good. True, the presence of almost any living being would have been welcome to the Mouser at this moment, but that it should be Ivivis was a bonus he could not help but appreciate.

"Dearest," he said sincerely, "I was feeling that I was perchance the last man on Earth. But now—"

"And acting as if I were the last girl, lost a year," she retorted tartly. "This is neither the place nor the time for amorous consolations and intimate pleasantries," she continued, half mistaking his motives and pushing back from him.

"Did you slay Hasjarl's wizards?" she demanded, gazing up with some awe into his eyes.

"I slew some sorcerers," the Mouser admitted judiciously. "Just how many is a moot question."

"Where are Gwaay's?" she asked, looking past the Mouser at the empty chairs. "Did he take them all with him?"

"Isn't Gwaay back from his father's funeral yet?" the Mouser countered, evading her question, but as she continued to look into his eyes, he added lightly, "His sorcerers are in some congenial spot—I hope."

Ivivis looked at him queerly, pushed past, hurried to the long table, and gazed up and down the chair seats.

"Oh, *Mouser!*" she said reprovingly, but there was real awe in the gaze she shot him.

He shrugged. "They swore to me they were of First Rank," he defended himself.

"Not even a fingerbone or skullshard left," Ivivis said solemnly, peering closely at the nearest tiny gray dust pile and shaking her head.

"Not even a gallstone," the Mouser echoed harshly. "My rune was dire."

"Not even a tooth," Ivivis reechoed, rubbing curiously if somewhat callously through the pile. "Nothing to send their mothers."

"Their mothers can have their diapers to fold away with their baby ones," the Mouser said irascibly though somewhat uncomfortably. "Oh, Ivivis, sorcerers don't have mothers!"

"But what happens to our Lord Gwaay now that his protectors are gone?" Ivivis demanded more practically. "You saw how Hasjarl's sendings struck him last night when they but dozed. And if anything happens to Gwaay, then what happens to us?"

Again the Mouser shrugged. "If my rune reached Hasjarl's twenty-four wizards and blasted them too, then no harm's been done—except to sorcerers, and they all take their chances, sign their death warrants when they speak their first spells—'tis a dangerous trade.

"In fact," he went on with argumentative enthusiasm, "we've gained. Twenty-four enemies slain at cost of but a dozen—no, eleven total casualties on our side—why, that's a bargain any warlord would jump at! Then with the sorcerers all out of the way—except for the Brothers themselves, and Flindach—that warty blotchy one is someone to be reckoned with!—I'll meet and slay this champion of Hasjarl's and we'll carry all before us. And if…"

His voice trailed off. It had occurred to him to wonder why he himself hadn't been blasted by his own spell. He had never suspected, until now, that he might be a sorcerer of the First Rank—having despite a youthful training in country-sorceries only dabbled in magic since. Perhaps some metaphysical trick or logical fallacy was involved…. If a sorcerer casts a rune that midway of the casting blasts *all* sorcerers, *provided the casting be finished*, then does he blast himself, or…? Or perhaps indeed, the Mouser began to think boastfully, he was unknown to himself a magus of the First Rank, or even higher, or—

In the silence of his thinking, he and Ivivis became aware of approaching footsteps, first a multitudinous patter but swiftly a tumult. The gray-clad man and the slavegirl had hardly time to exchange a questioning apprehensive look when there burst through the draperies, tearing them down, eight or nine of Gwaay's chiefest henchmen, their faces death-pale, their eyes staring like madmen's. They raced across the chamber and out the opposite archway almost before the Mouser could recover from where he'd dodged out of their way.

But that was not the end of the footsteps. There was a last pair coming down the black corridor and at a strange unequal gallop, like a cripple sprinting, and with a squushy slap at each tread. The Mouser crossed quickly to Ivivis and put an arm around her. He did not want to be standing alone at this moment, either.

Ivivis said, "If your Great Spell missed Hasjarl's sorcerers, and their disease-spells struck through to Gwaay, now undefended…"

Her whisper trailed off fearfully as a monstrous figure clad in dark scarlet robes lurched by swift convulsive stages into view. At first the Mouser thought it must be Hasjarl of the Mismated Arms, from what he'd heard of that one. Then he saw that its neck was collared by gray fungus, its right cheek crimson, its left black, its eyes dripping green ichor and its nose spattering clear drops. As the loathy creature took a last

great stride into the chamber, its left leg went boneless like a
pillar of jelly and its right leg, striking down stiffly though
with a heel splash, broke in midshin and the jagged bones
thrust through the flesh. Its yellow-crusted, red-cracked scurfy
hands snatched futilely at the air for support, and its right
arm brushing its head carried away half the hair on that side.

Ivivis began to mewl and yelp faintly with horror and she
clung to the Mouser, who himself felt as if a nightmare were
lifting its hooves to trample him.

In such manner did Prince Gwaay, Lord of the Lower
Levels of Quarmall, come home from his father's funeral,
falling in a stenchful, scabrous, ichorous heap upon the torn-
down richly embroidered curtains immediately beneath the
pristine-handsome silver bust of himself in the niche above
the arch.

The funeral pyre smoldered for a long time, but of all the
inhabitants in that huge and ramified castle-kingdom Brilla
the High Eunuch was the only one who watched it out. Then
he collected a few representative pinches of ashes to preserve;
he kept them with some dim idea that they might perhaps
act as some protection, now that the living protector was
forever gone.

Yet the fluffy-gritty gray tokens did not much cheer Brilla
as he wandered desolately into the inner rooms. He was
troubled and eunuchlike be-twittered by thoughts of the war
between brothers that must now ensue before Quarmall had
again a single master. Oh, what a tragedy that Lord Quarmal
should have been snatched so suddenly by the Fates with no
chance to make arrangement for the succession!—though
what that arrangement might have been, considering
custom's strictures in Quarmall, Brilla could not say. Still,
Quarmal had always seemed able to achieve the impossible.

Brilla was troubled too, and rather more acutely, by his
guilty knowledge that Quarmal's concubine Kewissa had
evaded the flames. He might be blamed for that, though he

could not see where he had omitted any customary precaution. And burning would have been small pain indeed to what the poor girl must suffer now for her transgression. He rather hoped she had slain herself by knife or poison, though that would doom her spirit to eternal wandering in the winds between the stars that make them twinkle.

Brilla realized his steps were taking him to the harem, and he halted a-quake. He might well find Kewissa there and he did not want to be the one to turn her in.

Yet if he stayed in this central section of the Keep, he would momentarily run into Flindach and he knew he would hold back nothing when gimleted by that arch-sorcerer's stern witchy gaze. He would have to remind him of Kewissa's defection.

So Brilla bethought him of an errand that would take him to the nethermost sections of the Keep, just above Hasjarl's realm. There was a storeroom there, his responsibility, which he had not inventoried for a month. Brilla did not like the Dark Levels of Quarmall—it was his pride that he was one of the elite who worked in or at least near sunlight—but now, by reason of his anxieties, the Dark Levels began to seem attractive.

This decision made, Brilla felt slightly cheered. He set off at once, moving quite swiftly, with a eunuch's peculiar energy, despite his elephantine bulk.

He reached the storeroom without incident. When he had kindled a torch there, the first thing he saw was a small girl-like woman cowering among the bales of drapery. She wore a lustrous loose yellow robe and had the winsome triangular face, moss-green hair, and bright blue eyes of an Ilthmarix.

"Kewissa," he whispered shudderingly yet with motherly warmth. "Sweet chick…"

She ran to him. "Oh Brilla, I'm so frightened," she cried softly as she pressed against his paunch and hid herself in his great-sleeved arms.

"I know, I know," he murmured, making little clucking noises as he smoothed her hair and petted her. "You were always frightened of flames, I remember now. Never mind, Quarmal will forgive when you meet beyond the stars. Look you, little duck, it's a great risk I run, but because you were the old Lord's favorite I cherish you dearly. I carry a painless poison...only a few drops on the tongue, then darkness and the windy gulfs....A long leap, true, but better far than what Flindach must order when he discovers—"

She pushed back from him. "It was Flindach who commanded me not to follow My Lord to his last hearth!" she revealed wide-eyed and reproachful. "He told me the stars directed otherwise and also that this was Quarmal's dying wish. I doubted and feared Flindach—he with face so hideous and eyes so horridly like My Dear Lord's—yet could not but obey...with some small thankfulness, I must confess, dear Brilla."

"But what reason earthly or unearthly...?" Brilla stammered, his mind a-whirl.

Kewissa looked to either side. Then, "I bear Quarmal's quickening seed," she whispered.

For a bit this only increased Brilla's confusion. How could Quarmal have hoped to get a concubine's child accepted as Lord of All when there were two grown legitimate heirs? Or cared so little for the land's security as to leave alive even an unborn bastard? Then it occurred to him—and his heart shook at the thought—that Flindach might be seeking to seize supreme power, using Kewissa's babe and an invented death wish of Quarmal as his pretext along with those Quarmal-eyes of his. Palace revolutions were not entirely unknown in Quarmall. Indeed, there was a legend that the present line had generations ago clambered dagger-fisted to power by that route, though it was death to repeat the legend.

Kewissa continued, "I stayed hidden in the harem. Flindach said I'd be safe. But then Hasjarl's henchmen came searching in Flindach's absence and in defiance of all customs and decencies. I fled here."

This continued to make a dreadful sort of sense, Brilla thought. If Hasjarl suspected Flindach's impious snatch at power, he would instinctively strike at him, turning the fraternal strife into a three-sided one involving even—woe of woes!—the sunlit apex of Quarmall, which until this moment had seemed so safe from war's alarums....

At that very instant, as if Brilla's fears had conjured up their fruition, the door of the storeroom opened wide and there loomed in it an uncouth man who seemed the very embodiment of battle's barbarous horrors. He was so tall his head brushed the lintel; his face was handsome yet stern and searching-eyed; his red-gold hair hung tangledly to his shoulders; his garment was a bronze-studded wolfskin tunic; longsword and massy short-handled ax swung from his belt, and on the longest finger of his right hand Brilla's gaze—trained to miss no detail of decor and now fear-sharpened—noted a ring with Hasjarl's clenched-fist sigil.

The eunuch and the girl huddled against each other, quivering.

Having assured himself that these two were all he faced, the newcomer's countenance broke into a smile that might have been reassuring on a smaller man or one less fiercely accoutered. Then Fafhrd said, "Greetings, Grandfather. I require only that you and your chick help me find the sunlight and the stables of this benighted realm. Come, we'll plot it out so you may satisfy me with least danger to yourselves." And he swiftly stepped toward them, silently for all his size, his gaze returning with interest to Kewissa as he noted she was not child but woman.

Kewissa felt that and although her heart was a-flutter, piped up bravely, "You dare not rape me! I'm with child by a dead man!"

Fafhrd's smile soured somewhat. Perhaps, he told himself,

he should feel complimented that girls started thinking about rape the instant they saw him; still he was a little irked. Did they deem him incapable of civilized seduction because he wore furs and was no dwarf? Oh well, they quickly learned. But what a horrid way to try to daunt him!

Meanwhile tubby-fat Grandfather, who Fafhrd now realized was hardly equipped to be that or father either, said fearful-mincing, "She speaks only the truth, oh Captain. But I will be o'erjoyed to aid you in any—"

There were rapid steps in the passage and the harsh slither of steel against stone. Fafhrd turned like a tiger. Two guards in the dark-linked hauberks of Hasjarl's guards were pressing into the room. The fresh-drawn sword of one had scraped the door-side, while a third behind them cried sharply now. "Take the Northern turncoat! Slay him if he shows fight. I'll secure old Quarmal's concubine."

The two guards started to run at Fafhrd, but he, counterfeiting even more the tiger, sprang at them twice as suddenly. Graywand coming out of his scabbard swept sideways up, fending off the sword of the foremost even as Fafhrd's foot came crushing down on that one's instep. Then Graywand's hilt crashed backhand into his jaw, so that he lurched against his fellow. Meanwhile Fafhrd's ax had come into his left hand, and at close quarters he stroked it into their brains, then shouldering them off as they fell, he drew back the ax and cast it at the third, so that it lodged in his forehead between the eyes as he turned to see what was amiss, and he dropped down dead.

But the footsteps of a fourth and perhaps a fifth could be heard racing away. Fafhrd sprang toward the door with a growl, stopped with a foot-stamp and returned as swiftly, stabbing a bloody finger at Kewissa cowering into the great hulk of blanching Brilla.

"Old Quarmal's girl? With child by him?" he rapped out and when she nodded rapidly, swallowing hard, he continued, "Then you come with me. Now! The castrado too."

He sheathed Graywand, wrenched his ax from the sergeant's skull, grabbed Kewissa by the upper arm and strode toward the door with a devilish snarling head-wave to Brilla to follow.

Kewissa cried, "Oh mercy, sir! You'll make me lose the child."

Brilla obeyed, yet twittered as he did, "Kind Captain, we'll be no use to you, only encumber you in your—"

Fafhrd, turning suddenly again, spared him one rapid speech, shaking the bloody ax for emphasis: "If you think I don't understand the bargaining value or hostage-worth of even an unborn claimant to a throne, then your skull is as empty of brains as your loins are of seed—and I doubt that's the case. As for you, girl," he added harshly to Kewissa, "if there's anything but bleat under your green ringlets, you know you're safer with a stranger then with Hasjarl's hellions and that better your child miscarry than fall into their hands. Come, I'll carry you." He swept her up. "Follow, eunuch; work those great thighs of yours if you love living."

And he made off down the corridor, Brilla trotting ponderously after and wisely taking great gasping breaths in anticipation of exertions to come. Kewissa laid her arms around Fafhrd's neck and glanced up at him with qualified admiration. He himself now gave vent to two remarks which he'd evidently been saving for an unoccupied moment.

The first, bitterly sarcastic: "...if he shows fight!"

The second, self-angry: "Those cursed fans must be deafening me, that I didn't hear 'em coming!"

Forty loping paces down the corridor he passed a ramp leading upward and turned toward a narrower darker corridor.

From just behind, Brilla called softly yet rapidly, penurious of breath. "That ramp led to the stables. Where are you taking us, My Captain?"

"Down!" Fafhrd retorted without pausing in his lope. "Don't panic, I've a hidey hole for the two of you—and even a girl-mate for little Prince-mother Greenilocks here." Then to Kewissa, gruffly, "You're not the only girl in Quarmall who wants rescuing, nor yet the dearest."

The Mouser, steeling himself for it, knelt and surveyed the noisome heap that was Prince Gwaay. The stench was abominably strong despite the perfumes the Mouser had sprinkled and the incense he had burned but an hour ago.

The Mouser had covered with silken sheets and fur robes all the loathsomeness of Gwaay except for his plagues-stricken pillowed-up face. The sole feature of this face that had escaped obvious extreme contagion was the narrow handsome nose, from the end of which there dripped clear fluid, drop by slow drop, like the ticking of a water clock, while from below the nose proceeded a continual small nasty retching which was the only reasonably sure sign that Gwaay was not wholly moribund. For a while Gwaay had made faint straining moanings like the whispers of a mute, but now even those had ceased.

The Mouser reflected that it was very difficult indeed to serve a master who could neither speak, write, nor gesticulate—particularly when fighting enemies who now began to seem neither dull nor contemptible. By all counts Gwaay should have died hours since. Presumably only his steely sorcerous will and consuming hatred of Hasjarl kept his spirit from fleeing the horrid torment that housed it.

The Mouser rose and turned with a questioning shrug toward Ivivis, who sat now at the long table hemming up two hooded black voluminous sorcerer's robes, which she had cut down at the Mouser's direction to fit him and herself. The Mouser had thought that since he now seemed to be Gwaay's sole remaining sorcerer as well as champion, he should be prepared to appear dressed as the former and to boast at least one acolyte.

In answer to the shrug, Ivivis merely wrinkled her nostrils, pinched them with two dainty fingertips, and shrugged back.

True, the Mouser thought, the stench was growing stronger despite all his attempts to mask it. He stepped to the table and poured himself a half cup of the thick blood-red wine, which he'd begun unwillingly to relish a little, although he'd learned it was indeed fermented from scarlet toadstools. He took a small swallow and summed up:

"Here's a pretty witch's kettle of problems. Gwaay's sorcerers blasted—all right, yes, by me, I admit it. His henchmen and soldiery fled—to the lowest loathy dank dim tunnels, I think, or else gone over to Hasjarl. His girls vanished save for you. Even his doctors fearful to come nigh him—the one I dragged here fainting dead away. His slaves useless with dread—only the tread-beasts at the fans keep their heads, and they because they haven't any! No answer to our message to Flindach suggesting that we league against Hasjarl. No page to send another message by—and not even a single picket to warn us if Hasjarl assaults."

"You could go over to Hasjarl yourself," Ivivis pointed out.

The Mouser considered that. "No," he decided, "there's something too fascinating about a forlorn hope like this. I've always wanted to command one. And it's only fun to betray the wealthy and victorious. Yet what strategy can I employ without even a skeleton army?"

Ivivis frowned. "Gwaay used to say that just as sword-war is but another means of carrying out diplomacy, so sorcery is but another means of carrying out sword-war. Spell-war. So you could try your Great Spell again," she concluded without vast conviction.

"Not I!" the Mouser repudiated. "It never touched Hasjarl's twenty-four or it would have stopped their disease spells against Gwaay. Either they are of First Rank or else I'm doing the spell backwards—in which case the tunnels would probably collapse on me if I tried it again."

"Then use a different spell," Ivivis suggested brightly. "Raise an army of veritable skeletons. Drive Hasjarl mad, or put a hex on him so he stubs his toe at every step. Or turn his soldiers' swords to cheese. Or vanish their bones. Or transmew all his maids to cats and set their tails afire. Or—"

"I'm sorry, Ivivis," the Mouser interposed hurriedly to her mounting enthusiasm. "I would not confess this to another, but…that was my only spell. We must depend on wit and weapons alone. Again I ask you, Ivivis, what strategy does a general employ when his left is o'erwhelmed, his right takes flight, and his center is ten times decimated?"

A slight sweet sound like a silver bell chinked once, or a silver string plucked high in the harp, interrupted him. Although so faint, it seemed for a moment to fill the chamber with auditory light. The Mouser and Ivivis gazed around wonderingly and then at the same moment looked up at the silver mask of Gwaay in the niche above the arch before which Gwaay's mortal remains festered silken-wrapped.

The shimmering metal lips of the statua smiled and parted—so far as one might tell in the gloom—and faintly there came Gwaay's brightest voice, saying: "Your answer: he attacks!"

The Mouser blinked. Ivivis dropped her needle. The statua continued, its eyes seeming to twinkle, "Greetings, hostless captain mine! Greetings, dear girl. I'm sorry my stink offends you—yes, yes, Ivivis, I've observed you pinching your nose at my poor carcass this last hour through—but then the world teems with loathiness. Is that not a black death-adder gliding now through the black robe you stitch?"

With a gasp of horror Ivivis sprang cat-swift up and aside from the material and brushed frantically at her legs. The statua gave a naturally silver laugh, than quickly said, "Your pardon, gentle girl—I did but jest. My spirits are too high, too high—perchance because my body is so low. Plotting will curb my feyness. Hist now, hist!"

In Hasjarl's Hall of Sorcery his four-and-twenty wizards

stared desperately at a huge magic screen set up parallel to their long table, trying with all their might to make the picture on it come clear. Hasjarl himself, dire in his dark red funeral robes, gazing alternately with open eyes and through the grommeted holes in his upper lids, as if that perchance might make the picture sharper, stutteringly berated them for their clumsiness and at intervals conferred staccato with his military.

The screen was dark gray, the picture appearing on it in pale green witch-light. It stood twelve feet high and eighteen feet long. Each wizard was responsible for a particular square yard of it, projecting on it his share of the clairvoyant picture.

This picture was of Gwaay's Hall of Sorcery, but the best effect achieved so far was a generally blurred image showing the table, the empty chairs, a low mound on the floor, a high point of silver light, and two figures moving about—these last mere salamanderlike blobs with arms and legs attached, so that not even the sex could be determined, if indeed they were human at all or even male or female.

Sometimes a yard of the picture would come clear as a flowerbed on a bright day, but it would always be a yard with neither of the figures in it or anything of more interest than an empty chair. Then Hasjarl would bark sudden for the other wizards to do likewise, or for the successful wizard to trade squares with someone whose square had a figure in it, and the picture would invariably get worse and Hasjarl would screech and spray spittle, and then the picture would go completely bad, swimming everywhere or with squares all jumbled and overlapping like an unsolved puzzle, and the twenty-four sorcerers would have to count off squares and start over again while Hasjarl disciplined them with fearful threats.

Interpretations of the picture by Hasjarl and his aides differed considerably. The absence of Gwaay's sorcerers seemed to be a good thing, until someone suggested they might have been sent to infiltrate Hasjarl's Upper Levels for a close-range thaumaturgic attack. One lieutenant got fearfully tongue-lashed for suggesting the two blob-figures might be demons seen unblurred in their true guise—though even after Hasjarl had discharged his anger, he seemed a little frightened by the idea. The hopeful notion that all Gwaay's sorcerers had been wiped out was rejected when it was ascertained that no sorcerous spells had been directed at them recently by Hasjarl or any of his wizards.

One of the blob-figures now left the picture entirely, and the point of silvery light faded. This touched off further speculation, which was interrupted by the entry of several of Hasjarl's torturers looking rather battered and a dozen of his guards. The guards were surrounding—with naked swords aimed at his chest and back—the figure of an unarmed man in a wolfskin tunic with arms bound tight behind him. He was masked with a red silk eye-holed sack pulled down over his head and hair, and a black robe trailed behind him.

"We've taken the Northerner, Lord Hasjarl!" the leader of the dozen guards reported joyously. "We cornered him in your torture room. He disguised himself as one of those and tried to lie his way through our lines, bumped and going on his knees, but his height still betrayed him."

"Good, Yissim—I'll reward you," Hasjarl approved. "But what of my father's treacherous concubine and the great castrado who were with him when he slew three of your fellows?"

"They were still with him when we glimpsed him near Gwaay's realm and gave chase. We lost 'em when he doubled back to the torture room, but the hunt goes on."

"Find 'em, you were best," Hasjarl ordered grimly, "or the sweets of my reward will be soured entire by the pains of my displeasure." Then to Fafhrd, "So, traitor! Now I will play with you the wrist game—aye, and a hundred others too, until you are wearied of sport."

Fafhrd answered loudly and clearly through his red mask, "I'm no traitor, Hasjarl. I was only tired of your twitching and of your torturing of girls."

There came a sibilant cry from the sorcerers. Turning, Hasjarl saw that one of them had made the low mound on the floor come clear, so that it was clearly seen as a stricken man covered to his pillowed head.

"Closer!" Hasjarl cried—all eagerness, no threat—and perhaps because they were neither startled nor threatened, each wizard did his work perfectly, so that there came green-pale onto the screen Gwaay's face, wide as an oxcart and team, the plagues visible by the huge pustules and crustings and fungoid growths if not by their colors, the eyes like great vats stewing with ichor, the mouth a quaking bog-hole, while each drop that fell from the nose-tip looked a gallon.

Hasjarl cried thickly, like a man choking with strong drink, "Joy, oh joy! My heart will break!"

The screen went black, the room dead silent, and into it from the further archway there came gliding noiselessly through the air a tiny bone-gray shape. It soared on unflapping wings like a hawk searching its prey, high above the swords that struck at it. Then turning in a smooth silent curve, it swooped straight at Hasjarl and, evading his hands that snatched at it too late, tapped him on the breast and fell to the floor at his feet.

It was a dart folded from parchment on which lines of characters showed at angles. Nothing more deadly than that.

Hasjarl snatched it up, pulled it crackingly open, and read aloud:

"Dear Brother. Let us meet on the instant in the Ghost Hall to settle the succession. Bring your four-and-twenty sorcerers. I'll bring one. Bring your champion. I'll bring mine. Bring your henchmen and guards. Bring yourself. I'll be brought. Or perhaps you'd prefer to spend the evening torturing girls. Signed (by direction) Gwaay."

Hasjarl crumpled the parchment in his fist and peering over it thoughtful-evil, rapped out staccato: "We'll go! He means to play on my brotherly pity—that would be sweet. Or else to trap us, but I'll out-trick him!"

Fafhrd called boldly, "You may be able to best your death-rotten brother, oh Hasjarl, but what of his champion?—cunninger than Zobold, more battle-fierce than a rogue elephant! Such a one can cut through your cheesy guards as easy as I bested 'em one-to-five in the Keep, and be at your noisy throat! You'll need me!"

Hasjarl thought for a heartbeat, then turning toward Fafhrd said, "I'm not mind-proud. I'll take advice from a dead dog. Bring him with us. Keep him bound, but bring his weapons."

Along a wide low tunnel that trended slowly upward and was lit by wall-set torches flaming no bluer-bright than marsh gas and as distant-seeming each from the next as coastal beacons, the Mouser striding swiftly yet most warily led a strange short cortege.

He wore a black robe with peaked black hood that thrown forward would hide his face entirely. Under it he carried at his belt his sword and dagger and also a skin of the blood-red toadstool wine, but in his fingers he bore a thin black wand tipped with a silver star, to remind him that his primary current role was Sorcerer Extraordinary to Gwaay.

Behind him trotted two-abreast four of the great-legged tiny-headed tread-slaves, looking almost like dark walking cones, especially when silhouetted by a torch just passed.

They bore between them, each clutching a pole-end in both dwarfish hands, a litter of bloodwood and ebony ornately carved, whereon rested mattressed and covered by furs and silks and richly embroidered fabrics the stenchful, helpless flesh and dauntless spirit of the young Lord of the Lower Levels.

Close behind Gwaay's litter followed what seemed a

slightly smaller version of the Mouser. It was Ivivis, masquerading as his acolyte. She held a fold of her hood as a sort of windbreak in front of her mouth and nose, and frequently she sniffed a handkerchief steeped in spirits of camphor and ammonia. Under her arm she carried a silver gong in a woolen sack and a strange thin wooden mask in another.

The splayed callused feet of the tread-slaves struck the stony floor with a faint *hrush*, over which came at long regular intervals Gwaay's gargly retching. Other sound there was none.

The walls and low ceiling teemed with pictures, mostly in yellow ocher, of demons, strange beasts, bat-winged girls, and other infernal beauties. Their slow looming and fading was nightmarish, yet gently so. All in all, it was one of the pleasantest journeys the Mouser could recall, equal of a trip he had once made by moonlight across the roofs of Lankhmar to hang a wilting wreath on a forgotten tower-top statue of the God of Thieves, and light a small blue fire of brandy to him.

"Attack!" he murmured humorously and wholly to himself. "Forward, my big-foot phalanx! Forward, my terror-striking war-car! Forward, my dainty rearguard! Forward, my Host!"

Brilla and Kewissa and Friska sat quiet as mice in the Ghost Hall beside the dried-up fountain pool yet near the open door of the chamber that was their appointed hiding place. The girls were whispering together, head leaned to head, yet that was no noisier than the squeaking of mice, nor was the occasional high sigh Brilla let slip.

Beyond the fountain was the great half open door through which the sole faint light came questing and through which Fafhrd had brought them before doubling back to draw off the pursuit. Some of the cobwebs stretching across it had been torn away by Brilla's ponderous passage.

Taking that door and the one to their hiding place as two
opposite corners of the room, the two remaining opposite
corners were occupied by a wide black archway and a narrow
one, each opening on a large section of stony floor raised
three steps above the still larger floor section around the
dried-up pool. Elsewhere in the wall were many small doors,
all shut, doubtless leading to onetime bed chambers. Over
all hung the pale mortared great black slabs of the shallowly
domed ceiling. So much their eyes, long accustomed to the
darkness, could readily distinguish.

Brilla, who recognized that this place had once housed a
harem, was musing melancholically that now it had become
a kind of tiniest harem again, with eunuch—himself—and
pregnant girl—Kewissa—gossiping with restless high-spirited
girl—Friska—who was fretting for the safety of her tall
barbarian lover. Old times! He had wanted to sweep up a bit
and find some draperies, even if rotten ones, to hang and
spread, but Friska had pointed out that they mustn't leave
clues to their presence.

There came a faint sound through the great door. The girls
quit their whispering and Brilla his sighs and musings, and
they listened with all their beings. Then more noises came—
footsteps and the knock of a sheathed sword against the wall
of a tunnel—and they sprang silently up and scurried back
into their hiding chamber and silently shut the door behind
them, and the Ghost Hall was briefly alone with its ghosts
once more.

A helmeted guard in the hauberk of Hasjarl's guards
appeared in the great door and stood peering about with arrow
nocked to the taut string of a short bow he held crosswise.
Then he motioned with his shoulder and came sneaking in
followed by three of his fellows and by four slaves holding
aloft yellowly flaming torches, which cast the monstrous
shadows of the guardsmen across the dusty floor and the
shadows of their heads against the curving far wall, as they
spied about for signs of trap or ambush.

Some bats swooped about and fled the torchlight through the archways.

The first guardsman whistled then down the corridor behind him and waved an arm and there came two parties of slaves, who applied themselves each to a side of the great door, so that it groaned and creaked loudly at its hinges, and they pushed it open wide, though one of them leaped convulsively as a spider fell on him from the disturbed cobwebs, or he thought it did.

Then more guards came, each with a torch-slave, and moved about calling softly back and forth, and tried all the shut doors and peered long and suspiciously into the black spaces beyond the narrow archway and the wide one, but all returned quite swiftly to form a protective semicircle around the great door and enclosed most of the floor space of the central section of the Ghost Hall.

Then into that shielded space Hasjarl came striding, surrounded by his henchmen and followed at heel by his two dozen sorcerers closely ranked. With Hasjarl too came Fafhrd, still arm-bound and wearing his red bag-mask and menaced by the drawn swords of his guards. More torch-slaves came too, so that the Ghost Hall was flaringly lit around the great door, though elsewhere a mixture of glare and black shadow.

Since Hasjarl wasn't speaking, no one else was. Not that the Lord of the Upper Levels was altogether silent—he was coughing constantly, a hacking bark, and spitting gobbets of phlegm into a finely embroidered kerchief. After each small convulsion he would glare suspiciously around him, drooping evilly one pierced eyelid to emphasize his wariness.

Then there was a tiny scurrying and one called, "A rat!" Another loosed an arrow into the shadows around the pool where it rasped stone, and Hasjarl demanded loudly why his ferrets had been forgotten—and his great hounds too, for that matter, and his owls to protect him against poison-toothed bats Gwaay might launch at him—and swore to flay the right hands of the neglectful ones.

It came again, that swift-traveling rattle of tiny claws on smooth stone, and more arrows were loosed futilely to skitter across the floor, and guards shifted position nervously, and in the midst of all that Fafhrd cried, "Up shields, some of you, and make walls to either side of Hasjarl! Have you not thought that a dart, and not a paper one this time, might silently wing from either archway and drive through your dear Lord's throat and stop his precious coughing forever?"

Several leaped guiltily to obey that order and Hasjarl did not wave them away and Fafhrd laughed and remarked, "Masking a champion makes him more dreadsome, oh Hasjarl, but tying his hands behind him is not so apt to impress the enemy—and has other drawbacks. If there should now come suddenly a-rush that one wilier than Zobold, weightier than a mad elephant to tumble and hurl aside your panicky guards—"

"Cut his bonds!" Hasjarl barked, and someone began to saw with a dagger behind Fafhrd's back. "But don't give him his sword or ax! Yet hold them ready for him!"

Fafhrd writhed his shoulders and flexed his great forearms and began to massage them and laughed again through his mask.

Hasjarl fumed and then ordered all the shut doors tried once more. Fafhrd readied himself for action as they came to the one behind which Friska and the two others were hidden, for he knew it had no bolt or bar. But it held firm against all shoving. Fafhrd could imagine Brilla's great back braced against it, with the girls perhaps pushing at his stomach, and he smiled under the red silk.

Hasjarl fumed a while longer and cursed his brother for his delay and swore he had intended mercy to his brother's minions and girls, but now no longer. Then one of Hasjarl's henchmen suggested Gwaay's dart-message might have been a ruse to get them out of the way while an attack was launched from below through other tunnels or even by way of the air-shafts, and Hasjarl seized that henchman by the throat and shook him and demanded why, if he had expected that, he hadn't spoken earlier.

At that moment a gong sounded, high and silver-sweet, and Hasjarl loosed his henchmen and looked around wonderingly. Again the silvery gong-note, then through the wider black archway there slowly stepped two monstrous figures each bearing a forward pole of an ornately carved black and red litter.

All of those in the Ghost Hall were familiar with the tread-slaves, but to see them anywhere except on their belts was almost as great and grotesque a wonder as to see them for the first time. It seemed to portend unsettlements of custom and dire upheavals, and so there was much murmuring and some shrinking.

The tread-slaves continued to step ponderously forward, and their mates came into view behind them. The four advanced almost to the edge of the raised section of floor and set the litter down and folded their dwarfed arms as well as they could, hooking fingers to fingers across their gigantic chests, and stood motionless.

Then through the same archway there swiftly paced the figure of a rather small sorcerer in black robe and hood that hid his features, and close behind him like his shadow a slightly smaller figure identically clad.

The Black Sorcerer took his stand to one side of the litter and a little ahead of it, his acolyte behind him to his right, and he lifted alongside his cowl a wand tipped with glittering silver and said loudly and impressively, "I speak for Gwaay, Master of Demons and Lord of All Quarmall!—as we will prove!"

The Mouser was using his deepest thaumaturgic voice, which none but himself had ever heard, except for the occasion on which he had blasted Gwaay's sorcerers—and come to think of it, that had ended with no one else having heard either. He was enjoying himself hugely, marveling greatly at his own audacity.

He paused just long enough, then slowly pointed his wand at the low mound on the litter, threw up his other arm in an imperious gesture, palm forward, and commanded, "On your knees, vermin, all of you, and do obeisance to your sole rightful ruler, Lord Gwaay, at whose name demons blench!"

A few of the foremost fools actually obeyed him—evidently Hasjarl had cowed them all too well—while most of the others in the front rank goggled apprehensively at the muffled figure in the litter—truly, it was an advantage having Gwaay motionless and supine, looking like Death's horridest self: it made him a more mysterious threat.

Searching over their heads from the cavern of his cowl, the Mouser spotted one he guessed to be Hasjarl's champion—gods, he was a whopper, big as Fafhrd!—and knowledgeable in psychology if that red silk bag-mask were his own idea. The Mouser didn't relish the idea of battling such a one, but with luck it wouldn't come to that.

Then there burst through the ranks of the awed guards, whipping them aside with a short lash, a hunch-shouldered figure in dark scarlet robes—Hasjarl at last! and coming to the fore just as the plot demanded.

Hasjarl's ugliness and frenzy surpassed the Mouser's expectations. The Lord of the Upper Levels drew himself up facing the litter and for a suspenseful moment did naught but twitch, stutter, and spray spittle like the veriest idiot. Then suddenly he got his voice and barked most impressively and surely louder than any of his great hounds:

"By right of death—suffered lately or soon—lately by my father, star-smitten and burned to ash—soon by my impious brother, stricken by my sorceries—and who dare not speak for himself, but must fee charlatans—I, Hasjarl, do proclaim myself sole Lord of Quarmall—and of all within it—demon or man!"

Then Hasjarl started to turn, most likely to order forward some of his guards to seize Gwaay's party, or perhaps to wave an order to his sorcerers to strike them down magically, but in that instant the Mouser clapped his hands together loudly. At that signal, Ivivis, who'd stepped between him and the litter, threw back her cowl and opened her robe and let them fall behind her almost in one continuous gesture—and the sight revealed held everyone spellbound, even Hasjarl, as the Mouser had known it would.

Ivivis was dressed in a transparent black silk tunic—the merest blackly opal gleaming over her pale flesh and slimly youthful figure—but on her face she wore the white mask of a hag, female yet with mouth a-grin showing fangs and with fiercely staring eyes red-balled and white-irised, as the Mouser had swiftly repainted them at the direction of Gwaay, speaking from his silver statua. Long green hair mixed with white fell from the mask behind Ivivis and some thin strands of it before her shoulders. Upright before her in her right hand she held ritualistically a large pruning knife.

The Mouser pointed straight at Hasjarl, on whom the eyes of the mask were already fixed, and he commanded in his deepest voice, "Bring that one here to me, oh Witch-Mother!" and Ivivis stepped swiftly forward.

Hasjarl took a backward step and stared horror-enchanted at his approaching nemesis, all motherly-cannibalistic above, all elfin-maidenly below, with his father's eyes to daunt him and with the cruel knife to suggest judgment upon himself for the girls he had lustily done to death or lifelong crippledness.

The Mouser knew he had success within his grasp and there remained only the closing of the fingers.

At that instant there sounded from the other end of the chamber a great muffled gong-note deep as Gwaay's had been silvery-high, shuddering the bones by its vibrancy. Then from either side of the narrow black archway at the opposite end of the hall from Gwaay's litter, there rose to the ceiling with a hollow roar twin pillars of white fire, commanding all eyes and shattering the Mouser's spell.

The Mouser's most instant reaction was inwardly to curse such superior stage-management.

Smoke billowed out against the great black squares of the ceiling, the pillars sank to white jets, man-high, and there strode forward between them the figure of Flindach in his heavily embroidered robes and with the Golden Symbol of Power at his waist, but with the Cowl of Death thrown back to show his blotched warty face and his eyes like those in Ivivis' mask. The High Steward threw wide his arms in a proud imploring gesture and in his deep and resonant voice that filled the Ghost Hall recited thus:

"Oh Gwaay! Oh Hasjarl! In the name of your father burned and beyond the stars, and in the name of your grandmother whose eyes I too bear, think of Quarmall! Think of the security of this your kingdom and of how your wars ravage her. Forego your enmities, abjure your brotherly hates, and cast your lots now to settle the succession—the winner to be Lord Paramount here, the loser instantly to depart with great escort and coffers of treasure, and journey across the Mountains of Hunger and the desert and the Sea of the East and live out his life in the Eastern Lands in all comfort and high dignity. Or if not by customary lot, then let your champions battle to the death to decide it—all else to follow the same. Oh Hasjarl, oh Gwaay, I have spoken." And he folded his arms and stood there between the two pale flame pillars still burning high as he.

Fafhrd had taken advantage of the shocks to seize his sword and ax from the ones holding them nervelessly, and to push forward by Hasjarl as if properly to ward him standing alone and unshielded in front of his men. Now Fafhrd lightly nudged Hasjarl and whispered through his bag-mask, "Take him up on it, you were best. I'll win your stuffy loathy catacomb kingdom for you—aye, and once rewarded depart from it swifter ever than Gwaay!"

Hasjarl grimaced angrily at him and turning toward Flindach shouted,—"I am Lord Paramount here, and no need of lots to determine it! Yes, and I have my arch-magi to strike down any who sorcerously challenge me!—and my great champion to smite to mincemeat any who challenge me with swords!"

Fafhrd threw out his chest and glared about through red-ringed eyeholes to back him up.

The silence that followed Hasjarl's boast was cut as if by keenest knife when a voice came piercingly dulcet from the unstirring low mound on the litter, cornered by its four impassive tread-slaves, or from a point just above it.

"I, Gwaay of the Lower Levels, am Lord Paramount of Quarmall, and not my poor brother there, for whose damned soul I grieve. And I have sorceries which have saved my life from the evilest of his sorceries and I have a champion who will smite his champion to chaff!"

All were somewhat daunted at that seemingly magical speaking except Hasjarl, who giggled sputteringly, twitching a-main, and then as if he and his brother were children alone in a playroom, cried out, "Liar and squeaker of lies! Effeminate boaster! Puny charlatan! Where is this great champion of yours? Call him forth! Bid him appear! Oh confess it now, he's but a figment of your dying thoughts! Oh, ho, ho, ho!"

All began to look around wonderingly at that, some thoughtful, some apprehensive. But as no figure appeared, certainly not a warlike one, some of Hasjarl's men began to snigger with him. Others of them took it up.

The Gray Mouser had no wish to risk his skin—not with Hasjarl's champion looking a meaner foe every moment, side armed with ax like Fafhrd and now apparently even acting as counselor to his lord—perhaps a sort of captain-general behind the curtain, as he was behind Gwaay's—yet the

Mouser was almost irresistibly tempted by this opportunity to cap all surprises with a master surprise.

And in that instant there sounded forth again Gwaay's eerie bell-voice, coming not from his vocal cords, for they were rotted away, but created by the force of his deathless will marshaling the unseen atomies of the air:

"From the blackest depths, unseen by all, in very center of the Hall—Appear, my champion!"

That was too much for the Mouser. Ivivis had reassumed her hooded black robe while Flindach had been speaking, knowing that the terror of her hag-mask and maiden-form was a fleeting thing, and she again stood beside the Mouser as his acolyte. He handed her his wand in one stiff gesture, not looking at her, and lifting his hands to the throat of his robe, he threw it and his hood back and dropped them behind him, and drawing Scalpel whistling from her sheath leaped forward with a heel-stamp to the top of the three steps and crouched glaring with sword raised above head, looking in his gray silks and silver a figure of menace, albeit a rather small one and carrying at his belt a wineskin as well as a dagger.

Meanwhile Fafhrd, who had been facing Hasjarl to have a last word with him, now ripped off his red bag-mask, whipped Graywand screaming from his sheath, and leaped forward likewise with an intimidating stamp.

Then they saw and recognized each other.

The pause that ensued was to the spectators more testimony to the fearsomeness of each—the one so dreadful-tall, the other metamorphosed from sorcerer. Evidently they daunted each other greatly.

Fafhrd was the first to react, perhaps because there had been something hauntingly familiar to him all along about the manner and speech of the Black Sorcerer. He started a gargantuan laugh and managed to change it in the nick into a screaming snarl of, "Trickster! Chatterer! Player at magic! Sniffer after spells. Wart! *Little Toad!*"

The Mouser, mayhap the more amazed because he had noted and discounted the resemblance of the masked champion to Fafhrd, now took his comrade's cue—and just in time, for he was about to laugh too—and boomed back,

"Boaster! Bumptious brawler! Bumbling fumbler after girls! Oaf! Lout! *Big Feet!*"

The taut spectators thought these taunts a shade mild, but the spiritedness of their delivery more than made up for that.

Fafhrd advanced another stamp, crying, "Oh, I have dreamed of this moment. I will mince you from your thickening toenails to your cheesy brain!"

The Mouser bounced for his stamp, so as not to lose height going down the steps, and skirled out the while, "All my rages find happy vent. I will gut you of each lie, especially those about your northern travels!"

Then Fafhrd cried, "Remember Ool Hrusp!" and the Mouser responded, "Remember Lithquil!" and they were at it.

Now for all most of the Quarmallians knew, Lithquil and Ool Hrusp might be and doubtless were places where the two heroes had earlier met in fight, or battlefields where they had warred on opposing sides, or even girls they had fought over. But in actuality Lithquil was the Mad Duke of the city of Ool Hrusp, to humor whom Fafhrd and the Mouser had once staged a most realistic and carefully rehearsed duel lasting a full half hour. So those Quarmallians who anticipated a long and spectacular battle were in no wise disappointed.

First Fafhrd aimed three mighty slashing blows, any one enough to cleave the Mouser in twain, but the Mouser deflected each at the last moment strongly and cunningly with Scalpel, so that they whished an inch above his head, singing the harsh chromatic song of steel on steel.

Next the Mouser thrust thrice at Fafhrd, leaping skimmingly like a flying fish and disengaging his sword each time from Graywand's parry. But Fafhrd always managed to slip his body aside, with nearly incredible swiftness for one so big, and the thin blade would go hurtlessly by him.

This interchange of slash and thrust was but the merest prologue to the duel, which now carried into the area of the dried-up fountain pool and became very wild-seeming indeed, forcing the spectators back more than once, while the Mouser improvised by gushing out some of his thick blood-red toadstool wine when they were momentarily pressed body-to-body in a fierce exchange, so that they both appeared sorely wounded.

There were three in the Ghost Hall who took no interest in this seeming masterpiece of duels and hardly watched it. Ivivis was not one of them—she soon threw back her hood, tore off her hag-mask, and came following the fight close, cheering on the Mouser. Nor were they Brilla, Kewissa and Friska—for at the sound of swords the two girls had insisted on opening their door a crack despite the eunuch's solicitous apprehensions and now they were all peering through, head above head, Friska in the midst agonizing at Fafhrd's perils.

Gwaay's eyes were clotted and the lids glued with ichor, and the tendons were dissolved whereby he might have lifted his head. Nor did he seek to explore with his sorcerous senses in the direction of the fight. He clung to existence solely by the thread of his great hatred for his brother, all else of life was to him less than a shadow-show; yet his hate held for him all of life's wonder and sweetness and high excitement—it was enough.

The mirror image of that hate in Hasjarl was at this moment strong enough too to dominate wholly his healthy body's instincts and hungers and all the plots and images in his crackling thoughts. He saw the first stroke of the fight, he saw Gwaay's litter unguarded, and then as if he had seen entire a winning combination of chess and been hypnotized by it, he made his move without another cogitation.

Widely circling the fight and moving swiftly in the shadows

like a weasel, he mounted the three steps by the wall and headed straight for the litter.

There were no ideas in his mind at all, but there were some shadowy images distortedly seen as from a great distances—one of himself as a tiny child toddling by night along a wall to Gwaay's crib, to scratch him with a pin.

He did not spare a glance for the tread-slaves, and it is doubtful if they even saw, or at least took note of him, so rudimentary were their minds.

He leaned eagerly between two of them and curiously surveyed his brother. His nostrils drew in at the stench, and his mouth contracted to its tightest sphincter yet still smiled.

He plucked a wide dagger of blued steel from a sheath at his belt and poised it above his brother's face, which by its plagues was almost unrecognizable as such. The honed edges of the dagger were tiny hooks directed back from the point.

The sword-clashing below reached one of its climaxes, but Hasjarl did not mark it.

He said softly, "Open your eyes, Brother. I want you to speak once before I slay you."

There was no reply from Gwaay—not a motion, not a whisper, not a bubble of retching.

"Very well," Hasjarl said harshly, "then die a prim shut-mouth," and he drove down the dagger.

It stopped violently a hairbreadth above Gwaay's upper cheek, and the muscles of Hasjarl's arm driving it were stabbingly numbed by the jolt they got.

Gwaay did open his eyes then, which was not very pleasant to behold since there was nothing in them but green ichor.

Hasjarl instantly closed his own eyes, but continued to peer down through the holes in his upper lids.

Then he heard Gwaay's voice like a silver mosquito by his ear saying, "You have made a slight oversight, dear brother.

You have chosen the wrong weapon. After our father's burning you swore to me my life was sacrosanct—until you killed me by crushing. 'Until I crush it out,' you said. The gods hear only our words, Brother, not our intentions. Had you come lugging a boulder, like the curious gnome you are, you might have accomplished your aim."

"Then I'll have you crushed!" Hasjarl retorted angrily, leaning his face closer and almost shouting. "Aye, and I'll sit by and listen to your bones crunch—what bones you have left! You're as great a fool as I, Gwaay, for you too after our father's funeral promised not to slay me. Aye, and you're a greater fool, for now you've spilled to me your little secret of how you may be slain."

"I swore not to slay you with spells or steel or venom or with my hand," the bright insect voice of Gwaay replied. "Unlike you, I said nothing at all of crushing." Hasjarl felt a strange tingling in his flesh while in his nostrils there was an acrid odor like that of lightning mingling with the stink of corruption.

Suddenly Gwaay's hands thrust up to the palms out of his overly rich bedclothes. The flesh was shredding from the finger bones which pointed straight up, invokingly.

Hasjarl almost started back, but caught himself. He'd die, he told himself, before he'd cringe from his brother. He was aware of strong forces all about him.

There was a muffled grating noise and then an odd faintly pattering snowfall on the coverlet and on Hasjarl's neck…a thin snowfall of pale gritty stuff…grains of mortar….

"Yes, you will crush me, dear brother," Gwaay admitted tranquilly. "But if you would know how you will crush me, recall my small special powers…or else *look up!*"

Hasjarl turned his head, and there was the great black basalt slab big as the litter rushing down, and the one moment of life left Hasjarl was consumed in hearing Gwaay say, "You are wrong again, my comrade."

Fafhrd stopped a sword-slash in midcourse when he heard the crash and the Mouser almost nicked him with his rehearsed parry. They lowered their blades and looked, as did all others in the central section of the Ghost Hall.

Where the litter had been was now only the thick basalt slab mortar-streaked with the litter-poles sticking out from under, and above in the ceiling the rectangular white hole whence the slab had been dislodged. The Mouser thought, *That's a larger thing to move by thinking than a checker or jar, yet the same black substance.*

Fafhrd thought, *Why didn't the whole roof fall?—there's the strangeness.*

Perhaps the greatest wonder of the moment was the four tread-slaves still standing at the four corners, eyes forward, fingers locked across their chests, although the slab had missed them only by inches in its falling.

Then some of Hasjarl's henchmen and sorcerers who had seen their Lord sneak to the litter now hurried up to it but fell back when they beheld how closely the slab approached the floor and marked the tiny rivulet of blood that ran from under it. Their minds quailed at the thought of those brothers who had hated each other so dearly, and now their bodies locked in an obscene interpenetrating and commingling embrace.

Meanwhile Ivivis came running to the Mouser and Friska to Fafhrd to bind up their wounds, and were astonished and mayhap a shade irked to be told there were none. Kewissa and Brilla came too and Fafhrd with one arm around Friska reached out the wine-bloody hand of the other and softly closed it around Kewissa's wrist, smiling at her friendlily.

Then the great muffled gong-note sounded again and the twin pillars of white flame briefly roared to the ceiling to either side of Flindach. They showed by their glare that many men had entered by the narrow archway behind Flindach and now stood around him: stout guardsmen from the companies of the Keep with weapons at the ready, and several of his own sorcerers.

As the flame-pillars swiftly shrank, Flindach imperiously raised hand and resonantly spoke:

"The stars which may not be cheated foretold the doom of the Lord of Quarmall. All of you heard those two"—he pointed toward the shattered litter—"proclaim themselves Lord of Quarmall. So the stars are twice satisfied. And the gods, who hear our words to each tiniest whisper, and order our fates by them, are content. It remains that I reveal to you the next Lord of Quarmall."

He pointed at Kewissa and intoned, *"The next Lord of Quarmall but one* sleeps and waxes in the womb of her, wife of the Quarmal so lately honored with burnings and immolations and ceremonious rites."

Kewissa shrank, and her blue eyes went wide. Then she began to beam.

Flindach continued, "It still remains that I reveal to you *the next Lord of Quarmall,* who shall tutor Queen Kewissa's babe until he arrives at manhood a perfect king and all-wise sorcerer, under whom our buried realm will enjoy perpetual inward peace and outward-raiding prosperity."

Then Flindach reached behind his left shoulder. All thought he purposed to draw forward the Cowl of Death over his head and brows and hideous warty winy cheeks for some still more solemn speaking. But instead he grasped his neck by the short hairs of the nape and drew it upward and forward and his scalp and all his hair with it, and then the skin of his face came off with his scalp as he drew his hand down and to the side, and there was revealed, sweat-gleaming a little, the unblemished face and jutting nose and full mobile smiling lips of Quarmal, while his terrible blood-red white-irised eyes gazed at them all mildly.

"I was forced to visit Limbo for a space," he explained with a solemn yet genial fatherly familiarity, "while others were Lords of Quarmall in my stead and the stars sent down their spears. It was best so, though I lost two sons by it. Only so might our land be saved from ravenous self-war."

He held up for all to see the limp mask with empty lash-fringed eyeholes and purple-blotched left cheek and wart-triangled right. He said, "And now I bid you all honor great and puissant Flindach, the loyalest Master of Magicians a king ever had, who lent me his face for a necessary deception and his body to be burned for mine with waxen mask of mine to cover his poor head-front, which had sacrificed all. In solemnly supervising my own high flaming obsequies, I honored only Flindach. For him my women burned. This his face, well preserved by my own skills as flayer and swift tanner, will hang forever in place of honor in our halls, while the spirit of Flindach holds my chair for me in the Dark World beyond the stars, a Lord Paramount there until I come, and eternally a Hero of Quarmall."

Before any cheering or hailing could be started—which would have taken a little while, since all were much bemused—Fafhrd cried out, "Oh cunningest king, I honor you and your babe so highly and the Queen who carries him in her womb that I will guard her moment by moment, not moving a pace from her, until I and my small comrade here are well outside Quarmall—say a mile—together with horses for our conveyance and with the treasures promised us by those two late kings." And he gestured as Quarmal had toward the crushed litter.

The Mouser had been about to launch at Quarmal some subtly intimidating remark about his own skills as a sorcerer in blasting Gwaay's eleven. But now he decided that Fafhrd's words were sufficient and well-spoken, save for the slighting reference to himself, and he held his peace.

Kewissa started to withdraw her hand from Fafhrd's, but he tightened his grip just a little, and she looked at him with understanding. In fact, she called brightly to Quarmal, "Oh, Lord Husband, this man saved my life and your son's from Hasjarl's fiends in a storeroom of the Keep. I trust him," while Brilla, dabbing tears of joy from his eyes with his undersleeve, seconded her with, "My very dear Lord, she speaks only nakedest truth, bare as a newborn babe or new-wed wife."

Quarmal raised his hand a little, reprovingly, as if such speaking were unnecessary and somewhat out of place, and smiling thinly at Fafhrd and the Mouser said, "It shall be as you have spoken. I am neither ungenerous nor unperceptive. Know that it was not altogether by chance that my late sons unbeknown to each other hired you two friends—also mutually unknowing—to be their champions. Furthermore know that I am not altogether unaware of the curiosities of Ningauble of the Seven Eyes or of the Spells of Sheelba of the Eyeless Face. We grandmaster sorcerers have a—But to speak more were only to kindle the curiosity of the gods and alert the trolls and attract the attention of the restless hungry Fates. Enough is enough."

Looking at Quarmal's slitted eyes, the Mouser was glad he had not boasted, and even Fafhrd shivered a little.

Fafhrd cracked whip above the four-horse team to set them pulling the high-piled wagon more briskly through this black sticky stretch of road deeply marked with cart tracks and the hoofprints of oxen, a mile from Quarmall. Friska and Ivivis were turned around on the seat beside him to wave as long a farewell as they might to Kewissa and the eunuch Brilla, standing at the roadside with four impassive guardsmen of Quarmall, to whom they had but now been released.

The Gray Mouser, sprawled on his stomach atop the load, waved too, but only with his left hand—in his right he held a cocked crossbow while his eyes searched the trees about for sign of ambush.

Yet the Mouser was not truly apprehensive. He thought

that Quarmal would hardly be apt to try any tricks against such a proven warrior and sorcerer as himself—or Fafhrd too, of course. The old Lord had shown himself a most gracious host during the last few hours, plying them with rare wines and loading them with rich gifts beyond what they'd asked or what the Mouser had purloined in advance, and even offering them other girls in addition to Ivivis and Friska—a benison which they'd rejected, with some inward regrets, after noting the glares in the eyes of those two. Twice or thrice Quarmal had smiled in too tiger-friendly a fashion, but at such times Fafhrd had stood a little closer to Kewissa and emphasized his light but inflexible grip on her, to remind the old Lord that she and the prince she carried were hostages for his and the Mouser's safety.

As the mucky road curved up a little, the towers of Quarmall came into view above the treetops. The Mouser's gaze drifted to them, and he studied the lacy pinnacles thoughtfully, wondering whether he'd ever see them again. Suddenly the whim seized him to return to Quarmall straightway—yes, to slip off the back of the load and run there. What did the outer world hold half so fine as the wonders of that subterranean kingdom?—its mazy mural-pictured tunnelings a man might spend his life tracing…its buried delights…even its evils beautiful…its delicious infinitely varied blacks…its hidden fan-driven air….Yes, suppose he dropped down soundlessly this very moment…

There was a flash, a brilliant scintillation from the tallest keep. It pricked the Mouser like a goad and he loosed his hold and let himself slide backward off the load. But just at that instant the road turned and grew firm and the trees moved higher, masking the towers, and the Mouser came to himself and grabbed hold again before his feet touched the road and he hung there while the wheels creaked merrily and cold sweat drenched him.

Then the wagon stopped and the Mouser dropped down

and took three deep breaths and then hastened forward to where Fafhrd had descended too and was busy with the harness of the horses and their traces.

"Up again, Fafhrd, and whip up," he cried. "This Quarmal is a cunninger witch than I guessed. If we waste time by the way, I fear for our freedom and our souls!"

"You're telling me!" Fafhrd retorted. "This road winds and there'll be more sticky stretches. Trust a wagon's speed?— pah! We'll uncouple the four horses and taking only simplest victuals and the smallest and most precious of the treasure, gallop across the moor away from Quarmall straight as the crow flies. That way we *should* dodge ambush and outrun ranging pursuit. Friska, Ivivis! Spring to it, all!"

A Nomad of the Time Streams
The Eternal Champion Vol. 4
New! Trade paperback omnibus **Available Now**
ISBN 1-56504-194-1
Also available in Hardcover - ISBN 1-56504-179-8

Sailing to Utopia
The Eternal Champion Vol. 8
Hardcover omnibus **Available in July**
ISBN 1-56504-183-6

MICHAEL MOORCOCK

"The Champion Eternal is what all stories are truly about, especially in
the writings of Michael Moorcock...In his dark fantasies, Moorcock
beautifully and tragically shows the Champion fighting not to destroy
Law or uphold Chaos, but instead to create a balance."
         —*BookPage*

Moorcock has written more than eighty works of fiction and nonfiction.
As creator of the multiverse in which Law and Chaos are permanently at
war, he is best known for his characters Elric of Melnibone, Prince Corum,
and Dorian Hawkmoon, all aspects of the Eternal Champion. He created
the first cyberpunk hero, Jerry Cornelius, and has won the World Fantasy
Award, the Nebula Award, the August Derleth Award and the British
Fantasy Award.